DEADLY

APPRAISAL

ALSO BY JANE K. CLELAND

Consigned to Death
Business Writing for Results

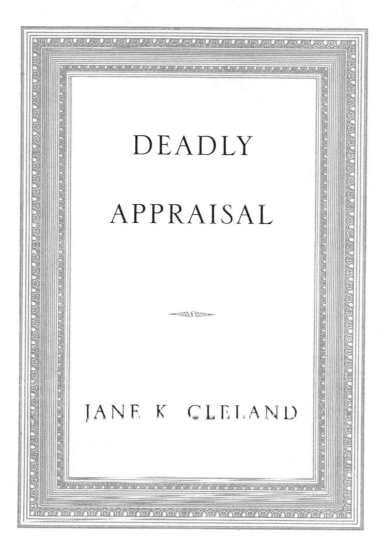

DEADLY

APPRAISAL

JANE K CLELAND

ST. MARTIN'S MINOTAUR

NEW YORK

www.minotaurbooks.com

Library of Congress Cataloging-in-Publication Data

Cleland, Jane K.
   Deadly appraisal / Jane K. Cleland.—1st ed.
      p. cm.
   ISBN-13: 978-0-312-34366-8
   ISBN-10: 0-312-34366-3
      1. Auctioneers—Fiction.   2. Murder—Investigation—Fiction.   3. New Hampshire—Fiction.   I. Title.

PS3603.L4555 D43 2007
813'6—dc22

                                                                2006051252

First Edition: April 2007

10 9 8 7 6 5 4 3 2 1

THIS IS FOR JO-ANN
AND, OF COURSE, FOR JOE

ACKNOWLEDGMENTS

I 'm grateful to Amy L., a forensic scientist, who wishes to remain anonymous. Amy, along with an associate, provided detailed explanations about poisons and trace evidence. Thanks also to Kevin Berean for answers to my legal questions, Leslie Hindman Auctioneers, Mary Ann Eckels, Susan A. Schwartz, Katie Scheding, Jo-Ann Maude, Linda Plastina, and Carol Novak.

It's a great pleasure to work with the entire St. Martin's Minotaur team of professionals, including David Rotstein, Jenness Crawford, and Julie Gutin, among many others. Special thanks to my editor, Ben Sevier, for his insight and care, and to my agent, Denise Marcil, for her wise guidance.

AUTHOR'S NOTE

This is a work of fiction. All of the characters and events are imaginary. While there is a Seacoast Region in New Hampshire, there is no town called Rocky Point, and many other geographic liberties have been taken.

DEADLY

APPRAISAL

CHAPTER ONE

So," Detective Rowcliff asked, "did you kill her?"

My lips parted, but no words came. I'd seen poor little mousy Maisy Gaylor collapse and die at tonight's Gala, and the horror of it was with me still. "What are you saying?" I managed. "Didn't she have a heart attack? Or a stroke? Or something?"

"Probably not."

"What do you mean?" I asked, confused and frightened.

"Let's stay on track here," he said impatiently, ignoring my question, his foot rat-a-tatting a staccato beat. "Did you kill her?"

"No, of course not," I said. "My God, no."

He stared at me, his eyes boring into mine. "Tell me what you saw," he said coldly.

I was so scared, I could barely breathe. I glanced away, then back at him, hoping for some sign of empathy or understanding. There was none. "What do you want to know?" I asked.

"How did Maisy end up onstage?"

I shut my eyes, letting the picture come.

My company's auction hall was decorated to the teeth in honor of the Portsmouth Women's Guild's Annual Black and Gold Gala. Even the banner stretched high over the stage was color-matched—the words PRESCOTT'S WELCOMES YOU were stamped in gold on a black silk background.

Dimmed chandeliers and wall sconces cast a soft glow and scores of candles flickered in tall crystal holders. Gilt-edged dishes, polished silver, and etched glasses gleamed in the amber light.

We were ready to go by six and guests started arriving about six thirty. By seven, clusters of people stood in small groupings near the antiques display. A brass quartet played classical music softly in the corner. Glasses clinked and people laughed. All around me, chitchat undulated in the background.

Most of the women wore all-black gowns, but several twinkled in black with gold sequins or metallic beads. All of the male guests wore black tie, and to keep to the black-and-gold color scheme, my male staff wore black suits with gold ties and the females, me included, wore long black skirts with gold silk jerseys.

A tuxedoed waiter passed by and I snared a flute of champagne. I scanned the room, seeking out people I hadn't yet met and trying hard to remember the names of those I had.

Just before we were called to sit for dinner, Maisy Gaylor, the Portsmouth Women's Guild's representative, approached me, grinning like a girl. She was wearing a fitted black dress, snug and cut low—an uncharacteristically sexy look for the normally all-business professional woman.

"Oh, Josie," she exclaimed, playfully grasping my arm. "*We did it!* All these weeks planning and working, and here we are! Aren't you just *so* excited?"

"Absolutely!" I agreed, smiling, her enthusiasm contagious.

"Oh, look! There's Britt!" Maisy flitted away in Britt's direction. Britt Epps, the honorary chair of the Gala and the most influential lawyer in town, was looking downright dapper, his bulk well disguised in a custom-made tuxedo. I watched as they air-kissed.

Later, after I'd greeted and chatted with dozens of attendees and finished a pretty good dinner, I realized that the event was on track to be a roaring success—the leaders of Portsmouth's social scene had come to my venue and were, by all appearances, having fun, which was excellent news for me, and they seemed to be bidding well on the antiques, which was excellent news for the Guild.

As the waiters cleared dishes, refilling wine for those of us who wanted more and pouring coffee for those who didn't, I sat idly chatting with my seatmate. Just as I picked up my dessert fork, my assistant, Gretchen, rushed across the room in my direction.

"All set!" she said, her emerald green eyes sparkling with delight, handing me the envelope containing the names of the winning bidders.

"Great!" I responded. Without opening it, I passed it on to Britt.

He stood up and leaned over to Maisy, seated at the table next to ours. "Maisy," he said in a stage whisper, waving the envelope to catch her eye. "We're ready to announce the winners."

Maisy jumped right up, her cheeks flushed with pleasure. Britt turned and motioned to Dora Reynolds, holding the envelope high above his head to flag her attention. Dora, the volunteer in charge of the event, nodded her understanding. She looked forty but was probably on the shady side of fifty. She was all gussied up in a full-length black silk slip dress that glittered with gold sparkles. As she approached us, she cooed to various people, working the room like a pro.

"I bet you've won the tureen!" she called to someone. "I have a witchy feeling about it! You'll see!"

Maisy squeezed Britt's hand. "I'm just so excited!" she exclaimed, beaming. "And curious!"

"Want to venture a guess as to how much we'll bring in tonight?" Britt teased.

Maisy giggled. "Oh, no! I just hope it's a big number!"

When Dora arrived at the front, Britt asked, "Ready, girls?" sounding more like a stage manager at a burlesque show than an important lawyer hosting a serious charity's most significant fund-raiser.

"Can I see the bid sheets before we announce the winners?" Dora asked.

"Of course," Britt replied, and handed her the envelope.

I stood with Maisy and Britt, barely listening to their nothing sayings while Dora thumbed through the bid sheets and slipped them back into the envelope. I sat. They filed onto the stage. Britt went first, his chest puffed out with pride and pleasure, followed by Dora, ethereal as always, almost gliding. Maisy brought up the rear, lifting the hem of her low-cut gown as she stepped up onto the low platform.

Just as Britt approached the podium, before he spoke a word and without warning, Maisy choked, uttered a desperate shriek, and tumbled forward, her wineglass shattering. She landed in a heap near my chair.

Detective Rowcliff began to tap his pencil, startling me out of my reverie. I opened my eyes and turned to him. He was chewing gum, as if he wanted to kill it, while watching me through uncaring eyes.

"So?" he prompted, sounding annoyed.

Taking a deep breath, I recounted the events of the night, answering his question about how Maisy had ended up on the stage.

"And then people rushed up and—" I faltered, unsure what to say next.

Rowcliff continued to tap his pencil, thinking about what I'd said. "Who wants Maisy dead?" he asked abruptly.

"No one. I mean, I didn't know her very well, but I can't imagine that anyone would want to murder her."

His angry eyes challenged me. "Well then," he demanded with a fierce rat-a-tat of his pencil, "who wants *you* dead?"

CHAPTER TWO

I stared at him. *What is he saying? His question makes no sense.* He stared back at me, watching me, waiting for my response.

"What?" I asked, giving voice to my confusion.

"I asked, 'Who wants you dead?' Got any enemies?"

"Why would you ask me that?"

"Answer the question," Rowcliff commanded.

"What has Maisy's death got to do with whether *I* have enemies?" I insisted.

He shrugged. "Maybe nothing. I'm just asking questions, trying to cover all bases." He paused, giving me a chance to speak, then added, waggling his fingers to hurry me up, "So . . .? Who wants you dead?"

"No one," I said, my voice barely audible.

"Right. No one ever wants to kill anyone," he said in an irritatingly sardonic tone. "Funny, isn't it, how a lot of people end up dead when no one has any enemies."

"Enemies? Are you saying that Maisy was killed by some enemy? Or are you saying that Maisy was killed by mistake and *I'm* the one with an enemy?"

He shifted position and tapped his pencil a few times against the table. "I'm not saying anything." After a long pause and a short series of taps, he said, "Describe her to me. What was she like?"

I considered how to express my jumbled thoughts. Maisy Gaylor had been my chief contact within the Portsmouth Women's Guild, and I couldn't recall that we'd ever shared a lighthearted moment, so it had been something of a shock to see her flitting about at the Gala, vivacious and effervescent. From my prior experience, I'd found her to be a painfully earnest, drab little woman, always quiet and often grim. Her atypical buoyancy had made me wonder at the time if she was high. And when she tumbled off the stage and died, I had the fleeting thought that maybe she had taken drugs and they'd killed her.

"I didn't know her well," I explained, offering a disclaimer. "But she seemed more high-spirited than usual. I couldn't help but wonder if she had taken something."

Another riff of rat-a-tat-tat. "Okay. Let's back up. How long have you known her?"

"About . . . four months. Once I accepted the sponsorship."

"Sponsorship of what? The Guild?"

"Not exactly . . . not the entire organization. My company sponsored the Gala."

"Which was a fund-raiser for the Guild."

"That's right."

He picked up the gilt-framed program that listed the evening's dinner menu, the Guild and Gala officers, the names of the musicians in the New Hampshire Brass Quartet, and the sponsors. He tapped the bottom of the program, indicating that he'd located my company's name. "Prescott's Antiques: Auctions and Appraisals," he read aloud. "Josie Prescott, president."

"Right."

"What does that mean—sponsoring? You pay the bills?"

"Well, yes. Some of them. I mean, the caterer discounted the food and the printer comped the invitations and the programs, but sponsoring an event like this involves more than just cash. This room," I said, gesturing, "is where we hold our monthly antiques auctions, so we're providing the physical space. We also donated some of the antiques that were auctioned off tonight. Plus, we researched all of them and prepared and produced the catalog."

He dropped the program on the table as if it were garbage and shifted in his seat. "Why?" he asked combatively. "Why be a sponsor?"

My father taught me that in business, as in personal relationships, it's crucial to deal only in facts. *When someone attacks your motive for doing something,* he instructed, *respond with facts. Don't get defensive. Don't attack back. Don't let your emotional reaction show in any way. Stay calm and stick to the facts.* I took a calming breath and reassured myself that no matter what Rowcliff was insinuating, there was nothing shameful about promoting my company's services.

"To help the Guild," I replied. "And to get my company's name out."

He picked up his pencil and gave a tap-tap, thinking what to ask next. "Were you and Maisy friends?" he asked.

"Not really. We worked together."

"No socializing, no lunches, no chitchat?" he asked, and from his demeanor, I had the sense that except for police-mandated standards, he would have added, *like most broads.*

"No. None. When we were together, we talked business."

He half-sneered in disbelief. *Yeah, right,* I could almost hear him thinking, *women—all business—I doubt it.* He punctuated his disdain with a quick tap-tap of his pencil. "Well then," he said, "let's try this. When did you first see her today?"

I ignored his attitude and focused on answering his question. "She got here early—midafternoon."

"When exactly?"

"About three thirty or four. She was excited and fluttered about, touching this and that, arranging flowers and so on." I smiled at the memory. She'd been almost giddy. "Mostly, to tell you the truth, she got in the way." I shrugged.

"Did you talk to her?"

"Then?"

"Ever."

"Sure. Lots. But not about anything special."

"Give me an example."

"Okay," I said. "About five, she asked me if I thought we had enough wine and I told her yes. Just before we sat down to dinner, she told me that she thought someone whose name I don't remember would bid over the estimate on the three-piece faience pottery set." I shrugged. "Things like that. Little nothings."

"What's a faience pottery set?" he asked.

"Faience is the French term for tin-glazed earthenware. This set includes two fruit dishes and a bowl. It's incredibly rare."

"How much is it worth?"

"About twenty-five hundred."

"You're kidding!"

I smiled. "Nope. Britt still has the auction sheets, I think, so you can see for yourself how it did."

"Why is it so valuable?"

"Aside from the fact that it's beautiful, the design is crisp and clean, and it's in perfect condition. Think about it—it's two hundred and fifty years old and it's unchipped and uncracked." I pointed. "Do you see it there?" He turned and tilted his head, squinting a little. "Notice how pure and bright the colors look even from this distance."

He nodded. "What else?"

"About the pottery?"

"No," he said, exasperated. "About Maisy."

I thought for a moment. "She told me a couple of times how great she thought the Gala was going." I shrugged again. "Nothing remarkable at all. I can't remember anything else."

He glared at me for a long moment, then stood up and looked around. "Looks like just about everyone's gone. Let's call it a night." He stood, shook out his pant leg, gestured to Officer Johnston, who was dutifully taking notes on the other side of the table, to follow him, and headed for the rear doors. I hunched my shoulders as a rush of icy air reached me. October in New Hampshire can be bone-chillingly cold.

Once the remaining guests and workers were processed out and Detective Rowcliff gave his final instructions to the police officers assigned to overnight sentry duty, he followed me through the warehouse into the main office and watched as I got ready to set the alarm.

He informed me in a tone that begged for argument that I had to leave my auction venue—to him a crime scene—unalarmed so the police could enter at will.

"No problem," I responded.

I retrieved my purse from where I'd placed it under a desk and turned to leave.

"When will you get in tomorrow?" he asked. He still seemed angry about something, but I figured that was his natural state, so I ignored it.

"I don't know. I'm sleeping late, I guarantee you that," I told him.

He didn't seem tired at all. Maybe murder energized him.

"I'm going to want to speak to you again in the morning."

"Let's talk when I get up," I said, making no commitment. I had a call in to Max, my lawyer, but even without his in-person support, I knew that I didn't have to agree to Detective Rowcliff's schedule.

"I'll call you," Rowcliff responded, and it sounded like a threat.

"Okay," I said.

I wiggled the door to be certain it was latched, told him goodbye, and walked across the lot to my car. Rowcliff's contempt was both irritating and intimidating.

He stood in place by the front door, unmoving. Waiting for the heat in my car to kick in, I sat still, staring at nothing. I glanced back through the rearview mirror. In the shadowy moonlight, it seemed as if his eyes were fixed on mine, and I shivered.

CHAPTER THREE

Pulling into my driveway about twenty minutes later, I turned off the engine and sat. The shimmering moon cast streaks of gray-white light on the meadow and pale shadows penetrated the stand of trees on the property's edge. Resting my forehead on the steering wheel, my father's favorite toast came to mind: *To silver light in the dark of night.* How I wished he'd be inside waiting for me, martini in hand.

When I allowed the memories in, my grief was as piercing and debilitating as the day he'd died six years ago. I moved my head a little, trying to ease the knotted muscles in my neck and shoulders. "Oh, Dad," I whispered, "tell me what to do."

Our relationship ran deeper than just loving daughter and father because of my mother's early death. I was only thirteen when she died of cancer, and as our way of coping, my father and I had circled the wagons. For the next sixteen years, until he died, we were a team, a rock-solid unit of two. He'd been the buttress on which I leaned, my biggest fan, and always, no matter what, a loyal ally. Neither time nor my move from New York to New Hampshire had eased the anguish of my loss. I'd endured, but I hadn't healed.

He would have agreed, I was certain, that leaving New York to start my own business, Prescott's Antiques: Auctions and Appraisals, was a smart move. But it had been terrifying to make the decision alone. And as exhilarating as it was to see my business grow, my success would have been far sweeter if I'd been able to share it with him.

Dad, I'd say, *our monthly auctions are increasingly well attended and profitable, the weekly tag sales are filled with repeat customers, and our newest promotional venture, Prescott's Instant*

Appraisals, has received participant acclaim and loads of positive media exposure. Plus, we've landed some good buys. Everything is going well, Dad. And I could hear his reply as clearly as if he were seated beside me in the car. *Way to go, Josie. Way to go.*

Until tonight. I'd set out to help the Portsmouth Women's Guild by sponsoring their annual autumn fund-raiser and I'd looked forward to receiving a kindly worded public thank-you for my company's efforts. Instead, a woman had died a horrible death in front of everyone. And as a result, not one of the 128 people in attendance would remember what a great job we'd done. What they'd remember was the murder at Prescott's.

I raised my head, reached my hand back and massaged my neck, trying to release the tension, and scanned the area around my house. Nothing stirred. It was so quiet, the world seemed vacant, maybe even dead. Yet when I cracked the window for air, life was apparent. Little clicks signaled that the engine was cooling off, an unseen animal skittered across the wooded path on the far side of the road, leaves crinkled as they were blown aside by a light breeze, and occasional squeaks and chirps alerted me that nocturnal birds were communicating among themselves. The sounds of night were loud and constant once I focused on them. *Perception is all,* I reminded myself.

I hate walking into dark places, especially a rental house that doesn't really feel like home, so I always leave a lamp on upstairs, in my bedroom. The small golden glow welcomed me, but tonight, it wasn't enough. As I went through the downstairs rooms turning on lights, I debated whether to take a shower and then have a martini, or whether I should have the martini first. I decided to take the shower, wrap myself in my favorite pink chenille robe, and then relax with the drink.

I was exhausted. My entire staff and I had worked long hours in the days leading up to the Gala. But it wasn't only a lack of sleep that had worn me down. It was a combination of fatigue, stress, and angst. Not only had I been on edge making certain every detail at the Gala was perfect, but I'd watched, shocked, as Maisy'd died in my auction room, and I couldn't stop reliving it. The memories played over and over again in an unending loop.

To make matters worse, Ty, my sort-of boyfriend and scheduled date for the evening, was unavailable to help me cope. I knew it was irrational, but his absence felt more like abandonment than an understandable reaction to a family emergency. When he told me that he needed to go to Los Angeles to care for his much-loved, ill aunt Trina, I'd said all the right things: "Go, Ty . . . Can I do anything? . . . Give Aunt Trina my best. . . . I'll send my good wishes west. . . . I'll be fine." While I felt sad for Ty and concerned for Aunt Trina, I also felt sad for me. I wanted Ty nearby. I sighed, trying to shake off my melancholy.

As I headed upstairs, aching with loneliness and tension, I again wondered why Detective Rowcliff had concluded that Maisy's death was murder. If Ty hadn't left, I could have asked him and he might have known. Or he could have found out. He could have called Rowcliff, one police official to another. Even though they were of different ranks and worked for different cities, as police chief of Rocky Point, Ty would have known the questions to ask the Portsmouth homicide detective to get the answers I wanted.

I thought back, trying to pinpoint an event that had led Detective Rowcliff to that startling conclusion, pausing as I relived the fatal moment.

An image of Maisy, her face contorted with horror as she fell, came to me. I forced the memory aside. But that vision was replaced with one that was worse—the cold practicality of the uniformed officials who'd loaded Maisy's body on a gurney and carted it away. Their businesslike "all in a day's work" attitude had left me feeling shaken.

I couldn't imagine why Detective Rowcliff thought Maisy had been murdered, and with Ty unavailable, I had no one to ask. I used to have my father and several good friends. Then, in a matter of months, everything changed, and now I was alone.

In New York, while still working at Frisco's, the famous auction house, I'd had to testify against my boss about the price-fixing scandal that had rocked the high-end antiques world. Despite the fact that I had done the right thing, even my best buddies shunned me, and it wasn't long before I was forced out of the company. A month later, my father's unexpected death shattered my world, and only weeks after that, my then boyfriend, Rick, decided that he couldn't handle my unremitting grief, and we'd parted company.

Since arriving in New Hampshire, my focus had been on work. That is, until I met Ty last spring. I still work hard, but now I make sure there's time for pleasure, too. I smiled, recalling the recent evening when Ty and I snuggled under an afghan to watch a Shark Week special on cable and flirted with the idea of taking a winter vacation to the Bahamas.

I climbed the last few steps and headed into my bedroom. The clock that rested on my bedside table read 12:31. I was surprised. It felt later. According to the red blinking light on my answering machine, I had three messages. *Please God,* I prayed silently, *let there be one from Ty.*

I pushed the button.

"Josie, it's Ty. I'm in Atlanta and had a sec before I get on the next flight, so I thought I'd leave you a good-luck message. I'm sure the Gala will go well. Thinking of you. Talk to you soon. Bye."

He'd left the message at six. I wondered if he'd heard about Maisy's death yet. Probably not. I bet he hadn't even landed in L.A. yet.

I pushed the button for call two.

"Josie, it's Wes. We need to talk."

Wes Smith, the young reporter from the *Seacoast Star.* He left his cell phone number and added, "Call me, Josie. You probably want to comment on something I plan to write."

Ominous, I thought. Wes had a gift for creating a sense of urgency. I jotted his number down, then braced myself for message number three.

"Josie, it's Wes again. Let's talk. Call me. Now."

The date and time marker revealed that his first call had been around ten, and the second one had occurred less than thirty minutes ago, just after midnight.

I felt out of control and upset. I'd done nothing, yet it was as if my world had tilted. I turned the shower up as hot as I could stand it, stood under the pounding water, and cried.

All at once, I felt dizzy, as if the shower stall were askew, just a little. I pushed against the steaming tiles and forced myself to breathe. A memory came to me, and I shut my eyes. When I was about eight, my mother and I entered a hall of mirrors at a fair, and I froze, unable to move, barely able to breathe. Not knowing what was real or which way to turn, I became paralyzed with panic.

"Come on, Josie," she whispered, stroking my hair. "Follow me."

I couldn't move. I couldn't think. Fright held me fast and my eyes stayed fixed on the shimmering mirror in front of me.

"Close your eyes and take a deep breath," my mother told me calmly.

I followed her instructions, but the uncontrollable terror remained intact. I felt myself begin to hyperventilate.

She took my hand and squeezed reassuringly. "Let's go. I'll lead us out."

A similar feeling of discombobulation came over me now, a sense that despite appearances, what was in front of me wasn't real. It was as if I'd tumbled into an unseen chasm through ground that appeared solid but suddenly no longer supported my weight.

Apprehension merged with a primitive and hopeless confusion. Just as I had endured skin-crawling anxiety that day when I was eight, overwhelming dread took hold of me now. I concentrated on my breathing, trying to find my way back to solid ground. Water streamed over my face and neck. I felt utterly alone and completely vulnerable. I wished Ty was with me to hold me, stroke my hair, and kiss the back of my neck. And to reassure me that everything would be all right, that Detective Rowcliff didn't really think I'd killed Maisy, that I wasn't the intended victim, and that Maisy's death was a tragedy but not a crime. "Please, God," I whispered, "let us all be safe."

I didn't know which was worse—to be unable to trust my perceptions or to recognize that there were things I couldn't understand or control. I'd had recurring bad dreams in the days following the hall of mirrors experience, and today, everything felt like a nightmare come true.

CHAPTER FOUR

A fter two martinis, I crawled into bed, unable to think because I was so tired, yet so tense that I was certain I wouldn't be able to rest. But after reading only a few pages of a favorite Rex Stout mystery I'd read a dozen times before, *Plot It Yourself,* I fell into a deep and dreamless sleep.

I jerked upright with a start, like a slice of bread popping out of a toaster. The phone rang. The clock told me it was nine thirty in the morning. I grabbed the receiver before it could ring a third time. "Hello," I said, agitated.

"Josie," Wes said. I recognized the *Seacoast Star* reporter's voice and could picture him hunched over the dirty steering wheel in his old car, pen poised in case I uttered a printable gem.

"Wes, why are you calling me so early?"

"What are you talking about? It's not so early. It's midmorning."

"It's not midmorning. It's early morning. And I was asleep."

"That's right, I forgot. You're always grumpy in the morning."

I slapped the sheet away and stood up, wriggling my feet into pink fuzzy slippers. "I'm not grumpy in the morning," I protested. I sighed loudly, resigned to the inevitability of talking to him. "What do you want, Wes?"

"A quote."

"Figures."

"Well, it's not every day you have a murder at your business."

"Do I now?"

"What do you mean?"

"How do you know it's murder?"

"I have sources," he said mysteriously. I'd heard that before. Wes always had sources. I snuggled into my robe and tied the sash tightly. It was cold. I reminded myself grimly that his sources were usually right.

"So," he continued, "what do you say about the theory that Maisy Gaylor wasn't the intended victim."

"Nothing. I say nothing."

"I'm going to quote multiple sources saying that there's confusion about the circumstances of Maisy's death and that you might have been the intended target. Do you want to comment?"

"No," I said, pushing aside the drapes that covered the side window. I shivered despite the warm robe and bright morning sun. Silvery white sparkles from sun-touched hoarfrost glistened on the lawn.

"I'm going to report that you're going to be reinterviewed by Detective Rowcliff this morning. Don't you want to comment?"

"No."

"Would you like to add anything?" he asked ironically.

"Wes?"

"Yeah?"

"What did Maisy die from?" I found myself almost whispering.

"No official word yet. They're pretty sure it was poison, though."

"Oh God. That's awful. That's just horrible."

"That's kind of a skimpy quote."

"Don't you dare publish a word I spoke. Not one word, do you hear me, Wes?"

"I'll promise if you give me an exclusive."

"I have nothing to say to you. I'm hanging up now."

I heard righteous sputtering as I gently replaced the receiver.

Memories of relentless media pressing in on me during the price-fixing scandal that had helped drive me out of New York stopped me as I headed downstairs to start coffee. I grasped the railing. "Not again," I whispered. "Please don't let them stalk me again." Then as now, I was innocent, the whistle-blower in New York and the cooperative bystander here.

The doorbell rang, startling me as I scooped coffee into the filter, and grounds sprinkled on the counter. "Damn," I said, sweeping the bits of coffee into the sink.

I peeked through the window on the front door but didn't recognize the dark-haired woman standing on the stoop. She was younger than I was by a few years, wore low-cut jeans with an orange turtleneck and an oversized orange-and-black flannel shirt, and had two children with her. A boy of four or five stood next to her, holding her hand. A girl of about two was cradled in her right arm, the little girl's head tucked into the woman's shoulder, her bottom resting on her hip.

"Hi," I said, opening the door wide.

"Oh my God, here I go again with lousy timing. You're still in your robe. Sorry."

"It's not a problem. How can I help you?" A missionary proselytizing, maybe, I thought, or a single mom selling cosmetics door-to-door.

She smiled. "I'm Zoe Dwyer. You're Josie Prescott?"

"Yes," I said. I didn't recognize the name.

"And this is Jake, and this little doll is Emma."

I smiled at each child. Jake pulled away from her and ran down the steps and into the field on the far side of the house, laughing and shrieking as he tried to catch a squirrel. Emma was drowsing, her face in soft repose.

"Jake, stay in sight!" Zoe called, watching him for a moment.

"Okay!" he called back.

" 'Quicksilver Jake,' that's what I call him." She turned back to me, smiling, and said, "Well, I'm sorry to disturb you, but I thought I ought to introduce myself."

"Sure."

Confusion must have shown on my face, because she said, "Sorry. I don't mean to be mysterious. I'm your new landlady."

"What? What happened to Mr. Winterelli?"

"My uncle. Wow, you didn't hear? Sorry to be the one to tell you, but he died."

"Oh, I'm so sorry. He was a nice man. I can't believe it. When did it happen?"

"Three weeks ago. He had a heart attack."

"Three weeks ago!" I did a mental calculation. We were in the final rush of Gala preparations back then. "I know I was busy at work," I said, "but I didn't know I was that busy. I'm so sorry."

"Thanks. Anyway, I was out in Colorado with my good-for-nothing husband, may God punish the f'ing bum—excuse my French." She hoisted Emma up higher on her hip and gave a short laugh. "I can't control my temper. I'm Italian. Sorry about that." She glanced at Emma. "Anyway, I said to him, 'You know what? I like New England. I grew up there, and I'm sure as shooting not happy here, so bye bye.'" She shrugged. "I packed up, picked up, and here we are. Anyway, I've moved in next door, so I thought I ought to come over and say hello."

Jake squealed as he ran toward the woods, and we both turned toward him. Two weeks past peak, the old maples that fringed the meadow still blazed with color. Most of the leaves were orange, but some shone with a yellow glint, and one entire tree glowed a pinkish red.

"Jake, stay close!" Zoe called.

"Wow, I'm just shocked," I responded. "Mr. Winterelli was so pleasant. Helpful and everything."

"Yeah. He always said nice things about you, too."

"Do you want to come in and have some coffee?"

"Thanks, I'd love to, but I can't. I loved my uncle to death, but he wasn't the best housekeeper, you know? There's a lot to do."

A collie came running full-tilt around the corner of the house, bearing a thick stick, which it dropped at Zoe's feet.

"This is Lassie. I know, not an original name, right?" She shrugged again. "What a great dog Lassie was. Do you remember that show? I must have watched a gazillion reruns growing up." She dipped down, keeping Emma in place, picked up the stick, and tossed it toward the back. Lassie dashed after it. Jake screeched a greeting to the dog and ran to meet her. "I better go. If you need anything, let me know."

"Thanks," I said. "Listen, if I can help you get settled, give a shout."

She waved as she headed down the steps, calling for Jake to come inside now. I watched as they made their way toward the big white house next door. The little house I rented was a smaller version, built a hundred years earlier as an in-law residence, an American version of a traditional British dower house.

As I shut the door, I felt sad and a little lost. It didn't matter that Zoe seemed like a lot of fun. All I could focus on was the unanticipated and unwanted change—nothing against Zoe, but I had liked Mr. Winterelli! *Just when I get used to something,* I thought, feeling fussy and allowing the door to slam, *it changes.*

The phone rang as I poured a cup of coffee. It was Detective Rowcliff, and he was brusque.

"I need to talk to you. When can you get here?"

"What about?"

"About Maisy Gaylor's death," he replied impatiently. I could almost hear him saying to himself, *What do you think I want to talk to you about? Duh.*

There was menace in Rowcliff's voice, and something else, too, but I couldn't put my finger on it. Some kind of energy—maybe excitement, maybe zeal. Was he on to something? We agreed to meet at my building in half an hour.

I hung up and dialed Max Bixby, my lawyer, my hand shaking uncontrollably. Last night's message hadn't conveyed the urgency I now felt. I got him at home and he agreed to meet me right away.

There was bad news awaitin'. I didn't know what, but I didn't doubt whether.

CHAPTER FIVE

I ran upstairs, threw on jeans and a sweater, laced up my work boots, grabbed my purse and jacket, and was out the door in nothing flat.

While I waited for the engine to warm up, a pleasant memory came to me. I was standing close to Ty. It was last spring, shortly after we met. I felt sparks between us and had sensed, from the warmth in his eyes, that he felt them, too. I grumbled that his car was too high to get into easily, and he told me that the police-issued SUV was more properly called a vehicle than a car, and that the problem wasn't that the vehicle was too tall, but that I was too short. It was a silly exchange, nothing special, really, just pleasant banter, the kind of innocuous conversation on which relationships are built.

Ty is a morning person, so even though it was still early in Los Angeles, I thought maybe I could catch him before he got busy with Aunt Trina and her doctors.

I dug my phone out of my purse and dialed his cell phone. After four rings, I heard the click that meant I was going to get his voice mail. "This is Chief Ty Alverez of the Rocky Point Police. Please leave a message."

He had a great voice, deep and strong. At the prompt, I said, "Ty, it's Josie. I got your message. Please give my best to your aunt, and know I'm thinking of you. Call when you can."

Not my best effort, but enough to touch base and acknowledge his message. He'd call when he was able. Never mind that I was consumed with worry and fear. It was important to me that I convey sensitivity to his situation with his aunt and that I not appear needy. Perception transcends reality.

As I approached my building, I could see that the parking lot was thickly quilted with vibrant gold and vivid vermillion leaves. Winter would soon be here, and the spectacular foliage scene would evolve into a setting seemingly devoid of life, tinted in brown and white. Nothing had ever looked as desolate to me as the New Hampshire coast in winter until I realized that beneath the veneer of barrenness, the land teemed with life, winter gardens and empty beaches revealing their own kind of beauty, spectacular in its way, once I took the time to look.

But today under the warming early-autumn sun, colors flickered opalescently as leaves fluttered in the light breeze. Lying on the ground, they appeared lush and supple, neither dry nor dead, but I knew that their good looks were deceptive; one good rain, and they'd become as dangerous as an unseen ice slick. I made a mental note to have them blown clear before next Saturday's tag sale.

I parked next to Sasha's car and noted that Fred was here, too, parked almost at the end of the lot, over by the tag-sale entrance. I bet it was our recent acquisition of a Picasso sketch that drew my two researchers into work on a Sunday morning.

Most of our acquisitions came from word-of-mouth referrals and responses to ads, plus, occasionally, walk-ins during our tag sales. Lately, as testimony to our growing reputation, we'd also attracted clients from other states.

Yesterday, a middle-aged woman, who'd introduced herself as Helen Finn, had arrived at our door without an appointment and with the Picasso drawing in hand. She'd explained that she was up from Arkansas on a leaf-peeping weekend, and after reading about us on the Internet, she'd decided to bring it with her, hoping we'd be interested in buying it. The sketch had been her mother's, she'd said, and now that her mother had died, she wanted to sell it.

The illustration was deceptively simple. It showed a sort of lion's head, swiftly rendered in thick sweeps of crayon on yellowing paper. Only a master could have wielded that crayon, executing his vision in one flowing movement, and also knowing what not to draw. While Fred did a quick Internet check to make certain a Mrs. Finn had, in fact, died, and that the sketch wasn't listed as stolen, Sasha consulted the Picasso catalogue raisonné on our reference

shelf and verified the sketch's dimensions and the signature. Delighted, I closed the deal. Ms. Finn was ecstatic to receive a ten-
thousand-dollar on-the-spot cash payment, and I was elated, too.
Properly marketed, it should sell for more than forty thousand dollars.

I sat for a minute, readying myself for the day ahead. The big
PRESCOTT'S ANTIQUES: AUCTIONS AND APPRAISALS sign perched atop the
building glinted in the sun, and looking at it, I allowed myself a
private moment of pride.

I remembered how Stella, the real estate agent who'd showed
me the property more than five years ago, had wrinkled her nose
as we turned into the parking lot. "You said you wanted space,"
she'd said. "That's about all this place has going for it."

The decaying building was a hodgepodge comprised of three
unequal sections. The largest area, the central unit, had been built
in the late 1800s by Millner Canvas Company as its spanking new
state-of-the-art factory. Millner's produced high-quality canvas
sails, bags, and shoes until the mid-1970s, when Doug Millner
moved the operation to North Carolina. Now it contained our offices and a cavernous industrial storage area.

When I'd bought the building, the area on the left—now my
auction venue—had been a retail shop—a latter-day factory-outlet
store selling products manufactured on-site at a discount. I'd replaced the small door that had separated the store from the factory
with custom-made sliding walls that allowed us to move big pieces
of furniture easily from the warehouse into the auction hall.

To the right of the original factory was an attached shacklike
structure we used for the weekly tag sales. I had no idea what its
original purpose was, and other than installing rest rooms and
bringing it up to code, I hadn't updated or redecorated it at all. Its
Spartan simplicity conveyed exactly the right mood for bargain
hunters.

An hour after Stella and I had pulled into the lot, I made an offer. Stella was stunned speechless, and I understood why. When
she viewed the property, she saw a run-down monolith, an un-
loved factory that had been abandoned thirty years earlier and ignored ever since. My perspective was different. What I saw was

the perfect place in a perfect location, just off I-95 and only minutes from downtown Portsmouth. There was plenty of space for
inventory, a layout that could have been tailor-made for my business model—running both auctions and tag sales—ample parking,
and if the engineer's report found that the building was structurally
sound, I could be up and running within a few months. Stella saw
a problem. I saw an opportunity. Perception is individual, and
real.

I stepped out of my car and saw that Officer Johnston, Detective
Rowcliff's note taker, was watching me from his post by the auction doors. I waved at him and mouthed hello, and he half-saluted
and nodded in return.

It was a beautiful day, and I wished I could assign myself the
duty of clearing the leaves so I could stay outside. With a sigh of resignation, I opened the front door, and chimes tinkled. Gretchen,
my assistant, had hung wind chimes from an eyehook high up on
the door about a month ago. When I'd asked her why, she'd
smiled sweetly and said, "Because it sounds nice." *Never overlook
the obvious,* I reminded myself.

"How can you say Matisse wasn't important?" Fred asked Sasha
now, sounding shocked.

"I didn't say he wasn't important. I said his importance was
diluted by the number of clever fakes on the market."

"That's insane. That's equivalent to saying that he was too talented for his own good."

"No, just that he was too popular too early on," Sasha said confidently. When discussing art, and only then, Sasha was completely
self-assured. "If no one had liked his work, no one would have
copied it, and his work would be easier to authenticate. People are
afraid to buy a Matisse. There are too many good fakes out there.
And that holds the prices down."

I hung my jacket on one of the hooks by the door and said,
"Hey. How are you?"

"Okay," Fred said. "You know. All things considered."

I nodded and turned to Sasha. "A little scared," she said, tucking
her hair behind her ear nervously. "How about you?"

I shrugged. "I've been better."

Sasha nodded, and after a momentary silence, I said, "Well, we seem to share a coping strategy—we work."

"Is it all right that we came in?" Sasha asked.

"Absolutely. It's a good thing. So tell me, what's today's debate?"

"Sasha says that Matisse's prices are artificially low because the prints are hard to authenticate," Fred said disdainfully.

Fred and Sasha were an odd couple. When Fred first joined the company last spring, I thought his imperiousness would alienate Sasha. To my surprise, they became friends, and I'd come to realize that their arguments revealed intellectual compatibility, not antipathy. They both revered analytical thinking and condemned lazy research. Their challenges of each other were all about scholarship, not personality. They interacted synergistically, and as a result, their work got better.

"You mean that if the art is easy to fake, it ends up having less value?" I asked.

"Yes," Sasha replied. "It's not whether the art is beautiful or worthy. It's whether it's easily reproducible."

"That's specious reasoning and you know it!" Fred insisted.

"No, it's not," Sasha responded. She turned to me. "Matisse once said that he'd produced fifteen hundred prints in his career and twenty-five hundred of them were in America."

"Ouch," I said.

"Exactly," she agreed, nodding. Fred made a derisive noise. "It's true," she insisted. "And the point is equally true about Picasso's line drawings. They're brilliant in conception and execution. That's not the issue. The issue is that they're easy to reproduce."

"And therefore easy to fake," I said.

"Right."

"And you, Fred? What don't you agree with?"

"Her premise is right. It's her conclusion that's dead wrong." He spun his desk chair and drilled Sasha with his eyes. "Whether or not a print is easy to reproduce is irrelevant. What's relevant is whether the piece can be authenticated with a high degree of confidence. When it comes to pricing, you know as well as I do, Sasha, how complex it is. Of course the beauty and originality of the piece figure into it. But so does its rarity, market trends, important or prestigious reviews, celebrity acceptance, and so on. But the number and quality of fakes available for sale is not one of the factors impacting price. Not when authentication is a straight-forward process. Which it is in this case. At least it's straightforward if you know what you're looking for."

Uh-oh, I thought, *here come the fireworks.* Instead, Sasha chuckled. "You're right, you're right, I know you're right," she said, rolling her eyes.

"Got it," I said, and added, "I'll be upstairs if you need me. Let me know when Max and Detective Rowcliff arrive, okay?" As I headed into the warehouse and up the spiral staircase to my private enclave, I heard Fred drive home his point.

"Assuming the art looks right, first test the paper," he said in a tone indicating that he was tired of repeating the obvious.

"Surely you're aware that you can buy genuine, period-specific paper with no problem," Sasha responded.

"I didn't say testing the paper was the only step. I said it was the first step."

Sasha's reply faded as I mounted the stairs. I crossed my fingers. Fred and Sasha were both intuitive and well-trained art historians, but neither was astute when it came to business. Assuming their conversation had something to do with the Picasso sketch we'd just bought, I hoped that their conclusion would be that we had underestimated its value, not that we'd overpaid.

Sasha buzzed on the intercom and told me that Max had arrived.

"Send him up," I said.

I walked to the door and waited for him. Max looked the same as always, although I hadn't seen him in several months. He wore a bow tie and tweed jacket, and his smile was easy and natural. He conveyed a comfortable combination of relaxation and legal tradition.

"Hey," he said, reaching the top of the staircase and extending his hand. "I haven't seen you in a 'coon's age. How are you?"

I shook his hand and smiled. "Boy, is it good to see you, Max! How's things?"

"Good, good. Our littlest one, Penny, she's sleeping through the night now, so all is well with the world."

I laughed, delighted at his mild joke, aware that much of my pleasure derived from relief. The future looked less bleak with Max in the room.

"Thank God for you, Max. You have no idea how hard it is for me to deal with this kind of chaos. With you on my side, it's easier."

He smiled and patted my shoulder. "I can't think of anyone's side I'd rather be on."

"Have a seat, and tell me what we do now."

Max hitched up his pants and lowered himself onto the yellow love seat. "The first thing we do is review what you know. Start by giving me an overview."

"An overview," I repeated, gathering my thoughts. "Maisy collapsed and died. At the time, I thought she had a heart attack or something, or that maybe she died from some sort of drug reaction or overdose—she was uncharacteristically euphoric before she died."

Max nodded and made a note on a pad of lined yellow paper balanced on his thigh.

"The only thing is . . ." I faltered.

"What?" he asked, looking up.

"Well, Detective Rowcliff—he's in charge of the investigation and he'll be here soon—well, he said that he didn't think she died from natural causes. He thought it was murder."

Max looked at me for a moment. "Why?"

I shook my head. "He wouldn't say."

"That's interesting, isn't it? Well, assuming he's right, let me get one question out of the way. Did you kill Maisy Gaylor?"

My mouth opened a bit. "Rowcliff asked me that, too."

"Oh, he did, did he? What did you answer?"

"I told him the truth. I told him no."

"Okay, then." He smiled reassuringly and I sank into a Queen Anne wing chair across from him. "So," he said, "talk to me. What else do you know?"

"Not much. Apparently, Rowcliff isn't even sure if Maisy was the intended victim. There's some uncertainty about whether maybe . . . well, it sounds silly when I say it out loud, but he seems to think that I might have been the target."

He nodded as if he'd expected that revelation. "Do you know why he thinks that?"

"No."

He gestured that I was to continue. "What else?"

I shook my head. "That's it. Really."

"Okay, then. When it comes to answering questions, if I tell you to stop talking, you do so, right?"

"Right."

"Keep your answers short and responsive. Don't volunteer information."

"Okay, but this is so unfair. I was just trying to promote my business and do a good deed, you know, by sponsoring the Gala. I barely knew Maisy."

"Still, something is making him think that someone might be targeting you, not Maisy."

I shook my head, not wanting it to be true. "It's not possible."

"Why not?"

I stared at him, then shook my head again. "It's just not possible," I repeated.

Max leaned forward and waited until he had my full attention. "Yes, Josie," he said softly, "it is."

CHAPTER SIX

I was still staring at Max, horrified, unable to think how I should respond to his terrifying comment, when Sasha called up that Detective Rowcliff had arrived. I asked her to tell him that we'd meet him in the auction room.

"Are you all right?" Max asked, standing and slipping his pad of paper into his briefcase.

"Not really," I confessed. "This is just awful."

He squeezed my arm, and I felt a little comforted.

"Remember . . . short answers, Josie. Okay?"

I smiled. "I remember. My lawyer once told me that one-word answers are good."

He smiled back and nodded. "Exactly."

"Have you ever met Detective Rowcliff?" I asked.

"No. But I gather from your tone that I ought to ask why."

I shrugged. "You'll see. He's pretty tough to take."

"In what way?"

"I guess mostly it's his sarcasm. I don't know. He looks at me and I feel like a bug under a microscope."

"Intensely examined?"

I thought for a moment before answering. "No, not exactly. More like despised and ready to be pinned."

"Yowzi. With that recommendation, I can hardly wait to meet him."

"Yeah," I said, heading for the stairs, feeling resigned to my fate.

"I won't let him pin you," Max promised.

"Thank you, but I'm not sure that even you could stop him if he has his sights on me."

I heard Detective Rowcliff before I saw him, the familiar tapping of his pencil alerting me to his presence. Sasha had escorted him to the auction room, and when I entered, he was squatting beside the podium on the stage, staring into the hollow area, examining the shelf. When he saw us enter from the back, he jumped down and hurried over.

I introduced them. Max said hello and Rowcliff nodded a sort of greeting.

Max glanced around the sad-looking room. On Rowcliff's orders, the caterer's team had left the tables untouched, and the litter contributed to the melancholy atmosphere. Maisy's collapse had interrupted dessert, and scores of unfinished apple tarts scattered about had long since hardened. Wineglasses stood partially filled, and crumpled cloth napkins remained where they'd been hastily tossed.

"Can Josie get this place cleaned up?" Max asked.

"Yeah, we're finished with it. I have a video camera with me, and after I get it all recorded, sure, then she can do what she wants."

Max nodded. "Okay, then."

Detective Rowcliff gave me a long look, then asked, "Did you have a good conversation with Wes Smith?"

"What are you talking about?"

"Talking to the media overnight. No grass grows under your feet!"

"What are you saying? All I told Wes was that I had no comment."

"I guess you don't subscribe to the *Seacoast Star*'s instant updates."

"I've never even heard of it."

" 'Quick Flash News,' they call it. It comes via e-mail. The department subscribes, and you're the big story."

He handed over a single sheet, a printout of an e-mail, and Max and I read it standing shoulder-to-shoulder. The headline alone made me feel faint. PRESCOTT INVOLVED IN SECOND MURDER. The article that followed was worse. Wes quoted me over and over again as saying, "No comment." I pursed my lips, impotent rage lashing me.

While what Wes wrote was literally true, the article left the vague impression that I knew things I wasn't telling, and it gratuitously referred to me as a suspect in the murder that had occurred in Rocky Point last year. Mr. Grant had been a potential client and he'd been killed, but to state that I was "involved" in his murder was either grandstanding or incendiary, or both. Damn him.

Wes ended by stating that maybe it was I, not Maisy, who had been the intended victim, implying that there were good, if unspecified, reasons for his conjecture. The article was intrusive and embarrassing, and I felt utterly betrayed. Stupid me. I'd thought Wes and I had an understanding. I clenched my fists to control myself and turned to Max.

"If I murdered Wes Smith, not a jury in the land would convict me," I whispered.

"That's probably true," he whispered back. "Stay cool."

To Rowcliff, he raised his eyebrows and asked, "What's your point, Detective? All she said was 'No comment.'"

"She shouldn't be talking to him at all."

"This is a free country," Max said coldly. "If she wants to talk to a reporter, she can."

There was a long pause while the two men stared at each other. My anger faded as I watched them bandy for position. With a smile that edged toward a smirk, Max handed back the printout and asked, "So, what can we do for you, Detective?"

Rowcliff accepted the paper, folded it, and slipped it into his pocket. "Ms. Prescott can answer a few questions."

Max gestured to some chairs near where we stood. "We'll be glad to answer your questions. Shall we sit?"

"Sure. Let me get Officer Johnston to take notes again."

"Again?"

"He recorded our conversation last night."

"We'll want copies of all of the notes—yesterday's and today's," Max said.

"No problem."

Johnston took his time getting situated. He was at my left and Max was sitting quietly on my right. I watched as Rowcliff tipped his chair back, eyeing Johnston, mentally hurrying him along.

"So," Detective Rowcliff said once Johnston was ready, "have you thought of anyone who wants you dead?"

Before I could answer, Max asked, "Why do you think Josie might have been the target?"

"Logic," he said sarcastically, glaring at me.

"Could you be a little more specific?" Max asked, his tone neutral.

Rowcliff stared at him, and from the look on his face, he was considering whether he could eliminate Max from our conversation. After a long minute, Rowcliff sighed, pursed his lips, then pulled them together so tightly, they formed a single thin line.

"Last night, I knew two things that made me wonder who the target was. Now I have additional information, and I'm still wondering. Nothing I've learned indicates whether Josie was or wasn't the intended target. Which means I need to evaluate all factors and consider both options."

"And these factors are?" Max pushed.

Rowcliff looked at Max, then back at me, unsmiling. He tapped his pencil on the table to a slower rhythm, calculating, perhaps, the likelihood of Max's allowing me to answer his questions without first giving his foundation for asking them.

He turned to me and sneered. "I guess I can tell you about it, since we plan on releasing the medical examiner's preliminary report to the media in about an hour."

What a jerk, I thought. Implying that anything he told me would inevitably go straight to the press. I wanted to tell Rowcliff what I thought of him. Then I wanted to hit him, to wipe the derisive smirk off his face. Max cleared his throat and sent me a warning look to keep quiet. It took willpower, but I managed to avoid reacting. I sat on my hands and stayed silent.

Holding up a finger, Rowcliff said to Max, "One, from all accounts, Maisy Gaylor sipped wine, gagged, collapsed, and died. Most people figured she'd had a heart attack or something. We were able to dismiss that idea pretty quickly."

"Why?" Max asked.

Rowcliff gave a short series of taps with his pencil. "I'll get there in a minute. But, if it was murder, you don't have to be Einstein to figure that something toxic was in the wine, so I asked everybody about it. Seems Maisy put her glass on the table near Josie as they were getting ready to announce the auction winners. Well, there was a lot of activity going on, and since both Josie and Maisy were drinking red wine, it got me thinking about whether the glasses could have been switched."

As he spoke, I pictured Maisy approaching the table last night. Her tight black dress looked odd, as if she were playing dress-up. Every other time I'd seen her, she'd worn clothes selected more for comfort than style—oversized sweaters, off-the-rack tweed blazers that weren't cut for her narrow frame, slacks that gapped at the knee.

I remembered how Walter, her husband, sat stiffly in his chair, watching her with a sour expression. Never having met him before, I didn't know if he was sulking over something in particular or whether pouting was normal for him. Regardless, I was glad he wasn't *my* husband.

"Is it time already?" Maisy asked as she reached me. "I can't believe it! The night has just flown by."

Oh God, I thought at the time, *is she for real?* Between missing Ty and making small talk, which I hate to do under the best of circumstances, to me the night seemed endless.

Rowcliff brought me back to the here and now with a tap-tap of his pencil. He raised a second finger and said, "Two, based on preliminary interviews, which I acknowledge in advance aren't definitive, absolutely no one wanted Maisy dead." He flipped a hand. "Everyone seemed bewildered more than anything else that someone would have killed her."

"No one even has a suggestion about a motive?" Max queried.

"Nope. Not a one. Maisy doesn't seem like a person who generated a lot of heat, if you know what I mean."

"I never met her. What was she like?" Max asked.

"From all reports, she was just what she appeared to be, a middle-aged, middle-class, happily married woman." He turned to me and asked, "Is that your impression of her, too?"

"I didn't know her well, but her husband seemed kind of, I don't know, dour. Happily married?" I shrugged. "I have no idea."

"Yeah. Maybe. It's early days. Still, with confusion about the wineglasses, and without any hint of a motive, I figured it was worth asking if Josie knew any reason why someone might be after *her*."

Max nodded, following Rowcliff's reasoning. I felt disconnected from the conversation, as if I were inadvertently eavesdropping on someone else's situation or watching a movie plot unfold.

Rowcliff stretched his legs out to the side. "The only out-of-whack comment I heard at all was that Maisy seemed happier than usual. So happy, maybe she was stoned. Right, Josie?"

I nodded. "I don't know. The thought occurred to me that something was different, that's all."

Rowcliff raised a third finger. "Which leads to point three. I now know that poison was, in fact, introduced into the wine. And it wasn't some kind of medication or recreational drug that killed her. No overdose or anything like that. It was homicide all right."

"What was it?" Max asked.

Rowcliff gave a long rat-a-tat, assessing me in some way I didn't understand. "Potassium cyanide," he said.

"Oh my God!" I exclaimed. "How awful!"

"Which you didn't smell?" Rowcliff challenged.

"What?" I responded, confused.

"Other people did—they smelled bitter almonds."

"No. I didn't smell anything."

"How come?" Rowcliff asked, his attitude demanding a defense.

Under his accusatory glare, I felt like a deer in the headlights, frozen in heart-stopping fear, and doomed because of it.

CHAPTER SEVEN

I shook my head helplessly and turned to Max for guidance. How could I answer a question posed as a negative?

"I'm not an expert," Max said, "but I know this much: Not everyone in a circumstance like this smells bitter almonds."

Rowcliff shrugged again, unconvinced. "So now I'm focusing on tracking who had access to the wine Maisy drank," he explained, ignoring Max's comment. "I'll have some questions for Josie about that later."

"Certainly," Max agreed politely.

"The fourth fact," Rowcliff said, raising another finger, "is a beaut. When Maisy dropped the glass, it shattered, except that a chunk of stem survived, enough for the technicians to identify fingerprints from two people. No surprise, Maisy's prints were on it, since she was holding the glass." He turned to face me directly. "The other prints were yours."

His point didn't register. I simply couldn't assimilate what he was saying. I knew my fingerprints were on file, but I couldn't understand why he seemed to be speaking with eager anticipation. When I applied for the job at Frisco's in New York, they'd performed a comprehensive background check, standard operating procedure for new employees before they got access to priceless treasures. And last spring, Ty took them again as part of the Grant murder investigation Wes had alluded to. I thought about what Rowcliff said, but the implications just didn't make sense.

"So tell me, Josie," the detective asked, "how did your prints get there?"

I stared at Rowcliff and tried to focus. *How did my prints get on Maisy's glass?*

"You mean, how *could* they have gotten there, right?" Max spoke up.

"Right," Rowcliff answered, irritated.

"Josie owns this place. And I've seen her attitude toward details. Presumably, she shifted some of the glasses around as part of the preparation process."

"Sure, that may explain it. But maybe she can remember touching that particular glass."

"Josie?" Max asked. "Do you?"

I closed my eyes, recalling the scene again. My assistant, Gretchen, had just delivered the bidding sheets, her long copper-colored hair shining in the golden light. I smiled a little, remembering how much she'd enjoyed being in the thick of it. She always loved celebrity gossip, even on a local scale, so she was completely in her element, happily seeing who did what with whom, when, and how, and noting fashions.

After Gretchen delivered the sheets, I signaled Britt that we were ready to announce the winners and he notified his two colleagues—Maisy, the Guild representative, and Dora, the Gala event chair—that we were ready for the highlight of the evening. Both Maisy and Dora acknowledged the signals, stood up from their respective tables, and headed our way.

Maisy arrived first. She placed her half-full glass of red wine on the table near me so she could accept Britt's proffered hand, and as her watch came into view, I was shocked that it was nine thirty. *Nine thirty!* I thought again of Ty.

I opened my eyes, chasing away the depressing memory, and found both Rowcliff and Max watching me. "I'm picturing the events," I explained.

"Good," Rowcliff said. "Do it aloud."

I glanced at Max and he nodded permission.

"Gretchen, my assistant, came to where I was sitting and handed me the bidding sheets. She was really into the evening, having a lot of fun. It was great to see her so into it."

"And then what?" Rowcliff asked, hurrying me along.

"I caught Britt's eye, and Britt told Maisy and signaled Dora that we were ready to announce the winners. They got up and made their way to the front. Maisy arrived first."

"From where?" Rowcliff asked.

I remembered how disagreeable Walter, Maisy's husband, had appeared as he watched her flit around the table. "From where she'd been eating dinner," I said. "She was seated next to her husband, Walter."

"How did he seem?"

"Walter?" I asked.

"Yeah," he replied, pronouncing the word *Ye-a-a-ah,* as if he thought I was as dumb as a doorknob to be asking.

I held on to the edge of my chair and forced myself to ignore his patronizing attitude. *Stick to the facts, Josie,* I told myself. *Ignore his manner.* "Walter seemed pretty gloomy all evening."

"In what way?"

I shrugged. "He looked bad-tempered. He never smiled."

"What happened when she arrived up at the front?"

"Britt said something and shook her hand." I glanced from Rowcliff to Max and back again. "That's when she put her glass on the table near me. To shake his hand."

Rowcliff was leaning forward, the pencil he'd been tapping on the table unmoving. "And?"

"And then Dora arrived. She took a little longer to reach us because she stopped a couple of times to chat en route. Britt turned to shake her hand, but she laughed, swept his hand aside with her little black clutch purse, and hugged him instead. She said, 'I want to get my arms around you, you handsome devil!'"

"What did he do?" Rowcliff asked, looking revolted at Dora's playful words.

Continuing to ignore his attitude, I said, "He chuckled happily and returned her hug." I shrugged. "It was kind of sweet. The three of them were so pleased, you know? The Gala was on track to be a huge success. It was nice to see."

"And then they walked up onstage, right?" Rowcliff asked, disregarding the emotional aspects of the situation.

"Yes. Britt invited me to join them, but I declined."

"How come?" Rowcliff asked, pouncing on my words as if he'd spotted a weakness.

I shrugged again, embarrassed. "I don't really feel comfortable in the limelight."

A quick rat-a-tat as Rowcliff paused to think. "Who went onto the stage first?"

"Britt."

"Followed by . . ."

"Dora. But she looked at the winning bids before they went to the stage."

"Why?"

"I don't know. She asked if she could peek before they announced the winners, and Britt said sure."

"Where was everyone while Dora was going through the bid sheets?"

"Standing around. Or sitting around. We all were. We made conversation, you know? While we waited for her to finish."

"What did you talk about?"

"Silly stuff, actually. Britt asked Maisy if she was ready to lead the applause, and she said absolutely, that she always wanted to be a cheerleader. That sort of thing. Mindless."

He nodded and thought for another moment. "Was anyone else nearby?"

"No one. I mean, there were other people at the table, but no one else was standing with us, if that's what you're asking."

"Did anyone pass by?"

I thought for a moment. "No. I don't remember anyone walking by. And I'm sure I would if someone had done so."

Rowcliff gave a double tap with his pencil as he thought about what he wanted to say next. "Did anyone approach you or them while Dora was looking at the bid sheets?"

"No, no one. Except the waiter," I added, suddenly remembering.

"Which waiter?" Rowcliff asked, focused and intent.

"I don't know his name or anything. He took my wineglass."

"When?"

"I'm not sure exactly. I didn't notice when he took it, but a little bit later, I reached for my glass, and it was gone."

"Why do you think the waiter took it?" Rowcliff asked, sounding exasperated.

"Who else could it have been?"

"Anyone. Someone at your table. Anyone."

"No. Let me explain. Once Dora finished reviewing the bid sheets, Britt led the way onstage and I settled back to enjoy the show. That's when I reached for my wineglass, but it wasn't there. I looked around and saw a waiter moving away, his tray filled with plates and glasses and miscellaneous debris." I shrugged. "I assumed he'd taken it away while I was standing and chatting with Britt and Maisy."

"Maybe," he acknowledged. "Did you try and get it back?"

"No. All I did was share a little joke with the guy sitting next to me."

"Who was that?"

"Greg. Greg somebody. I don't know his last name."

"You don't know him?"

"No, I met him last night for the first time."

"Okay. What was the joke?" he asked.

"Oh my God. It wasn't that good. It's not worth repeating."

"Probably true." Rowcliff smirked. "Tell me anyway."

I shrugged. "I said that it was a good thing it wasn't a martini that the waiter scooped up or I would have wrestled him to the ground to get it back." I smiled at the memory. "Greg was funny. He offered to challenge the waiter to a duel, but I told him there was no need, since it was only wine."

Rowcliff didn't appear to be amused. "Who else besides the waiter was nearby or passed by?"

I thought back. If the truth be told, I'd been pretty distracted at that point in the evening, tired of meaningless chat, missing Ty, and physically exhausted from the twelve-hour days I'd spent preparing for the Gala while maintaining a full schedule of auctions and tag sales. As Britt, Dora, and Maisy climbed onto the low stage, all I wanted was for the evening to be over, and if someone had been nearby, I simply didn't recall it.

I shook my head. "Sorry. No one else comes to mind."

Rowcliff leaned back considering what to ask next, and gave a quick tap-tap with his pencil. "Okay then," he said. "I think I've got a clear picture of what happened."

"And?" I asked.

"And I've got my work cut out for me." He turned to include Max, who'd been sitting quietly, making an occasional note. "I have plenty of lines of investigation to follow. One, who had access to potassium cyanide. Two, who could have put it in the wineglass. And three, whether I can find anyone who wanted Maisy dead." He paused, tapping his pencil quietly.

"That's a lot," Max agreed.

"Yeah," Rowcliff said. "And there's one more. Four, why someone might want Josie dead."

My heart flipped over. Rowcliff looked at me straight, no sneer, no smirk, and with no challenge in his eyes. "Josie, I've got to tell you . . . I've been asking a lot of questions of a lot of people since Maisy died, and guess what?" He pointed his finger at me. "I haven't discovered anything that says you *weren't* the target."

CHAPTER EIGHT

F orty-five minutes later, Max and I stood at the open door in the bright autumn sun and watched as Officer Johnston packed up the video camera and placed the carry bag in the backseat of his patrol car.

Max reminded Detective Rowcliff to get us a copy of the interview notes by the end of the day, and he agreed that I'd be available for further questioning as needed.

I closed my eyes and soaked in the feel and sounds of Indian summer. The sun was surprisingly warm for October, a nice treat after last night's icy blast. Fallen leaves rustled as they fluttered across the paved lot. I turned my face full to the sun, finding comfort in the heat.

"Josie, can I ask you something?" Max said.

I opened my eyes and looked at him. "Sure."

"Just between us—lawyer and client—you really don't know who might have it in for you, right? You aren't just doing a head-in-the-sand thing?"

"Really," I said, meaning it. "I have no idea." That someone was out to kill me made no sense. I lived a simple life. I worked hard, played fair, and paid my bills on time. If I had any enemies, I didn't know it—and I didn't know them.

He scratched the side of his nose, seeming to struggle for words. "Okay, then," he said after a too-long pause, sounding skeptical.

"Max, I'd tell you if I knew anything. But I don't. It can't be me."

"I believe you, Josie. But I can't get it out of my head. You know, no smoke without fire. Plus, I gather that Detective Rowcliff isn't an alarmist . . . anything but . . . so maybe there's something to it. I don't mean to upset you, but I think we need to consider the possibility seriously."

"I appreciate your concern. I really do. You know me—I'm a scaredy-cat." I gave an embarrassed laugh. "If there was any hint of a threat, I'd be running for the hills."

"Yeah, I know, but . . ."

We had a short, circular discussion about whether I was really in danger, until finally I interrupted him, saying, "Until I hear otherwise, I'm going with my gut. I have no enemies! Which means Maisy was the intended victim, and that's that. Hell, anybody can speculate about anything. For all I know, the world is flat."

"You mean it's not?" he asked, affecting surprise. He gave a gentle tap on my shoulder, allowing me to win the point.

"Ha, ha," I said, smiling.

"You call me if you need me, okay?" he said, his eyes on mine. "Anytime."

"I promise." I took a deep breath and watched as Max walked to his car. He gave a jaunty wave, and turned left out of the lot toward Portsmouth, heading, I presumed, home.

Watching his car disappear around the bend, I fought off a wave of loneliness and envy. Max had a place to go where people who loved him were waiting. I didn't. As the only child of only children, now that my parents were dead, I had no family. My isolation was ever-present, but on Sundays, the family day, the pain was more acute.

I turned away from the sun and locked the auction doors, bolting them on the inside. Walking across the empty room to the inner door, I made a point of not looking at the dirty tables.

The antiques sat undisturbed. Our display was impressive, well lighted, with ample room for viewers to circle each item. Large pieces stood near the inside wall, and smaller articles were positioned on pedestals under Plexiglas.

I smiled as I looked at the eighteenth-century egg-shaped sterling silver nutmeg grater. I wondered whether it had sold for more than its estimated thirteen to fifteen hundred dollars. It was a charming piece, a perfect collectible for a cook. My mother would have loved it.

Next to it sat the single most valuable piece we had up for auction, a Chinese porcelain tureen with a nine-inch diameter, designed for export and dating from the Qing dynasty, Yongzheng period, estimated to sell for upward of twenty thousand dollars.

Part of its value sprang from simple supply and demand. Not many tureens from the mid-1700s had survived in perfect condition. But it was also dazzlingly beautiful, decorated with the frequently copied "Birds and Flowers" design. Rose-colored enamel lotus flowers and meticulously painted mandarin ducks seemed to float across the shimmering surface of a peaceful lake. The colors were pure and bright and the craftsmanship was flawless.

I recalled overhearing Dora talking to a couple who seemed to love it, and I wondered if they had bid on it, and if so, if they'd won. I'd been impressed listening to Dora explain how we knew the tureen was intended for export. "Western dinnerware was bigger than Chinese dinnerware," she said.

Leaving the room through the back door, I entered the vast storage facility that separated the auction venue from the tag-sale quarters. Goods slated for future auctions were stored in small cubicles to the left and items scheduled to be offered at our weekly tag sales were stacked on plastic shelving to the right.

My footsteps echoed on the concrete flooring as I headed to the central office, and combined with the dim lighting, the vast space would have felt sinister if I had allowed myself to think about it.

As soon as I stepped inside the office, I saw that Sasha and Fred were still there, completely focused on their computer monitors.

"How's it going?" I asked.

"Huh? Oh, hi. What?" Sasha responded, looking up.

I smiled. "Sorry to interrupt. I was just wondering how things were going."

"Oh. Good. We're making progress. We think Picasso gave the sketch to a friend."

Fred ignored the interruption. He was absorbed with whatever trail he was following, typing on his keyboard.

"Interesting," I said. With a glance at Fred, I added, "I don't mean to disturb you."

"That's okay," Sasha said. "How did it go? Do you have any news? I mean, can you tell us anything?"

"It's pretty horrible."

"What?" she asked anxiously.

"It looks like Maisy was poisoned."

Fred looked up from the computer. Sasha semi-gasped, a small sound of surprise. I nodded in response to their looks of astonishment. "Yeah. It's awful."

"Who?" Sasha asked. "I mean, do the police know who—"

I shook my head. "No, not yet. They're investigating." After a moment, I added, "I'm going to leave in a few minutes."

"Um, we planned on staying a while longer. Is that all right?"

"Sure. You're in charge of closing up. The police are done with the auction site, so when you leave, you should alarm the entire building."

"Okay." As she turned back toward the computer, she spotted a slip of paper. "Oh, you have a message."

A woman named Verna had called, explaining that she and her husband were moving to Las Vegas and wanted to sell most of the contents of their house in nearby Newington. I felt a familiar anticipatory thrill. It's much harder to buy good quality antiques and collectibles than it is to sell them. An entire houseful of goods? I almost salivated at the thought. According to the note, I had an appointment to go through the house tomorrow at twelve thirty.

I tucked the note into my purse and used Gretchen's phone to call the caterer, Eddie. I left a brief voice-mail message, telling him that the police were done and he could come and clean up.

With a quick good-bye to Sasha and Fred, I left.

In times of trouble, I cook. I derive enormous comfort from using my mother's recipes. When my mother knew she was dying, she wrote out all of her recipes in a beautiful leather-bound book. On many of the pages, she added special instructions, suggesting what to substitute if I couldn't locate a certain hard-to-find ingredient, for instance, or recommending ways to balance flavors. "Josie, dear," she wrote on one, "Orange Chicken is sweet, so be certain to serve it with something salty like long-grain wild rice, properly seasoned."

The day she handed me her recipe book, I stood silently beside her bed, trying not to notice her sunken cheeks and downy-soft hair or alarm her with my weeping. But I couldn't stop the tears from running down my cheeks. Even at thirteen, I understood the importance of this solemn moment. Those recipes were an important part of her legacy to me.

I shook aside the memory, focusing instead on what to cook today. What was I in the mood for? Consulting my taste buds and cooking something to suit was a luxury. Since moving to New Hampshire, more often than not, I ate whatever was on hand.

When I lived in New York, it had been different. Most days, I'd stopped at the local market on my way home from work. As Valentino, the butcher, cut and trimmed whatever cut of meat or poultry I requested to my specifications, I strolled the vegetable aisles, and selected whatever looked freshest and most appealing.

In New Hampshire, I shopped weekly, sometimes even less frequently. I didn't have a butcher and I used more frozen foods. Adjusting to the new shopping pattern had been part of the culture shock of relocating.

On a whim, I decided to prepare Lobster Newburg. I hurried into the grocery store nearest my house and bought the fixings from memory, hoping I wasn't forgetting anything.

Waiting in the checkout line, idly scanning the magazine rack, I remembered the day, not long ago, when Ty had stood next to me as I waited to pay for the groceries. He leaned over and kissed me on the cheek. "Thank you for cooking for me," he whispered. I touched my cheek, the brush of my fingers on the spot he'd just kissed evocative and sensual.

And there it was—Wes's dastardly headline shouted from the front page of the Sunday late edition of the *Seacoast Star*. PRESCOTT INVOLVED IN SECOND MURDER, it screamed.

The news-flash e-mail that Detective Rowcliff had shown us earlier was bad enough, but this was outrageous. *I wasn't involved in Mr. Grant's murder,* I silently seethed, or *this one.* I'd done nothing wrong, yet here I was, publicly humiliated once again. Wes had triumphed, the bastard. I placed the paper on the moving belt upside down and bit my lip, paid for the groceries, and fled.

As I turned into my driveway, I heard Lassie barking. She was on her hind legs, clawing against an old maple, straining to get to something above her. I looked up into the half-bare branches and saw Jake swinging upside down on a leather strap. Zoe was pouring charcoal briquettes from a big bag into Mr. Winterelli's ancient grill. Emma sat on a blanket, playing quietly with a wooden push toy.

I stepped out of the car and called, "Hey, Zoe!"

"Hi! How are you doing?"

"Great," I lied. "Hey, Jake," I said over Lassie's barks.

"Hi!" he responded. "*Wheee!* Look at me!" He swung back and forth, holding on to the leather, righting himself, then tipping over backward, laughing and exclaiming with pleasure.

"Pretty impressive, Jake! Hi, Emma!" I called in her direction.

I carried my bags inside. I was glad Zoe and the kids were having Sunday family fun, but witnessing their pleasure made my loneliness worse. Keep on keepin' on, I told myself, and put the perishables in the refrigerator.

I headed upstairs to change into comfortable old sweats, my standard at-home leisure wear. As I entered my bedroom, I saw that the message light on my answering machine was flashing.

I sat on the bed, ready for bad news, while secretly hoping it was Ty. *Don't hope,* I warned myself. *Prepare for the worst.* My dad always used to say, *Expect the best, but prepare for the worst.*

The message was from Wes. "Don't delete this before you listen to it!" he said in a rush. He laughed awkwardly and added, "I know how you must feel. I didn't write the headline. My editor did. Sorry about that. Really, the headline I submitted was, 'Mysterious Gala Death Under Investigation.' Anyway, I've learned something about you. You'll be surprised—and intrigued. Really, no bull. We need to talk, and I promise I won't quote you unless you tell me it's okay. Call me."

I replayed the message and listened a second time. He sounded more collaborative than he had the last time he called, less combative. What could he have discovered about me? Against my better judgment, I allowed curiosity to overcome good sense, and I called him back.

CHAPTER NINE

At seven o'clock the next morning, Monday, I pulled my car onto the sandy edge of the road just beyond the Rocky Point Police Station, where Ty worked, and with an old wool beach blanket in hand, I stepped out into the autumn chill. Shivering from the damp ocean air, I clambered up the dune where Wes and I had agreed to meet and stood amid the tall grass, watching the waves. The water was dark green today, with a black sheen.

Wes screeched to a stop in back of my car and I flashed back to the nightmare ride I'd taken with him last spring. He was a terrible driver, speeding up for no reason, then slamming on the brakes, jerking back and forth, until I'd nearly gotten sick. I shuddered at the memory.

He hurried out of his car, notebook and doughnut-shop bag in hand, looking as disheveled as ever. He was probably a decade younger than me, in his mid-twenties, and he looked about the same as he had the last time I'd seen him, six months earlier—soft and a little pudgy. His skin was almost as white as the frothy waves behind me. I bet it had been a long time since he'd spent any time outdoors.

He smiled as he climbed the dune. "Hey, Josie."

"Wes," I replied, not smiling.

"Do you want to sit in my car so we can talk?"

"God no. Are you crazy? I remember your car. Everything is sticky."

"What are you talking about?"

"Never mind," I said, not wanting to get into it. "Let's sit on the beach."

"Okay."

We walked-ran down the dune toward the ocean. The waves grew louder as we approached. The beach was littered with stones and seaweed, and we walked for a minute until we came to a clear patch and spread out my blanket. Gulls stood nearby, eyeing us, hoping for scraps of food. Far down the beach, I saw two people walking away from us.

"Want a doughnut?" he asked, pulling a honey-glazed one out of the bag.

"No, I already ate—real food."

"There's nothing wrong with doughnuts."

"Not if you're having dessert."

"Ha, ha. Very funny. Be nice or I won't give you the coffee I brought for you."

"*I'm* always nice," I said, stressing the "I'm." I waved a hand to dismiss our fruitless blather and extended my hand to accept the paper cup. "Thank you. That I'll accept."

I opened the lid so the coffee could cool off while waiting for him to speak. I didn't admit it, but I was touched that Wes remembered that I took my coffee dark, no sugar.

He seemed to be having trouble getting started. Ignoring his discomfort, I stayed quiet. I didn't feel like making it easy for him.

"I am sorry, you know?" he said awkwardly.

I shrugged. "Even forgetting the headline," I answered, "you wrote the article so I'd look bad." I took a sip.

"No, I didn't. It's a bad situation is all, and that came through. It wasn't personal."

"Whatever." I looked out toward the horizon. The sky was brighter now and bits of gold flickered on the surface of the ocean. Maybe what he said was true, but it still stung.

He cleared his throat. "I have a question."

"Why? What's your interest? Pandering to the lowest common denominator?"

"What are you talking about?" he asked, hurt.

I shrugged, secretly pleased that I'd touched a sore spot.

"I'm doing a serious piece," he explained. "I plan on calling it

'Anatomy of a Homicide Investigation.' And I've cleared the title with my editor."

I shrugged again, feigning indifference. "Where do I fit in?"

Wes looked shocked. "What do you mean, where do you fit in? You're one of the principal players."

"I am not!" I protested.

"Look, like it or not, you're being investigated as both a potential murderer and a possible target. All I'm doing is searching along with the police. And you know, I'm pretty good at what I do. It's always possible I'll turn something up."

I took a moment and considered Wes's words. "What do the police say?"

He gave a sudden bark of laughter. "What do you think? They say go away and let the professionals do their work."

"To which you respond?" I asked with a smile.

"No." Wes's voice was quiet when he spoke the word, adding to its impact.

I nodded but didn't reply. He cocked his head, watching me closely.

"So, will you help me?" he asked.

I didn't want to reveal that I was terrified and desperate for information. Knowing Wes, he'd pounce if I revealed a vulnerability. While I knew that he was using me, I could see no advantage to letting him know that I was using him, as well. "Knowledge is power, and all that," I said vaguely. "So, anything I tell you is off the record?"

"Absolutely. Unless and until you tell me otherwise."

"What if you learn something from another source? I read once that if you have two independent sources, you can publish things you learn from me—even without my permission."

"Why? You have something to hide?" he challenged.

"Of course not! The point is that I don't want any more litanies of 'No comment' making me look like I crawled out from under a rock."

He nodded. "There may be facts I learn independently that involve you or that are central to the story that I'd go with. But I can guarantee you—I give you my word—that anything I learn *from* you is off-limits unless you tell me otherwise or until the case is resolved."

"Resolved how?"

"Resolved by an arrest being made."

I looked over at him. His chubby face held an earnest, concerned expression, which I found reassuring. In the past, his word had been good. "Okay," I said.

"I won't let you down."

I nodded. "Thank you. I'll hold you to that commitment." *He must be on to something,* I told myself. Otherwise, he wouldn't be so conciliatory. It made me wonder what he had up his sleeve. "What do you want to know, Wes?" I asked.

"How well did you know Maisy?"

"Only through working with her on the Gala. Why?"

He shrugged. "Learning as much as I can about Maisy is a logical first step in figuring out why she was killed."

I nodded, thinking how little I knew about her. "Sorry I can't help," I said, wondering who might have known her well enough to describe what she was really like—was she serious and unstylish, as she'd appeared to be during the months we worked together? Or was she bubbly and frivolous, as she'd seemed at the Gala?

"So you can't tell me anything about her?" Wes asked, sounding as if he didn't believe me.

"No. I barely knew her."

I gazed out toward the ocean. A ship—a tanker, it looked like—had appeared out of nowhere, heading south. It was so far away, it looked like a child's toy. After a few seconds, I added, "You said on the phone that you knew something about me."

Wes sipped some coffee. "Yeah. Well, it's kind of complicated."

"That sounds bad."

"I'm sure it's nothing. But I thought you'd want to know."

I turned to him with narrowed eyes. I didn't like the sound of that at all. "Have you ever noticed how when someone says they think you'd want to know something, you almost never do?" I said, joking.

"I'm serious, Josie."

"Me, too."

He sighed deeply, Wes-speak for his willingness to endure what he took to be my ill-timed jest because he had his sights set on some greater good. "I've come across what seems to be a pretty good motive for someone to want you dead."

"What? That's absurd."

"Don't be so quick to react. You may not know about it yet."

"What are you talking about?"

He looked at me and pulled his earlobe a couple of times, as if he had an itch. "Well, I checked out your background."

"*My* background! Why are you checking out *my* background?"

"It's just part of being thorough, that's all."

"And?" I asked, allowing my impatience to show.

"Do you know someone named Trevor Woodleigh?"

I recoiled as if I'd been slapped. Wes must have seen something in my face, because he immediately asked, "Are you all right?" He sounded worried.

I looked away from his knowing eyes, forcing myself to breathe deeply as I watched a series of low-rolling waves sweep toward shore and break with a frothy murmur.

Trevor Woodleigh had been my hero. As CEO of Frisco's, he'd been generous with his time and attention, helping me hone my skills as an antiques appraiser. From the first day I met him—during a new employee orientation workshop, at which he'd offered a gracious welcome to us all—until I wore the wire that caught him dead to rights conspiring with his chief competitor to hold commissions steady, I'd considered him a mentor, a leader, and an inspiration.

I still flinched when I thought of those months—my hero breaking the law; the sharklike press that circled around me for weeks, ready to attack; the unremitting icy contempt I endured from my colleagues; and the terse explanation from a newly hired acting CEO that they were concerned about my ability to function as a team player, and so, regretfully, I was being let go. I'd gone from golden girl with an unlimited future to pariah in a matter of months.

I shook my head, trying to regain my composure. "Yeah. I know him," I said.

"From what I read, your testimony was central to his decision to accept the plea bargain. What was the original charge?"

"Didn't you read that part, too?"

He looked a little self-conscious, but it was a prideful look. Wes was pleased with his comprehensive research. "Yeah, I did. Conspiracy to defraud. Racketeering. Perjury. I think there might have been a grand larceny charge as well, but that one was dropped as part of the plea bargain. Isn't that right?"

"Yeah."

I recalled how awful I'd felt when the prosecutor congratulated me for doing a good job, telling me that my testimony had led Trevor to accept the government's offer of a plea bargain. I hadn't wanted to do a good job. All I'd set out to do was tell the truth, but somehow my altruism was perceived as a betrayal of the firm, and by Trevor himself as a clever power-grabbing ploy. I'd learned a bitter lesson. Never again would I expect to be valued for doing the right thing. My testimony cost me more than my job; it cost me my innocence.

"Why did you ask if I knew him?" I said, watching a gull spike and dive into a wave in pursuit of a fish.

"Seems he just got out of prison."

I turned and stared at Wes. My mouth opened, but I couldn't speak. I took a sip of coffee and coughed. "Trevor's out of prison?"

Wes nodded. "Yeah."

"When?" I asked. "When did he get out?"

"Three days ago," he said.

I was speechless, stunned at the implication. A man who, from all reports, sincerely believed that I had conspired to entrap him in order to further my career by eliminating him as a rival was out of prison, free to exact revenge.

CHAPTER TEN

W here is he now?" I whispered.

"At his sister's house in Manhattan." He extracted a folded piece of paper from his jacket pocket and turned it over. "On East Sixty-fifth Street. Do you know where that is?"

"Yes," I replied, looking at the ocean. The tanker had passed out of sight.

East Sixty-fifth Street was a world away from New Hampshire, but less than six hours by car.

"Do you suspect that he . . . I mean, are you saying that he . . ." I left the thought unspoken.

Wes shrugged. "I'm checking further."

"What are you checking?"

"I'm looking into his whereabouts the night of the Gala."

My heart skipped a beat. *Can it be?*

Images of working with Trevor, of being with him, flooded into my head. Horrible courtroom moments and exhilarating work experiences came together in a confusing mix. On some level, I missed him, and that was sick. According to Wes, there was a chance he wanted to kill me.

"How?" I asked, trying to hide my fear from Wes.

"I have sources working on it," he said, sounding important.

I nodded, knowing enough not to ask for details. It wasn't just that he wouldn't want to tell me; it was also that I didn't want to know. I maintained a calm exterior, but the truth was that I was seriously shaken.

Until Wes put a name to the threat, it had seemed absurd to think that someone wanted me dead. But now I wasn't so sure. Sitting on a seaweed-strewn beach in New Hampshire, I'd assumed that I was safe. According to Wes, there was a good chance that I'd been wrong.

I kicked myself for not tracking Trevor's status, shaking my head in mute astonishment—it seemed that denial was a more powerful force than I'd realized. Despite Detective Rowcliff raising the potential that I, not Maisy, had been the target, it hadn't occurred to me that Trevor might be behind the murder.

Still, Trevor as cold-blooded murderer seemed incredible. Trevor was a thief, not a killer. But considering what I knew about Trevor Woodleigh, I began to question my automatic denial that he would plan and execute murder. My heart began to race.

Trevor was a man of impressive intellect, guided more by passion than reason. And he loathed me. If the anger that had simmered just below the surface throughout his trial had boiled over while he was in prison, I had no doubt that he'd have both the impulse to kill me and the smarts to pull it off. It was a terrifying realization.

"So what now?" I asked, trying to sound matter-of-fact.

Wes stood up and stretched, preparing to leave. "Now I keep digging," he said.

Me, too, I thought. *I've got to know where Trevor is and what he's up to—and I've got to find out quickly.*

"You'll keep me posted?" I asked.

"Give me an exclusive."

"Who else would I talk to, Wes?"

"Deal."

He flashed a quick **V** for victory and lumbered through the sand to his car. *Whose victory is he hoping to inspire?* I wondered. *Mine for my survival? Or his for writing a Pulitzer Prize–winning feature?*

I sat for several minutes trying to decide what to do first—follow up on Trevor or try to learn more about Maisy—but I reached no conclusion. *And,* I wondered, *is Trevor an immediate threat? Do I need a bodyguard?* I shook out the blanket, folded it up, and made my way across the sand to my car, all the while considering my options.

My father once told me that no matter what, it was always better to know the truth than not. He never said it wasn't frightening, just that it was better than the alternative. *Ignorance,* he said, *is never bliss.*

Leaves crunched under my tires as I drove through my parking lot.

The sound was evocative, bringing forth happy childhood memories of jumping into towering piles of raked leaves before my dad and I stuffed them into oversized trash bags. Life was easy then.

I saw that Gretchen, my assistant, was just getting out of her car, her ginger-colored hair hanging in gentle waves almost to her waist.

"You're here bright and early," I called. "It's not even eight thirty!"

"I couldn't sleep, so I finally gave up and decided to come in. It was either that or do laundry," she said, making a funny face.

I laughed, appreciating her lighthearted take on the world, even in the face of strife.

"Well, Prescott's appreciates being the beneficiary of your insomnia, even if you rank us just slightly above laundry." I unlocked the door and stepped inside. The chimes tinkled as I punched the code to turn off the alarm.

"I wouldn't put it that way," she responded with a giggle. "Laundry is way more important than work, but I finished it as a result of *yesterday's* insomnia, so I had no choice but to come in."

I smiled, signaling that I got the joke. "Why are you having trouble sleeping?" I asked.

Gretchen's normally luminous green eyes clouded over. She shrugged and turned toward her computer, her upbeat mood gone, as if she'd thrown a switch. "Maisy, I guess. It's stupid, I know, but I can't seem to stop thinking about her."

"It's not stupid at all. I'm having a hard time, too."

"I don't know what to do to stop my mind from replaying everything like a movie, you know?"

I nodded. "Yeah. Me, too."

"Have you heard anything? Do they have any leads?"

I paused, considering how much to reveal.

Gretchen was an enigma. She'd arrived on my doorstep the day I'd started in business, begging for a job, yet refusing to give me any information about her background or qualifications. She'd looked at me straight on, her expressive eyes revealing nothing, and promised that she'd work hard and help my company grow. In a strangely impulsive act for a methodical and research-oriented sort like me, I hired her on the spot, and have thanked my lucky stars ever since. She was a treasure, as much for her office skills as for her caretaking personality and upbeat attitude.

But she wasn't a friend, and outside of work, we had little in common. I liked her but felt no particular rapport with her. And knowing her fondness for gossip, I found it hard to imagine that she'd keep my secrets private.

"Nothing official," I said.

She sighed and nodded. "What do you do to turn off the replay?" she asked.

That one was easy to answer truthfully. "I work," I said.

She tried for a smile and almost made it. "You mean you don't do laundry first?"

I patted her shoulder as I started for the warehouse door. "Almost never. I've been known to buy new clothes rather than do laundry."

She laughed, and as I picked up the preliminary tag-sale financial report, a memory came to me.

Rick, my ex-boyfriend, had burst into my New York City apartment one evening about eight or nine years ago, excitement radiating from every pore.

"I got the assignment!" he exclaimed, pulling me away from the stove to do a fancy pirouette, spin, and dip.

"Oh, that's great, Rick! Congratulations!"

"Come with me!"

"Where?" I asked, thrilled that he'd want me to join him anywhere.

"Rome."

"They're sending you to Rome? For how long?"

"Just for meetings tomorrow and Monday. Which means I get the weekend in Italy—company-paid! Our flight is at eleven."

"*Our* flight? Tonight? You're kidding."

"Nope."

From his lopsided grin and eyes blazing with anticipation, I could tell that he was serious.

"But tomorrow's Friday. I have work," I objected.

"Call in sick," he said, his eyes promising fun and, I thought with a jolt, something deeper and more intimate, as well.

I felt my pulse race and I couldn't take my eyes off him. He pushed me gently backward until I reached the wall. His eyes seared into mine with passionate intensity. He leaned down and kissed me. My heart thudded and I pushed my hips against him in response. I lost myself in the moment, surrendering to his embrace.

"So, will you come to Rome with me tonight?"

"Yes," I whispered, my eyes still closed, smiling.

He did a quick jig. "Fantastic! Let's go!"

"But . . . I need to pack, and everything I own is dirty I was going to do laundry tonight."

"Who cares? While I'm working tomorrow, you can go clothes shopping."

And so I went to Italy with a toothbrush and my makeup case, and nothing else.

"I'll be upstairs," I called to Gretchen now, shaking off the memory.

I didn't miss Rick at all, but thinking of him made me miss Ty a lot. *Is Aunt Trina okay? Is he?*

CHAPTER ELEVEN

T he phone rang. Listening to Gretchen's side of the conversation, I could tell that it was Eddie, the caterer, letting her know he was on his way.

"Once Eddie's finished, call Macon Cleaners, will you? Tell them about the wine stains and see what they can do."

"Okay."

"I'll let Eddie in."

I left Gretchen to her work and walked through the morning-chilled warehouse toward my private office. Except for the clomping of my work boots, the quiet was absolute.

I decided to greet Eddie myself instead of sending Gretchen, so I could reassure him that I still wanted him to cater our upcoming auction dates. Maybe it wasn't a necessary gesture, but I was a little worried about him. Saturday night, after Detective Rowcliff had supervised the removal of Maisy's body, I'd spotted Eddie sitting alone in a far corner of the room, silent and morose. He'd put a lot of eggs in the Gala basket, and from his demeanor, I concluded that his situation was bleak. Catering my monthly receptions probably didn't represent enough business to save his company if things were as dismal as his manner Saturday night had suggested, but knowing that he hadn't lost an account might help him muster the energy to persevere.

As I walked across the shadowy warehouse en route to my office, I could see the outlines of hundreds of items in various stages of preparation. While Fred or Sasha worked on the appraisals, Eric cleaned and polished the pieces, readying them for sale. Lesser-quality goods went to the weekly tag sale, while better items were sent to auction. Except that sometimes I tucked a low-priced special piece into the tag-sale mix to encourage regulars to seek out bargains week after week.

The warehouse was a little more than half-full, and that was great news. Half-full meant business was good. A little more than half-full meant business was growing. As I passed by stacked shelves and roped-off areas filled with furniture, I smiled, proud of my accomplishment.

I sat at my desk and turned on my computer. While it booted up, I gazed at the old maple outside my window. Its branches swayed gently in the soft morning breeze and orange leaves fluttered to the ground.

I wondered what people in New York were saying about Trevor's release. I reached for my old Rolodex and found the entry for a former colleague named Shelley. We'd worked together at Frisco's for years—and she was still there. We'd never been close friends, but we'd always gotten along, and during my last days with the firm, she'd remained neutral. She hadn't rushed to my defense, but neither had she participated in the witch-hunt. I got her on her cell phone as she walked to work.

"Josie!" she exclaimed. "How ya doing?"

"Good. Really good. Business is strong up here. All is well."

"That's great to hear. Do you have snow yet?"

"Shelley, it's only October!" I chided, laughing at her chauvinistic view of the world outside New York City.

"Well, all I know is that you left us and moved to the frozen tundra or something."

" 'Or something' is closer than 'frozen tundra.' Listen," I said, trying for a casual tone, "I heard that Trevor got out of prison."

"Yeah, I heard that, too."

"What do you know?"

"Not much. I haven't seen him or anything."

"Have you heard what he's up to?"

"Just rumors that he's determined to clear his name and regain his, ahem, proper place in the antiques world."

Clear his name? I protested silently. *He confessed, for God's sake!*

I closed my eyes in an effort to steady my rage-fueled shaking hands. "Really?" I asked, aiming to convey playful disbelief. "How does he plan to do that?"

"Probably by trashing you," she said with an embarrassed giggle.

"Jeez," I whispered, stunned at the thought. Her answer was logical, but I couldn't help wondering if Shelley knew more than she was telling.

"Especially since you're not here to defend yourself," she added.

"Did you hear something in particular?" I asked as if it didn't matter one way or the other.

"No. I just know Trevor."

So do I, I thought. "You're so right, Shelley. Well, I guess it's another reason I'm glad to be out of the City. If I'm not in his face, maybe he'll ignore me."

"Maybe," she said, sounding unconvinced.

"So, how are you?" I asked, eager to change the subject.

We chatted about the new man she was dating and politics at Frisco's, the weather in New York and when it really started snowing in New Hampshire, and who was up for a promotion and who'd been passed over, and by the end of the conversation, I realized that I was truly thankful to be out of the corporate fray and on my own.

A truck rumbled into the lot.

Making my way down the spiral stairs, across the warehouse, and into the desolate auction venue, I turned on lights while avoiding looking at the spot where Maisy had stood. The vision of her tumbling forward, shrieking, "Ahhh . . . al . . . alahaaa . . . dah . . ." in a panicked screech was forever branded in my memory. I didn't want to remind myself of the scene. There'd be time enough to look at the platform again after the place was cleaned up.

I unbolted the double doors and swung them wide, enjoying the rush of autumn air. Eddie was opening his truck's back doors. I spotted two helpers.

Eddie was tall, maybe six three or more, and he was big all over, with thick arms and powerful thighs. His short red hair was turning gray.

"Hi, Eddie. How are you doing?"

"Hey, Josie," he replied. "I'm holding up pretty well, all things considered. How about you?"

"Good." I grimaced. "So-so, if the truth be known."

"Yeah. It's a helluva situation."

"Yeah. Listen, you have our auction schedule, right? We're still on for those dates."

He flashed a grateful grin. "Yeah. Thanks, Josie."

We weren't friends exactly, but he was chatty and open. Whenever he set out the wine and snacks for our monthly auction preview receptions and I was around, he told me more about himself.

"You never know, Josie, how things work out," he'd told me with a chuckle as he set up for the Gala. "Never say never."

He recounted how, last year, at forty-eight, he had, on a whim, quit his boring corporate job and signed up for a fancy cooking course. Three months later, with his certificate of completion in hand, he opened his catering business.

"With my contacts," he confided to me, "it should have been a snap. But I wasn't prepared for the competition."

We chatted briefly now and I watched as he directed his staff. After a minute, I said, "I'll be up in my office if you need me. Okay?"

"You bet. Thanks, Josie," he said, and though his eyes looked worried, he waved a cheerful good-bye.

I looked back as I reached the door to the warehouse. He stood between two of the display cases, overseeing his workers.

To one side was a Plexiglas case containing a nineteenth-century "Theatre Gringalet" clock entitled "This Evening Grand Representation." The elaborate scene showed a man playing a drum and a woman playing cymbals. Both figures stood on a stage, dressed in period costumes. Above them, a monkey looked down, observing their performance. Fabricated of metal, the clock measured fifteen by twelve inches and featured a French eight-day movement. The design was both practical and witty, and for someone who liked its style or who collected rare timepieces, it was a real find. We estimated that it would sell for around $2,300.

To Eddie's other side, also under clear Plexiglas, was the gorgeous faience pottery set I'd described to Detective Rowcliff.

As I stepped into the warehouse, I heard Eddie shouting directions to someone named Randy. He sounded so in charge, I thought that maybe I was wrong to worry about him. Perhaps the depression I'd observed on Saturday night was a natural reaction to the shock and sadness of Maisy's death, not, as I'd feared, from worry about his catering business.

Upstairs, as ways and means of discovering information about Trevor and Maisy simmered on my mental back burner, I reviewed the preliminary tag-sale numbers. Dolls and dollhouses continued to sell well, which meant I needed more inventory. Tea sets and porcelain figures were down. So were wooden tools. Quilts were holding steady. The pursuit of quality goods was unending.

I brought up a search engine and, with some trepidation, entered "Trevor Woodleigh" and "probation." Four seconds later, eighty-one links appeared.

The first one took me to the *East Side Trumpet,* a neighborhood newsletter serving the area where Trevor lived. The article confirmed what Wes had told me—Trevor had been released last week and was living with his sister.

A longer article appeared in *New York Monthly.* I winced as I noted that the author was Bertie Rose. She'd been one of a dozen reporters who'd made my life hell during Trevor's trial, following my every move, posing provocative questions, and trying hard to find a damning motive to account for my whistle-blowing. She still called me periodically looking for a quote, and I still refused to take her calls. I realized, stunned, that Trevor's imminent release must have been why she'd called within the last month and left an urgent message.

The phone startled me. It was Gretchen relaying the news that Dora and Britt would arrive at ten to discuss what to do about notifying the winning bidders. I glanced at the clock on my computer monitor. I had more than half an hour before they'd arrive. I turned my attention back to the on-line article.

The so-called exposé alleged that Trevor was determined to salvage his reputation as the world's premier expert on authenticating and appraising Impressionist art by writing a book on the subject. I was skeptical. Trevor's gift was his people skills. From what I'd seen over the years I'd worked with him, neither his scholarship nor his writing ability were in any way remarkable. But as Shelley had made clear, his actual talent notwithstanding, all that mattered was whether he could create the *perception* that he was an expert.

The story was probably colored by Trevor's wishful thinking—he was promoting the image he hoped to create. Pretty slick, if he could pull it off. To me, it seemed a pathetic effort to redeem himself, to reclaim his place in the art world. Surely he realized that we who knew him would recognize his efforts for what they were: disingenuous at best and specious at worst, a cynical attempt to sway opinion for his own ends. Did he think that we were stupid? It galled me beyond words that Trevor would try to fake his redemption.

I felt my throat tighten as I stifled an unwanted emotional display and I pressed the heels of my hands against my eyes in an effort to suppress my too easy tears. I stepped away from my desk and walked to the nearest window. The maple's orange and yellow leaves shimmied in the light breeze. *Why,* I wondered, *am I so irritated at Trevor?*

I knew the answer. He was trying to get what I sought, but without the work. I'd moved to New Hampshire to start anew, to build a business. He had no such intentions—he was manipulating the media to boost his status. My efforts at rejuvenation were sincere—I worked hard; Trevor's were false—he wasn't working at all.

If redeeming himself was his intention, however, why would he try to kill me? I quaked at the thought. I knew that answer, too. Killing me would allow him to feel vindicated. It was irrational—and completely in keeping with what I knew of his character.

CHAPTER TWELVE

N ew Hampshire was the most beautiful place I'd ever seen, filled with natural wonders. Everywhere you looked was something breathtaking: vivid reds and yellows in fall and subtle lilacs and cornflower blues in spring, opalescent whites in winter, and verdant greens in summer. It was a land of color, with every season representing hope. New Hampshire was my home. That Trevor might violate my adopted homeland with his presence made me crazy.

Don't speculate, I warned myself. *Don't guess about anything— neither Trevor's anger nor his alibi, neither Maisy's behavior nor her attitudes.* Research and consideration, not conjecture, answered questions.

Back at the computer, I searched for Trevor's name in conjunction with Saturday's date. A man determined to resume his place in the high-end art and antiques world in New York City might have attended a society event or gallery opening. And if he had attended something of that nature, his presence might merit a paragraph—or a sentence—in some publication. If I could confirm his attendance at the event, I could feel reassured that he hadn't been in my building killing Maisy, and forget about him. I tapped the Enter key and was immediately disappointed. Nothing. No relevant hits. *Now what?* I asked myself. *Should I sit back and wait for Wes to tell me more, hoping he can discover Trevor's alibi?* Way too passive for me. As my father repeated over and over again when I engaged in wishful thinking as a child, *Work, not wishing, makes it so.* I had to act.

I was certain that Wes would roar like a charging lion if he knew that I was going to report Trevor's existence to the police. But from where I stood, I had no choice. If there was any chance that Trevor was, in fact, out to get me, I had to protect myself. And unless I hired a New York City private eye to check out his alibi, I was out of options. I couldn't even consult Ty. I dialed Max's office.

"Max," I said when I had him on the line, choosing my words with care, "I've had a thought about someone who might actually wish me harm. I mean, I have no reason to think he is responsible for Maisy's death, but, well, you asked me to tell you if anything came to me."

"I'm glad you called. Tell me."

"His name is Trevor Woodleigh." I fought back unwanted tears, angrily brushing aside the dampness streaking down my cheeks, and forced myself to speak normally. "I testified against him at a trial a few years ago in New York, and it seems he's been released from prison."

"And he blamed you?"

"Yeah." I half-laughed. "Pretty much, he hates my guts."

"Well, this is certainly relevant information. I'll call Detective Rowcliff right away."

"I'm sure it's nothing."

After a small pause, Max said, "Probably you're right. Still, it can't do any harm to check it out."

In for a penny, in for a pound, I thought, quoting my mother. If I was going to check out Trevor, I ought also to see what I could learn about Maisy. I brought up another window and Googled Maisy's name.

Of the fifty-seven hits, only three were unrelated to Maisy's work with the Portsmouth Women's Guild. I went through them all, starting with the items connected to the Guild. I scanned newsletter articles about past years' Galas, press releases about awards the Guild had won, photos showing Maisy smiling as she handed someone a check or shook someone's hand—looking more stiff than comfortable—until finally, I came to the three non-Guild references.

The first one was a feature article in the *Seacoast Star* from two years ago, in which Maisy was quoted as supporting the arts in Portsmouth. The second reference was a photograph published in a service organization's magazine, showing Maisy, her features relaxed and her behavior buoyant, raising a glass of what looked to be sparkling wine with someone called Pam Field. And the third one was an issue of Maisy's church's newsletter—apparently, she had baked chocolate chip cookies for a fund-raiser last July.

I hit the back button until the magazine photograph reappeared. Maisy really did look lighthearted. The caption read "Maisy Gaylor and Pam Field celebrating Ms. Field's new venture, Field Design Studio." I studied the photograph. Pam Field looked familiar. Curious, I checked her name against the Gala invitation list—and there it was. She'd been at the Gala. The memory came back to me—I hadn't met her, but I had noticed Maisy and her, laughing. Anyone who was able to get Maisy to relax and have fun—well, that was someone I wanted to meet.

I found the Field Design Studio contact information in the White Pages and dialed the number. No answer. After six rings, a machine came on, but I hung up without leaving a message. I glanced at my computer monitor—maybe they weren't open yet. I jotted the phone number and address down and slipped it into my pocket.

As I walked downstairs, I wondered whether Pam Field would be able to shed any light on Maisy's unexpectedly sprightly performance at the Gala. Were they friends? I also wondered what Rowcliff would think about Trevor and whether he would follow up in person, and if so, how he'd react to what, no doubt, would be Trevor's vituperative condemnation of all things Josie.

CHAPTER THIRTEEN

D o you think they'll get divorced?" I heard Dora, the volunteer chairperson of the Gala, ask as I crossed the warehouse, heading toward the main office.

"I think so," Gretchen said. "It's so sad, isn't it? Their twins are only seven months old."

I wondered whom they were talking about. I didn't know anyone with seven-month-old twins.

"What do you think happened?" Dora asked.

"Same old, same old. He fell in love with his costar on the movie set. It happens all the time," Gretchen added, lowering her voice as if she were sharing a secret.

To the uninitiated, Gretchen probably sounded like she had inside knowledge, but I knew that her juicy tidbits came from weekly tabloids and on-line scandal sheets.

"You'd think that—" Dora said, breaking off abruptly as soon as she saw me. She slid off the desk where she was perched and walked to meet me, her hands outstretched. "Josie, how are you? Isn't this awful? Are you completely overwrought?"

I smiled in greeting, thinking how much I admired her graciousness. Reed-thin, Dora always looked like a million bucks. Today, she wore an ivory silk sweater set with a long gold chain-link necklace and dangling gold earrings. Her knee-length pencil skirt was rust-colored wool, and she wore high-heeled brown leather boots. She was stunning.

"It's no fun, that's for sure. How are you holding up?" I responded.

She grimaced. "I talked to that detective, Rowcliff, I think his name is. Isn't he horrible?"

"He's intense, I know that," I replied, avoiding saying anything negative. *Never gossip at work,* my father had warned me when I started at Frisco's. *If it would bother you to read it in tomorrow's paper, don't say it.*

Dora leaned toward me, her eyes expressing worry. "I got the impression that the detective thought *you* might have been the target. Is it true?"

Dora's question caught me off guard, and for a moment, I froze, aware that both Gretchen and Dora were awaiting my response.

Of course Rowcliff would have asked Dora if she knew any reason why someone would want to kill me, just as he'd asked me. In fact, as I thought of it, I realized that in all probability, he'd asked everyone.

I took in a deep breath and exhaled, trying to decide how I should answer. *Turn the headlights in another direction,* I thought, my pulse racing. All I wanted was to take the focus off myself.

In as playful a tone as I could muster, I said, "Nah, he's just covering all bases. Unless . . . Wait a minute. Gretchen, what do you think? Am I *that* tough a boss?"

I thought it was pretty lame, so I was pleasantly surprised when both Gretchen and Dora laughed a little.

"You're a great boss!" Gretchen exclaimed, sounding ready to argue with anyone who said different.

I was touched. "Thanks, Gretchen."

I turned to Dora. "I'm a simple soul. Who'd want to kill me?" I added, crossing my fingers behind my back for luck, hoping that what I said was true and that Trevor Woodleigh was busily plotting his redemption in New York City, not planning my murder in Portsmouth.

"I still can't believe it," Dora said, shaking her head sadly. "Poor Maisy."

My deflection worked and the discomfort I felt passed. My pounding heart began to slow and I took another breath. "How about if we head toward the back, Dora, and wait for Britt there?"

"Sure," Dora agreed.

She picked up her jumbo-size leather tote bag and together we headed toward the inner door that gave access to the warehouse.

"Gretchen, when Britt arrives, bring him back, okay?"

"Okay. It was nice talking with you, Dora," she said.

"Oh, you too! We'll catch up more another time." Dora gave an airy wave as we passed into the bone-cold warehouse.

Our footsteps reverberated off the concrete walls. When we were about halfway across the expanse, Dora asked, "Did you know them well? Maisy and Walter, I mean . . ."

I shook my head. "I never met Walter until the Gala. And Maisy, well, I got to know her a little, since we'd been working together. But nothing personal, you know? How about you?"

"I only met Walter once before the Gala. It was at a cocktail reception over the summer, one of those 'we're all working together on the Gala, so bring your significant others and let's bond,' things," she said, casting her eyes heavenward, a nonverbal commentary about what she thought of that idea. "I took Hank. You met him, right?"

"The trombone player," I said, remembering a tall guy with a blond ponytail. He'd been one of the brass quartet that had played soft music during the cocktail hour. He was maybe ten years younger than Dora, and cute as all get-out.

"Right. He's my honey."

"I didn't know," I said.

"He's a sweetie."

"That's great," I replied, unsure how to respond.

"Anyway," she said, "Hank is the most patient creature on earth, but after two minutes talking to Walter, he's tugging on my shawl and whispering in my ear, 'Get me away from this jerk before I pound him into the ground.'"

"Really? Wow, that's amazing. I mean, I got the impression that Walter was upset about something, you know? But I had no idea he'd inspire a patient man to violence." As I spoke, I opened the door that led into the auction hall and switched on the overhead lights. "Well," I said, "here we are."

Eddie was long gone, along with everything that wasn't nailed down or on display. It was a little creepy. Whereas an hour earlier there had been tables and chairs, linens, dishes, and candles, now there was nothing except the antiques we were there to discuss.

Dora glanced around and placed her tote bag against the wall near the display cases. I couldn't read her expression, but I sensed she felt as uncomfortable as I did.

"I wonder if Greg—he was my seatmate at the Gala—I wonder if he won the sideboard," I remarked. "Do you remember?"

"No," Dora answered. "I'm sorry, but I don't. But I do remember that it sold for more than its estimate."

"That's a good thing."

"It's an excellent thing!" Dora agreed. "What was it estimated to go for?"

"Nineteen thousand."

"That's a lot of money, isn't it?"

"Not really. Not for this piece."

Attributed to Anthony Quervelle from Philadelphia, and dating from 1830, the mahogany sideboard featured a backsplash that was carved with acanthine scrolls and a bowl of fruit. There was a central long drawer flanked by a pair of pedestal cabinets, each with a drawer over a cabinet door, and columns leading to scrolled paw feet. It was in pristine condition, having been lovingly maintained by the Hillshaw family for more than 175 years. I knew because Fred, my researcher, had personally confirmed its provenance.

"I don't like it, do you?" Dora asked, her hand on her hip.

"It's a magnificent example of American craftsmanship," I replied.

"Fair enough, but do you like it?"

"Well, yeah, I do, actually."

"Really? I didn't know anyone—"

Britt Epps stepped into the room. "Thank you, Gretchen, for the escort."

"My pleasure, sir."

I heard Gretchen's French heels tapping as she made her way back through the warehouse.

Britt spotted us and beamed. "Josie, it's so good to see you," he said, walking in our direction. "How are you holding up during this difficult time? Dora, my dear, how are you? Not that I need to ask. I can see that you're looking as beautiful as always. My, my,

I'm a lucky fellow this morning, aren't I, surrounded by two such lovely ladies."

"Oh, Britt, you are such a flatterer!" Dora teased.

"I never flatter, my dear."

I stood by, removed from their mindless interaction, half of me wishing that I could joke as deftly as they did and the other half wishing they'd just be done with it. After five long minutes of small tall, during which I smiled and said the little sillies that were expected of me, Britt finally got down to business.

He opened a flap of his oversized briefcase, closer to the big square ones used by pilots than the more traditional kind typically carried by lawyers, and began to paw through it.

"Here it is!" Britt exclaimed, standing up, waving the manila envelope containing the bid sheets that I'd handed him at the Gala. He closed the flap and latched it.

Twenty minutes later, we'd tacked Post-it notes with the names of the winners and the sale price on every piece of furniture and display case, and we'd begun to write a script for Gretchen to use when making the calls to the winners, when Gretchen's voice crackled over the PA system.

"Josie," she announced, "you have a call on one. It's Ty."

CHAPTER FOURTEEN

M y heart stopped.
I had to resist a white-hot urge to run full speed to the phone. Instead, I forced myself to smile politely and say, "Excuse me. I'll just be a minute," and walk at a normal pace toward the rear, where a telephone was tucked into a cleverly disguised cubbyhole.

"Hello?" I said into the receiver.

"Josie," Ty exhaled, "finally. How are you?"

"Fine," I said, my tone neutral, acutely aware that Britt and Dora were within earshot. "You?"

"Good. Aunt Trina is still undergoing tests—I have an appointment to review the results with the doctors later today. I couldn't believe it when I heard about Maisy. How are you holding up?"

"I'm okay. Actually, I'm sort of in a meeting right now," I said, clearing my throat. "Can we talk later?"

"Sure."

"How's six o'clock my time?" I asked.

"That won't work—I have that doctor's appointment." Ty paused, thinking. "How's one, your time?"

"That won't work for me. I have an appraisal."

"Maybe this evening," Ty said.

Neither Britt nor Dora spoke. I felt uncomfortably conspicuous. "Sure," I agreed. "Let's give it a try."

"Sorry about that," I said as I walked back.

"No problem," Dora said, smiling.

"I was just standing here considering something, and you know what?" Britt said. "I don't think this process needs to be so complicated. I mean, there's a lot of information we need to capture, but instead of writing a script, why don't we just explain what we need to Gretchen and let her ask questions?"

"That makes a lot of sense," I responded, relieved that we wouldn't have to take the time to write things out. Gretchen could take whatever notes she needed. And I could have some time to consider my next step in researching Trevor and Maisy before heading to my lunchtime appointment in Newington.

"Good idea, Britt, you clever dog, you!" Dora said. "Why don't you two go on ahead and talk to Gretchen. I'll just take one last look at the names to be certain they're spelled right. I know enough about donors to know that misspelling names is a surefire way to offend them."

"Are you sure? We could stay, if you want, and help," I offered politely while heading toward the warehouse.

"Nope, I'm all set. You both go on ahead and get started with Gretchen. I'll just be a minute."

I gestured that Britt should precede me, and when I glanced back, I saw Dora looking back and forth between the papers in her hand and the Post-it on the sideboard, her eyes narrowed in concentration.

Dora slipped into the office a few minutes later and placed a friendly hand on my shoulder for a moment, smiled, then sat next to Britt.

"So," Gretchen said, "in addition to gathering payment in-formation—check or credit card—I also need to confirm how they want the tax-deduction record to read, is that right?"

"Exactly," Britt said. "Some people might want their company to be the donor of record; others might want it to be recorded as an individual donation."

"What do I say if they ask about the tax rules?"

"Tell them that because every situation is different, they need to consult their own tax adviser."

Gretchen nodded as she wrote.

"Also, we need to consider how they want their names to ap-pear in the donor listings," Dora added. "John and Amy Smith, for instance, or Mr. and Mrs. John Smith."

Gretchen nodded again and jotted the instruction down.

As they continued explaining what Gretchen needed to do, I allowed my mind to wander, my thoughts drifting from antiques and tracking donations to Ty, then to Trevor and Maisy, then back to Ty. On the phone just now, Ty had sounded good. Pleased to be talking to me. My skin warmed at the thought.

Dora and Britt stood up, preparing to leave. I'd missed just about their entire conversation.

Glancing at the pink Mickey Mouse clock on Gretchen's desk, I was surprised to see that it was after eleven thirty. I'd need to get ready to leave soon.

Dora air-kissed me and Britt, chattering all the way out the door. "What a beautiful day! It's just gorgeous, isn't it? Don't you love this time of year? It's so good seeing you both. And you, too, Gretchen. We'll be in touch soon. Bye-bye. See you later!"

I stood by the open door and watched as Dora pulled out of the lot in her jazzy gold Jaguar. Britt shrugged into his trench coat and picked up his briefcase.

"Would it be possible to use the rest room?" he asked.

"Of course," I said. "Gretchen will show you where it is."

"This way," she said, leading him into the warehouse.

When she came back a moment later, I asked, "Are you clear on what you need to do?"

"Absolutely. There's a lot of bits and pieces of information Britt and Dora want me to capture, but it will be easy—I'll just add fields on the Gala spreadsheet to track the data."

I listened with half an ear as she summarized what they'd discussed and how she planned to approach the task.

"Let me know if you run into any problems, okay?" I told her.

"Sure."

"Thank you, ladies," Britt said as he hurried into the office.

"Gretchen will start on the calls today," I told him, and he thanked her once again.

I stood by the open door in a rectangle of sun and watched as he wedged himself into his silver Mercedes and took several minutes fussing with something or other before starting the engine. A careful man, I thought. Precise and thorough. No wonder he had the reputation of being one of the top lawyers in town.

I turned back to Gretchen and told her that I was leaving.

"Anything before I go?" I asked.

Gretchen glanced at her desk and computer screen. "Nope. I think everything's under control. I should have the tag-sale figures by the time you're back."

"Good. Do you know which day you're taking off this week?" I asked.

Because we all worked Saturdays, everyone got a weekday off. Eric, my all-around handyman and assistant tag-sale cashier, usually took Mondays. Gretchen was charged with reconciling the weekend tag-sale receipts, so she almost always worked Mondays and coordinated with Sasha and Fred so that there was always office coverage.

"I don't know. I have nothing going on this week, so I'll let Sasha and Fred pick first."

I nodded. "They were in yesterday, working on the Picasso."

"Oh yeah?" she said, spinning around to look at me. "What's the word?"

I raised crossed fingers and flashed a quick grin.

Gretchen smiled. "Great!"

I was halfway to Newington when my cell phone rang, interrupting my disordered thoughts. Between fanciful anticipation about my upcoming conversation with Ty and fretting about the implications of Maisy's murder, I was agitated and perplexed.

"Hello," I said, angling my head to keep the phone in place.

"Josie. It's Max."

"Hi, Max," I said, my worry meter spiking.

"I just spoke to Detective Rowcliff. He wants to see us this afternoon."

"Why?" I asked, not really wanting to know. My heart began to thud.

"Apparently, he has questions about a few things—including some about Trevor Woodleigh."

"Do you think there's a problem?"

"I think he just wants to clarify some things."

"That doesn't sound bad."

Max paused. "Well, Rowcliff isn't as forthcoming as I might like, so it's a wait-and-see situation, I think."

The studied neutrality of his response added to my anxiety. If Rowcliff had bad news, he wouldn't say a word to Max, no matter what Max asked, but if Rowcliff had good news, either he would have volunteered the information or Max would have discovered it. I felt a sense of impending doom.

"So," I said, knowing there was no alternative, "when?"

"How's three?"

I thought about how long I'd be at the Newington house. Verna, the woman who had called to schedule the appointment, was on her lunch hour, so I guessed that an hour was the outside limit. Twelve thirty to one thirty, a quick lunch, yes, I could get to Portsmouth by three o'clock.

"Sure," I said, feeling resigned to my fate.

"Rowcliff asked if we'd come to the police station. Are you okay with that?"

"Why? Why does he want to meet there?" I asked, on the edge of panic.

"His convenience. I could refuse, but that might make us appear uncooperative."

I swallowed as I turned onto Woodbury Avenue, pushing the panic aside. *You've done nothing wrong, Josie. You've done everything right.* "Sure," I said as calmly as I could. "No problem."

"Let's talk for a minute in the parking lot before we go in, okay?"

"Okay. About ten of?"

"Perfect. I'll see you there."

I tried to recapture the giddy pleasure of fantasizing about Ty, but unease about my impending interview with Detective Rowcliff had taken hold.

As I turned into Verna's street and searched for house numbers, I found myself fighting tears. I winked away the dampness as I pulled into the pockmarked driveway of 11 Melody Lane.

CHAPTER FIFTEEN

I was a few minutes early, so I sat in my car and dialed the number for Maisy's apparent friend, Pam Field.

"Field Design Studio," a woman answered briskly.

"Pam Field, please."

"This is she."

"We've never met," I said. "I'm Josie Prescott. I don't know if my name is familiar to you."

"Oh wow," she said, suddenly somber. "The Gala."

"Right."

"Poor Maisy. It's just so awful."

"Absolutely," I agreed. "I understand you and Maisy were friends."

"Yes. Very much so."

"I'm sorry for your loss," I said softly.

"Thank you. It was quite a shock."

I paused, trying to find the words to ask my questions without offending her or seeming too pushy. I decided to keep things vague. "I didn't know Maisy well. But now—well, this whole situation is so confusing—I'm trying to learn more so I can understand what happened."

"How can anyone understand murder?" she asked rhetorically.

"Of course." I cleared my throat. "Listen, you're located on Market Street, right?"

"Yes. Near Ceres."

"Can I buy you a drink later? Maybe we could just talk a little. I don't want to impose, but I'd be very grateful."

I could almost hear Pam thinking it through, and I crossed my fingers, hoping that she'd agree to meet me.

"Sure. A drink would be good," Pam said with confidence, her mind made up. "I'd like to hear about Maisy from your perspective if it wouldn't upset you to tell me about it."

"I'll tell you anything I can. When's good for you?"

"I'm finishing up a project—I'm a graphic designer . . . Ummm . . . how's eight? Is that too late for you?"

"Eight is perfect," I said, and suggested meeting in the lounge at the Blue Dolphin. She agreed.

As I got out of the car, I thought again of Ty. It would be good to talk to him. I was missing him, and missing him felt good. Also, I was looking forward to getting his professional take on Maisy's murder. Which made me think of my upcoming meeting with Rowcliff. All that interview promised was trouble.

One look at Verna's living room and all thoughts of trouble disappeared.

The room was packed with items that shined and twinkled. In a battered old curio case, rays of sunlight glinted off of several cut-crystal bowls. Silver candlesticks sat on a copper tray. And hanging on a rolling coatrack, the kind we wheeled in on auction days for attendees to hang their wraps, were a dozen or more sequined and beaded evening gowns.

"What exactly are you interested in selling?" I asked as dispassionately as I could.

She gestured to include the entire room. "Everything. You want it, it's yours."

I nodded. "Is that true of the entire house?"

"Pretty much. I mean, we're taking our clothes, of course, and some favorite pieces, but mostly we want it all gone."

I wondered why. I never get involved in the underlying reasons that drive people to sell their possessions, but sometimes I get curious. What would motivate a thirty-something woman and her husband to sell what seemed to be all of their possessions? Were Verna and her husband hoping to start fresh in Las Vegas? Or had they accepted a job that came with a furnished apartment, like managing one of the hotels on the Strip?

After surveying the house, I made an offer and was turned down flat.

"What?" Verna asked, shocked. "Eight hundred dollars? I would have expected more than that for the contents of the living room alone!"

"You have some nice pieces," I said without sounding overly enthusiastic. "But, with all due respect, most of the goods aren't special. Don't get me wrong—I'm not saying they aren't special to you and your husband. I'm simply talking from my business perspective."

She shook her head impatiently as I spoke. "No, no. I'm not talking about sentimental value. I'm talking business, too. I had another dealer in here and he offered me more than twice what you're offering."

"Really? Who was that?"

She tilted her head. "I don't think I should tell you."

I didn't believe her. Other than the good stuff on display in the living room, there wasn't much else. Amateur oil paintings hung next to chipped gilt-framed mirrors. There were two sets of flatware, both stainless, not silver or silver plate—and incomplete. Most of the furniture was painted and had been constructed of cheap veneer to begin with. She had a lot of stuff, and it would cost a few hundred dollars out-of-pocket to rent a truck and hire the temporary employees we'd need to help Eric pack and move everything. In situations like this, where there's a mixed bag of good stuff and junk, there are two options: cherry picking the good stuff or basing your bid on the good items but offering to take it all. Most dealers want the former and most owners want the latter. My strategy of bidding on everything has several advantages to Prescott's—it helps generate inventory for our tag sales, disguises where my true interest lies, and thus creates a barrier to competition. Because most dealers don't want to deal with an entire houseful of miscellaneous goods, I have a leg up, and almost never overbid.

I shrugged. "I think you should accept that person's offer. I doubt you'll do better." I headed for the door.

"Wait," she called after me. "Actually, that offer was contingent on our selling some of the pieces we decided to keep. You didn't see them. Eight hundred cash?"

"Yes," I said.

She looked at me for several seconds. "Okay. What the hell? Sold."

My offer was fair, but her attitude made our interaction seem somehow sleazy, a feeling I hated. *If a negotiation ends with anyone feeling bad or shortchanged, it's a failure,* my dad told me when I was first given bargaining responsibility at Frisco's. *It's more than "win-win,"* he explained, *which sometimes is more a matter of smoke and mirrors than substance. It's being fair.*

Do the right thing, kiddo, he added, *and you'll never be sorry.*

I stood with the sun on my back, straddling the front door threshold, promising that we'd be there at 12:30 tomorrow, cash in hand, and that we'd pack and move everything out right away.

As I walked to my car, I dug my cell phone out of my bag and called Gretchen.

"Hey, Gretchen," I said, "everything under control?"

"Absolutely. How did it go?"

"We got it!"

"Great!"

"Well, sort of. There's a few good pieces and a lot of junk. Got a pen?"

"I'm ready."

"Eric will need four guys and a twenty-footer, and they have to be there at twelve thirty sharp. Got it?"

"Got it."

"They'll only have a few hours, but that should be okay, because very little has to be packed carefully. Mostly, it's furniture, so simple padding will do."

"Okay."

"I'll talk to Eric, but if you speak to him first, tell him that he should focus on the living room and let the other guys take the rest of the house."

"What's in the living room?"

I took a quick glance at my notes. "Five cut-crystal bowls, two pairs of sterling silver candlesticks, and thirteen vintage evening gowns."

"Cool!" Gretchen exclaimed.

"Yeah. Be sure he has proper packing—there's lots of beading that can fall off."

"Okay."

"He'll need eight hundred in cash."

"I'll get it ready."

"Stress that he needs to count the gowns and bowls."

I wouldn't have put it past Verna to hold back one or two of those gowns, and if questioned, claim that they were favorites and weren't included in the sale. It happens a lot, sometimes for nefarious reasons, and sometimes out of pure sentimental attachment. Regardless, it's why I have a cast-in-concrete rule that the owner has to sign off on a listing of what we're buying.

"Will do. Are you on your way back?"

"No," I told her. "I have some other things to do. I don't know when I'll be back."

That's the truth, I thought as I ended the call. Knowing Rowcliff, I might be stuck at police headquarters all afternoon, enduring God only knew what innuendos and abuse at his hand.

CHAPTER SIXTEEN

Max was leaning against his car, his eyes closed, a small smile softening his determined-looking features.

I hated to disturb him and stood several paces away, watching him. Today's bow tie was dark green with small yellow polka dots. It went nicely with his cocoa-brown and green tweed suit and yellow shirt. His sandy hair was cut short and combed back. After a long minute, I cleared my throat and he opened his eyes.

"Were you six thousand miles away in Hawaii?" I asked.

"No, I was only about ten miles away, in my backyard, smelling the last of my tomatoes and wondering whether we could bring the basil inside for the winter, or whether it's doomed."

"Yum."

"Yeah," he agreed. He stood up and straightened his jacket. "So," he asked, "how are you holding up?"

"Good. Better than I would have expected. It helps that I just made a terrific buy. Most of a houseful of goods."

"Great!" He looked at me. "Are you ready for Rowcliff?"

"Nope. No one can properly prepare for a jerk."

He smiled. "I think he's a good cop, actually. I just think he's got a lousy bedside manner."

"Well, that part's true enough at least. Why do you say he's a good cop?"

Max looked over my shoulder, watching the traffic flow for a moment. "He asks good questions."

I nodded, remembering some of the pointed questions he'd asked me. "What should I expect?"

"No way to know. But regardless of what he does, I know what you should do."

"And that is?"

He shrugged and, with a twisted grin, said, "Tell the truth. Give short, responsive answers. Don't volunteer information. Follow my instructions if I tell you to stay quiet. You know, same old, same old."

"How scary is it that I'm getting good at handling homicide interrogations? Jeez. What does that say about me?"

"It says that you picked a good lawyer—one who's terrific at guiding his innocent clients." He lightly tapped my shoulder and I smiled at his attempt to reassure me.

Three police officers stood talking quietly in the lobby of the old building when we pushed open the heavy door and entered. One of them greeted Max by name, and each of them gave me a once-over.

Glancing around the entryway, I spotted a used copy of yesterday's *Seacoast Star* resting on a bench, and nearly choked. I felt hunted, unable to escape its censure—PRESCOTT INVOLVED IN SECOND MURDER. With a sideways peek to confirm that no one was watching me, I scooped the section up and folded it in half, hiding the headline, and stuffed it into my purse. Staring straight ahead, panic and embarrassment faded, and wrath simmered to the surface.

Detective Rowcliff entered the lobby through a door on the left and waggled his fingers, indicating that we were to follow him. His expression was severe, his gesture impatient. I wasn't intimidated at all. I felt pretty damn severe and impatient myself and utterly uncooperative. I didn't want to help anyone learn anything more about me.

Rowcliff led us down a serpentine corridor to a small conference room. A tiny window, up near the ceiling, was soot-stained and allowed almost no light to penetrate. It was austere, devoid of warmth.

I sat on a folding metal chair, facing the window, hoping he'd do something outrageous so I could justify telling him exactly what I thought of him. Wes wasn't handy, but Rowcliff would do.

As Max was extracting a pad of paper from his briefcase, the door opened and Officer Johnston appeared, notebook in hand. Max said hello and I nodded. We both watched as he got settled. Once Johnston recorded the date and time and indicated that he was ready, Rowcliff jumped in.

"Tell me about Trevor Woodleigh," he said.

"What do you want to know?" I groused.

"I want to know about your relationship," Rowcliff responded, his tone matching mine.

"He's my ex-boss," I said. "I have no relationship with him."

Rowcliff rolled his pencil back and forth on the pitted metal table. "Tell me about the relationship you used to have," he said, trying to convey patience and sounding patronizing instead.

"Oh, come on," I responded, fed up with Rowcliff's attitude. "That's so five years ago."

"Well, is there something about your relationship with Woodleigh you *don't* want to talk about?" Rowcliff asked provocatively.

Yes, I shouted silently. *Everything. I don't want you to tramp on the threadbare remnants of my pathetic hero worship.*

"Josie," Max interjected quietly, gripping my forearm.

I turned to him. His eyes conveyed a warning. *Stay cool,* they signaled. He leaned over and whispered, "Answer his questions, Josie. Short answers. Lose the sarcasm. Play it straight. Got it?"

"Okay, okay," I whispered back. The pulsating anger I'd felt in the lobby on seeing the newspaper faded to mere irritation.

Max nodded encouragingly and squeezed my arm before releasing it and resettling in his chair. I took a deep breath and after a short struggle pushed the last of my rebellion aside.

"Okay. Where were we? Is there something I don't want you to know?" I repeated, turning my attention back to Rowcliff, ready to fib. "Right. No. Ask away."

"Okay, then," he said, tapping his pencil on the table edge. "So?"

"So, I worked for him for a long time. I used to know him well. I've had no contact with him in over five years. What specifically do you want to know?"

"Has Woodleigh threatened you directly?"

"No." *Unless you count his courtroom stare, a hateful look that would have enlivened a marble statue to flee a garden perch,* I thought.

"You just said that you've had no contact with him since the trial. Is that right?"

"Yes. None."

"Has he tried to contact you? Left a voice mail, for instance, and you didn't return the call? Sent a letter and you didn't respond?"

"Nothing like that. No."

Rowcliff shifted in his chair, staring at me. "Why do you think he might be out to kill you, then?"

I paused, trying to think of how to express my amorphous concern. "I didn't. I don't. I can't imagine it. But you asked if I could think of anyone who might have a reason to kill me." I shrugged. "On paper, Trevor fits the bill. That's all."

Rowcliff nodded, thinking.

"Did you check him out?" Max asked.

"Yes. Two detectives from New York met with him." He turned to me. "You're not his favorite person. But he has no trouble explaining his whereabouts for all day Saturday."

"So he's out of it?" I asked eagerly, relieved.

"Not really. He went for walks, paid cash for entry into a museum and a movie theater, ate alone in Central Park, et cetera, et cetera. *Could* he have left New York at noon, driven to New Hampshire, killed Maisy, and driven back to New York before someone missed him? Yes. *Did* he? We're continuing to investigate."

"Which means . . ." Max prodded.

"Which means we have no idea and may never know. On the face of it, his alibi is perfect. Every minute is accounted for, and we can't—so far, at least—disprove anything he's said."

"What about the car?" I asked. "Does he own one?"

Rowcliff shook his head. "No."

"How about a rental?"

"Not under his own name," Rowcliff answered begrudgingly.

"What about not under his own name?"

"Who'd rent it for him?" he responded, his question a challenge, not an answer.

"His sister," I said, remembering how he'd often escorted her to company parties. "When I knew him, they were close."

Rowcliff nodded. "Who else?"

I shut my eyes. I recalled Trevor at work. He never walked from point A to point B. He'd stop at every cubicle, look at you straight on, without guile, and chat, or ask how it was going, or share a funny anecdote. And he always smiled. "That one may smile, and smile, and be a villain." Shakespeare knew.

"There were three people who were all geared up to testify at his trial on his behalf—character witnesses. No matter what facts were revealed, they remained loyal." I shrugged. "I wouldn't be surprised to hear that they still are."

Detective Rowcliff slid his notebook across the table and handed me a pen. "Write down their names."

I glanced at Max and he nodded. Feeling like a tattletale, I did as I was told and slid the notebook back across the table.

He looked at Max, then back at me, rhythmically tapping his pencil. Reaching a decision, he slapped the pencil down and leaned back in his chair, folding his arms behind his head.

"Here's the situation," Rowcliff said. "I have no viable theory of the crime. All I know for sure is that Maisy drank poisoned wine and died on the spot." He leaned forward and his chair legs made a sharp slapping noise as they hit the floor. "We'll continue checking his alibi, but I'm not holding out much hope. If we find anything out, it won't be through running down alibis." He turned to me. "Have you remembered anything else about your mystery waiter?"

"He's not *my* mystery waiter!" I responded, bristling. "All I said was that I didn't notice much about him, that's all."

"Did you happen to notice what Maisy said when she collapsed?" he asked sarcastically.

I wondered what Max would do if I walked out. I wondered what Rowcliff would do. Barely controlling myself, I answered as calmly as I could. "She screamed," I said.

"Can you describe it?"

"It was kind of a shriek. Is that what you mean?"

"Mimic it."

I looked at him, confused. "Me? Now?"

"Yeah."

"You mean I should yell?"

"Did Maisy yell?"

"It was kind of a guttural noise."

"Yeah, go ahead."

I shrugged. "Okay. Here goes nothing." I thought for a minute. "Maisy's eyes opened wide and she shrieked, 'Al-ahhhh! Aurrrruaghhh-alah! Aladah! Dahhh!'" I trembled, recalling the awful scene. "Something like that."

"Then what happened?" Rowcliff asked.

"I jumped up and my chair fell. I remember hearing it thud against the carpet. I couldn't believe my eyes. It was as if I were frozen, watching a horror movie." I closed my eyes for several seconds. "Maisy sank to her knees, then fell forward and rolled off the platform onto the floor." I looked up, to find Rowcliff's eyes fixed on mine. "I unfroze and rushed toward her. I heard gasps all around."

"Maisy didn't say or scream anything else?"

I shook my head. "No. That was it."

Rowcliff tapped his pencil and nodded.

"So where does that leave us?" Max asked.

"With a lot of questions but not a lot of answers. But if Josie was the intended target after all, someone might get impatient and try again. In which case, we'll catch him for sure."

"Gee, thanks. All someone has to do for you to charge him with Maisy's murder is kill me. Is that what I just heard you say?"

"No, don't be so quick to fire up," Rowcliff responded. "They don't have to succeed in killing you. All they have to do is try."

CHAPTER SEVENTEEN

About ten minutes after Rowcliff uttered his chilling comment, Max and I left the station and walked across the parking lot.

"What was up with that display of attitude?" he asked as we approached my car.

"What attitude?" I replied cheerily, hoping that my perkiness would distract him enough to skip the issue. In my current mood, the last thing I wanted was a lecture on proper decorum during police interrogations.

"Josie?" Max sounded stern, apparently unimpressed by my assumed insouciance. "It's a serious situation, and when you joke around, you sound defensive, not playful."

"I was trying for sassy, not playful," I said brightly, flashing a thousand-watt smile, still trying to distract him.

He didn't respond; he didn't smile back at me, and his eyes conveyed neither amusement nor reassurance. I brushed my hair aside, suddenly feeling childish in the face of his distress. What was I thinking—that I could wish the situation away? I looked aside again, girding myself to face the music.

"I'm sorry, Max," I said, sighing. "I know I shouldn't let him push my buttons."

"It's okay," he responded. "No permanent damage was done. But you shouldn't behave that way again." I nodded acquiescence, and he reiterated what I knew, that it was crucial that I stay calm, act professional, and not take anything Rowcliff said or did personally.

Listening to the lecture I hadn't wanted to receive, hearing nothing new, was tough. Tougher still was facing why I'd acted as I had. The bottom line was that I was full up with anxiety and worry, and as a result, my exterior toughness was worn down. It was as if my nerve endings were closer to the surface than usual, so that Rowcliff's normal sarcasm and cynical disdain were not merely irritants, but felt like sandpaper that had rubbed me raw. Regardless of the why of the situation, my reaction now struck me as sophomorically self-indulgent, dumb, and, worse yet, counter-productive.

I looked toward the street, embarrassed that my stupidity and immaturity had made Max's job more difficult.

As Max finished his comments, I noticed a woman driving a shiny red sports car with the top down. She slowed for the stoplight, her head bopping to music I couldn't hear, and I wondered what kind of songs she was playing and whether she felt cold in the brisk October air.

I bought my first car when I was almost seventeen, a used Fiat 850 Spider, and my dad and I cruised around for more than an hour with the top down even though it was a frigid, windy December afternoon. Even with the heat blasting on high, we nearly froze, but it didn't seem to matter at all. We had a blast. *Oh, Dad.*

I turned back to Max, who was waiting patiently for my response. "I'm really sorry. I just kind of lost it."

"Why?"

I took a deep breath. "I think that what put me over the top was seeing yesterday's *Seacoast Star*. They printed that goddamn article on the front page," I said.

He nodded. "Yeah. I saw it."

I began to cry and turned away from his sympathetic eyes, angrily sweeping away my tears. After a long minute, I gulped down the last of my emotion and said, "I'm sorry, Max. I'm just a mess."

"Don't keep apologizing, Josie. You're fine. Really. You're holding up very well, all things considered. I'm sorry I upset you." He patted my shoulder.

"You didn't. Wes did, writing such drivel." I sniffed, and when I opened my purse to find a tissue, I discovered the folded newspaper I'd stuffed in earlier, and I began to cry again. I wrestled the paper loose and thrust it toward him. "Here. I don't want the damn thing."

"I'll throw it away for you." Max accepted it and tucked it under his arm, out of sight.

"I'm okay now." I blew my nose and felt better, used the crumpled tissue to pat away under-eye mascara smudges, and took several deep breaths. "It sounds like Rowcliff is convinced that Trevor is out to get me, huh?"

"Rowcliff isn't giving up on any line of investigation, Josie. He's very thorough. Remember, he's checking on who could have acquired the poison and who could have put it in Maisy's wine, in addition to following up on Woodleigh."

"And he's still considering whether Maisy was the intended target," I added, forcing myself to sound at least a little hopeful. With any luck, I'd know more tonight, after I spoke to Pam Field.

"Right."

"Thank you, Max. Not just for your great lawyering but also for being so kind."

"Aw shucks, I'm blushing, little lady," he said, switching seamlessly into an old-style western cowboy dialect, shuffling his feet and looking theatrically ill at ease.

I smiled and felt comforted by his silliness. Competent and gentle. *What a guy.*

I didn't get back to Prescott's until just after 5:00 P.M. I could tell from the solitary car in the parking lot that only Sasha was still there.

I entered the office, the chimes jingling, and discovered Sasha, her coat in hand, ready to leave.

"Go on ahead," I told her. "I'll lock up."

"Are you sure?"

"Absolutely."

"Okay," she agreed.

"Will I see you tomorrow?" I asked.

"No, if it's all right with you, we agreed that I'd take tomorrow off, and Fred would take Wednesday."

"And Gretchen, Thursday?"

"Yes."

"Good. That's fine. Just one thing before you go."

Sasha turned to me, suddenly anxious. I had to watch my tone and my words when I spoke to her. Comments or questions that seemed to me innocuous were to her fraught with innuendo and danger. *Perception,* I reminded myself, *colors outlook. Don't underrate the power of perception.*

"What?" she asked.

I smiled. "The Picasso. Any news?"

She grinned, her worry dissipating in a flash. "It's very exciting, actually. It looks as if Picasso drew it in exchange for a meal."

"What?"

She nodded. "He did that sometimes. Not for the money, but as a tribute. Because his works were so highly regarded, if he favored a café, for example, he might create the drawing as a favor to the owner."

"And present it at the end of dinner?"

"Yes. Usually at the end of a big, expensive dinner!" she said with a grin. "In lieu of cash."

I laughed. "Smart fellow."

"Oh, he was. Absolutely."

I perched against a nearby desk. "And this particular drawing?" I asked.

"We're pretty sure we know which restaurateur he gave it to. We have some inquiries out."

I shook my head in mock amazement. "I can't believe you tracked it down. You're incredible! The best of the best."

Her smile was huge. "Thank you. Not really. I mean, it's work, you know. And Fred is just as good as I am."

"Ah, maybe. But you're my chief researcher, so you have to accept the accolades."

"Thank you," she said shyly, still smiling, unsure of what to do or say next.

"Go home now," I told her. "I'll see you on Wednesday."

"Okay. Thanks, Josie," she said.

As I watched her depart, I noticed that clouds had begun to move in from the west and the sky was streaked with gray.

I nearly skidded off the road as I realized that Trevor might have been on-site at the Gala. I slowed and righted my direction, focusing on the road. Trevor could be my mystery waiter. I pulled over and braked to a stop.

Perception, I thought. I'd never, not in a million years, have expected Trevor to be a waiter at the Gala, so I'd never have noticed him if he were there in that guise. He could have poured me wine.

It was hard to believe, yet even as I tried to chase the thought away as absurd, I realized that it was completely plausible. Not probable, perhaps, but possible.

I needed to talk to Eddie and glanced at the time display on the dashboard. It was almost five thirty. I found my cell phone at the bottom of my purse and scrolled through the phone log until I found Eddie's number and pushed the connect button.

"Eddie," I said when I had him. "I have a question."

"Sure, Josie. Shoot."

"It's going to sound stupid, but indulge me, okay?"

He chuckled. "Sure."

"The waiters for the Gala."

"Yeah?"

"Any newcomers? Any last-minute subs?"

"Sure. For a big job like the Gala, I always have new guys."

My heart started beating. "Can I stop by and show you a photo?"

"Of a waiter?"

"Of someone I'm wondering about. I want to know if he was a waiter."

"Who?"

"Just some guy," I responded, keeping it loose.

"Can we make it tomorrow, Josie? I'm on my way out the door."

"Sure," I replied, disappointed. "What time?"

We settled on nine, a late start for me, but early for a caterer who normally worked late into the evening. I was impatient for information.

As I stuffed my phone back into my purse and pulled out again, I shivered even though the heat was on. There was too much I didn't know for comfort, and in the face of my frightening realization about Trevor—that he could have been standing beside me, adding who knows what to my wine, unnoticed by everyone—I realized that I could no longer assume that I was safe.

Ty, I thought. Now I had another reason to talk to him—beyond missing him, I was confident that he'd be able to provide direction or suggestions.

When I turned into my driveway, my headlights swept over my new landlady, Zoe, as she sat alone on the front stoop of her house. She looked harassed.

"Are you okay?" I asked as I got out of the car.

"Am I okay?" she repeated in a musing tone. "Well, the police aren't here and it's been over an hour, so that's a good thing."

"Zoe, my God! What happened?"

She rubbed her forehead a couple of times, then said, "Do you know Mrs. Wilson?"

"Sure. Nice lady. Lives with her husband next to the Frost place."

"Right. Well, she stopped by to drop off a cherry pie as a welcome gift."

Zoe must have seen my confused look, because she added, "She saw Emma—you remember my two-year-old, don't you? Well, Mrs. Wilson rings the bell, takes one look at Emma in the cage, drops the pie, and flees!"

Curiosity burned hot. "Why was Emma in a cage?" I asked.

"It's Lassie's cage. For transporting her. Since she's new to the house, I left it in the front hall, you know, to help her settle in, so she could go inside to a safe, secure, familiar place if she wanted to. Lassie's blankie is in it, and some food and water." Zoe sighed and rubbed her forehead again. I figured she had a headache. "And her favorite rawhide bone," she added.

I nodded. "So what happened?"

"So Emma toddled in and fell asleep. She looked so cute, I didn't have the heart to wake her, and I said to myself, Why should I? Let her be."

"That's logical. She wasn't going anywhere, right?" I smiled, hoping to ease the tension.

"That's what I figured. But still, given the look of abject horror on Mrs. Wilson's face, I wonder why she *didn't* call the cops."

"Maybe when she got home and told her husband what happened, he warned her to lay off the booze, and they're still fighting about it."

"Maybe." Zoe laughed. "So tell me, how was your day?"

"Oh, special. I had a very special day," I said. "Are you ready to laugh again?"

"Always," she replied.

"I spent a chunk of the afternoon with a homicide detective, discussing who wants to kill me and why."

"Oh my God. Tell me."

"It isn't funny," I said, "so I don't know why I feel this overwhelming urge to laugh." I sat beside her.

"Me, too. The flip side of crying maybe. Give me an overview so we can really share a chuckle."

"Okay. Have you heard how Maisy Gaylor was killed at the Gala this weekend?" I asked.

"No. All I hear about are nursery issues."

"Well, you have to be the only person around who's unaware of what happened." I sighed. "She drank some wine spiked with cyanide while hosting an event my company was sponsoring." I sighed again. "I was proud to be the sponsor. Can you imagine? God, it's been awful."

"What's the funny part?"

"They're not sure whether the poisoned wine was intended for me and poor Maisy died by accident."

"You're right," she said, turning to look at me. "It's not funny."

"No, I guess it really isn't."

Zoe reached her arm around me and gave me a quick shoulder squeeze. "We're quite a pair, aren't we?"

I smiled. "In a good way."

She smiled, too. "I agree."

We sat in companionable silence for a long minute. I heard soft crackles as small animals traipsed on fallen leaves across the road, on the other side of the old stone wall, sharp clicks as insects said their good nights, and, in the distance, the forlorn, echoing cry of a seagull.

"Josie?" Zoe asked.

"What?"

"Thank you. I don't know what I would have done without this conversation. It's really helped lighten the load, you know?"

"Me, too," I said.

"You know what?" Zoe asked, standing up.

"What?"

"We gotta go inside. It's f'ing freezing out here."

"I can't. I've got a call. I've got to get ready."

"You've got to get ready for a phone date? What's involved? Cheetah-print lingerie and a Web cam?"

I laughed. "I wish."

"So-o-o?" she asked, shaking her head a little, trying to draw me out. "Who is he? Where is he? Fill me in."

"Oh, just a fellow I've known for a while," I said evasively, not wanting to share that part of my life, not yet.

She pushed a little for details, not too much, and finally we hugged good-bye. As I started across the leaf-strewn lawn that separated our houses, I looked back. "Zoe," I called.

"Yeah?" she replied.

"You can use me as a character witness with Children's Services anytime."

She laughed, thanked me, and disappeared inside.

Under the dim wattage of the lone bare lightbulb that illuminated Zoe's porch, everything was washed with a soft golden glow, the color of joy and contentment. An omen, I thought, and hoped it wasn't an illusion.

CHAPTER EIGHTEEN

I had one message, from Wes.

It was brief and menacing. All he said was that he needed to see me as soon as possible. He sounded severe. Remembering Sunday's paper, I felt no inclination to talk to him, let alone see him, but his message scared me. Calling him seemed the lesser of two evils. I didn't want to speak with him ever again. But I was more afraid not to know what he had to say.

With some trepidation, I dialed his number, and he answered on the first ring, as if he'd been waiting for my call.

"Wes," I said. "It's Josie. What's up?"

"I have information for you. And a question."

"What?"

"Not on the phone."

"God, Wes, you're so dramatic."

"I am not. I'm prudent."

Maybe he's right, I thought. "Is it really that urgent?"

"Pretty much so. Can you meet now?"

"Not now. How's morning?"

"It shouldn't wait," he responded, lowering his voice for effect.

I thought through my schedule. I wanted to grab something to eat before I met Pam at eight o'clock. And I hoped to talk to Ty before that. If his doctor meeting was brief. "I can meet you for a few minutes around seven thirty."

He sighed, the sound of Wes disappointed, but capitulating. "Okay-y-y," he said, drawing the word out, signaling that he thought delay was a bad idea. "Where?"

I thought for a minute. I wanted someplace easy to get to, where we could talk without interruption—and somewhere clean,

I reminded myself, remembering Wes's sticky and litter-filled car.

"How about by the salt pile?" I suggested, thinking of the huge mountain of salt used to de-ice Portsmouth's streets throughout the winter. It was located just outside of downtown, not too far from the Blue Dolphin, where I was meeting Pam afterward.

"Too public. Let me think for a minute." After a pause, he asked, "You know Mill Pond Way?"

"I'm not sure," I said, trying to picture the street.

"It's off Dennett."

"Oh, right. I know where you mean."

I'd bought a lovely Wedgwood teapot from a woman who lived on that street. I recalled its fancy enamel work in pink, green, black, and yellow, the acanthus-molded spout, and its scroll handle. Sasha identified the design as "Chintz" pattern, and she authenticated the pot as a David Rhodes original, produced in the Wedgwood factory in 1775. It was a beautiful piece.

"It's a dead-end street, isn't it?" I asked Wes to confirm my memory.

"That's it," he said, and we finalized our plans.

Ty hadn't called by the time I needed to leave to meet Wes. I figured he was still tied up with Aunt Trina's doctors. *Maybe later,* I thought.

I parked at the very end of Mill Pond Way, near North Mill Pond, and got out of the car. I stretched. It was cool, and the air was fresh with a smell of rain.

My smile faded as soon as I saw Wes. The creep. I was still mad at him for his scurrilous writing, but although I'd never admit it to anyone, I secretly admired his unrelenting determination to dig deep and get the facts.

I wondered if I was smart to meet him. If he wrote another article insinuating that I had guilty knowledge of a murder, I might just prove the truth of his words by killing him.

He was standing with his back to me. "Wes," I called softly as I approached.

He turned and looked at me. I was wearing a black wool cape, warm enough for the evening cool, yet dressy enough to suit my mood, over clean jeans and high-heeled green lizard cowboy boots.

"How come you're all dressed up?" he asked.

Always a reporter, I thought, *wanting to know.*

"I have plans," I responded, then turned the subject before he could ask for details. "So did you get a bonus?"

"For what?" he asked.

"Your article made the lead story in the paper. Your editor must be thrilled." I hoped my sarcasm made him feel bad.

"I'm really sorry about it," he said, looking contrite.

"Ha."

"Really. I told you already."

I relented. "Still."

"Tomorrow's article focuses on tracking the purchase of the poison. You're barely mentioned."

"What do you mean, 'barely mentioned'?" I demanded wrathfully. "Why am I mentioned at all?"

"There's no record of you having purchased any," he said, as if he expected me to be thrilled to get the update.

"Oh my God."

"What?" he asked, sounding more hurt than ever. "It's good news for you, isn't it?"

"Good news? That's like the old joke: 'So how long has it been, Mr. Smith, since you stopped beating your wife?' Don't you get it, Wes? Saying that I didn't buy poison is implying that someone had reason to think I might have done so."

"Well," he said, annoyingly rational, "they did."

"Wes," I said, ready to pull my hair and stamp my foot, "the point is that I don't want my name associated with a murder investigation in any way."

"I understand, Josie," he said patiently, as if he were talking to a four-year-old. "But you *are* associated with a murder investigation. I didn't involve you; I'm just reporting the truth."

I gave up. I understood his point of view, and I knew he was right. But that knowledge didn't quiet my angst. "Okay, whatever.

Forget about it. Is that what you wanted to tell me? That I didn't buy any poison?"

"Not exactly. I have a question, and it's important." He looked at me as if gauging whether I might fire up again, or whether it was safe to proceed.

"What?" I asked, resigned.

"I understand from my sources that the police have found no record of anyone involved in the case purchasing potassium cyanide. Not a surprise when you think about it, since only a fool would openly buy poison he or she intended to use for murder, and there's no reason to think that the killer is a fool."

"True," I agreed.

There are other ways to get cyanide, I thought, *besides buying it. Do photographers still use cyanide?* I knew they used to years ago. Images of Trevor supervising photographers came to me. One photographer in particular, Lewis somebody. Old-school, temperamental, talented.

I remembered walking into Lewis's photography studio in the Chelsea section of New York City for the first time. Trevor had introduced me as his bright new star. Despite all that had passed, recalling the moment when Trevor spoke those words brought a flush of pride, just as it had when I first received the tribute.

Some photographers probably still used the old way of developing, the one that called for cyanide. I bet Lewis was one of them. *Is Trevor still in touch with Lewis?* I wondered.

"What are you thinking about?" Wes asked, watching me with hawklike intensity.

"Nothing." No way was I sharing information with Wes. "What's your question?"

"If you wanted to get your hands on cyanide, how would you go about it?"

"I wouldn't!" I responded, outraged. "What a question!"

"No, no," he said. "I meant theoretically."

"What do you want to ask me, Wes? Stop being cagey."

He sighed, disappointed that I wouldn't allow him his dramatic lead-in. "Okay, okay. Here's the point. Since the police still don't know whether you or Maisy was the intended victim, it got me thinking. Potassium cyanide has many industrial applications. For instance, it's frequently used in the jewelry business. You know, gold plating. So I was wondering—do you have a relationship with anyone who does any gold plating?"

The wind off the pond was biting and I flipped my cape's hood up. "No, no one. I don't know any jewelers," I said.

"How about jewelry designers? Anyone you know do amateur designing? Anything of that nature?"

"No. Not that I know of."

"What about for your work? Don't you ever have things plated? You know, restoration stuff."

"No. What are you doing? Trying to see if you can find evidence that I'm a murderer?"

"Of course not!" he assured me, sounding shocked. "I'm thinking maybe someone set you up. If I can trace the poison, then we can find out who has it in for you."

I was appalled at his calmly expressed suggestion of a diabolical plot against me. "That's outrageous, Wes."

"Maybe. It's just one line of thinking I'm investigating."

"It'll be a waste of time."

"Probably. So, how come you don't use any gold platers in your business?"

I stared at him for a long moment. His idea about seeking out people who used industrial cyanide had merit. His thought that I was being framed did not. It was absurd even to think about.

"That's just not what we do—we don't restore things. We sell things as is. If they're in rough shape, they go to the tag sale. The better items go to auction. But we don't do restoration."

"Think, Josie," Wes insisted. "It's important. Any source of metal plating?"

I shook my head. "Nothing comes to mind."

"No neighbors who are jewelers?"

"Not that I'm aware of."

"Former neighbors?"

I shook my head again.

"Do you know Frank Connors?"

"No, why?"

"How about Michelle Piper?"

"No. Who are they?"

"Gold platers in the area. Maybe you know someone and just don't know what they do for a living. The last one is named Labelle Brown. Do you know her?"

"No. Truly, I have no idea of anyone who has access to cyanide," I stated firmly, pushing thoughts of Lewis aside.

"Except that someone did, in fact, acquire and use cyanide."

"Good point," I acknowledged.

And if I can identify the source of the cyanide, I might get a clue about who obtained it—but I can't believe someone got cyanide, and used it to kill Maisy, in order to frame me.

"How's your research coming?" I asked him, changing the subject.

"Pretty good," he said, sounding unconvinced. "I'm trying to follow the same logic as the police. That's the foundation of the article I'm writing—you know, 'Anatomy of a Homicide Investigation.' "

"Uh-huh. And?"

"So I've gone back to the basics, just like they have."

"Wes, it's cold. Do you have anything else to tell me or ask me?"

He looked hurt, as if he would be happy to spend hours standing in the dark on a cold October night discussing the ways and means of conducting journalistic research. He sighed. "I was hoping to fill you in and solicit your opinion about what I've learned. Not because you're involved," he added quickly, "but because you know the situation from a close-up perspective."

I wasn't flattered. Plain and simple, Wes was an opportunist and I represented access to information he wanted. But I decided to play along both because I was curious and because I thought there was a good chance I might learn something that would help me cope with my increasingly frightening situation. "Okay," I said, resigned to the inevitable. "Talk to me."

"So," Wes said, putting his notebook away and clearing his throat. "You told the police about Trevor Woodleigh. How come?"

I nodded and pulled the cape close as a gust of wind whipped off the water. Wes hunched his shoulders as it hit.

"I had to tell them."

"I figured it was you. You should have talked to me first."

"Why? So you could argue with me about it?"

"No, so I'd know what was going on. I wasted time trying to track how they found out about him."

I nodded, acknowledging his point. "Sorry."

"It's okay. I understand why you told them. You were scared."

He made it sound like I was a sissy. "It's reasonable for me to be scared, Wes. There'd be something wrong with me if I wasn't."

"So you're now thinking that you were the target after all?" he asked, poised to strike.

"No. I'm saying it was only prudent to learn more. You should have reported it to the police yourself."

"I didn't have any reason to think he was a suspect," he responded, sounding righteous.

"Whatever," I said, dismissing the discussion as pointless.

"What did they tell you about Woodleigh?"

I thought for a moment about how much I should reveal, and decided to tell him nothing. I would use Wes to help me find answers to specific questions, but I'd confide in him not at all. "Nothing. Just that they were investigating."

"I hear he has no alibi," Wes said.

"That's not what I hear," I responded, my curiosity piqued.

"What do you mean?"

"Apparently, Trevor can account for all of his time on Saturday."

"Right, but nothing is verifiable."

"I guess," I acknowledged, not wanting it to be true.

Wes nodded. "I'm thinking of going to New York and talking to him."

"Lucky you."

"If I do, I'll let you know what he says, okay?"

"No, don't. He hates me and I don't need to hear about it again."

"I'll keep you posted in a big-picture way, okay?"

I shrugged acquiescence and we said good-bye. I hurried toward my car, anxious to get out of the cold and to get away from Wes. He was thorough, I thought as I drove, and very good about following up every lead. He was also good about staying in touch

and making me feel important. Which, considering my uncontrollable rage at seeing his damnable article plastered across the front
page of the *Seacoast Star,* was quite an accomplishment.

I turned the heat on high. A raw dampness had gotten into my
bones from standing outside so long. From the feel of it, I knew
there'd be rain before long. I was looking forward to the crackling
fire I knew would be burning in the old fieldstone fireplace in the
Blue Dolphin's lounge.

I turned onto Market Street and began the search for a parking
space, keeping one eye on the rearview mirror. It wouldn't surprise me at all if Wes followed me, eager to learn more about my
plans.

CHAPTER NINETEEN

T he Blue Dolphin was located at the intersection of Bow and Ceres streets, in the heart of town and about two blocks away from where I parked on Market Street, the closest spot I could find. Its position at the end of a gentrified little road added to its charm. Ceres Street was filled with trendy restaurants, ocean-themed bars, and froufrou gift shops.

Shivering, I sped up as much as my boots—whose heels were made for strutting, not running—allowed.

I rushed past a row of old wooden and stone four-story buildings with shops and stores at street level and offices and apartments on the upper floors. Everything was closed—the beauty parlor with wigs on faceless white foam heads in the window; the hardware store with signage from the forties; two women's clothing stores; a shop that sold hand-dipped candles and aromatic oils; and a tanning salon with part of its neon lighting on the blink.

I crossed a narrow driveway that gave access to the backs of the buildings, and then the Blue Dolphin came into view. A copper overhang shielded the entrance and bow windows gave an unobstructed view of Portsmouth Harbor.

Eager to get there and warm up, I increased my pace a little. I passed another block of shops, including a real estate broker with listings taped to the front window; a café; a bookstore with pyramids of books on display; and a gift shop offering goods as varied as picture frames and Christmas ornaments, linen napkins and teapots, and pewter vases and wooden trunks.

There was no foot traffic, and all at once I became extra aware of the darkened stores and shops around me. A quiver of fear flew up my spine. I looked over my shoulder. Nothing. I didn't understand what had startled me. Maybe it was just being alone on such a dark night. I heard faint bursts of laughter and the hint of music from the establishments on Ceres and farther up Market, but on this section of the street, there was no sign of life.

Reaching the restaurant, I pushed open the heavy wooden door and gave a sigh of relief as heat enveloped me. I told Karla, the hostess who offered to take my cape, that I'd keep it, then entered the lounge just after eight o'clock.

Pam Field looked just like her picture. She sat at a window seat with what looked to be a Cosmopolitan on the copper-topped table in front of her, facing the fire. I had trouble picturing her and Maisy as friends. They were about the same age, I guessed, somewhere in their forties, but whereas Maisy had looked like a dowdy matron most of the time, Pam seemed way more hip. Her dark hair hung in angular layers to her chin, her jewelry was big and shiny, and she wore all black.

"Hi," I said, introducing myself. "I'm Josie Prescott."

"Hi," she replied.

I ordered my usual—Bombay Sapphire on the rocks, with a twist—and settled into an armchair across from her.

"Thanks for meeting me," I said.

She nodded and gazed at the fire. "Maisy spoke about you a lot."

"Really? I'm surprised."

"How come?"

I shrugged. "We didn't know each other all that well. What did she say?"

"She admired you. She thought you worked really hard."

"That's nice to hear. I admired her dedication to the Guild, too."

We ran out of small talk. Suddenly, I felt awkward and silly being there, being in this place with this woman I didn't know, preparing to ask questions I hadn't framed, trying to learn I couldn't imagine what.

"Anything I can do to help," she said, sparing me the necessity of finding a way to start. "I want to. I want to help find my friend's killer."

"I understand that and I appreciate it."

"What do you want to know?"

"It's complicated. I don't know—no one, it seems, knows whether Maisy was killed by misadventure and whether, well, *I* was the intended victim. If whoever poisoned Maisy wanted her dead—then that's a tragedy and the police can work to find the murderer. But if not, well, I need to do something to protect myself—although I'm not sure what."

Pam nodded but didn't speak.

"So I was hoping you'd tell me about her . . . give me some insight into her life, so maybe I can figure out what's going on," I explained.

She leaned in and picked up her drink, her hair swooping forward. "It's pretty hard to imagine someone killing Maisy on purpose."

"Why?" I asked.

Pam finished her drink and signaled Jimmy, the bartender, for another.

"Maisy was awfully self-contained, you know? Not so easy to get to know. Pretty reserved. It's hard to picture anyone hating her enough to kill her."

"It doesn't need to be hate," I said. "It could be envy. Fear. Money. Love."

Pam grunted a little, a disdainful sound. "No envy. No fear. Money? No. Love? Did you know Walter?"

"Not really," I replied. "I met him only once, at the Gala."

"Once is enough."

"Yeah," I acknowledged, recalling his unpleasant attitude. "Were they happy?"

Pam sipped the drink that Jimmy slid across the table. She met my gaze, but I couldn't read her expression.

"Maisy expected Walter to walk out on her," she said after a long pause. "She was planning on leaving him first."

"Really?" I asked, stunned. "I had no idea. Why would Walter leave her?"

" 'Cause he'd fallen like a ton of bricks for a bookkeeper in his office."

I couldn't see how his infidelity provided a motive—unless Walter *wasn't* going to leave Maisy. That would provide a pretty solid reason for the bookkeeper girlfriend to want Maisy dead.

"What are the chances he was stringing the bookkeeper along?"

Pam shook her head. "Not according to Maisy. She told me it was for real. He had a lawyer's appointment and everything."

"What was Maisy's attitude toward her marriage ending? Was she going to contest the divorce?"

Pam half-smiled and said, "No, she was okay with it. She was a little hurt, but she was prideful, too."

"What was Walter doing at the Gala?" I asked. "Do you know?"

"Maisy asked him to show up to put a good face on things. They intended to file for divorce right after the Gala."

I nodded. *Envy. Fear. Money. Love.* What I had originally perceived as Maisy's over-the-top enthusiasm was, it seemed, a studied reaction to her troubles with Walter. *I'm fine,* she was signaling the Gala crowd. Maybe her euphoria hadn't been a sign of insipidity, but a mark of bravado.

Perception can be wrong, and often is.

If that was what had been going on. I had only Pam's word for it, and I wondered how deep in Maisy's confidence she'd really been. Maybe Maisy had been seeing someone herself. Hard to imagine, but she wouldn't have been the first middle-aged woman to succumb to the lure of illicit love. That also might explain her giddiness. Maybe her animation hadn't been intended to camouflage her hurt. Perhaps the answer was one of cause and effect—if she had been caught in a tidal wave of passion, it was possible that she simply could no longer keep her exhilaration under wraps. Would Pam know? And if she knew, would she tell me?

"I hope you don't mind my asking . . . but is there any chance that Maisy was having an affair?"

"No way."

"How can you be so sure?"

"You didn't know her or you wouldn't ask. That kind of deception just wasn't in Maisy's makeup."

I nodded, noting that Pam didn't say that Maisy wouldn't have an affair, just that she wouldn't lie about it. Which could be true—

or Maisy could have been a better liar than her good friend Pam knew. I felt utterly out of my depth. I was gathering miscellaneous information, but I didn't know what was meaningful and what wasn't. I began to feel frustrated.

"How about money? Were she and Walter comfortable?" I asked, thinking that it might have been cheaper for Walter to kill Maisy than to divorce her.

"Yeah, I guess. But they weren't more than comfortable, if you know what I mean. She told me once that she needed to work."

I nodded. "If she'd gotten divorced, what would she have done? Do you think she planned to stay in the area? Keep working at the Guild?"

"She talked about taking a trip. She was so excited when her passport arrived! Her first one ever. She described it to me. You know, telling me it was dark blue with pretty gold printing." Pam looked away, shaking her head a little, a sad smile on her face.

"Where was she going? Did she say?"

"A cruise. One of those around-the-world cruises."

"That isn't cheap," I commented.

"No," Pam agreed.

"How could she afford it?"

"I don't know. I guess I figured she was going to take part of her divorce settlement and kick up her heels a little. She asked me to join her."

"What did you say?"

"'No can do, I'm afraid.'" She half-laughed. "I told her I didn't have the money and couldn't take the time. We toyed around with my joining her somewhere at one of her ports of call."

"That sounds good," I said, smiling. "Where were you thinking?"

"We were debating between Cannes and Hong Kong."

"When Maisy said 'around the world,' I guess she meant it!"

"She sure did," Pam agreed.

"Do you know which ship she was thinking of?"

"Yeah. What was its name?" she asked herself. After a sip of her drink, she shook her head. "I don't remember the name, but I have the brochure somewhere. I could give it to you if you want."

"Thank you. That would be great." I dug out a business card and wrote my home address and phone number on it. "Would you send it to me at home?" I asked, thinking that Gretchen, who opened my mail at work, would have a field day if an expensive travel brochure arrived in the mail.

"I'll look for it first thing in the morning. I'm pretty sure I know exactly where it is."

I nodded, then turned to look out the window. Gazing into the deep darkness of the moonless night, I couldn't see anything but my shimmering reflection. I didn't know what else to ask.

"Would you tell me something?" Pam asked softly.

"Sure."

"Do you think Maisy was putting on an act for Walter, or do you think she really had fun at the Gala?"

I had no idea, but I inferred that Pam would find some comfort in believing that Maisy had had fun. "Given that there's no way of knowing for sure, I can tell you my strong impression."

"Okay," she said.

"Did Maisy have fun? Absolutely. She had a ball! She genuinely seemed to be having a good time. Right up until the end."

"That's great to hear. Really great. I thought so, too." Pam picked up her purse and said, "I've got to go. Did anything we talked about help?"

"I don't know. It's all pretty confusing."

She nodded, pushed her half-full drink aside, and fixed me with her eyes. "Maisy was a good woman. Strong and kind. She was a good friend to me."

I nodded. "She was lucky to have you as a friend."

"Thank you." Pam blinked away a tear.

I insisted on paying the check, and after Pam left, I sat alone, watching the flames consume crackling apple wood, thinking about Maisy until my drink was gone. *Envy. Fear. Money. Love.* I felt as if I knew less about Maisy's murder than when I'd walked into the Blue Dolphin, and that uncertainty was terrifying.

Outside, I swung my cape over my shoulders, extracted my car key from the pocket, and ran. It had begun to sprinkle. "Great," I said aloud, "I get to run in heels in the rain. A fitting end to a stressful day."

The rain grew steadier and I ran faster and tripped on a crack in the sidewalk, almost going down, but righting myself at the last moment. Just as I reached to open the driver's-side door, I heard a car motor gunning. When I looked up, I was blinded by headlights on bright and froze until I realized that a car was heading straight at me.

I reacted in the only way I could think of. I slapped the palms of both hands on my car and catapulted myself over the hood, landing on the grassy edge of the sidewalk and rolling away from the curb just as the oncoming vehicle slammed into mine.

I screamed, covering my head with my arms, and curled up in a ball.

CHAPTER TWENTY

First a man arrived, then the police, then an ambulance. Then I stopped screaming.

I struggled to sit up, but before I could, I was lifted onto a stretcher and whisked away. When we arrived at the emergency room in a frenzied rush, with lights flashing and the siren shattering the night, I thought I saw Ty, but since I knew that was impossible, I wondered if the man I saw was a look-alike or if I was hallucinating.

Every part of me ached or throbbed and the noisy pandemonium added to my anxiety. The commotion didn't stop until X-rays were taken and I was wheeled back to the ER. An aide left me alone in a big room with an opaque white curtain pulled halfway around my bed, explaining that someone would be in after the radiologist reviewed the X-rays. Apparently, the examining physician thought there was a chance that my left ankle had broken when I landed on it.

Broken or not, I felt thoroughly battered, as if I'd strained every muscle and scraped every inch of flesh. I felt emotionally beaten, too, worn and weary and without the internal fortitude to fight on. Tears seeped out of the corners of my eyes and I didn't have the strength to stop the flow. The terror that had electrified me the moment that I realized the car intended to hit me was with me still. I closed my eyes.

I was a believer now—someone wanted to kill me, but I had no idea who or why, and that was almost as scary as the mere fact itself.

My father would have agreed. I remembered the warning he issued the day he told me to find out immediately who was telling malicious tales about Trevor and me—untrue innuendos alleging an affair. *An unknown enemy is more dangerous than one you know,* he declared. *Once you know who you're up against, you can outmaneuver the son of a bitch.*

Taking my dad's counsel to heart that day, I asked around and quickly discovered the source of the gossip, a vile woman named Hattie, an assistant in the restoration department, with big hair and disapproving eyes. I'd taken her aside and with a bright smile—my thousand-watter—I'd threatened her with mayhem if she didn't cease and desist, and she did.

I never learned what drove her to try to sabotage my career and ruin my reputation. Jealousy that I, and not she, was Trevor's golden-haired girl, perhaps. The experience taught me that the *why* of things rarely mattered, and that my focus needed to be on the *what*. *What* she did was diabolical; *why* she did it was irrelevant.

Lying on the too-hard hospital bed, raw and weak and frightened, I had no idea what I could do to stop whoever wanted to kill me from succeeding.

"Are you asleep?" Detective Rowcliff asked briskly.

"Yes," I replied, recognizing his voice. I kept my eyes closed.

"Can you tell me what happened?"

"A car aimed at me and tried to hit me. I don't know how I did it, but I flipped myself over the hood of my car to get away, and the other car smashed into mine."

"How do you know the car was aiming at you?"

"What do you mean? Look at me."

"Maybe it was an accident."

I turned to him, cringing at the pain. I groaned a little. My neck didn't want to rotate. Max's words warning me to take Rowcliff's questions seriously echoed my father's instructions to ignore sarcasm and deal only with the content, and remembering both admonitions helped me control my impulse to address him derisively. Instead, I spoke in a serious, calm tone.

"Someone tried to run me down, to kill me," I said. "First, they got me full in their headlights and then I heard the car's motor roar. It wasn't an accident. It was on purpose."

"Did you see the car or driver?"

"Not really. He or she—or they—had the car's brights on. It was blinding."

"Were you able to see its shape? Was it a car or a pickup truck, for example? A van? An SUV?"

I closed my eyes for a moment, thinking. "I can tell you that the car was medium-sized and dark. Black or deep green or blue. Now that you mention it, I do seem to recall the shape of the car. I'm pretty sure it was a sedan. Ordinary."

"We'll get some illustrations in here and maybe you can narrow it down further."

I nodded and stopped halfway when my neck objected—again.

"What else do you remember?" he asked.

"Nothing."

Rowcliff persisted in questioning me. His growing impatience with my short answers and lack of information was obvious, and his agitation irritated me. It was as if he were an insect buzzing in my ear, not actually biting or stinging me, but annoying enough that I had to respond. An hour later, Rowcliff had left and the doctor gave me the good news that my ankle wasn't broken, merely badly sprained. She assured me that it was common for a person to pull ligaments and muscles when executing a fly-over-the-car move.

"You'll begin to feel better in a few days," she explained, "but don't be surprised if you're still experiencing some discomfort a month from now—and it may take as long as three months, or even a little longer, before you're a hundred percent better. Also, you shouldn't be alone tonight. Just in case. Who can we call for you?"

Oh Dad. I wish you were here to care for me, I thought. The doctor looked up from the chart, surprised, it seemed, by my silence. My mind was blank. *Who would stay with me tonight?*

Ty was a continent away. One of my staff—either Sasha or Gretchen—would rush to help. But I couldn't bear the thought of my employees seeing me in this miserable state. I just couldn't bear it. I began to cry because I was all alone and had no friends and my dad was dead, and then I thought of Zoe.

With painkillers in hand, and with my boots in my lap, I was processed out of the ER and cleared to go home.

Zoe pulled up in her old car and I saw the kids strapped into their car seats in the back. Apologizing for taking so long, she held my arm as I struggled out of the wheelchair that the ER insisted had to be used to transport me to the exit door, then guided me gently into the passenger seat.

"I'm sorry to get you out at this time of night," I told her.

"Don't be silly. I'm glad to help." As she closed the door, she added, "I put the seat all the way back, but the car's pretty small. Here, let me latch the seat belt for you."

I didn't argue. I didn't care. The painkiller and sedative had begun to work, and as my fear and pain dulled, I just wanted to go home and go to sleep. I dozed as she drove, lulled by the motion of the vehicle and the hum of the motor.

I awoke with a start at the sound of her door closing and looked around. The kids were asleep. We were home.

"Wait here," Zoe said, and got the kids out of the car, running them inside one at a time.

I dozed again.

"Come on, Josie," Zoe said. "I pulled out the sofa bed. You'll be warm and toasty."

"No," I semi-whined. "I want to go home."

"In the morning," she said.

I didn't have the strength to refuse. Zoe settled me in the living room, where I'd never before set foot, and handed me a steaming mug of tea. It might have felt awkward if I hadn't been three parts asleep. She encouraged me to keep sipping the tea, and when I was done, she helped me get situated under a thick down comforter.

After she had gone, I closed my eyes and listened to the night noises for what seemed like a long time.

I awoke at 8:00 A.M. and struggled up and out of bed, groaning and wincing.

Zoe had placed a fresh toothbrush on the sink and taped a note to the mirror:

> Josie, I hate to leave you, but I've got to take Jake to pre-school. I'll be back in a flash. Call me on my cell when you wake up. There's some food in the fridge and coffee on the burner.
>
> Zoe

Standing in front of the full-length mirror, I took stock of my condition. I didn't look as bad as I'd expected. I couldn't put much weight on my left ankle, but I could hobble with no problem. My muscles had stiffened, my scrapes hurt to the touch, and my joints ached. A yellowish purple bruise circled my left eye. But I was vertical and mobile, and as I swallowed a painkiller, I felt ready to get on with business.

As I entered the kitchen, my ankle throbbing, I realized that the house was oddly dark. All of the curtains and shades were pulled. *Zoe thinks that whoever wants to kill me might try shooting through a window next,* I realized with a rush of panic.

I didn't feel up to a shower, but I used a washcloth to clean up, folded the comforter, and, with a groan, horsed the sleeper sofa closed. Borrowing a pair of Zoe's sneakers that I found in the hall by the door, I peered deep into the sun-streaked trees across the street. *Go,* I told myself. *Don't think about it. Just go.* I saw nothing that shouldn't be there and, with my heart thudding, limped out-side. I felt vulnerable and exposed.

Leaning heavily on the banister, I wobbled down the porch steps and staggered across the small patch of lawn that separated our houses. Inside my own place, I sank into a kitchen chair and tried to quiet my still-pounding pulse. As the wave of dread re-ceded, I took stock: My ankle throbbed. My neck was stiff. I didn't know what to do. I felt terrified and overwhelmed and alone. Part of me wanted to do nothing but sink into a hot, bubbly bath, then go back to bed. But a bigger part of me knew that if I stayed home, all I'd do was fret, my reasonable fear mounting into paralyzing panic. *Plus which,* I reminded myself, *the doctor told me to keep moving or I'd stiffen up.* I decided to go in to work.

I called Zoe. She answered on the first ring.

"Hi," I said. "It's your houseguest. Thank you for the rescue."

"Hi. My God, you're up early for someone who looked as battered as you did. How are you doing?"

"Not as bad as I expected."

"Good. Where are you?"

"Home—my home. Why?" I asked.

"Keep the blinds down, okay?"

Feathery shivers ran up my spine, and instinctively, I looked out the back window. The rain had stopped during the night, and the morning was bright and sunny. Golden meadow stretched into distant woods.

"I noticed they were drawn in your place," I said, trying for a light tone. "You think there might be a sniper, huh?"

"No way to tell," Zoe replied crisply. "Better to be careful."

Her words were unnerving. "Right. Good point." I thanked her again for her help, and as soon as I hung up, I lowered the shades and drew the curtains in all the ground-floor windows. My heart was racing. When I was done, I stood in the kitchen, leaning heavily against the counter, and waited for my pulse to slow.

"Okay, then," I said aloud.

I stared at the staircase. Clean clothes and my answering machine were up there, but from where I stood, it looked like a mountain. Taking a deep breath, I started up. After only three steps, I had to sit for a while and rest. After another few steps, I rested again, taking the last several steps in one final push.

Triumphant, I reached the top landing and struggled into my bedroom. The little lamp next to the bed that was always on as a welcome-home greeting burned brightly. I sank onto my bed and collapsed, allowing myself a few minutes to regroup. When I felt able to sit up again, I turned toward my answering machine. I had seven messages. I leaned over and pushed the Play button, my muscles protesting the motion. *Mental note to self,* I thought, *don't lean.*

Wes had called twice, both times wanting a quote for the article he was working on about the newest attempt on my life. His tone was pantingly curious. I deleted both messages.

Max had called and wanted to know where I was and asked that I call him and tell him that I was all right.

Britt, the honorary chair of the Gala, had called to express concern. Thoughtful.

Eddie, the caterer, had called, saying he was shocked to hear from Britt that I was the intended target after all and to let him know if he could do anything—and let him know if I wanted to reschedule our meeting.

Ty had called, saying he was sorry he missed me and he'd call me later and that I should try him, too, though he said that in the hospital he had to keep his cell phone off.

Gretchen had called, crying, but trying to pretend she wasn't. I dialed her number and got her at home.

"Oh, Josie, thank God. Are you all right?"

I was touched by her emotionalism and a little embarrassed. "You bet, Gretchen. I'm fine. Well, almost fine. When you see me, don't faint. I'm very colorful."

"Are you in the hospital?"

"No, no, I'm home. I'll be in to work in a while."

"You're able to come to work? Oh, that's wonderful!"

"I'm a little shook up, but you know me—I'd always rather work than sit around."

Once we got down to details, I told her to call Eddie and ask if he could come by in the early afternoon.

"Of course," she said, jotting notes.

I explained that she was to go over everything about the pickup at Verna's with Eric. "Stress that he needs to tick off the items on the list one by one."

Eric was young, barely out of his teens. He was a willing worker, but I'd discovered the hard way that he was literal, not imaginative. If I gave him specific and detailed instructions, he did a meticulous job. But if my instructions were broad, he'd miss things and skip steps that, to a more experienced person, were self-evident.

I reached Max at his office and told him what I knew, and he said he would call Rowcliff for an update and get back to me.

I lay down again, wondering whether I had the strength to persevere in the face of my physical wounds and emotional distress. Apparently, Trevor was determined to kill me, and I felt utterly unable to stop him.

--

CHAPTER TWENTY-ONE

Max called back and told me that Rowcliff would be talking to me later. "No news so far," he said.

"Do you know where my car is?"

"The police have it."

"When will they be releasing it? Did Rowcliff say?" I asked.

After a pause, Max said, "I think it's pretty much totaled, Josie."

"Oh, wow, I hadn't realized. I guess that means I should call my insurance agent."

"Yeah."

"And get a rental car," I added, thinking aloud.

"Are you able to drive?" Max asked, sounding doubtful.

"If my right ankle was the one that had gotten messed up, it would be more problematic," I said, brushing off his concern.

"Before we hang up," he said, "there's something you need to think about."

"What's that?" I asked warily.

"I think you need someone with you," he said.

"What do you mean?"

"Some security —someone to keep an eye out."

I paused before I responded, trying to think logically. "Can't I just be super careful or something?"

"It's not so simple," he explained, his voice even and unemotional. "You've never been trained to know what to be careful about."

His words were terrifying. "Detective Rowcliff said he'd have someone around," I offered.

"No doubt he'll do what he can," Max said, "but the truth is that he can't do much. He doesn't have the manpower. And you don't live in Portsmouth proper, so he's got to ask another department to increase its patrol when you're at home. Don't get me wrong. He will ask. And so will I. And they will help out as best they can. But it's not enough."

How do you find a bodyguard? I wondered. *Do I look in the Yellow Pages under* B *for "body guard" or* G *for "guard, body"?*

"What should I do?" I asked.

"I can call someone I know."

"Okay," I agreed, the burden of fear weighing me down.

"I'll let you know when I hear from him," he added. "If he's not available, I know other good men I can contact."

"How much will it cost?" I asked.

He gave me a range and I did a quick calculation. It wouldn't take many days before the fees added up to many thousands and made quite a dent in my savings. But what choice did I have? If there was a realistic alternative, I couldn't think of it.

I redialed Gretchen's number and asked her to arrange for a rental car and then pick me up ASAP. Twenty minutes later, she pulled up in front of my house, leaped out of her car, and ran up the pathway. I stepped out of my front door. I'd expected her to do something like clutch her heart and scream when she saw me, but I was wrong. She took one look at me and zipped into high-octane caretaker mode.

"Take my hand," she offered when she reached me.

"I'm okay, Gretchen," I responded, waving her away. "Just moving a little slowly. Please don't fuss."

"I put a pillow on the front seat so it would be more comfortable. Sorry the car's so small. You're going to be pretty scrunched. I saw you limping. If you'd like, I can move the pillow to the floor and you can use it to support your leg. What do you think? Would that be better? Is anything broken? No, of course not, because if it was, you'd have a cast on. Can you see out of that eye? It's swollen. I can't believe this happened to you. I'll be quiet now because I can tell that you're in pain and are just being strong the way you always are."

She didn't stop chattering until we reached the rental-car location on Route 1 in Hampton. I had her wait outside while I limped into the small office alone. The clerk sneaked apprehensive looks at me as she hurried to complete the paperwork, and having seen myself in the mirror, I understood completely. My face looked bad.

Out on the lot, I found my car and sat for a moment familiarizing myself with its gauges and setting the mirrors, and then I headed off to work. It felt odd to drive a strange vehicle and odder still to look into the rearview mirror and see Gretchen following me.

When we got to Prescott's, I parked close to the front door and used the rearview mirror to scan the lot. Nothing. I stepped out and walked in the warming sun to the door, holding it so Gretchen could enter first.

Unlike Gretchen, who calmly accepted my bruised and battered appearance, Fred took one look at me and almost fainted. He bounced up from his desk, then froze, his mouth agape, the color fading from his face.

"Sit here," Gretchen told me, swooping down on the guest chair, sliding it out, and holding it in place until I sat, then hovering nearby. "I'll make tea. What else can I do? I could move up this other chair for your ankle. I can't believe you decided to come in today, but you're in good hands. I'll make sure that everything you need is close by, okay? Fred, do you see? Josie is doing fine and—"

I held my hand up to stop her stream of blabber. "Thank you, Gretchen. I'll take the tea, but as to the rest, as you can see, I'm okay."

I turned to Fred, whose mouth was still hanging open. He was about Gretchen's height, taller than I, but short for a man, and slight. I knew that he was young, in his mid-twenties, but his demeanor was serious and he looked and acted older. He pushed his glasses up on his nose and asked, "Are you really okay?"

I smiled as best I could and said, "You bet."

Fred was a terrific researcher, methodical and cautious, but interpersonal skills were not his strong suit. He gawked.

I tried another smile and said as casually as I could, "You can stop staring now."

He closed his mouth and sat down.

I wanted to shift our conversation to work-related issues. I didn't want to review my injuries or discuss how I was feeling. Talking about work would distract me from pain and worry, and confidently directing a technical discussion would succor me.

"How are you doing, Fred? Is everything under control?" I asked, hoping he'd follow my lead.

"Absolutely," he replied quickly, probably as relieved as I was to move the conversation to more familiar ground.

"Where are you with the Picasso?" I asked, shifting a little, trying to find a more comfortable way to position my ankle.

"I have an inquiry out to the grandson of the restaurateur about the Picasso sketch."

"Really? What did you ask him?"

"Well, we're having trouble following the print across the ocean."

"Tell me," I instructed.

"We know that Mrs. Finn—you remember, the lady we got the sketch from—well, we know that her mother bought the print from a Little Rock dealer in 1973—we spoke to the gallery owner himself, and he was able to verify the sale by looking through his old ledgers. But the boxes with the records of purchases were lost in a fire twenty years ago. And he doesn't remember how he acquired it." He shrugged. "It's a complete dead end."

"So then what?" I asked.

"We start at the other end. We've verified that the Picasso was, in fact, given to the owner of the café, M. Roi, as payment for a meal."

I smiled. "That's terrific. How did you do that?"

"Sasha found a photo of the sketch in an old Paris newspaper."

"Terrific. When from?"

"Nineteen fifty-two. It was in a restaurant review. M. Roi was standing next to it, gesturing toward it proudly."

"That's great work," I commented admiringly.

"Yeah. But from that newspaper photograph in 1952 until the sale in Little Rock in 1973, we have no information. That's a gap of twenty-one years."

That was bad.

I nodded, and my head began to throb painfully. In order to sell fine art for top dollar, we needed to be able to document an object's provenance. Without demonstrating an unbroken chain of ownership, we couldn't offer a guarantee of authenticity. And without that warranty, we couldn't expect big money. I bit my lip and closed my eyes for a moment until the dull ache faded.

"What else do you know?" I asked, trying to ignore my discomfort, hoping for at least a glimmer of good news.

"The restaurateur, M. Roi, died that same year, just a few months after the review appeared. We located his death certificate, and his will. According to the will, his estate was divided equally among his three children, but we don't know which one got the Picasso or whether it was sold upon his death. The worst part is that all three of the children are dead, too." He paused and thumbed through a manila file on his desk, looking for something. "Two of them died in a car wreck in 1980, along with their spouses. The other one never married and died of a heart attack in 2000."

"How many grandchildren are there?"

"Four. We've heard back from one, who says she knows nothing, but she put me in touch with her cousin—the grandson I mentioned contacting."

I nodded. "And the other two?"

He sighed. "One is a missionary in the Philippines. The other is traveling in a caravan in Scotland—I gather a caravan is like an RV."

"Egad. I don't suppose they have e-mail."

He shook his head. "Nope."

"Well, I'll keep my fingers crossed," I said, shifting position again as more muscles made their presence felt. "What else are you working on?"

"I'm dating Mrs. McCarthy's silver."

Rosie McCarthy had called one day and asked me to come and take her silver away. "I want it all gone," she explained with a self-conscious laugh. "I haven't used it in years—decades, if the truth be told. My kids don't care about it. At eighty-four, it's time for me to lighten the load."

"These are beautiful things," I said, lifting a sugar bowl, appreciating its heft.

"Well, it used to be beautiful when I kept it looking good." Another embarrassed laugh. "Now everything needs polishing. After my husband died, I tried to keep it up, but after a while, well, it was just too much for me."

I nodded. "Where did they come from?"

"My husband's aunt. Augusta Mayberry. She was from Londonderry, you know, never married, and her passion was collecting silver. We were very fond of her."

"Did she buy it all locally?" I asked, knowing that Londonderry, like many small New Hampshire towns, was home to several excellent antique shops.

"No. Well, some she did, but she bought most of the pieces in England. She traveled there every June with her friend Hazel Waters."

"Well, they're wonderful pieces and I'm sure whoever owns them next will love them."

She smiled warmly and patted my hand. "That's very thoughtful of you to say so, dear. Thank you."

Eric, my jack-of-all-trades, had inventoried the thirty-seven tarnished items—eighteen bowls, five pitchers, and fourteen serving pieces—and polished every one to a mirrorlike shine. And now, one unit at a time, Fred was authenticating their pedigrees and estimating their values. His desk was covered with files and notes and Mrs. McCarthy's silver.

"Are you having any trouble identifying hallmarks?" I asked Fred, referring to the small symbols stamped or engraved on items to designate various attributes, usually the town and date of manufacture, the quality of the material, the maker, and, sometimes, that taxes had been paid.

"Not yet. So far, every mark is on the date chart," Fred said, pointing to the guides we kept on our reference shelves, books that displayed every symbol ever used by silversmiths to identify their wares.

I wasn't surprised at his answer, since Augusta Mayberry had collected English silver, and authenticating it is almost always a straightforward process.

"Where's that one from?" I asked Fred, pointing to a medium-size pitcher with fruit swags and paw feet.

"Chester," he replied without hesitation. "Eighteen ten. Gregory Winslow, maker."

"That's just great," I said as I stood up, my motions a little rickety.

I turned to Gretchen, who'd begun fussing with the tea. "Is Eric here?" I asked.

"Yes. He's getting packing stuff together," she told me.

"Good. I'm going to make my way—slowly, I admit—to my office. Give me half an hour, then send him up, okay?"

"Sure," Gretchen replied. "I told him what you said," she added, "about checking things off on the list and packing each cut-glass bowl separately." I pictured Verna's living room. The vintage evening gowns would be snapped up early on Saturday at the tag sale, but the glassware needed appraising to determine whether it was worthy of going to auction. Whether it was rare and valuable or merely pretty, it wouldn't be worth anything if it was chipped.

"Excellent," I said. "Good job."

She smiled and her pretty features lit up.

"Would you take the tea upstairs?" I asked.

"Of course."

"And order pizza for us all to be delivered around eleven thirty. Eric needs to leave around noon, and I want him to be sure and get a slice or three before he goes."

She nodded and wrote a note.

All I wanted to do was crawl into a fetal position and suck my thumb, but I knew from experience the positive effect of work. During the months when I was shunned by my coworkers at Frisco's, before I was let go, it was only the hands-on work with antiques that enabled me to maintain my equilibrium. And in the weeks after Rick and I broke up and the dark days after my father died, it was my ability to concentrate in the midst of turmoil and heartbreak that got me through.

I hobbled toward the warehouse and the spiral staircase that led to my private office.

CHAPTER TWENTY-TWO

S itting at my desk upstairs, waiting for my computer to boot up, I reached for a pad of notepaper and a pen. Even that small motion hurt.

"Lewis," I wrote, followed by "cruise money," and "Trevor's alibi."

I wanted to know whether Trevor's favorite photographer, Lewis, was still in business; if Maisy had had the money to go on a long cruise—and if so, how she'd acquired it; and whether Trevor had been at the Gala disguised as a waiter. I could research Lewis's current whereabouts and I had some thoughts about how to discover more about Maisy's cruise plans, but investigating Trevor's alibi had me stymied. Wes might uncover something, especially if he went to New York. So might Rowcliff, if he took the threat seriously. All I could think of to do was approach the question about Trevor's whereabouts from the other angle—not whether he could have traveled from New York to New Hampshire, but whether he had, in fact, been at the Gala disguised as a waiter.

I knew it was a far-fetched idea, but having had the thought, it was like an itch I couldn't scratch. Until Eddie confirmed that he hadn't hired a waiter who looked just like Trevor, or a stranger who appeared out of the blue on his doorstep, I couldn't relax.

I turned toward the maple outside my window. The opalescent leaves fluttered in the soft breeze, glowing in pink and gold, orange and red, and bright, glossy yellow. I marveled at their colors and satin smoothness, and as I watched, a small brown bird landed on the tree branch closest to my window. It dipped its head, seeming to listen to some private message. After a moment, with a head bob and a ruffling of its tail feathers, it flew away. I turned back to watch the leaves sparkling in the sun. The quiet, restful moment was interrupted when Gretchen buzzed up that Max was on the line.

I thanked her and picked up the receiver. "Hey, Max," I said, trying to sound perky.

"Josie. You sound pretty good for a woman who was nearly run over."

"Painkillers and grit."

"Especially grit, I suspect. Well, let me tell you. I just got off the phone with Detective Rowcliff."

My heart began to pound against my bruised chest. "And?" I asked.

"I called him to find out if he had any news before I called you. I knew you'd want to know."

"Right. Thank you." *And? So tell me! What did he say?* I nudged silently.

"Unfortunately, it looks like there were no witnesses. You know how little traffic there is that time of night."

"But what about the man who came to help me?"

"He came on the scene after you were already on the ground. He heard your screams, but the car that hit you was long gone."

"Oh," I remarked, disappointed.

"There's a little good news, though. The forensic evidence is significant. It seems that they'll be able to pinpoint the make and model of the automobile that ran into your car from paint scrapings and glass particles. The car broke a headlight."

"That's great! Did he give you specifics?"

"No, but he said to tell you that he'll probably be calling later to ask you some questions. Do you remember that he wanted you to look at illustrations of vehicles?"

"Yes. I remember."

"Well, apparently they expect to be able to narrow their search by measuring the height of the impact."

"That makes sense."

"So between the color of the paint and the height of the car, the number of options is limited. Based on that, Rowcliff wants you to look at some automobile shapes."

"Sure. When?" I asked.

"Later today, probably. I told him to call you directly. I don't need to be there unless you want me to."

"You're making me face Rowcliff alone in my battered condition? That's cold," I said in a determinedly playful tone.

"You know what to do. Don't rise to his bait. And if he asks you about anything other than the hit-and-run, or if you feel uncomfortable at any time, call me."

"Okay." I paused. I turned to look out the window and forced myself to focus on the sun-dappled maple tree instead of my embarrassment at discussing personal issues.

"One more thing," Max said. "I asked Rowcliff about security. He said he thought that police protection would be adequate but that if you'd feel better having private coverage, he wouldn't discourage you."

"Okay, then. It's better to be extra safe, I guess, until we know what's going on." I noted how calm I sounded, when the truth was that I was agitated and upset.

"I agree. Just to be sure, I checked up on that guy I mentioned, Chi."

"What's his name?" I asked, uncertain I'd heard right.

"Chi." He spelled it.

"Chi?" I confirmed.

"Yeah."

"That's an unusual name, isn't it?"

"He's Asian. Chinese, I think. He told me once that the word *chi* means 'energy.' "

I cleared my throat. "So, how did you check up on him?"

"One of my clients, a woman whose ex wouldn't leave her alone, used him last summer. I wanted to hear her views, so I called her."

"Well, the fact that she's still alive to talk to you is a good sign."

"Good point."

"And?" I asked.

"And she was very encouraging. So I called Chi. He's available and can start today. I'll ask him to check in with you, introduce himself, take a look around, okay?"

"Sure."

"You won't necessarily see him, his associates, or the police patrols, but someone will be keeping an eye on you."

I trembled at the thought that I needed watching out for. But I acknowledged that no matter what was going on, it was reassuring to think that the good guys were keeping an eye on me. "Thank you," I said quietly.

As I hung up the phone, Gretchen appeared at the door with a steaming mug in her hand.

"You are so good to me," I said.

"Wait 'til you taste the tea," she said with a giggle, her titian colored hair glinting with mahogany highlights as she passed through the rays of sun that stippled the carpet. "I think I made it too strong."

She placed the mug on my desk and said, "You remember that Mitch Strauss and his wife, Rochelle, won the Qing dynasty soup tureen?"

"Right."

"He's picking it up today, coming with someone named Dr. Kimball, an expert from Boston, I think it was, to authenticate it. They should be here around three."

"Good. The quicker we can move stuff out, the happier I'll be."

The phone rang and Gretchen answered it at my desk. "Prescott's," she said, as cheery as ever. "I'll check. Please hold." Turning to me, she said, "It's Detective Rowcliff. He says it's important."

She handed me the receiver, and as I accepted it, I told her she could go. "Don't forget," I said, "get Dr. Kimball's card. You never know when we might need an outside expert on Chinese porcelain."

She said she would, and headed out slowly.

I could tell that she didn't want to go, no doubt hoping that she could pick up a spicy nugget of gossip if only she were allowed to stay. I waited until I heard the click-clack of her heels against the concrete flooring at the bottom of the stairs before pushing the button that took Rowcliff off hold.

As I girded myself for the interrogation I was certain would follow, I crossed my fingers. *Please, God,* I said to myself, *let him tell me I'm safe.* It was probably a futile hope, I knew, but still, it could do no harm to pray that he was calling with answers, not questions.

CHAPTER TWENTY-THREE

D etective?" I said. "This is Josie."

"I was thinking I got cut off," he complained.

Ignore the tone, I reminded myself. *Deal only with the content.*

"Sorry you were on hold," I said, keeping my apology simple.

"How's the ankle?" he demanded without compassion.

"Okay, I guess."

"You're able to get to work, I see," he said in a tone I took to mean that if I was really hurt, I wouldn't have been able to do so.

"Thank you for your concern," I replied, my voice neutral. If he couldn't tell I was being sarcastic, did it count?

He cleared his throat and said, "So. I have a question."

"Okay."

"Have you spoken to Bixby?"

"Max? Yes. Just now. Why?"

"Then you know that the forensic evidence looks good. We're probably going to be able to ID the model of automobile by the paint and the kind of glass that was used in the headlight—you know, the one that shattered. Plus, we've got good information about the size of the car by analyzing the point of impact."

"Yes, Max told me. That's great."

"While the lab does its thing, I thought I'd try a shortcut. That's why I'm asking."

"Okay."

"Who do you know who drives a black sedan?" he asked.

A black sedan. Nothing came to mind. "No one."

"Your staff?"

"No."

"What kind of cars do they drive?"

"Why are you asking about my staff?"

"Just covering all bases," he said. "It's not personal."

"But why?"

He sighed. "I want to see what kind of automobile memory you've got."

I knew if Max were here, he'd tell me that Rowcliff's reasoning was clever, not insulting. "Sasha's car is a red compact. Eric drives a tan truck, an old four by four. Gretchen has a blue Mini Cooper. And Fred's car is white. I don't know about the part-timers or temps."

"How many of them do you have?"

"It varies. We have a couple of regular part-timers and we add on as needed."

"I'll need their names."

"Why?"

"Because I need to be sure their cars weren't involved," he stated, sounding irritated at my question.

So it wasn't *just a test of my automobile memory,* I thought. "I'll have Gretchen prepare a list for you."

"Go back a year, okay?"

"Sure."

"What about neighbors? What kind of cars do they drive?"

I tried to picture Zoe's car, but nothing came to mind. When I was in her vehicle last evening, I was drugged and weak. "I don't know. I've never noticed."

"Business associates?"

"Like who?" I asked.

"I don't know," he snapped. "That's why I'm asking."

I took a breath and forced myself to refrain from snapping back. Instead, I said, "Nothing comes to mind."

"I want to show you some automobile shapes anyway. If you think of anything else, you can tell me then. What time this afternoon is good for you?"

My heart rate increased at the thought of having to interact in person with Detective Rowcliff without Max by my side. I tried to think when it would be best to meet him.

"Four o'clock," I said. "Could you come at four?"

He agreed and I hung up the phone, relieved that the call was over. I wondered if everyone he questioned had the same reaction to him that I did. I called Gretchen and told her to prepare the employee listing for Detective Rowcliff and to send a copy to Max. Was it possible that one of my own employees was out to kill me? No. Rowcliff was just being thorough.

To calm myself, I sipped some tea, and after a few moments, I was hit by a sudden wave of exhaustion. I leaned back and closed my eyes.

I slept.

I awakened about fifteen minutes later when Eric cleared his throat. I opened my eyes and saw him standing at the threshold, looking concerned and unsure whether he should enter the office.

"Come on in," I said, sitting forward, brushing hair out of my eyes, smiling.

He walked in, still troubled. "Are you okay?" he asked.

"Absolutely. Better than I look, for sure."

He nodded, and when I told him to have a seat, he did so.

Eric was the second person I hired when I started Prescott's; he'd started only days after Gretchen. At first, he worked a few hours during the week and all day on Saturdays. When he graduated from high school, I offered him a full-time job, and with a shy smile, he accepted, confessing that he'd never been much good at school and was glad to be done with it and get going with "real life."

Today, he seemed girded for bad news, signaling through his body language that he was expecting to hear criticism, a lifelong *C* student's best-learned lesson—low expectations. Poor Eric.

I wondered if his self-image would improve. I wasn't optimistic. It hadn't budged yet, and he'd had ample opportunity to feel good about himself, since I was generous with praise as well as money.

Looking at him anxiously waiting for me to explain why I'd called him in, I realized for the hundredth time how young and vulnerable he was. He was very tall and boyishly thin, with a wisp of peach fuzz mustache and a sallow complexion. I hoped he'd be pleased with my announcement. I didn't think he had a lot of joy in his life, and maybe this reward would give him a boost.

He lived in Dover, a small town a dozen miles northwest of Portsmouth, with his crabby widowed mother and two big dogs. There weren't a lot of young men just out of their teens who'd be content with such a circumscribed life, but if he was dissatisfied, it didn't show at all. He expressed only kindness and patience.

One time when I'd answered the phone and his mother asked for him, I told her what a valuable employee he was, what a hard worker. He stood nearby, listening, embarrassed, but obviously pleased. She didn't respond, not a word, and after a moment, I said I'd get him for her. I gathered from listening to his side of the conversation that she wanted him to stop and pick up something from the grocery store on his way home. When he hung up the phone, he paused before heading out of the office.

"I'm sure she appreciates it, you know, the nice things you said. She just doesn't show a lot because, well, life has been pretty hard on her, you know?"

I didn't know what to say, so I'd patted his shoulder and half-smiled. A shoulder pat can mean anything.

Over the years, I'd come to realize that he had no hidden agenda. He was just what he seemed to be, a thoughtful and loyal son, a young man who took responsibility seriously and loved his dogs, and a humble and uncomplaining employee who followed rules and always did his best.

I considered delaying the conversation I was about to initiate, then decided it was important to proceed with as much normal day-to-day business as I could. It felt good to put my aches, and my fear, aside and work to keep my company running smoothly, but meeting with Eric wasn't simply a way to distract myself from pain and worry. It was crucial. "Time waits for no man." If I didn't keep up with the demands of business, I'd give my competitors an edge.

"I have good news, Eric," I said, jumping in. "You're getting a promotion and a raise."

His eyes cleared and his focus shifted from resignation to hope. "Really?" he asked.

"Yup. We're growing, and at this point, there's too much work for you to do alone."

"I could work more hours."

"No, that's not the answer." I paused, thinking how best to explain. "One metric I use to keep a handle on how we're doing is how long it takes us to get new inventory to auction or out to the tag sale, not counting the items we're keeping back on purpose, of course."

He nodded, listening hard, and I understood why. Managing inventory was one of the most complex aspects of the business, and he wanted to learn.

No matter what we acquired, or when, where, how, or how much we paid for it, as soon as it arrived on-site, Eric entered it into our computerized inventory-control system. Then it was up to Fred and Sasha to conduct a quick-and-dirty assessment. The best items were set aside for a more exacting appraisal, while everything else went to the tag sale.

"And it's not just the inventory management. You're also responsible for cleaning items and stocking shelves. Plus, you do all the moving, help set up displays, oversee pickups and deliveries, and—whew—you're also the assistant cashier at the tag sale!"

"You're right," he said with a grin. "I need a raise."

I laughed. "Hey! Not so quick! You're well paid for your current job. It's your *new* responsibility I want to reward."

"What's that?"

"Supervisor."

"Supervisor? Me? Who will I supervise?"

"The new person we hire. Or the two new part-timers."

"To do what?"

"To help you with various things. Your job is too big for one person, Eric. I want to identify what other people can do, and train you to supervise them while they do it."

"I don't know . . ." he began, his eyes clouding over again.

I recognized his reaction and held up a hand to stop him. His visceral fear when faced with learning new things was ingrained after years of struggling in school and achieving only a mediocre academic record.

"You're going to be a good supervisor," I said. "I'm sure of it because I know you. You're smart, hardworking, and fair. I'm guessing that you're hesitating because you're aware of how much you don't know. Am I right?"

He nodded.

"That's okay. I promise I'll teach you everything you need. And I guarantee that you can learn it. Really."

He didn't say anything.

"I'll prove it to you. The first thing I want you to do is write down everything you do and how long it takes you to do it. Okay?"

"Everything?" he asked, startled.

"Yup. Once we know where your time is going now, we can figure out who we should bring in to help."

"But how do I do that?"

"Work with Gretchen to identify broad categories. Here," I said, handing him a pad of paper, "jot these down." He took the pad, selected a pen from the holder on my desk, and waited for me to talk. "Entering new items into inventory. Moving furniture. Cleaning and polishing antiques. Driving to pickups and deliveries." I waited for him to finish. "Do you see what I mean?"

He nodded.

"Tell Gretchen what we're doing and ask her to help you brainstorm category titles and then create a spreadsheet so you can track your time in, oh, let's say fifteen-minute increments. We'll do it for a week or so, until we feel like we really have a sense of how long it takes to do various tasks."

"Okay."

"During this time, while you're working on this log, when you do something that's not on the list, write it down and tell Gretchen so she can add it in."

He nodded again.

"Can you do that?" I asked him.

"Yes. Absolutely."

"See," I said, smiling, "I told you I'd prove it to you. You *can* learn what you need to be a supervisor."

"I'll do my best, Josie. Thank you."

"I know you will," I said, and when I told him the raise I had in mind, he smiled again, a big grin that went from ear to ear and lit up his eyes.

CHAPTER TWENTY-FOUR

A bout twelve thirty, just as I was finishing reviewing Sasha's first draft of next month's auction catalog, which featured an unusual collection of American weather vanes, Eddie called on my cell phone and asked how I was doing.

After expressing conventional words of concern, he said, "Josie, I wanted you to be the first to know—well, almost the first," he said, chuckling.

"Know what?"

"I'm closing the catering business and moving."

"You're kidding! Eddie, when? And why?"

He chuckled again. "When? Now. I'm on the road already. Why? What the hell, Josie, you know I was having a hard time. I told you."

"Yeah, but—"

"Nah, it's good. Nothing like failing at business to help you get over a midlife crisis."

"Oh, Eddie, I'm sorry."

"Don't be, kiddo. You're the best. My favorite client, so I wanted to tell you directly. You'll be getting an announcement."

"Did you sell out?"

"Sell what? Who'd want to buy a lot of nothing? I just closed the doors."

"I can't believe it, Eddie! What about the investigation? You know, Maisy. Is it all right for you to leave?"

"Hell, Josie, I'm not disappearing. I'm just moving. Sure, I told the cops. I'm keeping the same cell phone—they've got the number."

"Where are you going? What are you going to do?"

"I got a job out west. Can you believe it? Me and the cowboys."

"Are you okay, Eddie?"

"Relieved as all get-out, Josie. I guess I don't have what it takes to be an entrepreneur after all." He chuckled again. "I'm looking forward to getting back to being a working stiff and letting the other guy take the headaches home."

"I'm so surprised and sorry, Eddie. I've really liked working with you."

"Me, too, Josie."

I sat forward and closed my eyes to help me concentrate. "So you won't be stopping by today?"

"Sorry, Josie. It was time to head out, you know? We were going to leave later this week, but then I said to my wife, 'What the hell? Let's get outta here.' So we did."

"Wow. I'm just stunned."

"Never mind that. Tell me how you're doing?"

"Okay, all things considered," I said, ignoring the daggerlike stabs in my ankle and my achy, stiff muscles.

"That's good. It's a helluva thing. I couldn't believe it when Britt told me about it."

"Britt?" I said, surprised. *That's right*, I thought, remembering Eddie's mention of Britt in his voice-mail message, the one waiting for me when I'd returned home from Zoe's.

"Britt. You know Britt. Britt Epps. He's my lawyer." Eddie chuckled. "I cleared my quick getaway with him."

How had Britt learned of my injuries? I pondered. At the time, in my battered and weary condition, I'd considered their calls thoughtful gestures, nothing more. Now they seemed ominous.

"How did he hear about what happened?" I wondered aloud.

"Who knows? Bad news spreads fast, that's for damn sure."

"I guess," I responded, just to say something. "Eddie, can I ask you something?"

"Sure. What?"

"About the waiters—"

"You bet. What can I tell you?"

"I'm interested in anything you can tell me about the new ones. The ones who started just before the Gala."

"I think I might have given you a wrong impression about that," Eddie said.

"What do you mean?"

"I told you there were new guys—and there were. But everyone was either known to me or recommended by someone. You know, a friend of a friend, someone's cousin, that sort of thing. No strangers."

"Really?" I asked, a groundswell of relief beginning to grow. The odds that Trevor was a waiter at the Gala just lowered—a lot.

"Absolutely."

We chatted another couple of minutes about the details of his move, the job itself as manager of someone else's catering business, and how he and his wife had heard only good things about his new home, Tulsa.

"I wouldn't have thought of Tulsa as 'out west,'" I remarked.

"What do I know? I'm an Easterner—it sure seems 'out west' to me!"

With a final exchange of good-luck wishes, we hung up. I called Gretchen on the intercom.

"Eddie just called me," I said when she picked up. "Guess what? He's moving away. He closed the business and took a job in Tulsa."

"You're kidding!" she exclaimed.

"Nope. Can you believe it? Anyway, he sounds fine. You know what that means?"

"We need a new caterer."

"Exactly. Get me some possibilities, okay?"

The reality sank in: In all likelihood, Trevor Woodleigh hadn't disguised himself as a waiter during the Gala. *Unless Eddie's lying.* I didn't think that Eddie would deliberately mislead an investigator if he thought he had information that would help find a killer. But I could easily imagine that he would take a more flexible view of truth telling when it came to discussing an idea he'd probably see as far-fetched, and that occurred during an event that was, to him, old news. In the hours before he drove off to start a new life, he might have decided that it would be easier to fib and say he knew the entire wait staff—at least a little—than it would be to get more deeply involved in an ongoing murder investigation.

I shook my head, aware of feeling unreasonably sad and apprehensive. I liked Eddie okay, but it wasn't that. What was upsetting
was having to endure more unwanted change. Nothing stayed stable,
it seemed. Nothing.

Gretchen buzzed to say that Wes was on hold, and on a whim, I
decided to take his call.

"Josie," he complained when I was on the line, "you didn't call
me back."

"I wasn't really up for chatting."

"Why not?"

"I'm in kind of tough shape right now."

"What do you mean, 'tough shape'? According to the reports,
you're okay."

"What reports?" I asked.

"The official statement from the police."

"What official statement? What did it say?"

"Just what I told you," he replied impatiently. "Why? Is it wrong?
Did they exaggerate?"

This was the Wes I knew, wanting to acquire new information,
not share that which he already possessed.

"No, no, I guess it's fair to say, all things considered, that I'm
okay."

"Fill me in. Specifically, what's your condition?"

His wording made me feel as if he wanted a report on the status
of a specimen in a jar, not an update on a woman who'd been attacked.

"I hurt, what do you think?" I responded petulantly.

"How bad?"

"Wes, you're flipping me out here. Why do you want to know?"

"For tomorrow's paper."

"Wes, I swear to God, if you print one word, I'll . . . I'll steal your
pencil and snap it in two. Off the record, remember?"

"Even about your condition?" he asked, sounding shocked.

"Yes," I said firmly.

He sighed, the sorrowful sound of Wes expressing acute disappointment. "All right," he said, sighing a second time, "no problem. Let's start again. Are you okay, really?"

"More or less, I guess. I'm a little shaky, a little scraped, and, to tell you the truth, a lot frightened."

"Could be worse, right?"

"Oh God, Wes, you smooth talker, you."

"Huh?"

"I hardly know the words to tell you how touched I am by your concern."

"What are you talking about?" he asked.

Getting Wes to understand that he sounded like an insensitive jerk would be like asking a squirrel to bark. I gave up. "What do you want, Wes?"

"We need to meet."

"Why?"

"I have news." His lowered tone implied importance.

"Good or bad?"

"I don't know. Interesting."

Wes using the word "interesting" reminded me of that ancient curse: "May you have an interesting life."

"I can't."

"Josie—" he whined.

"Wes, give me a break. I'm battered, bruised, and exhausted."

"I understand," he said, apparently trying to placate me, as if he were doing me a favor by being so flexible. "Let's meet later this afternoon, then. You pick the time. We can meet at our regular place—the dune, okay?"

"I can't," I said again.

"Why not?"

"I can't exactly scramble up a sandy hill right now. My ankle's pretty badly sprained."

"Just at the edge, then. You can sit in your car if you want," he said, sounding as if he were making a great concession.

"No," I said slowly, trying to gather my thoughts before I spoke, "that won't work. It's not going to be so easy speaking to you privately."

"How come?" he asked.

"The police are sort of, you know, protecting me," I said.

"Oh, wow, yeah, I hadn't thought of that. I get it. So for you and me to get together, you've got to figure out how to slip away from them."

"No, Wes. I don't want to get away from them. I *want* their protection."

"Then how are we going to meet?" he asked.

I shook my head in mute amazement at Wes. For someone as smart as I knew him to be, he sure could sound dumb. It was one thing to be focused, but it was another to lose sight of important side issues. I decided to ignore the implication that my safety was secondary to his nailing a story, thinking instead about the issue at hand—I wanted to hear his news.

"Maybe," I ventured, "we can cover everything on the phone. Anyone checking the records knows we're talking anyway."

"They'd learn that calls were made, but not the content of those calls. What if your phone is tapped? We can't assume it's not."

True enough, I thought. "If you come here," I said, "I'll arrange it so we can talk privately."

I could meet Wes at the edge of the paved parking lot, out of sight and hearing of the office, near a cluster of birch trees at the rear of my property. I glanced at the spot. The white-barked trees were spectacular with their lush gold and smooth, soft yellow leaves shimmering in the sun. Too open, I realized. It would be more private to meet in the deserted tag-sale area. I told him to park down the street and walk through the woods to the tag-sale entrance on the far side of the warehouse. "I'll be at the door," I said. He agreed to be there at one fifteen, but only after a little more give-and-take, and his impatience made me wonder what he had up his sleeve. Wes was tactless to the point of rudeness, but he usually had the goods.

CHAPTER TWENTY-FIVE

I must have fallen asleep again, because I woke up disoriented and upset. Hairs prickled on my arms and my heart pounded as if I'd awakened from a nightmare—but if I'd had a bad dream, I couldn't remember it.

I looked around fretfully, straining my neck. My office was quiet, the phones were silent, and no one was nearby. My fearful awakening seemed inexplicable. It was eerie and unsettling. Stretching gingerly, I looked at the clock. Only a few minutes had passed.

To throw off my hazy discontent, I decided to do some research, and I figured I'd start with Lewis, the photographer, who might still stock cyanide. I could understand why Trevor felt betrayed by me, even though from where I sat, it was he who betrayed Frisco's and, by extension, me. But I couldn't understand how his rage could lead him to plot to kill me.

I couldn't imagine him doing such a thing. Then I could. Then I'd tell myself I was being foolish. Then I'd recall Max suggesting I was doing a head-in-the-sand thing. I was on an emotional roller coaster and it was exhausting. But one thing was likely: If he did kill Maisy, he got the poison from Lewis.

I Googled "Lewis" and "photographer" and "New York City" and got more than a hundred hits. The first link connected me to the National Art and Antiques Photographers Association's Web site, and there I learned that Lewis had died two years ago. According to the site, his widow had closed his New York City studio shortly after his death and then moved to Scottsdale. *If the studio was closed, Trevor couldn't have acquired cyanide there.*

As I allowed myself to relax a little, my father's words came back to me: *Irrational and random events happen,* he told me, *but not nearly as often as people would have you believe. If it's not logical, it's probably not true.*

That Trevor was guilty of murder was illogical, and therefore, it probably wasn't true. His release from prison a day before Maisy's murder was, it seemed, nothing more than a coincidence of timing. Sure, he *could* have acquired the cyanide from another source— or even hired someone to kill me. *But I just don't believe it,* I thought. *It's just not credible that he'd sneak into a fancy community event like the Gala and slip cyanide into a drink. Nor that he'd hire someone to kill me with poison or by running me down. Too dicey.*

In fact, I felt reassuringly closer to answering the most basic question springing out of Maisy's death: Was she the target? Or was I? *It's not me,* I concluded, overwhelmed with relief.

The tag-sale room gave out to a large uncovered area separated from the parking lot by a tall wooden fence. During nice weather, we put several table displays outside, but the rest of the time, the space was empty.

Just before one fifteen, I opened the door in the fence that gave access to the parking lot and waited. Within minutes, Wes came trudging out of the woods at the rear of the property, brushing aside low-hanging branches as he stepped onto the asphalt. He saw me and hurried over.

Inside, we sat on high stools in back of the cash registers. I left most of the lights off, so anyone outside looking in couldn't identify us. There was a crossbeam under the counter at just the right level for me to rest my left foot, and by pushing my stool up to the wall, I could stretch my leg out and take advantage of it while also getting some back support. I wasn't in pain, exactly, but I was uncomfortably aware of my various muscle pulls and skin abrasions.

"Your face looks pretty torn up," Wes remarked as he got settled.

"Yeah," I agreed, wishing he'd used less descriptive language.

"Are you ready for a shockeroonie?"

"A 'shockeroonie,'" I repeated, eyeing him warily. "I'm not sure."

"You're joking, right?"

"Right. Sort of. Okay, tell me. I'm ready to be shocked."

"Guess who Maisy consulted last week?"

"Who?"

"Britt Epps."

I stared at him, his pudgy cheeks puffed with pleasure at delivering hot news.

"Wow," I said. "What do you figure that means?"

"I don't know. What do you think?"

I turned away and stared out the salt-stained window on the far side of the room. The trees were close to the building back here, mostly evergreens, dark and thick.

"Gala business, maybe," I ventured.

"Not likely, since she paid him in cash."

"How do you know that?" I asked, amazed at Wes's ability to uncover potentially significant information.

"A source," he said.

"How good a source?" I asked. "This might mean something."

"It's solid," he insisted. "A source in Britt Epps's office verified the payment."

"So Britt wasn't trying to hide the cash," I said, thinking aloud.

"It looks that way," Wes agreed. "Why, do you think it's significant?"

"If it were a business matter, she'd have used a Guild check. Even if it was personal, but in the open, she'd write a check. Paying a lawyer in cash is unusual."

"That makes sense," he agreed.

"I mean, think about it. Lawyers are expensive, you know? It's not like buying a fifty-cent newspaper or even fifty dollars of food at the supermarket."

Wes nodded, reached into his inside coat pocket, and pulled out his notebook. He wrote something, then looked up and asked, "What could it indicate?"

I thought for a moment. "She didn't want someone who had access to her checkbook to know that she was consulting a lawyer. Like her husband, maybe. Or perhaps she asked Britt to do something illegal or unethical and didn't want to leave a paper trail. And Britt," I speculated, "wanted to be sure that no one thought he was doing anything other than on the up-and-up, so he made darn sure the cash payment was entered into his company's books." I paused again while Wes jotted notes. "Also," I added, "it could be that she tried to bribe him. And just because the payment was recorded doesn't mean that he didn't accept the bribe." I shrugged again, a small one, as my shoulder muscles announced the move. "Or maybe it was about the divorce, and Britt was the only lawyer she knew except for the one she and Walter used as a couple, and she wanted someone who would be *her* lawyer, not *their* lawyer, if you know what I mean."

"That explains her choice of Britt, but not the cash."

I nodded. "Okay—maybe it's really simple. It's possible that it's just that she was one of those people who pays for everything in cash."

"I can check that out," Wes said, scribbling a note.

"How?"

"Charge records," he said.

"How can you access her credit-card receipts?" I asked, appalled that he was able to uncover Maisy's financial information with such ease.

"I have sources," he said in a lofty tone.

Wes and his sources. *I wish I had them,* I thought, the question about how Maisy had paid, or planned to pay, for her around-the-world cruise in the forefront of my mind.

"What do you think about this?" he asked. "Maybe she was in cahoots with him about something."

" 'Cahoots'? About what?"

"I don't know. Maybe they were stealing money that had been donated to the Guild."

I looked at him straight on. "Do you think it's possible?"

Wes shrugged. "Britt Epps has a top reputation, so probably not," he replied, sounding disappointed.

"Was that the hot news?" I asked.

"Yeah. I think Maisy and Britt having a relationship outside the Guild might be significant, don't you?"

Wes's use of the word "relationship" got me thinking. Could Maisy and Britt have had a little something on the side? *Nah,* I thought, *not possible.* "I have no idea, Wes. None. I don't know anything about anything."

After Wes left, promising to call me as soon as he got more information, I limped over to the bank of windows at the rear and stood staring out into the sun-flecked forest. *Think,* I told myself. *Be methodical.*

A squirrel caught my eye as it dashed across the leaf-strewn grassy patch at the edge of the woods, an acorn in its mouth. "Hurry, baby," I whispered. "Get home!" It disappeared into the underbrush. I shut my eyes and leaned my head against the cold glass. It hurt my neck and I grimaced and pulled back.

I pressed myself to process Wes's information quickly so I would know what to do next. As I stared into the middle distance, the PA system crackled and Gretchen announced that I had a call—Chi.

I took it in the tag-sale room, back over by the cash registers. He gave me his cell phone number and told me that he was on-site and ready to go. He added that after today, I probably wouldn't see him, or anyone on his team, often or much, unless, of course, I needed help, but they'd be there. I didn't know he had a team, but I liked the sound of it. He told me to call him if I was going to do anything out of my routine, so they could plan for it. I thanked him and hung up, comforted to know Chi was in place.

I sat for a while longer, weighing my options, considering alternative plans; then when I was ready, I locked up and headed into the warehouse. By the time I reached the front office, moving slowly, ready for another painkiller, I knew my next step.

CHAPTER TWENTY-SIX

ould you run upstairs and get my purse?" I asked Gretchen after I'd settled myself into a guest chair positioned near her desk.

"Sure," she said. She hurried toward the warehouse, glad to have a way to help.

While she was gone, I used her phone to call Pam Fields.

"Pam," I asked after a brief exchange of greetings, "by any chance, did you find that brochure? You know, the one for the cruise ship?"

"I'm sorry, Josie, I haven't had a second to look. I promise I'll get to it today."

"That's fine. What I'm really after is the name of the travel agent Maisy used. Do you know it?"

"I should remember," she said slowly, as if she was thinking hard. "I know she mentioned it. But I just don't recall the name. I'm striking out for you today."

I reassured her that it didn't matter and she again promised to track down the brochure.

I called the Guild. A woman answered, maybe Maisy's assistant, and I said, "Hi, this is Josie Prescott. I'm hoping you can help me."

"Of course."

"Maisy always told me how happy she was with the Guild's travel agency, and I'm calling for the name."

"Sure," she said. "We've used them for years. It's Victory Travel."

The address was close—a storefront in a strip mall only about a five-minute drive away.

"A travel agent? Going somewhere fun?" Gretchen asked pro-

vocatively, overhearing me reading back the address. She handed
me my purse.

"Afraid not. It's for a friend," I responded, keeping it vague.

"Want me to enter the information into our vendor file?" she offered.

"Good idea." I handed her the slip of paper.

While she typed, I dug out the bottle of painkillers from the bottom of my purse.

"All set," she said, passing the paper back.

Under Gretchen's vigilant observation, I swallowed the pill.

"How are you doing?" she asked.

I made a face.

"Do you think you should leave—you know, take the rest of the
afternoon off?"

"I'm fine, really. Besides which, Detective Rowcliff is coming at
four and I should be here."

"He could meet you at home," she argued.

"I'm okay," I said dismissively as Eric entered the office from the
warehouse. Glad for an excuse to take the focus off of myself, I
turned away from Gretchen to ask him how the pickup at Verna's
house had gone. I was glad to hear that there'd been no
problems—no discrepancies, no breakages, and no attitude from
Verna. Good news, and a relief.

I told Gretchen I'd be back in a while, and in the face of her
patent disapproval, I headed out.

Chi, assuming the slender, dark-haired Asian man behind the
wheel was him, drove an old dark blue Alfa Romeo, and at first,
he followed close. From the sharp maneuvering I witnessed
through the rearview mirror, the car was in race-ready condition.

I pulled into a parking space right in front of Victory Travel's
door. I stood in the sun and looked all around. There was no blue
sports car in sight, and I didn't know if that was good news and
Chi was deftly avoiding exposure, or bad news and he'd already
lost me.

A bell chimed as I pushed open the door. The agency had one long room. There were eight desks, four to a side, with a central aisle. Six of them were staffed. There were no customers. Posters showing Greek islands, Mexican ruins, the Eiffel Tower, and African elephants walking in the savanna lined the walls.

A woman wearing a fluffy pink sweater greeted me without stopping what she was doing at her computer. "Can I help?" she asked.

"Thanks," I said, and waited. Finally, she looked up, registered my battered appearance, and looked away, avoiding my eyes, then, after a moment, openly stared at my face.

A name placard on her desk read GERT. "Are you Gert?" I asked, pointing to the nameplate.

"Yes. That's me." She giggled, as if she'd said something funny.

"I feel better than I look." I smiled as best I could.

"Sorry for staring," she said, sounding embarrassed.

"It's okay." I tried smiling again. "I'm Josie Prescott."

"Hi."

"Hi. Listen, this agency was recommended by the Portsmouth Women's Guild, and I was hoping I could talk to their agent."

"Sure. Do you have the agent's name?"

"Sorry, no."

"Oh." She pursed her lips. "Let's see." She typed something into her computer, and within seconds reported that Christie Jax was the Guild's agent.

"Is she in?" I asked.

Gert gestured to a dark-haired woman sitting at the last desk on the right, talking on a headset. "That's Christie."

"Can you let her know I'm here?" I asked.

"Sure," Gert said, standing up. "Have a seat, why don't you, while you wait."

She slipped a note under Christie's eye and I saw Christie glance at me and nod. While I waited, I flipped through a bunch of brochures describing vacations to the Bahamas.

"Sorry to make you wait," Christie said as she waved me over.

"No problem."

Responding to the unspoken question in her eyes, I explained that I'd been in a car accident, then, smiling, repeated that I felt better than I looked. "I was hoping you could help me."

"Sure. Any way I can."

"Thanks. It's about Maisy. Maisy Gaylor."

Her smile faded. "It's horrible what happened."

I nodded agreement, and after a small pause, I said, "Maisy told me she was thinking of a cruise and that you were enormously helpful in helping her select the right one."

"Oh, isn't that just like her? So sweet! I hope I helped, but the truth is, she knew exactly what she wanted—I just needed to locate it."

"What did she want?"

"Very high-end. Very exclusive."

I nodded. "Which one did she settle on?"

Christie typed something into her computer. "The *Richmond Queen*—an around-the-world tour—it's a beautiful ship."

"When was she planning on leaving?"

Christie rubbed her chin as she met my gaze, signaling her doubts. "May I ask what your interest is?"

I smiled again and looked down. "Maisy got me so excited talking about her plans, I began to toy with the idea of booking a cruise myself."

"Really?" She smiled, her attention captured.

"No promises," I said. It was one thing to *sort of* imply that I might become a paying customer, but it was another thing altogether to *really* imply that she was about to close a sale. "I figure I might as well capitalize on her research. She sure seemed to check all her options."

"That's true. She wanted *all* the details."

"That was Maisy! Well-organized."

"And practical!"

"What do you mean, 'practical'?" I asked, surprised by the word choice.

Christie smiled and leaned back. "She was going on this expensive—I mean really luxury-level tour—but she wanted to know about whether washing machines were available for passenger use on board and if I had lists of Internet cafés in the various ports of call." She leaned forward and lowered her voice. "I mean at this level, the crew does your laundry—no extra charge, you know what I mean? And Internet access is included on board, too."

"Proving she doesn't come from money."

"That's true. People from *old* money *assume* everything's included."

I smiled at her observation. "When was she planning to start the trip?" I asked.

"Let me see here." Christie typed something else into the computer, then reached into her desk drawer; after a moment's search, she extracted a file folder. She laid it open on her desk.

"I haven't updated the computer yet," she explained. "She'd just decided on the departure date."

I focused on reading upside down as Christie turned the pages one by one. From what I could see, the papers appeared to be contact and other information, some kind of liability release, and an insurance form. While she was hunting for departure information, I spotted an unexpected paper—an electronic transmit authorization form.

Christie looked up at me, and seeing my eyes on the papers, unobtrusively folded her hands to block my view. I played dumb, smiling innocently. After a long pause, she decided not to make an issue of it. "Her departure date was November first from New York City," she said.

"So soon!"

"Yes, from the beginning, Maisy was looking at November departures."

I nodded. "And her trip is all paid for. So sad."

She glanced down and saw the form. She pulled it out and put in on top. "No, just a deposit, but she signed up for the insurance, so she won't lose anything. Or rather, her family won't lose anything." She smiled. "How about you? Would you be thinking of a November departure, too?"

"No, that's too soon for me. What's available in March?"

While she typed the inquiry and waited for the answer, I pulled out a small spiral-bound notebook from my purse and, holding it low on my lap, out of sight, copied down the account number and bank address. The bank was located in someplace called Campione d'Italia. *Italy? Why in God's name would Maisy have had a bank account in Italy?*

With a printout of the *Richmond Queen*'s schedule for the entire year in hand, I shuffled to my car.

I knew more than when I'd walked into the travel agency, but I wasn't sure what any of it meant. I needed to think.

CHAPTER TWENTY-SEVEN

J ust before I reached the turn-in to my parking lot, I saw a flash of blue go by as Chi unexpectedly passed me. I pulled into a spot near the front, and as I opened my car door, he was standing with his back to the building, methodically scanning the area.

I nodded in his direction and trudged inside. I felt exhausted, confused, and worried. I was pushing myself too hard and I needed to rest. Learning about Maisy's overseas account and her meeting with Britt added no clarity, except that it showed how little I knew about Maisy. And on the drive back, I'd realized that my hope for absolution notwithstanding, even if Trevor was out of it, that still didn't explain why someone had tried to run me down last night. *But,* I thought, stepping out of my car and hurrying into the office, *I've already racked my brain for answers as to who might want me dead.*

The chimes tinkled as a reason occurred to me, and I froze — *could it be . . . was it possible . . . could I have seen something damning at the Gala?* If someone had poisoned Maisy's glass before she arrived at my table, I might not have seen anything. *Which means no one would be trying to kill me because of what I observed,* I told myself. I shook my head, frustrated at the complications.

"Hi," I said, dragging my attention back to the present moment. "Anything going on?"

"Nope," Gretchen said. "Just waiting for Dr. Kimball."

"Oh, yeah," I acknowledged, remembering, "the Chinese porcelain guy. He's due at three, right?"

"Exactly."

I glanced at the clock on Gretchen's desk. I had about forty-five minutes. "I'm going to my office."

"Are you up to the stairs?" she asked.

"Absolutely," I fibbed.

She looked doubtful, but wisely, she stayed silent. I wasn't in the mood to argue, and she knew it. I turned to Fred tapping away on his computer.

"How are you, Fred?" I asked.

"Fine. Working steadily."

"Good." I allowed his imprecise answer to stand. None of my staff ever wasted time. Lucky me.

After struggling up the stairs one at a time, I was glad to sink into my comfortable chair and rest. *Assuming, for the sake of argument,* I thought, closing my eyes, relaxing, *I* did *see something at the Gala that, if known, would reveal the murderer's identity—what was it? Pretend you are a video camera. Don't interpret. Just report.*

I closed my eyes again and took myself back to Saturday night.

My seatmates had been talking and laughing, but I wasn't really listening to their conversation. I smiled when appropriate and responded when addressed directly, but otherwise, I was in my own world.

Just before Gretchen arrived and delivered the bid sheets, I finished my wine, and within moments, a waiter refilled my glass. I remembered that I'd been impressed at the quick service. I took a sip, then idly watched the crimson swirls that formed as I tilted my glass this way and that. I gasped now as I realized the significance of that memory: *As of that moment, my wine was untainted. No one had tampered with my wine before Maisy's arrival,* I thought. I was pleased that my tactic of focused reminiscence was working. *All right, then. What happened next?*

Gretchen came hurrying up.

I was hit by a wave of nausea as a horrific thought came to me. *Could my always-thoughtful, sunny-spirited assistant, Gretchen, have poisoned the wine?* Even posing the question made me sick. *It can't be. Not Gretchen!*

I opened my eyes and watched through the window as a red-and-gray bird swooped down momentarily, then flew away. I shut my eyes again. *What happened next?*

Gretchen approached in a rush. She squatted near my chair, radiant, her green eyes ablaze with excitement, and leaned over to hand me the envelope. "The bids are excellent," she whispered. *Oh, Gretchen. Could it be?* Since she was there, it would seem that she had the opportunity. I forced myself to consider whether she also had a motive.

No! my heart answered, but the truth was that I didn't know much about Gretchen's background, and even after all these years, she had never opened up about her past. She was a master of the art of friendly evasion. A few years ago, Sasha had asked her if she was going home for Christmas. She cheerfully responded, "Home is where the heart is! How about you?"

"The past isn't over. It isn't even past," Faulkner wrote. I simply couldn't believe that Gretchen had a motive. Could she be insane? The kind of person who killed for pleasure or imagined slights? Absurd! Yet, I had to think objectively. It was one thing to dismiss as ridiculous the idea of Gretchen as a homicidal maniac. It was another altogether to ignore the facts—she was there by my side and she refused to discuss her past.

During her job interview, she told me that she'd moved to Portsmouth from up near the Canadian border because she wanted a fresh start. She joked that she didn't want to recount the sad story of her past. Her comment struck a chord with me—I, too, moved to Portsmouth to begin a new life—and I, too, didn't want to talk about my past.

Sitting here alone in my office, stiff, frightened, and in pain, I wondered. I knew my own secrets, but what was in Gretchen's past that she refused to talk about? She was young, only twenty-five or -six now, so she would have been no more than about twenty-one when she joined my firm. What had transpired in the years leading up to her arrival on my doorstep that was too painful or too damning to recount?

Should I investigate? Tears welled up and moistened my cheeks. Even to think of spying on her was shudderingly horrible. But if it had to be done, I would do it. I swept the wetness from my face and took several deep breaths for strength. *Think. Where did I leave off?*

Gretchen was squatting beside my chair at the Gala, jubilant and exhilarated as she reported the auction's success. "Great!" I said, responding as much to her enthusiasm as to the Guild's good fortune.

She stayed a moment longer, then stood up, and I took a sip of wine as I watched her skirt the tables, heading for the back.

I gasped as I recalled this now. *I sipped wine!*

I clasped my chest, almost hyperventilating with relief. *Thank God.* From the moment Gretchen crouched by my chair until the moment she stood and sauntered away, I'd sipped my wine steadily—and lived to tell about it. Which meant Gretchen was innocent.

I began to cry, weak from the sudden release of tension. "Oh, Gretchen, forgive me for even asking the question," I said aloud. I lowered my head and sighed. Whatever her secrets, they could stay safe. I took another deep breath and raised and lowered my shoulders as I tried to relax my knotted muscles.

Forcing myself back to the Gala, I remembered how Gretchen left my side. *What happened next?*

After Gretchen headed off, I passed the envelope to Britt, who, as the Gala honorary chairman, was responsible for announcing the winning bids. He was sitting on the far side of my table.

I now recalled feeling relieved that the seemingly endless evening would soon be over. Mostly, if the truth be told, I'd thought about Ty, wondering how he was doing, and hoping he was okay.

Breathing deeply to calm my jagged nerves now, I forced myself to picture the envelope as I handed it to Britt at the Gala.

Then what?

With the envelope in hand, Britt leaned over to Maisy as she sat at a nearby table and said, "Maisy—we're ready to announce the winners."

"You bet!" She jumped up and came over to our table, carrying a glass of red wine. Her vivaciousness wasn't merely out of character; it was so saccharine, I figured it had to be a charade. *God*, I thought at the time, *is she for real?*

Was it possible, knowing what I now knew about Maisy's apparently secret bank account and evident plans to leave the country, that her cloying effusiveness masked something? *What?* Was she publicly declaring that all was well with her? Did she want the Gala participants to witness her contentment? Or was she sending a message, targeting one person in particular? Maybe she wanted her husband, Walter, to know that she didn't care that he was divorcing her. Perhaps her upbeat demeanor masked nothing more than pride and had nothing at all to do with murder.

I shook my head in frustration. I had no way of knowing Maisy's motivations, and her behavior was open to so many interpretations, it was hopeless to try to sort it out.

Walter watched Maisy, too. Perhaps the look he gave her that I'd perceived as bitter wasn't that at all, but contemptuous. Maybe he understood the message she was trying to convey and was sending one back—that he thought her efforts at camouflage were pathetic. I wondered what Detective Rowcliff had learned about their relationship. I shrugged, acknowledging that no matter how comprehensive the investigation, or what role Walter might have played in Maisy's murder, it was unlikely that anyone could ever know what had fueled the dynamic between them. Including Pam.

Pam Field had sat at their table, I now recalled. *How well does she know Walter?* I wondered. Had Pam hung out at her good friend Maisy's house? Did she develop a relationship with him separate from her friendship with Maisy? I shook my head. There was no way to know.

Once again, I asked myself, *What happened next?*

Britt gestured to Dora, who was sitting with a boisterous group across the room. She acknowledged his signal and, taking her time, joined us.

I smiled now, remembering how much I'd admired her ability to work the room. Another memory came to me. Before she began her trek, weaving through the tables, Hank, her boyfriend, the trombone player, smiled at her lovingly. She smiled in response, and her eyes glinted momentarily with sensuality and promise, a barely perceptible change in affect. It was a private look, intended just for him, and I felt unholy envy as I watched their intimate exchange. He was younger than she was by a lot and very handsome, tall and fit, with a blond ponytail. *I miss you, Ty,* I'd thought as I turned away, ashamed, feeling like a voyeur.

Maisy said something, I couldn't remember what, and sipped her wine. *Wait! Maisy drank some wine and she was fine!* My mouth fell open at the significance of the memory. I took a deep breath and struggled on. *After Maisy sipped her wine, then what?*

I thought back, picturing Maisy standing to the side. She placed her glass on the table next to mine just as Dora arrived and hugged Britt. Britt handed the bid sheets to Dora and moved aside with Maisy, chatting, while Dora scanned the pages.

"Think!" I whispered aloud.

All I was doing was reliving the same experiences again and again. It was as if I were watching a movie, frame by frame, yet nothing new was revealed.

Focus. What happened next? Britt and Maisy kept talking. I couldn't recall now what they'd said.

I ran the film back several frames.

Britt reached across and handed Dora the bid sheets.

I opened my eyes now, stunned.

Britt's arm had been extended over our wineglasses as he passed the papers to Dora. Could he have had the cyanide in his hand, maybe in a fold of cloth or tissue, and dropped it in the wine as his hand passed over the glass?

That would have required the dexterity of a magician, and no sleight of hand had been possible, because everyone was looking at him. He was standing at the front, the focal point of everyone's attention.

Maybe.

I, at least, *hadn't* been looking at Britt. I'd been looking at Dora. She looked so gorgeous with her easy smile and beautiful gown. Her dress was black silk and covered with glittering gold sequins. I'd hoped we might become friends.

A piercing shriek of seagulls overhead brought me back to the here and now, my mouth hanging open, astonished. Britt could have poisoned the wine and I wouldn't have noticed. I'd been there with my eyes open and yet saw nothing.

Murder in plain sight. Was it possible?

I closed my eyes again, willing more memories to come.

Dora scanned the bid sheets. I noticed her shimmering shawl, draped artistically, barely resting on her shoulders, drooping low at the back and dangling from her elbows. A small black clutch purse was tucked under her arm.

I looked at Dora; then I moved the wineglasses, shifting them aside, away from Dora's shawl. *The shawl's too close; it will dip in the wine,* I thought as I watched Dora.

In the waning afternoon light, the trees visible through my window appeared dense and dark. I allowed my eyes to stay fixed in the middle distance as more freeze-frame memories came to me.

When Dora had finished reading, she rearranged her shawl a bit and turned toward Britt. She was excited by the results—the Guild had raised a lot of money. He accepted the bid sheets from her and said something to Maisy that I couldn't recall now, then spoke to me, inviting me to join them at the podium. I declined.

When did Maisy pick up her glass? I shook my head. I had no recollection. What I did remember was that as soon as Britt approached the platform, Hank's brass quartet segued into the fanfare, as scheduled. Britt climbed the few steps to the low stage, stood behind the podium, and looked out over the crowd with self-important satisfaction. *Was he feeling prideful because of the success of the Gala,* I wondered, *or because of his handiness at poisoning the wine?*

I didn't know anything about Britt's relationship with Maisy, beyond what Wes had revealed. Wes discovered that Maisy had consulted Britt on what we assumed was a non-Guild matter and paid in cash. Why? And was that act related to her death?

Maisy was far more complicated than I'd realized. Maybe everyone was once you scraped the surface of their veneer.

CHAPTER TWENTY-EIGHT

I turned toward my computer and Googled Campione d'Italia. *Who knows?* I thought.

Campione d'Italia was an Italian tax haven completely surrounded by Switzerland, on the shore of Lake Lugano, a tiny place with huge financial impact. Unique. A little piece of Italy where people could have unfettered access to Swiss services—including Swiss banks.

I called Wes.

"What ya got?" he asked as soon as he heard my voice.

I swallowed, wondering whether I needed to be circumspect on the phone. No. I assumed that Detective Rowcliff had found some reference to Maisy's overseas account, so even if my phone was tapped, I wouldn't be revealing anything he didn't already know. "Maisy had booked a cruise leaving in November."

"And?"

"And she paid for it by electronic transfer from a bank in a place called Campione d'Italia." I explained what it was and rattled off the bank's name and Maisy's account number.

"We should meet," Wes said, warning me to keep quiet.

"I can't. And I'm sure that there's nothing I know that the police haven't already learned."

"Fair enough. That's true for me, too."

"What are you talking about?" I asked, mystified.

"Great minds," he said. "After we talked about Maisy paying in cash, I checked with my financial sources. They told me Maisy charges a lot, so the cash payment is unusual, as we speculated it was. Plus, the police apparently found an e-mail on Maisy's work computer confirming that a Swiss bank account was opened and that a big deposit was received, but there's no indication of the origin of the money, and the bank won't say—at least not yet. The police are working on it."

"How much?" I asked.

"Two transfers totaling four hundred thousand U.S."

I whistled softly. "That's a lot of money."

"Tell me about it," Wes said, agreeing.

"She deposited that amount?"

"Nope. The money came from another source—not from any of her accounts."

"What source?"

"That's unclear," he stated, and I could picture his mouth twisted in frustration, hating it that there was something he didn't know.

"So you've confirmed that someone deposited money in her account, but you don't know who?"

"Exactly. The deposit was electronic, from another offshore account."

"What do you think it means?" I asked.

"Maybe Maisy was planning to move there."

"No way," I said. Even a cursory look at Web sites related to Campione d'Italia showed a jet-setting lifestyle, way beyond what most people could afford. "Unless she has more accounts than that one, it's not possible. This is the sort of place the megarich live. Four hundred thousand sounds like a lot of money, but in that world, it's not."

"So, then, why would she open the account there?" Wes asked.

"Maybe she wanted the privacy of a Swiss bank."

"But if that's the case, why wouldn't she just have opened an account in Geneva or Zurich?"

"It seems that's the beauty of this place. There's no tax." Clever little Maisy. "Wes?"

"What?"

"Maybe the money was a blackmail payment," I ventured.

"I was thinking the same thing. You knew her. Does that idea fit?"

"No way. But I shouldn't speak—the truth is that I didn't know her at all. It's almost as if she lived a double life."

"Or was getting ready to."

"Yeah. Good point."

"Except that if Maisy really was blackmailing someone, maybe she was the intended murder target after all," Wes said.

"But someone really did try to kill me yesterday."

"That's true," he replied.

We agreed to talk later, and as I hung up, I swung my chair toward the window and watched my maple tree as I continued thinking.

Wes and I speculated that Maisy had blackmailed someone—$400,000 worth of extortion. *Was it possible,* I wondered, *that she had, in fact, done so, and that Britt was her target?* If so, maybe I'd found a viable motive. Perhaps the cash payment that someone in Britt's law office had recorded was a fake, that Maisy went to his office to extort money, not to get legal advice. It was possible that Britt took money out of his own pocket and handed it over to his bookkeeper to create the illusion that Maisy was a client.

I needed to talk to Max, to get his read on my shocking revelation, and to ask him how he thought I should proceed. Would he believe me? Or would he think I was fanciful, embellishing the facts in my effort to find answers?

I wondered whether to call Wes back. Maybe. Knowing him, he'd have a source who would be able to ferret out Britt's financial dealings. A $400,000 withdrawal from any of Britt's accounts might indicate that I was onto something. As I stood, stabbed by throbbing pain, I decided that I *should* call Wes. It wasn't idle curiosity. It was self-preservation. Screw protocol. I wanted to know everything I could that might help me stay alive. My father didn't just say, *Ignorance is never bliss.* He also told me, *Knowledge is always power.* Later, maybe, I'd call him. But not now. Now I needed support more than information.

As I shuffled across my office floor and walked down the spiral steps one slow stair at a time, slowly limping through the vast warehouse space into the auction venue, I felt weak from the searing intensity of my Gala memories and my brush with death. I had to face the fact that it was entirely possible that Britt was a killer—and that now he was out to kill me.

When Britt stood next to me, perhaps concentrating on sliding the powdery poison into the wine, he'd have had no way of knowing that I wasn't paying any attention to him at all. It was entirely possible that he would be surprised to know that my focus was divided between admiring Dora's stunning appearance and missing Ty, and that, therefore, I hadn't observed a thing.

I shook my head as I switched on the lights and adjusted the thermostat to take away the afternoon chill. Surely Britt—or whoever was responsible—knew by now that I was no threat. I hadn't told the police anything against him, or anyone, and I wasn't a blackmailer.

Maybe, I thought with a flash of hope, *there will be no further attempt to kill me.* My optimism faded soon enough.

"Hope is the thing with feathers," Emily Dickinson wrote.

It didn't matter whether I had seen anything. What mattered was whether the murderer believed that I had. "Perception," I whispered. "Perception becomes conviction." I shook my head, confused and troubled, picked up the phone, and dialed the only person I felt I could trust—Max.

CHAPTER TWENTY-NINE

I s everything all right?" Max asked when I had him on the line.

"Yes. Thank you, Max. Detective Rowcliff is due at four."

"Good. What's up?"

"I remembered something. And I think maybe it's important."

"I'm in a meeting, Josie, so I can't talk for long. Can it wait?"

I paused, unsure how to respond. *Could it wait?* Yes. *Should it?* No. "I think Britt had an opportunity to add the poison. I don't know that he did, but I recall his hand stretching over the glasses."

I heard Max breathing, but he didn't speak for several seconds. "I'll stop by about quarter to four and we can discuss this further. All right?"

My tension melted away. Max would tell me what to do, and he'd be here when Rowcliff arrived to show me the automobile illustrations. What a relief.

"Thank you, Max," I said, my voice cracking unexpectedly. "That's great."

I hung up and leaned against the wall, trying to decide what to do next. It hurt to move, and I closed my eyes until the throbbing pain diminished. "Whew," I said, and glanced at the clock built into the thermostat display. It read 2:45 P.M.

Soon Mitch and his expert would arrive to pick up the Chinese tureen. I was exhausted, but the high-charge energy racing through my veins made resting impossible. *I'll go to bed early,* I thought. Groaning with effort, I stretched and walked toward the front office to wait.

As I stepped in, I saw Gretchen half-hidden by a pink aluminum

Christmas tree that she was holding up. Fred was on his knees, counting branches. A short middle-aged stranger with a Vandyke beard was leaning against the door frame, waiting. He glanced at me and I gathered from his double take that he was shocked by my bruised appearance, but he didn't comment.

"Hi, Josie," Gretchen said with a giggle. "Mr. Dublin is wondering about his tree."

"And ornaments," the stranger added, pointing to an old cardboard box on the floor next to him.

"I see," I responded. "I'm glad you stopped by, Mr. Dublin. Anything I can do to help, Fred?"

"No, I'm okay," he answered, still counting.

"Would you like some coffee, Mr. Dublin? Tea? A Coke?"

"Nope. Thanks, though."

I sat on Gretchen's chair, and in a moment, Fred stood up.

"You said you don't have the original box," he said. "How about the paper sleeves the branches were shipped in?"

"No. Why? Does that matter?"

Fred nodded. "Original packaging always enhances value."

Dublin shrugged. "We threw all that stuff away when we first got the tree."

"When was that?" Fred asked.

"Mid-sixties."

I smiled a little. Fred was so focused on research, he'd forgotten that Gretchen was still supporting the tree. "How did you transport the tree?" he asked.

I sent Gretchen a private signal, and she nodded, indicating her understanding, and unobtrusively placed the tree gently against the wall.

"In my truck," Dublin replied, shooting his thumb over his shoulder toward the parking lot.

"Loose?"

"The branches weren't in the pole," Dublin responded, "if that's what you mean. I rolled them in a blanket. The pole was loose."

"Gotcha. I'll just be a couple of minutes," Fred said, turning toward his monitor.

Fred was right about the value of original packaging. Most collectors are glad to pay a premium of 20 percent or more for it. But there was another, less obvious advantage to acquiring items in their original packaging. Antiques and collectibles stored in whatever was designed to protect them are much more likely to be in good condition than goods stored haphazardly. Knowing that the aluminum branches were rolled in a blanket meant we'd need to examine them much more closely than if each one had been tucked into its sized-to-fit paper sleeve. Of course, on a two-dollar item, it didn't much matter, but aluminum Christmas trees were hot right now, especially pink ones, so we were talking way more than two dollars, and determining its value was definitely worth the effort.

The phone rang and Gretchen reached across her desk to answer in her usually happy tone. "Prescott's. May I help you?" She listened. "The tag sale runs every Saturday."

As she informed the caller about our tag-sale hours and gave directions, Dora arrived in a flurry of excitement and resolve.

"Oh, Josie!" she exclaimed. "Look at you. Isn't this just awful?"

I smiled a little, touched by her concern. "I'm okay."

"Are you, really?" she asked earnestly.

I nodded. "I am. Thank you, Dora."

"You have such a good attitude, Josie."

Unsure how to respond to the compliment, I introduced her to Mr. Dublin, explaining that Fred was pulling together some information for him about his Christmas tree and ornaments.

"Don't you love these things!" she exclaimed, running her manicured nails through the aluminum frills. "I'm too young to remember them, of course! I meant that I loved seeing them on old TV shows!"

Mr. Dublin laughed. "Me, too! Both about loving seeing them on TV and being too young. It's my mother's tree," he added with a wink.

"Really?" she asked, her eyes twinkling merrily. "Looking at you, I would have thought it must have been your grandmother's!"

He chuckled with delight. Dora had a gift all right.

Gretchen's call ended, and as she greeted Dora, Fred ripped a sheet from his notepad and handed it to me as he walked toward the box of ornaments. Under the printed maroon heading that read PRESCOTT'S, Fred had printed "Net retail $700."

I folded the note and slipped it in my pocket.

After a polite exchange of pleasantries, during which Dora declined Gretchen's offer of coffee or tea, Dora asked me, "Have you heard anything about who did it?"

All eyes turned toward me.

CHAPTER THIRTY

I shook my head, feeling conspicuous. "Nothing yet. At least not that I'm aware of."

Dora sighed, communicating worry and concern. "You must be terrified," she said.

"I'm okay," I repeated, uncomfortable in the face of her anxiety.

"Are the police watching you?"

"They're increasing their patrols," I said, casting an embarrassed glance in Mr. Dublin's direction. He was openly eavesdropping.

"Is that enough to keep you safe?" she asked.

"Actually," I said with a small smile, "you'll probably laugh, and to tell you the truth, it makes me feel a little like a rock star, but I've got some extra security."

She nodded, satisfied. "Good. I'm glad to hear it. You're smart."

I shrugged. "Well, until we know what's going on, it's hard to say if it's smart or paranoid. But I figure it can't do any harm, right?"

"Absolutely."

Dora followed my eyes, and together we watched as Fred separated the ornaments into clusters of three and four. From what I could tell, he was segregating them by the materials used to create them. Some were fabricated of glass, others carved of wood, and a few appeared to be crocheted. I noticed a preponderance of pink.

She turned to Gretchen. "Britt told me he's going to call you later to get an update on the auction pickups. How have things been going?"

"So far, so good," Gretchen responded. "I've either reached everyone in person or left a message. Our first pickup is scheduled for . . ." she said, drawing out the last word as she glanced at her watch, "now."

"Well, I'll keep my fingers crossed that everyone shows up," Dora remarked. "You never know with pledges." She swung around and faced me. "Josie, I'm actually here for a business reason. Are you certain you're able to talk? I can wait if you prefer."

"Well, it depends. I'm taking painkillers, so anything involving advanced economic theory or existential philosophy will have to wait. But other than that, I think I'm good to go."

"All right, but only if you promise to tell me if you want me to go away."

"Okay." I wondered what business she had that involved me. "Should we go to my office?"

She tucked her blond hair neatly behind her ear and shook her head. "It's not private and it will only take a minute."

I looked questioningly at her.

"You may know that the Guild isn't my only interest," Dora said. "I'm also involved with a wonderful little group called Literacy Matters. Have you ever heard of them?"

"No, I don't think so."

"Well, I'm not going to tell you about them now." She laughed, a musical sound, and leaned forward again to touch my arm with a feathery brush. "I'm hoping you can attend a luncheon I'm giving on the group's behalf this Friday. If you come, I promise you delicious food, excellent wine, and engaging company, and the only thing I ask is that you listen to a five-minute description of the group's important work—and that you bring your checkbook." She laughed again. "But if you're not feeling up to joining us, I'll understand completely. I do this periodically, and I'll invite you again."

As Dora spoke, a happy memory came to me. It had been a bitter cold February day, with icy gusts bringing tears to my eyes as I hurried along Lexington Avenue in New York. My good friend Katie was hosting a clambake in her tiny studio apartment. She'd organized the elaborate faux beach party in support of a charity. I remembered admiring her commitment to the cause, and the camaraderie I'd felt as I and all of her guests pulled out cash or checkbooks in response to her appeal. *And this is how a support-ive society is supposed to work,* I'd thought at the time. *Someone asks and others who are part of that community trust the person's judgment and say okay.*

I was more than pleased that Dora had invited me—I was elated. *Maybe,* I thought, with fingers crossed, *this week will mark the beginning of the end of the isolation I've endured since moving to New Hampshire. Ty is different,* I told myself. *No matter how ter-rific a man may be, he can never replace a girlfriend.* Maybe Zoe, my landlady and neighbor, would become a friend, and Dora, my covolunteer, another. *Is it possible,* I wondered, *that I've found the beginnings of a community that will last?*

"I'd love to go," I said. "I'm sure I'll be able to—just as long as you don't think my appearance will scare your other guests away."

"Don't be silly, Josie. Everyone is very upset about what's going on and thrilled that you're all right."

"Thank you, Dora," I said, discomfited at the thought that people were discussing me.

"I'm going now," she said, flashing a smile in Gretchen's direc-tion, "I'll call Gretchen tomorrow and give her all the details."

"Great," I said, meaning it. "Thank you for including me."

Five minutes later, I sat in the guest chair, sipping another cup of tea, resting as Gretchen and Fred worked in companionable si-lence. Fred was almost done with his on-the-spot appraisal. The phone rang—another inquiry about Saturday's tag sale. In the midst of all my strife, I allowed myself a private "woo hoo!" Busi-ness was good.

"Are you interested in selling the tree and ornaments?" Fred asked Mr. Dublin.

"Nope. It's my daughter, Irma. She's getting married next month. As part of her wedding gift, her mom and I thought we'd give her all the Christmas stuff. I just want to know what it's worth, so when it's my other daughter's turn to walk down the aisle, we can be fair to Kenna."

"Okay, then," Fred told him, "but you need to help me understand what you mean by 'fair.' The thing is that replacement value is different from 'I gotta get cash' value, you know?"

"Understood," Dublin said, nodding. "I don't need an exact number. I just need a ballpark figure."

"Well then, you might as well use full retail," Fred told him.

"Okay," Dublin agreed.

"Keep in mind, this is the top-dollar price for the tree. I'm not saying you could get this amount, but you might."

"Got it. And?"

"Full retail is around seven hundred dollars."

Dublin looked pleasantly surprised. "That's more than I expected. How about the ornaments?"

"To tell you the truth, there's nothing special there. I mean, there's no item that's worth more than a dollar or two, even though there are some nice things."

Tag-sale value, I thought, using our unofficial code to indicate that there was nothing significant.

"So, soup to nuts," Dublin asked, "you're talking what? About seven fifty?"

"Not even. Realistically, you should call it seven hundred, seven twenty-five, maybe," Fred responded matter-of-factly.

Dublin smiled and nodded. "Fair enough. Thanks." Working together, he and Fred disassembled the tree. He shook my hand, thanked Fred for his work, scooped up his tree pole and branches and the box of pink ornaments, and, with a final smile and a wave, left.

No money changed hands, but with any luck, Mr. Dublin would refer friends to us and return if and when he ever wanted to buy—or sell—antiques in the future.

"Good job," I told Fred.

Mitch Strauss's expert, Dr. Miles Kimball, arrived a few minutes later. He stepped into the office and announced to no one in particular, "Please tell Ms. Prescott that Dr. Kimball has arrived." He looked as snotty as he sounded.

I placed my mug on Gretchen's desk, stood up, and said, "Hi. I'm Josie Prescott." I extended a hand and smiled as best I could.

Dr. Kimball took my hand, shock at my appearance registering on his long, bony face.

"Josie," Mitch Strauss exclaimed, entering the office a moment later. "Good God. Look at you. Should you be here? Shouldn't you be in the hospital? At least at home?"

"I feel better than I look," I assured them both, using my stock line, trying again to smile.

"I'm glad to hear that," Dr. Kimball said coldly.

Mitch wouldn't allow my disclaimer to stand and said something else about how I ought to be resting. If I'd let it, his effusive concern would have embarrassed me into silent misery. Instead, I deflected the attention. "Thanks for your concern. So tell me, are you excited to pick up your tureen?" I asked.

"You bet! I can't wait to get it home and on display. Rochelle has cleared out a cabinet—'the place of honor,' she calls it."

During the Gala, Mitch and his wife, Rochelle, had carefully examined each item up for auction, but I'd noted that, like most investors, they seemed to care more about the value of the antique than they did for the item itself. When I started at Frisco's, I learned quickly that for many collectors, the concept of value is complex. Sure, for some, the beauty, rarity, or cultural importance of the antique matters. And so, too, does its cost, of course. But for most, it's the status that possessing the item confers on its owner that seems to matter most.

Right out of college and filled with naïve idealism, I'd expected people to buy an antique because of the piece's splendor or significance, and had been stunned and disappointed to learn that such reasons were, in fact, the exception, not the rule. Most buyers made purchase decisions based on their personal perception of value, and usually that meant some combination of investment potential and prestige. *Perception again,* I thought. *It always comes back to perception.*

I led the way through the warehouse into the auction venue,

and I noted that Mitch kept his eyes down, never once glancing toward the stage, where Maisy had stood only three days earlier. I limped over to where the "Birds and Flowers" tureen stood. Mitch and Rochelle had won the object with a bid of $21,800, almost 10 percent above our estimated selling price.

Even before I could lift the Plexiglas cover, Dr. Kimball snorted scornfully. "This is a fake."

CHAPTER THIRTY-ONE

hocked, I stared at him for a quick moment, then turned toward the tureen and saw at a glance that he was right. Instead of the vivid rose-themed duck and lotus flower design, I saw a crude illustration in faded pink.

Stunned, I lifted the Plexiglas display case cover and gently rotated the bowl to reveal its bottom. I stared, disbelieving. "Made in China. Not for food use. May poison foods," the orange legend read, indicating the dangers of lead paint.

I couldn't believe my eyes. My stomach flip-flopped and I thought I might pass out. I couldn't move. I couldn't speak. Not only was the tureen a fake, it wasn't even a good fake. Notating the country of origin by name didn't begin until the mid-twentieth century, and adding toxicity warnings was an even more recent development. Even at a glance, I knew its pedigree. It was the sort of import marketed as a "reproduction" through scores of specialty gift shops nationwide, and probably it retailed for about a hundred dollars.

Since no one could possibly think that this fake would fool a professional—witness Dr. Kimball's immediate recognition—it was a placeholder, nothing more, an item to put on display so our attention wouldn't be caught by an empty case.

I felt completely mortified. *What must Dr. Kimball and Mitch think?* I wished a trapdoor would open and allow me to escape. *I should have checked it out before bringing them in to appraise it,* I thought, rebuking myself. *How could this have happened?* I stared into space, shocked and ashamed. *It's my fault.* I could have kicked myself.

Horrified at the potential impact this debacle might have on my reputation and future prospects, I was unable to speak, but my brain was running at top speed. I didn't know who had stolen the tureen or when. But on the face of it, it didn't seem like a garden-variety theft. It seemed worse—more carefully plotted—as if someone was trying to ruin me.

Dr. Kimball left, his heavy footsteps pounding across the concrete floor of the warehouse.

"I'm sure there's some logical explanation," Mitch assured me. "You know, a misunderstanding of some sort. Or a joke."

I stared at him and tried to appreciate his efforts at minimizing the situation, but I couldn't. My initial shock had morphed into white-hot anger, and my wrath was growing by the minute.

"Thanks for the thought, Mitch," I replied calmly. "But whatever is going on, it's no joke. It's a major theft. I'll be calling the police immediately, of course." I nearly choked on the words as I added, "I assume I don't need to tell you that I *did not* substitute a cheap fake for the real thing."

"No, no, of course not. Please excuse Dr. Kimball's brusqueness. I'm sure he would never think such a thing, either."

I didn't comment. From the look Mitch gave me, I could tell that what he'd just said was a lie. Dr. Kimball was probably already on his cell phone, spreading the word that Prescott's was a sham and I was a charlatan.

"Well, I guess I'd better go," he said after an awkward pause.

"Can you find your way out?" I asked.

"Absolutely," he said, and headed for the door.

I limped to the wall and sat down on the floor. I needed to think about what I should do, but I was having trouble focusing. My rage ran deep, but it couldn't eliminate the shock. I felt sucker punched.

Mitch's footsteps had barely faded away when I heard the familiar click-clack of Gretchen's heels.

"Josie?" she said as she entered the room. "What's wrong?"

I looked at her. "Please call the police and report that the Qing dynasty tureen has been stolen."

"What happened?" She started toward me, concern apparent in her expression.

"Not now, Gretchen," I replied sharply. "Call them."

She must have heard something in my tone and seen something in my expression, because she stopped short, turned, and ran to the phone.

"This is Prescott's," she said when someone came on the line, then gave the address. "We've had a theft . . . a rare tureen—an antique. . . . Oh my God, I didn't think . . . no, I don't know. Hold on, please." She placed the mouthpiece against her chest and said, sounding awed, "Josie, they want to know if the intruder is still here."

I stared at her for a long moment, numb and frightened; then I turned toward the double doors that gave way to the parking lot. The heavy bolt was in place. That meant that this was probably an inside job. I couldn't believe it—had one of my employees, Gretchen, Sasha, Fred, or Eric, all of whom had the run of the place, done this terrible thing? *I can't trust anyone,* I reminded myself. *I'm alone.* I shivered as if it were cold, though it wasn't. What gave me goose bumps wasn't the temperature—it was the chill of isolation. The police had asked if the thief was still here. *Maybe.* I turned to look at Gretchen, who was waiting for my reply.

"Tell them I don't know," I said.

I was still sitting on the floor, deep in thought, when Gretchen escorted a uniformed policewoman named Officer Shirl into the auction room and introduced us.

It took me a minute to get to my feet. I felt beyond tired and wondered if I could go on much longer without collapsing.

"Are you all right?" Officer Shirl asked, watching me struggle and wince.

"Not really," I admitted. "But I'm hanging in for now."

"Shall I bring over a chair?" Gretchen asked.

"No, thanks," I said, and as she seemed inclined to linger, I added, "I'll take it from here. You get back to work and hold down the fort, okay?"

"Are you sure?" she asked, looking scared.

Of what? I wondered. *The situation? Or her role in it?*

"I know I can count on you to take care of whatever comes up."

She flashed a quick appreciative grin. "Okay, then," she said, and left.

"Whenever you're ready, please tell me what happened," Officer Shirl said.

"A valuable tureen was stolen. It's an antique."

"What kind of tureen?" she asked.

"It was Chinese. A beautiful piece. Quite rare."

"Can you describe it?"

"It would be easier to show you. Here," I said, handing her a catalog, one of a score still piled on a display case nearby. "Turn to page eight."

She nodded, flipped to the entry, and began reading, her eyes widening when she saw the twenty-thousand-dollar estimate. "Is this right? Twenty thousand dollars?" she asked, sounding as if she wasn't 100 percent convinced she'd read it right.

"More."

"Who bought it?"

I gave her Mitch and Rochelle's names and added, "Gretchen can give you their address and phone number."

Officer Shirl made a note. "And they arrived to pick up the tureen?"

"Mitch did. He brought an expert named Dr. Kimball."

"Why the expert?"

I shrugged. "It's not unusual. He wanted to authenticate the tureen before handing over the check."

"And Dr. Kimball discovered the theft?"

"Yes," I replied, mortified at the memory.

"How did Dr. Kimball know it was a substitution?"

"Anyone would have noticed. He didn't even examine it."

"But you didn't notice it, did you?"

Her tone belied the words. She wasn't implying that I should have noticed anything. She was just asking.

"I noticed it, too," I told her.

She smiled a little and said, "Tell me about it."

I closed my eyes for a moment, reliving the shock of the discovery. "Dr. Kimball announced that it was a fake. I looked up and saw it." I opened my eyes, looked at her, and shrugged. "Really. That was it. One glance."

"Then how come it took an expert to discover it? How come you didn't see it before?"

"It didn't take an expert. It took someone focusing on it, that's all."

I explained my theory that whoever had substituted the fake tureen intended to delay discovery, not trick a pro. "No way would anyone who knows anything think that this tureen was an antique."

"Why do you suppose you hadn't noticed the substitution before?"

I leaned against the wall, resting my still-aching ankle. "I didn't look. That's all. I had no reason to. I wasn't in this room at all today. If I'd looked at it, I would have seen it had been switched."

She nodded and asked, "When did you last notice it?"

I paused for a moment, trying to gather my scattered thoughts into some semblance of order. "Yesterday. Britt, Dora, and I put Post-its"—I pointed to a couple of the yellow sticky notes still in place—"on every item. The tureen was where it was supposed to be then."

"Britt? Dora? Who are they?"

"Britt Epps, the honorary chairman of the Gala. Dora Reynolds, the chair. That's what all of these antiques were being auctioned for. It was a charity event."

She nodded. "When were you here with them?" she asked.

"I'm not sure exactly. Morning."

"And since then?"

"I haven't been back in here."

"Who has?"

"I don't know for sure. I haven't been here the whole time."

She persisted. "As far as you know, who?"

"No one."

"Who else would know?"

"Gretchen. She's my assistant. The woman who brought you in here. She might have some ideas."

All at once, I had an unaccountable urge to cry. Anger had degenerated into self-pity. It was just too much. First Maisy's murder. Then worrying about Ty and Aunt Trina and missing him, when having him around would have been such a comfort. Then my attack. Now a theft. I felt overwhelmed and underprepared to deal with the madness. I took a deep breath, trying to stop. When I opened them, I found Officer Shirl watching me with professional interest. *To her I'm a suspect,* I realized, and all at once, I felt faint.

CHAPTER THIRTY-TWO

I 'm sorry," I said, embarrassed at my emotional display.

"It's okay," she said. "Do you want to sit down? Can I get you a glass of water?"

"Thanks. No. I'm okay. Please, just continue. What else can I tell you?"

"You own this business?"

"Yes."

"How many employees do you have?"

"Four full-time and a couple of part-timers."

"Their names?"

Officer Shirl was writing down their names when I heard footsteps and Max arrived, escorted by Gretchen. From his solemn expression, I gathered that Gretchen had filled him in.

"Hi, Max."

"Josie." He turned to Officer Shirl and introduced himself.

"Gretchen," I said, "Officer Shirl was asking about yesterday. Britt, Dora, and I were in here putting up the Post-its—until when? Do you remember?"

"Around eleven thirty, I think."

"That sounds right," I agreed. "I left for an appointment not long after that, so I would have no way of knowing if anyone entered later." I turned toward Gretchen and asked, "Do you? Do you know if anyone came in here after eleven thirty yesterday?"

"Yes," Gretchen replied, sounding frightened.

"When?" the policewoman asked.

"Who?" I asked simultaneously, then smiled and said, "Her first. When?"

Gretchen paused to think. "Around two."

"Who?"

"Me."

"You?" I asked, surprised.

"Why?"

"I wanted to be sure the doors were locked. You remember, Josie, Eddie had been in and out and I didn't even know if the doors were closed."

"Who's Eddie?" the police officer asked.

"Oh, sorry. The caterer. He was in taking everything away. You know, tables and plates and things. Cleaning up after the Gala."

Officer Shirl nodded and made a note. "When you checked, were they locked? The doors?"

"Closed but not locked."

I looked at Gretchen, stunned. "So anyone could have walked in until you locked them?"

"I guess," she acknowledged.

"And you're sure you did, in fact, lock them?" Officer Shirl asked.

"Yes. I turned the dead bolt and moved the sliding bolt into place."

"At two?" she asked, confirming Gretchen's recollection

"About then. Fred might recall. He was in the office, working at his computer. I asked him to cover the phone because I wanted to come back here and check."

Whether Fred remembered the exact time or not, a doubtful prospect given his absentminded professor–like proclivities, the fact remained that for a period of more than two hours, anyone could have walked into the room from outside, substituted the fake tureen, and spirited away the original.

"Josie left the room at eleven thirty and you entered at two. Are you aware of anyone who came in between those hours?" Max asked, joining the conversation for the first time.

"Just Eddie," Gretchen replied.

"No, no," I clarified, "Eddie was here early on. Before Britt and Dora arrived. Max is asking about after they left."

"Eddie came back," she explained.

"Really?" I asked. "Why?"

She shrugged. "He said he forgot something. He popped into

the office and said he'd just run around back. Actually, that's why I thought about making sure the doors were locked." She turned troubled eyes toward me. "That was okay, wasn't it, Josie? To let him show himself in? I mean, it was Eddie. He's here all the time. Or he was."

"What do you mean 'was'?" Max asked, pouncing on her word choice.

"Well, he moved, right? To Oklahoma, isn't that what you said, Josie?"

Officer Shirl aimed laser-sharp eyes at me. "What?" she asked.

"That's right. He called me from the road to tell me good-bye. He said his business went bust and he'd taken a job in Tulsa. I asked if it was okay for him to be leaving in the middle of a murder investigation, and he said he had the police's permission."

"Who did he tell?" Officer Shirl asked, sounding as if she disbelieved him—or me.

"That's a question for Detective Rowcliff, who's handling the investigation, and," Max said with a quick glance at his watch, "is due here any minute."

"You called him about the theft?" Officer Shirl asked, confused.

"No, he scheduled an appointment related to the Gaylor murder investigation," Max explained. "You probably know that Maisy Gaylor was murdered here last Saturday during the Gala charity event."

"Got it," the officer said, nodding. "Prescott's is hosting some kind of crime wave, huh?"

"As far as we know, the theft is unrelated to any other event," Max deadpanned. I wondered if he believed it.

"Let me get this straight," Officer Shirl said. "Eddie, the caterer, had been in this room earlier in the day yesterday, and then he came back—what time?"

Gretchen paused before answering. "Right about one thirty, I think. I was still eating lunch at my desk."

"How long did he stay?"

"Just a minute or two. I didn't notice in particular, but I'm pretty sure I heard his truck drive off almost right away."

Eddie, the glib bastard, had sneaked into my building and stolen the most valuable antique in the room. Probably he took a copy of the catalog home after the Gala, then spent Sunday weighing his options. What did he figure? That this would be an easy way to get a stake for his new life? And that my insurance would cover it, so it was no big deal?

Officer Shirl continued to ask questions, but I stopped listening. I was so angry I could spit.

CHAPTER THIRTY-THREE

T he PA system crackled and Fred's voice announced that Detective Rowcliff was on the phone. *What now?* I thought. I cast a panicked look in Max's direction.

"Would you like me to take it?" he asked, responding to my unspoken plea.

"Thank you, Max. Yes."

As he walked toward the phone in the cabinet on the back wall, I took a deep breath, preparing for what I was certain would be more bad news. Officer Shirl stood nearby, respectfully silent and attentive. Gretchen's eager eyes glinted with excitement. I knew her well enough to understand that she wasn't taking pleasure in my pain—she just loved the drama of the moment.

"Detective?" Max said into the phone.

He stood with his back to us, looking relaxed. I couldn't imagine talking to Rowcliff and feeling at ease. Gretchen edged closer to Max, the better to hear his side of the conversation.

"This is Max Bixby. Yes, Josie is here, but she's pretty worn down, so I thought I'd take the call. . . . Yes. . . . No, she's okay, just tired out. Well, the doctor said she'd be sore for a while, so it's not unexpected. . . . Well, sure, it's physical, but also, I'm sorry to report that there's been a theft here. . . . Of course we did. . . . Officer Shirl. . . . One of the antiques auctioned at the Gala . . . a soup bowl—a Chinese porcelain tureen. . . . I don't know. I just got here myself. . . . That's right. Officer Shirl. . . . Yes. . . . Sure. She's right here. Do you want to speak to her now? . . . Okay. . . . I'll put her on when we're done. . . . Okay. . . . Really? . . . That's great news. . . . Hold on. I'll ask Josie."

Officer Shirl's intelligent eyes followed along as Max turned to face me.

"Josie," Max called, "good news. Using only forensics, they were able to ID the car that almost killed you. It's a 2003 Mitsubishi Lancer ES. Black. Does that ring a bell?"

I thought for a moment, then shook my head. "No. I've never known anyone who drives a Mitsubishi. How can they know the specific model or year?"

"The paint."

I nodded, impressed. "Wow. That's incredible."

As Max turned back and began to speak into the phone again, I limped over to the wall and sat down on the floor. Stretching out my leg eased the throbbing a bit. I ached and hurt everywhere. My nerves were stretched tight and my emotions were so tangled, I couldn't even find a thread to try to sort through the mess. I closed my eyes and listened to Max.

"No, she doesn't recognize the car at all. Maybe the choice of a Mitsubishi was opportunistic—maybe whoever attempted to kill Josie stole it. . . . Really? . . . That's quick work, Detective. . . . Now what do you do? . . . That makes sense. . . . Already? And? . . . Nothing?"

I wondered what he was referring to.

"Okay. . . . Then let's talk in the morning. . . . I don't know," he said. "I'll check."

I opened my eyes as he turned to me and asked, "Josie, what's your schedule tomorrow?"

I couldn't remember. *Tomorrow? What day is that?* I asked myself. Wednesday. All I planned to work on was finding Eddie, the bastard.

"I don't know," I replied. "I mean, I can't remember. Tomorrow is Wednesday, right? I don't think I have anything scheduled. Gretchen? Can you remember?"

"No outside appointments," she concurred, vamping like an actress pleased to finally have a line to speak.

"Okay, then," Max said. Turning to face Officer Shirl, he added, "When I'm done, Detective Rowcliff would like to talk to you."

"Of course," she said, nodding.

He turned back to the wall and spoke to Rowcliff. "Josie is open all day, so why don't you and I talk in the morning and we can decide from there. . . . Okay. . . ."

He listened awhile longer, then handed the phone to Officer Shirl. Looking concerned, he came over and asked me when I was planning to go home.

"Soon. Once I know our next steps." I turned to Gretchen. "You can head back to the office now, Gretchen. If Officer Shirl needs more info, I'll have her talk to you there, okay?"

"Sure. Would you like a cup of tea or something? You look kind of tired."

I smiled at the understatement. "Thanks, but no."

She flashed her megasmile, then left. Officer Shirl stood arrow-straight, listening.

"Yes, sir. That's excellent, sir, thank you."

"I wonder what he's saying," I remarked in a low tone.

"He told me that he was going to offer Officer Shirl support. Whatever resources she needs."

"That means he thinks the theft is related to the murder."

"He doesn't know, Josie, any more than we do. He's committed to checking everything out."

I nodded, wondering if the answer wasn't right in front of us. *Eddie. Did Eddie kill Maisy? And steal the tureen? The cretin.*

Officer Shirl hung up the phone. I took a deep breath, pushed against the wall, and got up from the floor. Max, towering above me, reached down to help, but I waved him off. "I'm too tender to touch, but thanks," I explained.

Officer Shirl reached us as I stood. *"Whew,"* I said from the effort of standing.

"Detective Rowcliff filled me in," she said. "We'll be taking a look at things from the dual perspective, theft and murder."

"Good. Let us know if we can help," Max said.

"Thank you," she replied, nodding.

"Do you have any other questions for Josie at this time?"

"No. Not now."

"Then we'll leave you to it. We'll be in her office for a little while if you need us."

"And after that? When do you close?"

"Normally around five," I told her.

"The crime-scene work may take longer than that," she said, glancing at her watch.

"I'll ask someone to stay as late as you need," I assured her.

Max and I stopped in the office and I asked Fred to stay until Officer Shirl was done, and then lock up. He was a night owl, so it wasn't a huge imposition, although I knew it might make for a long day for him.

"Sure. No problem. Maybe I can finish up the silver," he said, glum.

"Have you run into trouble?" I asked.

"Yeah. One of Mrs. McCarthy's bowls is French," he said.

That explained his moroseness. Not every country made it as easy as England to authenticate silver. While France, for example, had standardized its marks since the 1200s, they also allowed a huge variety of symbols. Often the identification process resembled a needle-in-a-haystack hunt more than methodical research.

At a guess, the piece Fred was struggling to identify was one of Mrs. McCarthy's aunt Augusta's local purchases. We were relatively close to Quebec, so it wasn't unusual to find French-produced silver in New Hampshire antiques stores. French silver was often brought to the French Canadian province by immigrants and later acquired by Americans on vacation.

"Good luck," I said with an empathetic grimace.

"It's good that I like a challenge," he acknowledged, looking content.

"It's more than good; it's terrific." I turned to Gretchen and raised my foot to relieve the pounding pressure on my ankle. "Is Eric still around?"

"He'll be back in a few minutes. He's returning the truck."

I'd been so absorbed in the events in the auction venue, I hadn't heard the rumble of the rented twenty-foot truck as it rolled out. It made me wonder what else I'd missed.

In business, try hard never to be wrong, my father told me years ago. *You're not allowed a lot of errors in the big leagues. And the easiest way to avoid big mistakes is to consider everything—gather the facts and weigh them appropriately. The biggest trap is selective perception.* That's what happened to me at the Gala, I realized. I'd perceived some things but hadn't noticed others. Same as now. I'd been so focused on solving the theft of the tureen, I'd missed Eric's departure. *And you can't avoid it,* my father warned. *Selective perception happens all the time. So avoid arrogance at all costs. Never be positive—never be wrong.*

"Anything for me?" I asked, shaking off the thought.

"A message," Gretchen replied, handing me a slip of paper.

Pam Field had called. She'd just read about my attack in the paper and wanted to know if I was all right.

"Anything else?" I asked.

"That's it. I'm all set."

Upstairs, I saw that it was almost five. Once Max got situated in the yellow wing chair closest to my desk, I asked, "So Rowcliff isn't coming?"

"Right. No need to show you illustrations, since they've ID'd the car."

"What else did he say?"

"He told me that the car hadn't been reported stolen, nor was it in a body shop getting worked on."

"In Portsmouth?"

"In New England."

"Wow," I said, "that's quick work."

"Gotta love computers."

"Really. What does he do now?"

"He cross-references ownership records from the DMV and gets a list of owners of black 2003 Mitsubishi Lancer ESes."

"And then?"

"Then they show you the list and hope you recognize a name."

I felt my heart begin to pound. "When?"

"Tomorrow."

"Sounds like they're making progress."

He nodded, looked at his watch, and said, "Are you up to telling me about Britt?"

"Yeah." I paused, refocusing on my earlier revelation. "I remembered something," I said. "Something that makes me wonder if Britt's the killer."

CHAPTER THIRTY-FOUR

W hat?" Max asked.

"When Britt handed the bid sheets to Dora, his hand passed over my glass and over Maisy's. He reached across the table, then pulled his hand back. That's opportunity."

His brow wrinkled in confusion. "You saw him do something that makes you think he poisoned the wine?"

"No. No, not at all. Max, the truth is that I was a million miles away, involved in my own thoughts, and sort of watching Dora, but I definitely remember that Britt's arm stretched across as he handed her the bid sheets."

"Okay. What else?" he asked, sounding unimpressed.

"I know, I know, it sounds unbelievable, but it's not. I heard from someone—I don't remember who—" I said smoothly, looking down to pluck an invisible thread off my thigh, hoping to deflect attention away from the fact that I wasn't mentioning my source, "that Maisy consulted Britt professionally, and paid in cash."

"Really?" Max asked, intrigued and surprised.

"So, maybe there's a motive there somewhere," I said. "I don't mean to harp on the point, but as far as I know, Britt is the only person who *could* have poisoned the wine."

"Why do you say that?"

"I remember drinking my wine and seeing Maisy drink hers, and we were both fine. Then Maisy put her glass on the table alongside mine, and a few minutes later, she picked up a glass, drank from it, and was dead." I shrugged. "I was there. No one but Britt could have done it."

"Whoa! Hold your horses, young lady," he said lightheartedly.

"You remember seeing Britt's arm reach over the wineglasses— although you say you weren't actually looking at him—but okay, even if that's true, there was a roomful of people. Someone would have seen him."

"I know. Except that no one did."

He nodded and ran his fingers through his hair. "Point taken. But let's go back to the motive thing. How do you know that Maisy consulted Britt? Or that she paid in cash? How can you possibly know these things?"

Before I answered, I swung my chair to face the big maple tree, which was barely visible in the late-afternoon dusk. The parking lot's perimeter lights were on, and in the stark white brightness, the autumn leaves glowed an iridescent ruby red.

"I heard from Wes Smith, the reporter."

"Josie," Max said sternly, and I knew I was in for it.

"Yeah?"

"Look at me."

I spun back.

"Why are you talking to a reporter?"

"Wes has access to information I want."

"It's not smart, Josie."

"Why?"

"How can you ask that? Look at the articles he's written, for God's sake!"

"We have an off-the-record agreement now." I shrugged, fighting a wave of fatigue. "I'm scared, Max, really scared, and when I can ask questions and get answers, I feel less frightened."

"What kind of questions?"

"Well, for instance, Wes and I think maybe Maisy was blackmailing someone. She just got a passport and she put four hundred thousand dollars—not a fortune, but not hay, either—in a Swiss bank account."

"Wes told you all of that?"

"No. I found some out on my own. But Wes told me about Maisy consulting Britt and the cash payment."

Max nodded and stroked his nose, thinking. "And?"

"That's it so far. I was thinking that maybe someone could check

194

on Britt—check if he withdrew four hundred thousand dollars, or sold some assets. It would be quite a coincidence if he had."

Max shifted position and glanced at his watch again. "I'm going to have to go." He smiled. "I've got to pick up Mackenzie, my eldest, at ballet."

I smiled, too, and nodded, but I didn't speak.

"We need to tell Detective Rowcliff what you've remembered," Max continued. "And we need to do it now. I'll call him on my cell en route to the ballet school. But you need to know something. I'm betting that the police know about Maisy's account—her finances have been scrutinized, I'm sure. And you can bet that they're using every available means to trace the origin of the money she deposited in Switzerland. But—and it's an important *but,* Josie—until and unless they trace the money *back* to Britt, they won't find where it came from. *The police can't go fishing.* And I've gotta tell you this: I can't imagine how Wes can find out private, confidential, nonpublic financial information like the fact that Maisy paid Britt in cash. It's *outrageous.*"

I started to respond, to tell him that I didn't know, either, but he held up a hand to stop me.

"It's not you doing it, is that correct? It's Wes, right?"

"Yes."

"Good. I'm an officer of the court and I cannot, and will not, have anything to do with any illegal activity. Which is to say, I'm relieved to hear that you're not doing anything illegal, and I'm glad that I don't represent Wes."

I didn't speak for a moment. "I have no reason to think Wes is doing anything illegal."

Max smiled. "Good."

"So you're saying that we shouldn't suggest that Rowcliff look at Britt's accounts?"

"Of course not. We should describe the incident you remembered—and not interpret it. We should talk about what you know, not gossip that you've heard. Short statements that are based on fact. All the same rules apply, Josie."

"Should I talk to Wes?" I asked.

"It would be completely inappropriate for me to recommend that you talk to a reporter—especially one who apparently uses illegal methods to find out people's personal financial information."

I wished my mind was sharper. Given the fear, stress, fatigue, and quantity of information rattling around in my brain, I couldn't be certain, but I thought that Max had just told me to ask Wes without letting him know about it. Max said that it would be inappropriate for *him* to recommend that I consult Wes—but he didn't say that it would be inappropriate for *me* to proceed.

"Okay," I said, meeting his clear-eyed, inscrutable look.

He stood up and shook out a trouser leg. "I'll call Rowcliff now, and I'm sure he'll want to meet with you tomorrow about this and to see if you recognize any Mitsubishi owners' names."

"Max," I said, my voice cracking and my eyes watering. "Thank you."

"Go home, Josie. Get some sleep. Things will look better in the morning."

I nodded.

"Have you met Chi yet?"

"Someone was around and then he wasn't there. I guess that was Chi."

"That sounds like him. Good. You think of anything else, you call me. Okay?"

My smile wavered. "Thank God for you," I managed to say.

"Ah shucks, little lady, you gonna make me blush like a girl."

I listened to his quick-moving steps as he hurried down the spiral stairs, and only when they faded away did I reach for the phone to call Wes.

CHAPTER THIRTY-FIVE

es," I said when I had him on the line, "it's me—Josie."

"What's up?"

"I can't meet in person, so I'm going to be discreet."

"Okay," he said, "shoot."

"You know the appointment we discussed? The one Maisy paid cash for?"

"Yeah. What about it?"

"I'm wondering if there's a chance that *he's* the victim?"

After a pause, he asked, "What do you mean by 'victim'?"

Damn, I thought. *How can I be clearer without naming people?* "Wes, do you remember the European place we discussed?"

"Yes," he replied, sounding excited.

"Right," I said, reassured that he understood my reference to Britt and the Campione d'Italia bank account. "Maybe *he* was the source of the funds."

"Yeah, okay, got ya. Why? What do you know?"

"I remembered something that I can't tell you now."

"Josie," he whined, "I need to know."

"No, you don't. I'll tell you later, when we're back on the record. Now we're off the record, right, Wes?" I said, allowing myself to sound intense and, I hoped, almost threatening.

"Okay, okay," he agreed, backing down.

It was empowering to try to intimidate quick-talking Wes and, in my battered and weary condition, succeed.

"Do you think you'll be able to find out?" I asked.

He chuckled. "Oh yeah, I'll get the goods. No sweat." He sounded bloodthirsty.

"Good. Okay, then."

"I'll call you tomorrow," he said.

If he could find out whether Britt Epps had transferred $400,000—or had gotten that amount in cash—I might be that much closer to finding answers that would help keep me alive.

Ty called and got me on my way home. I pulled off to the side of the road, which was banked by pine needle–covered grass under an arbor of elms and sycamore. I kept the motor running for warmth and turned on the blinkers for safety. The night was dark. Clouds were thickening, promising more rain.

"I heard the news. How are you?" he asked.

"Okay. I'm okay. But it's been pretty much a nightmare from start to finish."

I felt the familiar rush of electricity course through me just hearing his voice. I wished I could see his eyes. I loved his craggy, rough-hewn appearance. He looked weathered, as if he'd been buffeted by harsh storms and survived, with the brown patina and self-confidence to prove it.

Until I moved to New Hampshire, I'd counted on men taking care of me, but I'd learned the hard way that it doesn't work that way. Having lost my father, my boyfriend, and my boss within months of one another, I knew that being independent wasn't an option; it was mandatory. Still, listening to Ty's deep voice, the truth was that all I wanted to do was have him take charge.

Chi passed me, then backed up and pulled even with my car.

I gave him a thumbs-up and pointed to my phone. He nodded and backed up a ways farther. He turned his headlights off and disappeared into the night.

"How come you didn't call?" Ty asked.

"I didn't want to worry you. I'm okay."

"Are you sure?"

"Medium-sure," I said, adding, "how's Aunt Trina?"

"She's having a tough time." He filled me in about her condition, and his concerns. He sounded tired. "I just heard about the theft," he said, changing the subject.

"So fast?" I asked.

"Yeah. I called into work and it was on the scanner."

"It's horrible, Ty. I just can't believe it."

"Any ideas?" he asked.

"Eddie, the caterer."

"How come?"

I shrugged and winced at the motion. I needed this day to be over. "I'm just worn to a nub, Ty. Can I explain details later? I need to get home and eat and go to bed."

"Sure," he said, immediately empathetic. "Just tell me that the police know everything you know."

I pictured surly Detective Rowcliff. "Are you kidding me? Detective Rowcliff?" I joked. "He knows way more than me. Just ask him."

I was starving. After the blissful relaxation of a lavender-scented bath, I was so ready for bed that I debated skipping dinner, then quickly dismissed the idea. The aromas wafting upstairs from the leftover chicken soup I'd put on the burner to warm up enticed me back downstairs. Wrapped in my pink robe, I sat at the oak dinette table to eat. The storm had started as misty drizzle, but the rain quickly became steady. Inside, warm and at ease, I felt cozy.

Ty called. "Are you eating?"

"Just sat down. Why?"

"I thought I'd keep you company."

"What a great idea. Thank you."

"Are you able to answer questions?"

"Able? Sure. Willing? Oh, please don't make me!"

"You sound completely worn out."

Empathy, I knew, was an effective investigative technique. Had Ty called with a professional, not a personal, agenda?

"When did you last see the tureen?" he asked as I blew on a spoonful of soup to cool it. "I mean, when are you *certain* you last saw it?"

"When I was with Britt and Dora reviewing the auction winners. We looked at each item one by one."

"When was that?"

"Monday morning."

"And after that?"

"I didn't see it again until Mitch arrived with Dr. Kimball—that's the winner and his appraiser—a little after three today."

"Who had access to the auction venue between Monday morning and when you discovered the fake?"

"My entire staff—Eric, Gretchen, Sasha, and Fred—and Eddie."

"Eddie's the caterer, right?"

"Right."

"Have I ever met him?"

"I don't think so," I said, considering the question. "But you've heard me talk about him a lot."

"He's the guy with the midlife crisis."

"That's the one."

"And that's it? What about part-timers?"

"No part-timers were on-site, but I suppose anyone could have entered. Gretchen didn't lock up until after Eddie's second visit in the afternoon. But that's a pretty big stretch. Someone would have had to know the place was open *and* know the value of the tureen *and* acquire a fake. Not likely." I took another spoonful of soup.

"What would motivate Eddie to steal the tureen?"

"Money. Did I tell you that he closed his business and moved to Oklahoma to take a job?"

"He did?" I could imagine Ty's face—it would reveal only mild curiosity. Ty wasn't a gambler, but he could have been. Even when he felt things deeply, he didn't show it.

"With Rowcliff's permission, apparently."

"It happens."

"So maybe Eddie needed a stake to start over out west and figured to grab the most expensive piece in the auction. Estimates were listed in the catalog, so he could have easily figured out what to take. Find a Chinese-style tureen, and bada-bing, bada-boom, he's done. Probably he didn't even attempt to replicate the actual tureen. He just wanted something that would delay discovery long enough for him to get out of Dodge. And guess what? It worked."

"What could he get for it?"

"Quickly? A few thousand. If he got it appraised and advertised it in the right circles, more. Maybe as much as ten thousand."

"What was your estimate?"

"Twenty thousand."

"Why the discrepancy?"

"Stolen art and antiques have a limited market. Most collectors would be leery of buying such a valuable piece without a detailed provenance." I shrugged. "Some wouldn't."

"If he advertises it, wouldn't he risk getting caught?"

"Probably not. Most likely, he'd offer it to a shop on consignment, so they'd be the one advertising it, not him. And the tureen isn't unique. Even with the police sending out alerts, there are so many small antiques stores and so many small newsletters and Web sites that it would be like trying to find a ceramic teapot hidden in a pottery store. Pretty much, it would be a long shot."

"And you told Rowcliff your suspicions about Eddie?"

"Officer Shirl—she was the police officer assigned to the theft— I told her. But I didn't go into any detail or anything. Max has drilled it into my head that I should give only brief, directly responsive, fact-based answers when speaking to the police. Sad to say, at this point, I seem to have a fair amount of experience with doing so."

"So that's what he tells you, huh?"

"No comment." I pushed my soup bowl aside. "Back to Eddie," I said, "I have his cell phone number. I was thinking of calling him myself."

"And saying what?"

"Well, that's the problem, actually. I can't figure out what to say or ask him. I mean, after 'Did you steal my tureen?' then what? I can't figure out a follow-up question when he says, 'No, I didn't.'"

"Leave it to the police," he said. "They know the questions to ask."

I shrugged and stayed quiet, unwilling to agree, but lacking the strength to argue.

"How hard would it be to acquire the phony tureen?" Ty asked.

"I don't know exactly. The fake isn't a high-quality one. There are thousands of them out there."

"Where would you buy it?"

"Specialty gift shops. Like Weston's on Market Street," I added, naming a local example.

"How does the theft connect to Maisy's murder?"

I shook my head. "I have no idea. I don't understand any of it."

"What does Max say?"

I thought about my recent conversation with Max and my subsequent call to Wes. I didn't want to tell Ty about it, and I knew why. I wanted to avoid an argument I knew I couldn't win. If I revealed my take on Max's strictures—including what I perceived as Max's faux outrage and veiled encouragement and my call to Wes—Ty would be upset. I could hear him telling me to leave it to the experts—the police. I understood his position, and I disagreed. As Max had said, the police were limited by the law. And from all I could tell, Wes was not. But while I was confident in my decision, I felt too frazzled, overwhelmed, frightened, and exhausted to debate the issue.

Ignoring my father's oft-repeated warning, *If you have to rationalize it, it's probably the wrong thing to do,* I selected part of the truth. "Nothing," I said.

CHAPTER THIRTY-SIX

I slept from eight o'clock Tuesday evening to seven o'clock Wednesday morning, and I would have slept even longer if I hadn't set the alarm. With my eyes closed, I felt around until I located the clock radio's button and quieted the buzzer. After a long minute of drowsing, I slowly sat up.

As I stood in the bathroom, looking at myself under the merciless fluorescent glare, I realized that I wasn't distracted by the throbbing of my ankle. The sharp pain had been replaced by a mild, pulsating ache. When I shrugged, it didn't hurt. The purple surrounding my left eye had faded to a mottled gray, and a greenish yellow hue had been added to the mix. The swelling was down and I could see just fine. My scrapes were still somewhat painful from the recent abrading, but my smile would no longer frighten small children. I was getting better and it felt good to see and feel improvement.

I took a quick shower to wake up, and while I still leaned on the banister as I made my way downstairs, I was relieved that movement hadn't led to wincing or tears. I'd need less grit to get through the day.

I was just about to put my coffee cup in the dishwasher when the phone rang.

"Josie," Zoe whispered, "I'm on my porch watching some guy sneaking around the back of your house. He's in the flower beds by the kitchen. Jesus, Josie, I think you got a stalker."

I pressed my back against the wall and edged toward the hall. I'd left the curtains drawn overnight, but that didn't quell my panic. I couldn't breathe, I was so frightened. "What's he doing now?" I asked.

"He's testing one of the windows, but don't worry, I got my Beretta 391 aimed at the MF's head, the son of a bitch. He tries to get in, he's dead."

I clamped my eyes closed. "Zoe, who is he?"

"I've never seen him before."

"What's he look like?"

"Asian."

"Chi!" I exclaimed, opening my eyes and moving away from the wall.

"What?"

"My bodyguard. He's Chinese. His name is Chi."

"What kind of name is Chi?"

"It means 'energy.' But that's neither here nor there. The point is that you need to stop aiming your gun at him!"

"Okay, okay. But are you sure? Because he's out of sight. He just turned the corner, circling the house."

"I'm sure it's him. Who else could it be?"

"I don't know," she said. "But I don't like it that I can't see him."

"You're scaring me, Zoe," I said. "Where do you think he went?"

"Either into the woods or on the other side of the house. But why was he in the backyard anyway?" she asked.

"Checking things out, I guess. Still, you'd think he would have told me first before he started skulking around."

"Yeah," she said with a small laugh, "that way, you could have told me what he was up to and I wouldn't have aimed a—uppp . . . uggh . . ."

I heard a click, and nearly fainted. "Zoe?" I stupidly called into the phone. "Zoe?"

The doorbell rang a moment later, and I ran to the door. I saddled up to the door and peeked out at a handsome Asian man who stood calmly facing me. He was taller than I expected and lean, like a runner.

"Who is it?" I called.

"Chi."

I swung open the door and saw that he was gripping Zoe by the upper arm. He held her shotgun, business end pointing down, in his other hand.

"You know her?" he asked.

"Of course! Zoe, are you okay?"

"Yeah, I got surprised in a rear attack," she said, making a funny face. But it was clear from her wavering voice that she was shook up, too.

I stared at him, shocked. "What are you doing? Let her go."

"She had a weapon pointed at your back door," he said.

"I was on the phone with her. She was pointing the weapon at you."

He released her, broke open the gun and examined it, then swung it in her direction. "It's unloaded."

She rubbed her arm and took the gun. "Of course it is!" she said to him. "I've got kids."

"Zoe, you crack me up. Protecting me with an empty shotgun."

With the hand not holding the weapon, she pointed her index finger at me. "I meant what I said before. You need me, you call. Okay?"

"You bet."

Chi and I both watched Zoe's progress down the steps and across the October-brown grass to her yard.

"What were you doing around back?" I asked, my heart still racing.

"Looking."

"Looking for what?"

"Just looking."

"You scared us to death! Why didn't you call and tell me what you were doing?"

"I did. Twice."

"What?" I asked, surprised. "Oh, wow, I must have been in the shower."

"May I come in for a minute?"

"Sure." I stepped back to give him room to pass, wondering what he wanted. Inside, he blinked a couple times, his eyes adjusting to the dim inside light, then scanned the entryway and looked through the arch into the kitchen. I had the sense that he was memorizing the layout. His intensity was both frightening and reassuring.

"Do you have a weapon? A gun?" he asked.

"Why?"

He met my eyes, unsmiling, for what felt like a long time. "Mr. Bixby said you wanted protection. I'm trying to provide it."

I nodded, a little discomfited by his stern attitude. "Makes sense. Yes, I own a gun."

"Do you carry it?"

"No."

He nodded and reached for the doorknob.

"Should I?" I asked.

"Do you know how to use it?"

"Yes."

He shrugged. "Think you'd be able to use it for real?"

"Yes."

"Got a permit?"

"Not to carry."

"Up to you, then."

I paused to consider how I felt. My Browning 9mm was upstairs in a drawer of my bedside table. *Would it feel empowering to know I had the means to protect myself from my unknown enemy?* I asked myself. *No,* I decided. The last thing I wanted was something else to be concerned about, and if I had a gun in my purse, I'd worry all the time.

"No," I said, smiling. "I won't take it with me."

He nodded indifferently. "Are you ready to go?"

"In a minute," I responded, thinking I wanted to tidy up the kitchen before I left.

At the sound of a car approaching, I looked up, beyond Chi, and recognized Dora's gold Jaguar. She turned into the driveway.

"Hi, Dora!" I called as she got out.

"Hi there! You got a sec?"

"Sure," I responded, "come on in." She started up the porch steps and I introduced Chi, who nodded coldly in her direction.

"I'll be in my car whenever you're ready," he said.

"Thanks. I won't be long."

"Is that your . . . you know . . . your guard?" Dora whispered as she watched, wide-eyed, as he walked toward his car.

I nodded. "Yes." I held open the door for her to enter. "You're up and about bright and early," I added, eager to change the subject.

"And I'm already done with a meeting!"

"You're kidding!"

"Nope." She laughed a little, embarrassed. "When I saw you on the porch, I couldn't resist stopping. I have good news."

"Excellent!" I said. "I love good news. Come into the kitchen. Do you want a cup of coffee?"

"No, thanks. My meeting was a *breakfast* meeting."

"That's important-sounding."

She smiled again, opening her purse as she followed me into the kitchen. She extracted a slip of blue paper and handed it to me.

It was a personal check made out to the Portsmouth Women's Guild for ten thousand dollars. The signature was neatly written and easy to read, and it was a name I thought I ought to recognize, but I couldn't place it—Marcus Boyd.

"Wow," I said, handing it back. "Who's he?"

"Didn't you meet him? He was at the Gala. He's the CEO of Armitage Flooring," she explained, lowering her voice dramatically.

I nodded, recognizing the company and Boyd's name—the firm was one of the area's largest employers, located near where I lived, and his name had been on the Gala invitation list.

"Congratulations," I said. "You're quite a fund-raiser."

She smiled. "I am, aren't I?" she responded with a soft giggle.

"It's great," I said. "The Guild is lucky to have you."

I slipped my coffee cup into the dishwasher and used a paper towel to wipe down the counter.

She sighed. "Now especially, when there's no one at the helm."

"Have you heard the board's plans?"

"They're meeting tonight to discuss it. Maisy's shoes will be hard to fill."

I nodded, thinking that this, at least, was true. Maisy had been a dedicated employee, seemingly sincerely devoted to the cause.

"You know that the funeral is scheduled for tomorrow?" Dora asked.

Thursday. Only five days since she died. It already felt like weeks. "No. I hadn't heard. When and where?"

"St. John's," she said, "at ten."

"I want to write that down. Where's my purse?" I asked rhetorically. "On the stairs!" I limped over to the staircase, where I'd left my handbag, then dug out my calendar and a pen and noted the time and place on the block labeled THURSDAY.

"Josie, I'm shocked!" Dora mocked as she joined me in the hallway. "You use an actual calendar? I didn't know *anyone* still wrote things down."

"I know, I know. I'm completely old-fashioned."

Dora smiled. As she reached for the front doorknob, she paused and turned back to face me. "It's so good to see you up and about," she said.

I watched through the window until she drove around the bend and disappeared from sight.

When I stepped outside, ready to go, Chi approached me. "What route do you normally take?" he asked.

"I-95."

"Go another way today. You can get there by taking Route One, right?"

"Yeah. Or Ocean Avenue," I said, preparing to slide into the front seat of my rental car.

"That's fine. Take whichever route you want, Route One or Ocean Avenue. Just not 95. Not today."

I agreed and started the engine. *He thinks someone has been watching me, and now, knowing that I almost always take I-95 to get to Prescott's, thinks that whoever wants to kill me might be lying in wait.* With a fresh stab of fear, I wondered if he was right.

CHAPTER THIRTY-SEVEN

I took Ocean Avenue for the view. Dune grasses lay almost flat, blown sideways by the strong easterly wind. Fast-moving gray clouds streaked by, leaving the sky dark and foreboding, and whitecaps dotted the midnight blue ocean waters. From the look of it, we'd have more rain before noon.

I pulled into my usual parking space and made my way across the leaf-strewn lot to the door. As I entered, the phone rang. According to the clock on Gretchen's desk, it was eight twenty-five. I started speaking the routine Prescott's greeting, when the caller interrupted.

"You suddenly remember that Epps could have poisoned the wine and you decide to keep it to yourself?" Detective Rowcliff barked.

"No," I sputtered, "not at all. I mean that I told Max as soon as I remembered and I'm—" I stopped and took a deep breath. *Don't defend reasonable behavior,* I told myself.

"Well, what did you remember?" he asked sarcastically.

I took another deep breath. "Let's talk later. Right now, I'm hanging up and calling Max." And I did.

At ten o'clock, Max and I sat across from a still-wrathful Rowcliff. We were upstairs in my office. I was behind my desk. Max and the detective sat in yellow guest chairs angled to half-face each other and half-face me. Together, our chairs formed a comfortable conversation triangle, but there was little comfort in the room.

"I've read Officer Shirl's report," Rowcliff said, his tone icy.

"And I've spoken to her. So I'm up-to-date. Unless you've remembered some other detail about the theft that you neglected to tell her?"

"No," I said, doing a good job of ignoring his sarcasm, "nothing."

"Are you in the habit of leaving twenty-thousand-dollar antiques out in public?"

"No, of course not. The tureen wasn't in public. My auction venue is secure."

"Except that it wasn't. It was wide open."

"Right. It was an oversight—the doors should have been locked."

"But you let people in unsupervised all the time," he said combatively.

"Only people we know and trust."

He snorted derisively, and I felt stupid in the face of his contempt. Worse, I knew that he was right. It was inexcusable that the outside doors had been left open, and it was probably unwise to let people in unsupervised—even people I knew well, like Eddie, or employees of companies that were bonded, like Macon Cleaners. Worse still, and I hoped I'd never have to tell him, we had a vault that we rarely used, since it was inconvenient to access. I knew better, too. At Frisco's, neglecting to place an object in the vault was a fireable offense.

He took a pencil from an inside pocket and began tapping on his thigh. "Tell me what you remembered about Britt Epps."

I glanced at Max for support, and he nodded encouragingly. "My memory is hazy, but I do remember his reaching across the table." With halting words, I explained what I'd seen.

Rowcliff stopped tapping and listened. "Tell me how the theft and the murder are connected," he said.

"I have no idea."

I met his eyes, waiting. I was telling the truth, but under his uncompromising gaze, I began to feel guilty, as if I were withholding information or lying.

"Do you recognize any of these names?" he asked, pulling a sheaf of papers from an inside pocket.

I accepted the packet and smoothed the fold lines. "Are these the owners of Mitsubishis?" I asked.

"Yeah." He turned to Max. "Still no reports of stolen vehicles or bodywork."

"Max?" I asked, waving the papers.

Max nodded. "It's okay. Take a look."

"What am I looking for?" I asked Max.

"Detective?" Max asked.

Rowcliff looked as if he'd rather drink beer laced with horseradish than solicit my help, but he did so. "First, see if you recognize any names. The car might be owned by someone who lives with someone you know, so, second, see if any address looks familiar. Third, see if any of the tags—the license plates—mean anything to you. Maybe there's a clue in a vanity plate. You know, SNO BUN means 'snow bunny' and GRT CHF means 'great chef.'" He shrugged. "Keep an open mind and see what strikes you."

I nodded and looked down, flipping pages. "How many names are there?"

"A hundred and forty that fit our profile."

"Including all of New England?" I asked.

"Mostly New Hampshire. Other places, too." Rowcliff shrugged.

There were five pages, twenty-eight names to a page. I began to read. Rowcliff shifted position so he could tap his pencil on my desk.

In my first scan through the names, I recognized nothing. Karl Abington was first on the list. He lived on Greene Street in Hanover, and he had an all-number license plate. Marcus Wiggins of Main Street in Manchester, who also had a numbers-only plate, was last.

I shut my eyes for a moment, disappointed, and began again.

Britt, I knew, lived and worked in Portsmouth, and I spotted three cars with in-town addresses. *Surely,* I thought, *if his address is on the list, Rowcliff would have flagged it.* "Did you check if any of the Portsmouth names have anything to do with Britt Epps?"

"Not just the Portsmouth listings. We looked at Epps, your staff, and Trevor Woodleigh."

"How about Eddie?" I asked.

"Sure. All your vendors. And you."

"Me?" I asked, startled.

He leaned back, smirking. "You never know."

"Josie," Max said quietly, "continue looking. See what you notice."

I nodded, pushing my outrage aside. I knew that Max was right: The quickest way to get rid of Rowcliff was to do as he wanted. Righteous arguing or fussing in any way would only delay the inevitable. I took a breath, looked down, and started at the top.

I decided to focus on local names first. Someone named Vivian Bodier from Grove Court in Exeter had license plates reading LDY N WHT. I wondered what it meant. *Lady in white? Lindy and Whitey?*

Also from Exeter were Saul Panzer on Summer Street and Fred Durkin on Haven Lane, both of whom had numbered plates. Henry Avery on Old Locke Road and Sam Rhodes on Sea Road were both from Rye Beach and had numbered plates. Marlie Blanders lived on Wallis Road in a nearby neighborhood known as Wallis Sands. Her license plate read MFB LV DS, and it made me wonder the name of the person she loved. Edward Roland of Pine Road in North Hampton owned one with numbered plates, as did Brooke Stadler, who lived in Newington. Nothing rang a bell.

I took one last look, name by name, and finally gave up. "I'm sorry," I said, putting the pages on my desk, and looked up, trying to hide my disappointment. "Nothing."

Half an hour later, Rowcliff was still at it. I was becoming increasingly irritated and achy, and after a while, I dug the bottle of painkillers out of my purse, shook one into my hand, and swallowed it with water.

"So," Rowcliff said, "I've checked out your staff's backgrounds and cars. No one has any history of arrest, and no one, including your part-timers, drives a Mitsubishi. What do you think of them? Do you like them? Can you imagine any of them involved in any way in any aspect of the murder, the theft, or the attack on you?"

I answered truthfully. "No, I can't. It's incredible to even think about. I've known everyone for years, except Fred, and he came to us with recommendations from a highly respected employment agency that specializes in placing art and antiques professionals."

"How long ago?"

"Six months," I responded.

"Do you know any of them outside of work?"

"Not really. We don't socialize, if that's what you mean."

"Why do you think Eddie is in Oklahoma?" he asked, shifting gears.

"Because he told me he'd accepted a job in Tulsa."

"Have you any new thoughts about why someone would attack you?"

"No. I wish I did."

Rowcliff paused, marking the time with a steady rapping of his pencil.

"Can I ask you something?" Max asked, looking at Rowcliff.

"Sure." The detective narrowed his eyes.

"Does anyone have an alibi for Monday evening when the attack on Josie occurred? Has anyone been eliminated?"

"Just her old boss from New York, Trevor Woodleigh," Rowcliff replied. Max seemed surprised, and I stayed quiet. "We checked out whether anyone rented a car for him last Saturday, and no one did that we can find. But that's pretty much beside the point, since we discovered that he was front and center at some charity event on Monday—the evening you were attacked." He shrugged. "So he's out of it."

"How about Eddie? Have you reached him yet?" Max asked.

Rowcliff twisted his lips, apparently irritated by the question. He leaned forward, aiming his eyes in my direction but speaking to Max. "No. That's why I asked Josie why she thought he went to Oklahoma. We have him in Arizona."

"What?" I exclaimed. "I don't understand."

Rowcliff turned his laser focus in my direction. "What don't you understand?"

"What it means. Do you think he lied?" I asked.

"We're looking into it," Rowcliff replied sharply.

Max caught my eye just as I was about to ask a follow-up ques-

213

tion, and shook his head a little, signaling that I should back off:
Short answers, Josie. Don't volunteer information. How often had
he repeated those words to me? I was champing at the bit to get
details about what seemed, potentially, a huge break in the case,
but I was prepared to obey Max's unspoken instructions, so I simply nodded instead.

"All right, then. Let me ask you this. Are you certain that you
don't know the origin of the fake tureen?" Rowcliff asked out of
the blue.

"That's correct—I don't."

"Yet you recognized it as a reproduction right away. How?"

"I'm an antiques appraiser. Part of what I do is recognize fakes."

"Just because she recognized the tureen as a fake doesn't imply
she knows where it comes from," Max said sternly.

Rowcliff tapped his foot for a long beat, then said, "We tracked
down the importer, and from them, the distributor. Seems they
have a policy of limited distribution. They sell only to specialty
shops and interior-design studios—no mail order or Internet sales,
although there may be some secondary sales on-line. Turns out
there are two design firms and six specialty stores within a hundred miles that stock those tureens. Do you know any interior designers?"

"Sure."

"Who?"

"Several—we sell them things."

"What kind of things?"

I swept my arm wide. "All sorts of things. Period antiques and
bindings, mostly."

"Bindings?"

"Leather-bound books. Collectors care about the book. Designers care about the binding. Will it look pretty on the shelf? We sell
them by the yard."

Rowcliff's lip curled and he shook his head.

"When do you expect to have information about where it was
purchased?" Max asked.

"I have two people making calls tracking sales. We'll know
where we stand by the end of the day, tomorrow at the latest."

A hundred miles—the distance Eddie could realistically have traveled in the hours between when gift stores likely would open on a Monday morning—10:00 A.M.—and his return that afternoon around 1:30 P.M. *Would someone remember selling the tureen to Eddie?* I wondered.

Rowcliff shifted position again, leaned back in his chair, and gave another quick trill of tapping. "Back to the Mitsubishi. Do you maintain customer records?"

"What kind of records?" I asked, bewildered by his question.

"Some kind of database? For mailings, that sort of thing?" he asked impatiently.

"Yes, we do."

"Let me have it. I want to compare names and addresses," he said, reaching for the listing. From his tone, I could tell he thought I was dimmer than a twenty-watt bulb.

"That's a great idea," Max said, jumping in, deflecting Rowcliff's annoyance. "Can you e-mail the file to Josie? Maybe she can do an electronic comparison of some sort."

"Sure." He whipped a cell phone out of his pocket, flipped it open, pushed a quick-dial button, and barked instructions to someone named Feldman. He picked up one of my cards from the little holder on my desk and read off the e-mail address. Sliding the phone back into his side pocket, he added, "It'll be here pronto."

"We'll get right on it," I assured him.

"Good. We'll need yours, too."

"Why?"

"So we can compare them as well."

Max leaned forward and asked in a semiwhisper why I was hesitating. I whispered, "My customer list is valuable to us. I don't want it out of my control."

"Josie is concerned about confidentiality," Max said.

"What is she—a priest? Whoever heard of a customer list being protected?"

Before I could respond, Max raised a hand to quiet me and said to Rowcliff, "We're talking about competitive protection here. She wouldn't want the list to get into the hands of a competitor."

Rowcliff shook his head. "We promise not to hand your list over to another antiques store."

"I don't have a store," I said coldly.

"Whatever."

"With that assurance, Josie will be glad to send her list over. Where do you want it sent?"

Rowcliff took a business card from a leather case and told me to send it to that e-mail address. I passed the instruction on to Gretchen on the intercom.

"Next subject. Officer Shirl tells me that except for yours, there were no clear fingerprints on the Plexiglas display case that contained the tureen. Only smudges. I figure that either it was wiped in a hurry or cleaned badly. So, when was it last cleaned?"

"Gretchen would know for sure, but I think it was Monday. We called Macon, my cleaning service, after you gave the all clear."

He nodded and looked at me. After a moment, he said, "Want to give her a call and ask?" His attitude implied that I was either stupid or uncooperative not to have done it already.

"Sure," I said, and picked up the phone, hating him. When Gretchen answered, I asked, "Has Macon cleaned the auction room yet?"

"No," she replied. "They're coming tomorrow."

"Wow. Why so long?"

"No reason. I didn't think there was any hurry, and Macon was busy. Is there a problem?"

"Nope, no problem. Just curious."

I hung up the phone and turned to Rowcliff. I glanced at Max, wanting to include him in my comment. "Macon hasn't been near the place—and that means it was wiped off sometime after we left the room Monday morning after sticking the Post-it notes on the furniture."

With a final tap of his pencil, Rowcliff stood up. "I'm taking over the investigation—the theft of your tureen. Officer Shirl and I agreed that since the theft and the murder are probably related somehow—or might be—it made sense to put the investigations together."

"What does this mean to Josie?" Max asked.

"It means that if she thinks of anything else," he said, turning to me, his voice low and threatening, "she calls me, not Officer Shirl—and not a reporter."

Before I could react to his menace and insult, Max spoke. "As always, Detective, Josie is glad to cooperate."

"Call me later," he said to me, "and let me know what you discover when you compare lists." Every word Rowcliff uttered was, it seemed, intended to intimidate. Some people would have spoken the words so they sounded collaborative, but Rowcliff turned them into an accusation, as if I'd planned on withholding the information.

"She'll call me," Max said in a friendly voice, "and I'll call you."

"This afternoon," Rowcliff insisted.

Max looked at me. I shrugged. "We'll do our best," I said. "If the database fields are identical, we can do a merge/purge quickly and easily. If not, and we have to compare lists by hand, it'll take longer."

"I'll call you later," Max said to Rowcliff with a friendly smile, "and give you an update."

Rowcliff nodded and paused at the door to add, "Call my cell."

"You bet," Max assured him.

Once his footsteps had faded away, Max turned to me and, still smiling, said, "Down, girl!"

I controlled myself and forced a smile. "Yeah. He does have that effect on me, doesn't he?"

Max shook his head good-naturedly. "Oil and water is all."

"That's one way of putting it." I took a deep breath as I tried to calm myself. "Now what?" I asked.

"Now we let the police do their work and you get going on identifying the Mitsubishi," he replied with a reassuring smile as he slid his notepad into his briefcase, preparing to leave. "And you let me ask the tough questions."

"What do you mean?" I asked.

"Like whether Eddie has disappeared."

I nodded, understanding that Max was trying to protect me from Rowcliff's anger. If Max asked the questions, the detective's rage would be directed at him, not me.

The rain began. I turned to look out of the window. The sky was solid gray and the branches on the maple tree swayed in the rain-swept wind. Dark red and gold leaves fell heavily to the ground.

"Oh my God!" I exclaimed.

Max stopped what he was doing to look at me. "What?" he asked.

It was so obvious, I couldn't believe it hadn't occurred to me before: All Eddie would have had to do was spike the wine in advance and deliver it to Maisy. He was on the floor throughout the Gala, overseeing the service and assisting his wait staff. No one would have noticed.

"I just thought of something," I replied, shocked. "I just realized that Eddie could have delivered the poisoned wine directly into Maisy's hands."

"But what possible motive could he have had to kill her?" Max asked after I explained, sounding unconvinced.

"I don't know," I acknowledged. "Maybe Maisy saw him steal something at some event. Or maybe she caught him overcharging someone." I shrugged. "Obviously, I don't have any idea what she found out—if she learned anything, which is, of course, purely a guess on my part—but I do know this much: If Maisy discovered Eddie doing anything illegal or immoral, and *if* she threatened him with exposure, his business was doomed. And maybe that was the threat she held over his head to blackmail him—pay or I ruin you."

Max nodded, following my logic.

"And that would have made him desperate . . . maybe as desperate as a cornered rat."

"Next time I talk to Detective Rowcliff," Max said, capping his pen, "I'll work it into the conversation and see what he says."

Something my father had told me years earlier came to me. I couldn't recall the circumstances leading up to his warning, but I remembered well the apprehension his words engendered. *Remember, Josie,* he said, *cornered rats almost always survive.*

CHAPTER THIRTY-EIGHT

As Max was saying good-bye, the intercom rang. It was Gretchen.

"I'm sorry to disturb you, Josie. Britt Epps is here. I told him you were in a meeting, but he said it was urgent, so I thought I'd better call up."

"Give me a sec, Gretchen," I said, and pushed the hold button. I turned to Max. "Gretchen tells me Britt Epps is here—something urgent, he says. Do you want to stay?"

"Absolutely."

"What should I do?" I asked him, uncertain of my ground.

Max sat down again and looked at me as if he'd find the answer on my face. "Do you have any idea what he wants?" he asked.

"No."

"Let's hear him out."

"Okay." I reached for the phone. "I wonder if he ran into Detective Rowcliff. God, if he did, Britt is going to think I'm a suspect myself."

"Nah," Max said, reassuringly. "Whether he says anything or not, I'll mention that we just were finishing up a meeting with Detective Rowcliff. There's nothing wrong with letting him know that you're working closely with the police to get to the bottom of things."

"Are you sure?"

"Yes," he said, smiling.

I nodded and pushed the hold button to release Gretchen from telecommunications limbo. "Bring him up, will you, Gretchen?"

The rain was steadier now, and the wind brisker. The maple

tree's limbs softly pattered against the building. While we waited, I checked my e-mail.

"Detective Rowcliff's e-mail has arrived," I said to Max.

"Forward it to me, okay? You never know. I may recognize something."

"Good point," I said, and did so, sending it also to Gretchen, adding that I'd explain why later.

I heard the click-clack of Gretchen's heels and the solid thud of Britt's sturdier shoes as they made their way across the warehouse floor and up the stairs. Gretchen politely knocked on the open door before stepping across the threshold.

"Britt," I said, pushing myself upright as he entered, his oversized pilot's case in hand, "welcome. How are you?"

"I'm fine. Just fine. And you?" he asked, nodding to Max. "I hope you got my message, Josie. Terrible. Terrible."

"Thank you, Britt. I'm feeling much better today."

I gestured to the chair that had recently been occupied by Detective Rowcliff and said, "Have a seat, Britt. What can I do for you?"

He cleared his throat and glanced again at Max. "Are you sure I'm not intruding?"

"We were just finishing up," Max said. "We had a very productive meeting with Detective Rowcliff. You know him, of course, don't you?"

"Certainly. A terrible thing, terrible," he said, and I wondered if he was still referring to my attack or if he was thinking of Maisy's murder. "Any news?" he asked, lowering his voice portentously.

"Not that I'm privy to, but apparently, the police have several good leads," Max responded, sounding as if he knew more than he was telling. "Josie is helping all she can, of course."

"As are we all!" Britt said. "Josie," he continued, giving an awkward cough, "I need to discuss something with you, and I hope you won't be offended if I'm very direct."

My heart began to throb at his words. *Oh no,* I said to myself, *please beat around the bush and drive me crazy with innuendo.* "Absolutely, Britt. You know me—I always prefer direct."

"All right, then," he said, nodding, his tone low and serious. He shifted position, crossing his chunky legs and leaning forward. "Have you heard from any of the winning bidders?"

His question was so completely unexpected, it took me a few seconds to respond. "I'm not sure I know what you mean. Gretchen has been in touch with *all* the winning bidders."

"Well," he said with a sigh, and a quick glance at Max, "given the scandals that continue to come to light, I just have to wonder if we were going to lose anyone." He added, "I have to think of what's best for the Guild. I'm sure you understand."

I was appalled, both by the implication that Prescott's was so riddled with problems that no one would want to do business with us and by the fact that Max was listening. It was humiliating. Yet I knew that he was right. One whiff of scandal and customers flee.

I was depressingly familiar with both the transitory nature of fads and the insidious influence of snobbery. Right now, it was fashionable to support the Portsmouth Women's Guild, but if the winning bidders thought that they might be tainted by associating with us, they'd find excuses not to honor their pledges. On some level, I felt grateful to Britt for raising the issue; on another, it just made me mad. But knowing how easily perception becomes reality, I knew I needed to push aside my indignation and fear and switch into crisis-management mode. It was crucial that I convey confidence—step one in trying to change perception. Step two would be to receive official vindication. And step three was to ensure that I received an onslaught of positive media coverage positioning me as a stoic victim. With any luck, Wes would write my story as news, so it wouldn't read like self-congratulatory fluff. I smiled, thinking that he would be pleased to know I was including him in my plans.

I gave what I hoped sounded like a reassuring chuckle. "No one's backed out, Britt," I said with a warm smile. "Everything looks fine."

"What about the theft?" he asked, lowering his voice dramatically. "I heard about it, and it won't be long before everyone does."

Because you'll tell them, you nosy old Parker.

"And I wondered what the Guild should do to distance itself from the scandal. You understand, I'm sure, Josie, the difficult position this puts us in."

I knew he was correct, but I was livid nonetheless. *How dare he insinuate that Guild members need to distance themselves from my company!* I wanted to pound the desk, order him off my property, and never speak to the pompous ass again. Instead, I took a deep breath. "I think you're overstating it, Britt. Sadly, a theft isn't that unusual—things happen. Plus, the antiques speak for themselves."

"I don't know. . . ."

"Have you heard anything specific?" I asked, praying the answer would be no. "If so, I'd be glad to talk to people directly to reassure them."

"Maybe that's what we should do . . . call everyone and invite them in for some sort of explanatory meeting," he said enthusiastically, no doubt envisioning another opportunity to be the big man on campus.

"I really think that's making too big of a deal of what is, after all, an isolated incident, Britt," Max said, jumping in.

"Do you?" he asked, sounding dubious.

I understood why Max voiced his objection, and I was grateful. Britt seemed determined to whip a minor worry into a frothy witch's brew of trouble. Max was equally determined to help me maintain control and solve the problem.

"Why don't I make some exploratory calls to confirm the pickups? Assuming things are still a go, that should reassure you," I said, trying not to sound patronizing.

"That's a good idea. In fact, let me give you some suggestions about whom in particular you should call. I know everyone, you know," he added in a semiwhisper, as if he were revealing a secret, "so I'm in a good position to say who's most likely to run shy."

"Sure," I said without sarcasm, "that would be helpful."

"Let me just get the list. . . . It's right here in my case. . . . I won't be a second. I have the results here somewhere," he said as he leaned over, opened the case's flaps, and began to paw through his files. "I'll be just one more sec. . . . That's the downside of having such a big case! I can never find anything in it." He gave a self-conscious chuckle.

And then I remembered. My mouth gaped open and Max, watching me closely, leaned forward to catch my eye as Britt continued his hunt. He mouthed, "Are you okay?"

I couldn't speak, not to Britt, still rustling through his papers, nor to Max, his concern visibly mounting as he stared at me. All I could do was stare into the middle distance, a stricken look on my face.

How could I have forgotten? I thought, rebuking myself.

After we'd finished applying the Post-its to the displays, Gretchen and I stayed in the front office while Britt went to the rest room, carrying his pilot's case—his *oversized* pilot's case.

CHAPTER THIRTY-NINE

Max got rid of him and said he wanted to call Detective Rowcliff right away. I stood while he scanned through his cell phone's outgoing-call log looking for Rowcliff's number. "I'll tell him about how Eddie could have delivered the wine, as well," Max said.

"But wouldn't Eddie's fingerprints have been on the glass?"

"Easy enough to hold it with a napkin or something," Max said, shrugging.

My shoulders felt stiff with tension. "I'll be downstairs," I said. "I want to get Gretchen started on the Mitsubishi project."

"You okay?" Max asked as I started off toward the stairs.

"About what you'd expect," I responded with a smile that probably looked more sad than happy.

"Also," Gretchen said to Eric as I entered, "you work on the mailings."

"Well, not really. I mean, it's not really part of my job or anything. I just help out."

"Eric!" Gretchen protested with a small laugh. "You've stuffed more envelopes than anyone else for every mailing we've ever done!"

"It's not a big deal," he said with a shrug.

"That's not the point," Gretchen told him firmly. "We're supposed to list everything you do—not just those tasks that you think are important." Gretchen turned to me and smiled. "You have a message," she said. "Dora called. Here's the address for Friday's Literacy Matters luncheon."

I accepted the slip of paper and read the address—Old Locke Road. "I didn't know she lived in Rye Beach," I remarked.

Gretchen giggled, and I could tell she'd love to have a good gossip about it. "She doesn't. The lunch is at Hank's place—her boyfriend. Remember him from the Gala? He was *so* cute. The trombone player."

Eric looked painfully uncomfortable.

"Right," I replied. "I remember. Did she say why she's holding it there and not at her own place?"

"She said his place has the better view—it's on the ocean."

I nodded. "Anything else?"

"Nope. That's it!"

"So, Sasha," I said, turning in her direction. "How are you doing?"

"Great, actually. I heard from Monsieur Roi's grandson." Her eyes were dancing. "The Picasso sketch was sold by this fellow's father in the late sixties to a family friend who'd married an American woman. Guess where she was from?"

"Tell me it was Arkansas."

"Yes! And I spoke to her myself—she sold the print to the gallery in 1973—the same year Mrs. Finn's mother bought it!"

"Which means you've done it! You've confirmed its history!"

She slid her desk chair back on the plastic carpet protector and smiled confidently. "Yup!"

"Isn't that great!" Gretchen chimed in.

"Have you called Fred?" I asked, thinking that he wouldn't object to the interruption on his day off.

Sasha blushed and looked down. "I did. I couldn't wait."

"And?" I asked, smiling.

"And he shouted, he was so happy," she said with another blush, embarrassed, I suspected, at Fred's unprecedented exclamation of victory.

"This is just great. Good job, Sasha." She blushed again, this time with pleasure and pride. "Next step: Would you prepare a list for me of which museums have collections of Picasso—and if you can find out, which ones want to?"

"Yes," she replied, her smile fading into a look of concentration, her mind already on the job.

"How's it going for you guys?" I asked, turning back to Eric and Gretchen.

"Fantasmic!" Gretchen answered, never shy. "Eric is in a state of shock, I think, now that he sees in black and white how much he does!"

I glanced at him and saw that he was smiling awkwardly, enjoying Gretchen's teasing.

"No wonder he looks so tired!" I joked, playing along.

"I'm not," he protested, still smiling.

"Well, you should be!" Gretchen said, laughing a little. "And I have the spreadsheet to prove it!"

Eric stood up. "Are we done for now? I've got work to do," he said with a self-conscious laugh.

"We'll pick up tomorrow," Gretchen said. "Keep thinking!"

He nodded, and as he pushed through the door to the warehouse, the phone rang.

Gretchen swung around to answer it. "Prescott's," she said with her usual verve, and a moment later, she said, "Absolutely. We'd be pleased to look at it. Anytime, until five."

As she hung up, she said, "A woman who inherited a box of old leather books wants to sell them and wondered if she could stop by later today."

"Excellent!" I said, hoping they were volumes of interest, and that she'd cover them in plastic to protect them from the rain.

I was stockpiling rare books for an auction I hoped to hold next year, and it would be terrific if we could acquire some additional volumes of merit—eighteenth-century English literature, for example, or important volumes published in America. Maybe, with luck, tucked into the box might be a first edition of something written by Samuel Johnson, the one so many people know only as "the dictionary fellow." Or perhaps there would be a book or two of hand-colored illustrations of flowers or costumes used in opera. *Just don't let it be filled with battered textbooks from the thirties,* I thought. Those little leather volumes were charming, yet they had essentially no resale value.

Refocusing on the pressing issue at hand, I asked, "Were you able to open Detective Rowcliff's attachment?"

"I can open it with no problem," Gretchen assured me. "The file's from the same database program we use."

I explained what we were looking for and she nodded, listening hard.

"I can do a dupe check. No problem."

"A 'dupe check'?" I asked.

"Yeah. I can eliminate duplicate entries, so if I create a new file containing both our database and Detective Rowcliff's, I can use that function for this purpose."

"Good. Let me know as soon as you learn anything. Okay?"

"Anything?" I asked Max when he entered the office. I hadn't heard him come down the stairs.

"Rowcliff thanked you and said he'd be in touch," he said.

"You shouldn't do an ad hoc revision," I told him, trying to keep the mood light. "Rowcliff never thanked me. But I can believe that he said he'd be in touch."

Max laughed. "True enough. I did use a little editorial license."

"So, tell me the truth. Is he mad at me again?"

"Nothing he won't recover from. I told him to call me to schedule an appointment whenever he's ready to meet with you again."

I tried to smile, but I didn't have the strength to fake it. Max shrugged into his coat and turned up the collar. He gave me an empathetic shoulder pat, then ran for his car.

CHAPTER FORTY

S oon after Max left, the chimes sang out, announcing an arrival. I turned and saw Wes's stocky form awkwardly pushing through the door. He was breathing hard, winded by the run from his car to our office. He wasn't wearing a raincoat and the small black umbrella he carried had a broken spoke. Drops of water dripped steadily on the floor.

Gretchen popped up from her desk and took the sodden umbrella from his hands. "Oh, wow, it's really coming down, isn't it?" she said with her bright, welcoming smile. "I'll just put your umbrella here in the stand, okay?"

"Thanks. It's pretty wet," he agreed.

"Hey, Wes," I said.

"Got a sec?"

I couldn't imagine why he was here. After all our circumspection, for him to boldly walk in was an anomaly that smacked of danger. My trouble meter whirred into high alert. "Sure," I said. "Follow me."

I led the way through the warehouse and unlocked the door to the tag-sale area where we'd met before. Tomorrow, Thursday, the place would become a beehive of activity as Eric and a gaggle of temporary and part-time workers began to set up the displays for Saturday's all-day tag sale. By Friday midday, they'd be done. But today, the tables were bare.

Sometimes I questioned my policy of returning all unsold items to inventory and starting the setup from scratch each week, because the procedure added hours of extra work, but I couldn't think of an easier way to ensure that our displays always looked fresh. Over the years, I'd concluded that merchandising was an art form. For instance, I'd observed that a cobalt blue bud vase looked different when it was positioned among glassware than it did when it was placed next to a lamp in a display of living room knickknacks. One buyer wouldn't even notice the vase in the midst of all the glasses, but would leap on it in the living room display. Another buyer, who collected only items made of cobalt-colored glass, might not even visit the living room display area.

"I'm surprised you're here," I said. "I expected you to call, not just show up."

Wes nodded. "I need to talk to you. On the record."

Rain pounded at the building and rivulets of water streamed down the windows. It was a good day to be inside. I turned on the lights and the globe-covered high-wattage bulbs overcame the dull grayness of the stormy day.

I tilted my head, considering him. "What about?"

"The theft of the tureen."

Damn, I thought, *just what I need—another hit of bad publicity.* "What do you know about the theft?" I asked.

"Why? So you can see how little you have to tell me?"

"I don't have to tell you anything, Wes," I said, unyielding.

"I'm writing tomorrow's lead about it—and don't be thinking that it's covered by our off-the-record arrangement, because it's not. That only applies to the murder."

"Wes, if you write one word about this, you'll be sorry forever. I promise you. Not one word, do you hear me?"

"Josie, it's my job to write about crimes. Theft is a crime. Talk to me. Control the spin," he said, his tone reasoned.

The more rational Wes sounded, the more worried I became. The inevitability of seeing my name in print in the morning loomed large. I flashed on Detective Rowcliff's last admonition—not to talk to reporters—and smiled. *How could I resist?* Talk about killing two birds with one stone. With one innocuous quote, I'd help Wes and irritate Rowcliff.

"Okay. Here goes. Are you ready?"

Wes pulled his crumpled notepad out of his pocket and nodded. "Go," he said.

"Everyone at Prescott's is shocked and appalled by the theft. The circumstances are under investigation by the police and we have every confidence that the tureen and the perpetrator of this terrible crime will be located quickly. All staff members at Prescott's are cooperating fully with the police. It was an isolated incident, a fluke, an unfortunate onetime event. Prescott's has state-of-the-art security and a highly professional staff." I paused to think if there was anything else I should add, taking solace from the thought that Wes must hate my white-bread statement.

"Come on, Josie. That sounds like a press release."

"Well, why not? You're the press. Those are my only words on the subject. Our other arrangement stands, right, Wes?"

"What did you discuss with Detective Rowcliff?" he asked.

"The theft. He asked if I knew who stole it and I told him no."

"What else?"

"That's it."

"No way, Josie." He looked up. "All you told me was that you met with the police."

"No comment."

"Okay, okay. Let me ask you to verify some facts."

Wes peppered me with questions that revealed a detailed knowledge of the crime, once again suggesting that he had access to inside sources. He knew about the smudged fingerprints, Eddie's surprise reappearance at my building Monday afternoon, and the limited distribution of reproduction tureens. Britt, I guessed, the old gossip, was responsible for some of his inside scoop. But he also had to have a police source.

I neither confirmed nor denied anything. "Would you agree that I have refused to discuss the details of the case with you?" I asked.

"Hell, yes!"

"Do you have any reason to think I have any guilty knowledge of the theft?"

"No." He looked at me for a minute. "Why?"

"I expect to read both of those facts in your article tomorrow."

He made a note. "Fair enough."

"I'll tell you something else—but it's got to be off the record," I said.

He sighed, acting put-upon. "Okay. What?"

"Eddie is MIA."

"What do you mean?"

"You heard me—but you can't quote me. The police can't find him."

Wes's eyes lit up in anticipation of a new lead. "What do you know?" he demanded, all business.

"The police think he's in Arizona. I have him in Oklahoma."

"Got it." He made a note. "What else?"

"That's it. They can't reach him." I shrugged and paused as he wrote. "Can I ask you something?" I said when he looked up.

"Sure," he replied.

"Do you have any new information about the origin of the money in Maisy's account?"

"Yeah. It takes us nowhere, though."

"How so?"

"It was moved through six U.S. cities—starting in New Orleans and ending in Atlanta. From there, it went to Montreal, and then offshore to Belize."

"And then to Europe?"

"No record. Belize keeps banking private."

"I thought those days were gone."

"No way. Have you ever heard of the MLAT?"

"No. What's that?"

"The Mutual Legal Assistance Treaty. Belize doesn't adhere to it."

"Wow. So the whole point of moving the money around is to muddy the waters?"

"Exactly. To make it harder to trace."

"But it sounds as if you were able to do so."

"Yeah, but tracking it is of no real value, because at each stop along the way, there's a different name. Some accounts are personal, some corporate. Sometimes the money moved in one lump payment, sometimes in several payments over a few weeks."

"All electronic transfers?"

"Yup."

"I wonder who's behind it."

"That's the sixty-four-thousand-dollar question," Wes said.

"My mom used to say that. 'The sixty-four-thousand-dollar question,'" I commented, remembering.

"Mine, too."

Funny to think about Wes having a mother. I smiled at him but didn't pursue the conversation. Instead, I asked, "What about Britt? Were you able to trace the origin of the four hundred thousand?"

"No dice. Britt Epps has not made a big withdrawal, nor sold any asset of record, during the last year."

"Really?" I asked, astonished. *How can that be?* I thought. *I was so certain that we were onto something.*

"Yup, looks like he's not the one we're looking for."

I sat for a moment, thinking. "Unless he keeps a lot of money under his mattress or something."

"I suppose," he said without enthusiasm. "To tell you the truth, Josie, I think it's another false lead."

"Yeah, maybe."

"And you know what that means. No money, no blackmail. No blackmail, no motive."

I shook my head. "Yeah."

He gave me a long, penetrating look. I didn't flinch.

"Anything else?" I asked indifferently.

"Yeah, but you won't discuss it."

"My word is good, Wes. You know that," I responded, knowing the importance of maintaining good relations with the press. "As soon as I can tell you more, I will. Exclusive to you."

He shrugged. "Okay, then."

"You'll let me know about Eddie?" I asked as I led the way back toward the warehouse.

"Yeah. So how are you, anyway?" he asked as we walked.

Ignoring the fact that his solicitous inquiry was his last thought, not his first, I told him I was improving.

Wes was in a hurry to leave and seemed oblivious to Gretchen's good-natured chat as he got his umbrella opened; then, with a final wave, he dashed across the lot to his car. The rain seemed to be coming sideways now, heavier than ever.

It has *to be Britt,* I thought. *How can it* not *be?* But if Wes was right, and it wasn't Britt who'd poisoned Maisy and funded her Swiss account, who had? *Eddie?* No way did he have access to that kind of money. *Unless,* I thought, shocked at the idea, *he has, in fact, been stealing for a while, and the four hundred thousand dollars sitting in Maisy's account are the ill-gotten proceeds of his thievery.*

Britt or Eddie? Or, I suddenly wondered, was there someone else responsible for the murder, theft, and the attack on me? Someone I hadn't even considered as a possible suspect? I had no idea. I was overwhelmingly confused. Not knowing who might lurk around the next corner, or what they might do next, was terrifying. I had no control over events, and I knew it. And I was on my own.

Shivers of fear rippled up my arms like goose bumps.

CHAPTER FORTY-ONE

G retchen called to say there were no matches between our database and the police listing of Mitsubishis. "I ran a dupe check for each field," she said.

I sighed. I'd felt so hopeful, and now I was, once again, baffled and disheartened.

I racked my brain trying to think of who else might own the Mitsubishi—or if it had been stolen specifically to attack me, why it hadn't been reported missing. *Maybe the owner is out of town,* I thought, *and no one has noticed that it is gone.* If so, the report would come in sooner or later, I supposed. I shook my head, frustrated.

A thought occurred to me and I gripped the phone in a spasm of panic. *Unless Gretchen lied*—all she'd have to do is delete one of the entries in our database before sending it on to the police and comparing the lists herself, and neither the police nor I would ever know that we had a hit. It felt as if I'd catapulted through time into the petrifying hall of mirrors of my childhood and I could no longer trust my perceptions.

Work the problem, I reminded myself. *Don't make things worse by panicking.* I took a deep breath and closed my eyes for a moment. *How can I test Gretchen's integrity?*

"How many names are there in the combined file?" I asked, opening my eyes and reaching for the up-to-date customer list that I kept in a three-ring binder on my desk.

One of Gretchen's thousands of duties was replacing the pages whenever she updated the database so that I always had a hard-copy backup, just in case of computer failure. I flipped to the last page—a man named Martin G. Yardley was last on the list, customer number 1,429.

"Let me see . . ." Gretchen said. "Fifteen hundred and sixty-nine."

The 140 names on Rowcliff's list plus 1,429 on ours totaled 1,569. Tears stung my eyes, but I managed to thank her and hang up without revealing my emotionalism. I felt drained. *I can't take the anxiety—the struggle—the not knowing who's out to get me,* I thought. *I'm so sorry, Gretchen, for doubting you. I just can't stand it.* But I knew I could—and would—endure. After a moment, I took a deep breath and considered what to do next.

I swiveled toward the window, anxiety fading away. It was early afternoon, but darker than dusk. Most of the branches had been stripped bare by the relentlessly driving rain. I turned back to my desk and dialed Max.

"No luck, Max," I said when I had him on the line. "There's no match."

He paused. "That's too bad, isn't it?"

"Yeah. And worse, I think I'm going crazy." My voice cracked. "This whole thing is making me see devils in the shadows."

"What do you mean?"

"I just did a check on Gretchen, to see if she'd deleted any names."

"Why would she do that?" he asked.

"I have no reason to think she would, but she *could* have. So I checked. I added the one hundred and forty names on Detective Rowcliff's list to the number of entries in our database and had her confirm that that's the number she had in the combined file."

"That's pretty clever, Josie. I'm not sure I would have thought of that."

"Desperate times lead to suspicious thinking. On the one hand, I'm completely relieved that she passed my test. On the other, I'm disgusted with myself for even considering that it was possible that she wouldn't have."

"I take a different view. I think you're smart, Josie. You know the saying: 'Trust, but verify.'"

"Yeah—I guess. I keep thinking that the switch of tureens must be an inside job."

"You can't know one way or another until we have more information. And until we find out what's going on, you can't be too careful."

"Do you think we'll ever know?" I asked, fighting tears as a wave of hopelessness washed over me.

"You bet. I have a lot of confidence that one of the avenues Detective Rowcliff is pursuing will pan out."

"Why? Nothing has so far."

"You'll see. I've got a good feeling about it. . . . There's going to be a break soon."

"Thanks, Max."

"No problem. I'll call Detective Rowcliff and let him know the results."

I hung up the phone, exhausted and discouraged. I scanned my office. There were no projects that enticed me, no deadlines that had to be met, and nothing that was waiting for my immediate attention. I didn't know what to do. *Stop it,* I chastised myself. *When you don't know what's best to do,* my father once advised, *pick the least bad of the alternatives. If you still don't know what to do, stop thinking about it. Instead, call a friend and have some fun for a while.* I called directory assistance and got Zoe's phone number.

"Hello," she said, a cacophony of clattering in the background.

"My God, Zoe! It sounds like World War Three has broken out in your living room."

"That's about right. Except that I'm in the kitchen. It's Emma making war. She's commandeered all of the pots and pans. And the lids."

I laughed and felt better already. "I'll let you get back to your peacekeeping duties. I was hoping you and the kids could come to dinner tonight."

"You're a lifesaver. I was just thinking that I wouldn't be able to cook because I had no pots or pans!" She laughed heartily.

I smiled, thrilled by her acceptance. "Come about seven, okay? Is that too late for the kids?"

"Nope, it's perfect."

"Anything you're allergic to? Anything you hate?"

"You cook it, I'll love it!"

"How about the kids?"

"They're easy. . . . I'll bring mac and cheese and they'll be happy."

"Are you sure? I can make it."

"Not like Mama you can't! No, I'll bring their mac and cheese, their jammies, and a bottle of wine; you do the rest. How's that?"

"Great! See you at seven."

I allowed myself a small *attagirl* for finding the strength to make the call to my new maybe friend, the first step, perhaps, in finding a chink in the wall of my self-limiting isolation.

I closed my eyes, allowing myself to enjoy the relaxation that came from thinking of my mother's recipes. *What should I make for dinner?* After considering and rejecting several options, I decided on roast chicken with homemade stuffing, and following my mother's instructions to add complex flavors to balance the simplicity of the chicken, herb-stuffed tomatoes, broccoli with a lemon-tarragon sauce, and chocolate bundles for dessert.

I wrote the grocery list, and called Chi to alert him that I was going grocery shopping, then home. He thanked me for calling and told me he was on the property and ready when I was.

Downstairs, I entered the office just as a young woman with pink-tinted hair and six earrings in her right ear perched on a guest chair. Her eyes were intent on Sasha as she sorted through a box of leather-bound books.

I could tell by the undistinguished gold-tooled spines that most were uninteresting twentieth-century volumes, but a couple bound in mahogany-colored leather looked intriguing, and I noted that Sasha had set those aside.

Sasha straightened up, twirling her hair, a sure sign that she was nervous. "You said you wanted to sell them. Is that right?" Sasha asked.

"Yeah. That's right," she responded.

"I can offer you forty dollars."

That worked out to about four dollars a volume, a fair offer for leather-bound books of no particular value.

"No way," the pink-haired woman argued, looking shocked. Another seller with an unrealistic notion of value.

"I'm sorry I can't offer more," Sasha said softly. She began to replace the books in the box.

"Oh, man, jeez. Are you trying to rip me off?"

"No, no," Sasha said, appalled. "It's just that that's what they're worth to us."

Pink hair flying, the woman jumped up and slammed the remaining books into the box. *Don't take it out on the books,* I silently entreated, wincing.

"What a joke," she snorted. She lifted the box as if it had some heft and shielded it from the relentless rain with her body. I watched as she quickly walked to an old beat-up Chevy truck waiting in front with its engine idling. She ripped open the passenger door, hoisted the box onto the seat, and jumped in. The truck screeched away.

"Anything there?" I asked Sasha, who stood with her head down, looking troubled.

"Not really," she said. "Maybe I should have explained why the price was so low."

"Maybe," I said, acknowledging her remark with a shrug. "But it probably wouldn't have made any difference. You win some, and you lose some. It's no big deal."

Gretchen wasn't in the office. I inferred that she was on break, because I could see the home page of one of her favorite celebrity gossip Web sites on her computer monitor. Instead of tracking her down, I asked Sasha to tell her I'd left for the day.

Zoe arrived in a laughing fuss of backpacks, umbrellas, children, bedrolls, and plastic containers. I accepted coats, packages, blankets, and a bottle of wine. Jake began a running survey throughout the downstairs rooms, screaming, and Emma wailed, wanting to be picked up.

"Come on, sweetie! Are you going to help Mama get the bedrolls ready?"

"I can't believe you brought bedrolls!"

"Are you kidding? By eight, I hope they're both dead to the world. I love them to death, but they're exhausting." She turned to Jake, still tearing through the house. "Jake, come here, darlin'! Look!"

He paused long enough to glance at the sliding-piece puzzle she was handing him, happily screeched, "I can do it!" and plunked down on the living room carpet.

"Zoe?" I said, having become aware of her raiment. She wore a full-length floral-patterned flannel nightgown with little ruffles at the hem and cuffs.

"What?" she responded, guiding Emma in unrolling the bedroll on the carpet.

"Why are you wearing a nightgown?" I inquired, bemused.

"Oh God!" she exclaimed, spinning around to face me, her eyes huge. "Don't tell me there are other guests."

"No, no, just us."

"Okay, then," she said, and turned back to her task.

"But why?"

"They wouldn't put on their jammies unless I put on mine," she said in a tone of abject resignation.

"Of course," I replied, and started laughing.

By the time Zoe left around ten o'clock, I felt calmer and more prepared to cope with my confusing situation than I had in a long time. We dashed back and forth carrying Jake and Emma, both fast asleep and swaddled in their bedrolls, and all their supplies, laughing as we leaped puddles. My muscles and ankle complained, but not much.

On her final trip, she told me, "This was great! Thanks, Josie. Best damn chicken I've ever had!"

"It meant a lot that you were here."

And then she was gone and I was alone.

Ty phoned around eleven. I was in bed reading *Plot It Yourself.*

"Aunt Trina seems to be weakening," he told me.

"How come?"

"They don't know."

"That sounds frightening."

"It happens."

"And you're okay with that?"

"What do you mean?"

"Well, it sounds a little unclear is all. Do you think you should get a second opinion or something?"

A too-long pause made me feel as if I'd said the wrong thing. "We'll be fine," he finally responded.

"What does that mean?" I asked, sitting up, slapping the book aside, spine side up.

"Nothing."

"What do you mean 'nothing'?"

"Not now, Josie."

"Right. No problem."

I hung up, gently cradling the phone, looked at the blank wall across from the bed, the one I intended to decorate with seashells, or family pictures or something, and thought, *Why bother? If Ty doesn't want to confide in me, so be it. If I have to watch every word I say for fear of offending him or overstepping his unspoken boundaries, forget it. Maybe he's not quiet and deep like I thought. Maybe he's emotionally unavailable or domineering. Maybe he just can't stand a woman who voices an opinion that implies he might have made a mistake.* I shook my head. *Would he let Aunt Trina continue to weaken, maybe even die, rather than accept unsolicited advice? No way. Not Ty. Ty is reasonable and rational and open,* I reassured myself. *Unless my perception that he's a good man is wrong.*

Doubt and despondency once again replaced hope. I had no energy for anything but switching off the light. I turned toward the window. Usually, slivers of moonlight were visible at the outer edges of the shades, but not tonight. Tonight, the sky was blacker than ink, and the windswept rain hammered the house unceasingly. I plumped the pillow and tried to sleep, but I couldn't seem to find a comfortable spot.

The phone rang, but of the people who were likely to be calling, there was no one to whom I wanted to speak—not Wes with his unrelenting demands for information, nor Ty with his closed heart and glib explanations, nor Rowcliff with an emergency question. No one. I let the machine pick up. It was Ty and his words were utterly disarming.

"Please pick up, Josie. . . . Josie, please. . . . I'm sorry. I don't know why I froze exactly, but—"

I picked up the phone. "It's me, Ty."

"Josie."

"It's okay. Apology accepted."

"Thanks." He paused, then added, "I got a second opinion this afternoon."

"Good." After an awkward silence, I added, "That gives you more confidence, I'm sure."

"Yes."

Another pause. *Reach out,* I thought. "Are you okay?"

He gave a nonfunny laugh. "I've been better. But, yeah, I'm okay. How about you?"

"Yeah."

"When this is over—well, I was thinking—"

"What?" I asked, my heart beginning to race. *Tell me!*

"Let's go away."

"Away like sell our possessions, change our names, and move to Vegas? Or away like a vacation in the Bahamas?"

He laughed a little, this time sounding amused. "The latter. I'm thinking heat, water, drinks with little umbrellas, tropical nights."

"Oh God, let's go now."

"Soon," he said.

I smiled. "Date."

We ended the call promising to talk in the morning, and I lay back down, pleased but still concerned. Could I meet his expectations? Ty was reserved, but when he opened up, he had a lot to give. If asked, would he say the same about me?

I forced myself to be still and try to sleep, but instead, I thrashed and rolled from side to side until the sheets were tangled around my neck, the quilt was on the floor, and my pillow somehow had ended up under my feet. Resigned to wakefulness, I sat up in bed and rested my head on my hands. *How will I endure the night?* I wondered.

CHAPTER FORTY-TWO

I must have slept, because when I awoke, I was cold to my bones. The quilt was once again on the floor. Hurrying into the bathroom, I caught a look at myself in the mirror in the gray morning light. I looked like hell. My skin was white-blue pale, my eyes were rimmed in red, and my bruises had faded to a sickly green.

I took a fast hot shower, then went back into the bedroom, wrapped in my pink chenille robe. After putting on some makeup, trying to disguise my green-tinted, too-pale skin, I dressed for Maisy's funeral. The black slacks, moss-colored blouse, black-and-green tweedy blazer, and black leather ankle boots were appropriate for church, but not for work, so I packed jeans and a flannel shirt, my standard work wear, along with my work boots, in a large tote bag.

As I walked slowly downstairs, leaning heavily on the banister, I felt overwhelmed with fatigue and barely controlled panic. I was in no shape to cook. Instead, I treated myself to breakfast at the Portsmouth Diner.

I bought a *USA Today* from a vending machine just inside the front door—I didn't want any local news—and sat in a small booth at the rear of the restaurant for almost an hour, relishing the companionable hum of early-morning customers.

I decided to call Ty, just to check in, but didn't reach him. It was early. I left a message on his cell phone, reminding him that I'd be at Maisy's funeral until around noon.

When I got to my building, I sought out Eric and found him in the warehouse, loading inventory onto a cart for transport to the tag sale. I wanted to be certain he included the six boxes of highly sought-after 1950s vintage barware, all in good shape, I'd recently acquired.

"Perfect," I said, "for Christmas gift buying."

We discussed display ideas for about ten minutes; then I went upstairs to my office, fighting the anxiety and fear that threatened to paralyze me. It took all of my willpower to sit and review last month's financials.

I had gotten to Maisy's funeral a few minutes early and I sat alone in a pew near the back. I scanned the room for people I knew, recognizing several.

Mitch and Rochelle, the winning bidders of the stolen tureen, sat fairly close to Maisy's husband, Walter, in the front row. Walter looked shell-shocked. Pam sat alone, about halfway back. Dora was off to the right, near the front, skewed around, chatting earnestly with a couple I'd never seen before. Britt was nearby, sitting next to a couple I'd seen at the Gala but hadn't met.

No one spoke to me until Detective Rowcliff slid into my pew. I felt my heart begin to thump, and I scooched my purse toward me, as if it were a buffer that could somehow protect me from him.

"I need to talk to you," he whispered fiercely.

"Sure," I responded.

"Later today."

"I'll talk to Max and we'll arrange something."

"I'll call him," he said. "Let's try for two o'clock. We have a lot to talk about."

Ominous, I thought. "Sure. If Max is available," I said.

Rowcliff got up and moved to the far corner—the better to see everything that was going on. I kept alert, too, but noticed nothing that provided a clue. Still, my anxiety level continued to rise, and I didn't know why.

I left the church as soon as the service was over. It was still raining, and it, along with the mournful hymns and sorrowful eulogy, left me feeling sad in addition to panicky. I noticed a patrol car three cars back, following me. I was glad to get to work, and gladder still when I saw the glint in Fred's eye. *Let there be good news,* I thought.

"What?" I asked him as I placed my dripping umbrella in the stand near the door.

"One of Mrs. McCarthy's bowls isn't just a bowl," he said. "It looks like a bowl, but it's not. I called her and asked about it. She looked around and called me back."

"And?"

"And she found something in an old trunk."

"How intriguing. What?"

"A nearly black centerpiece with lions and tigers and other figures positioned around a palm tree. Eight black supports extend from the tree and lead to black circles. Seven supports have black bowls with cut-glass inserts suspended from the circles—one black bowl is missing." He pushed his glasses up, smiling. "I had her describe them."

"And?"

"And she said that they all were simple in design, with only a fancy pattern along the rim for decoration. Here," he said, handing me a silver dish, "look."

I reached for it, noted the gadrooned border, and turned it over. On the bottom were three hallmarks—an anchor, a lion passant, and a lower case *a.*

"Birmingham," I said, recognizing the anchor. "Nineteenth century?" I guessed.

"Right."

"Cut to the chase, my friend. What have you got?" I asked him, smiling, handing back the bowl.

"I don't know, but I think we ought to get our hands on that piece quickly."

I understood the implication. If Fred's instincts were correct, the black centerpiece would metamorphose into silver when polished. Lions and tigers? The piece sounded like a nineteenth-century epergne, perhaps unique, and potentially valuable.

"Is she interested in selling it?" I asked.

"Yes." He smiled, looking proud of himself.

As well he should be. "Great catch, Fred," I said, impressed.

I glanced at the Mickey Mouse clock on Gretchen's desk. "Give her a call, will you?" I asked. I wanted to get my hands on it before Mrs. McCarthy called another dealer. "See if I can stop by today. Four, four thirty?"

"Sure," he said.

The phone rang and Sasha answered it. "Prescott's," she began, "how may I help you?"

I was pushing through the door to the warehouse, intending to see how Eric was faring with the tag sale, when Sasha gestured for me to come back.

"It's Max," she said, her voice hushed.

I nodded and took the call at Gretchen's desk. "Max," I said.

"I understand you saw Detective Rowcliff this morning."

"Don't remind me."

"Sorry to break it to you, but we have an appointment with him at two thirty."

"Two thirty?" I questioned. "I thought he wanted two."

"He asked for two. I held out for two thirty."

"How come?"

"'Cause he seems to think we're at his beck and call, and I decided it was time to show a little independence."

I laughed and brushed hair out of my eyes. "I knew it was only a matter of time before he got to you."

"Yeah. Well, I made my point."

"What's his problem?" I asked.

"Persistent jerkitis, as far as I can tell." He chuckled a little, and added, "Don't get me wrong—Rowcliff has a reputation as a top detective, diligent and creative, but no one ever said he was personable."

I laughed again and felt a slight lightening of the melancholy weighing me down, but I didn't comment.

"Do you know what he wants to discuss?" Max asked.

"No clue."

"Well, we'll know soon enough."

As I hung up, I turned to Fred. "Mrs. McCarthy—four thirty."

The phone rang again, and Sasha said that I had a call from Wes on line one.

"Josie," Wes said, without even a hello, "I have news. We have to get together right away."

My heart skipped a beat. "That will be difficult," I said.

"If you can't get away, let's meet at your place, same as before. I'm right around the corner and can be there in two minutes."

"Okay," I said after a moment's consideration.

"Two minutes," he repeated, and hung up.

As I walked toward the tag-sale area, Sasha's voice came over the PA system. "Eric, Gretchen on line one," her voice crackled.

Odd, I thought, that Gretchen would be calling Eric on her day off.

I opened the door that led into the tag-sale room and spotted Valerie, a long-term part-timer, putting the final touches on a sewing display. Quilts hung on black bars, and thimbles and pincushions were encased in a glass-topped cabinet. We chatted for a moment. Eric hung up the phone, saw me, and hurried over, looking worried.

"Is everything all right?" I asked, walking to join him.

"Yeah, why?"

"You look concerned," I said.

"I thought maybe I did something wrong," he replied.

"Why?"

"You don't usually come in to check on me this early in the setup."

Wow, I thought, *am I that intimidating?* "Nah," I told him, and play-punched his arm, "you didn't do anything wrong. I'm heading outside to see about something is all."

I smiled and continued down the center aisle. I noticed that Valerie was now sorting art prints by subject matter.

The rain had tapered off to a thick mist, not quite a drizzle, yet more than fog. It felt good on my skin, rich with moisture. Still, it was cold. Wes was waiting outside the locked gate, and with a glance over my shoulder to ensure that no one had followed me, I unlocked it and let him in.

"There are people working just inside, so we ought to be quick," I explained, leading him to a corner, out of the direct line of sight.

"Sure, sure," Wes agreed. "Listen, here's the thing. It's about Eddie." Wes exuded excitement, and I knew the look—he was hot on the trail of something.

"What?" I asked.

"The police can't reach him," he said.

"That's not news. The police think he's in Arizona, and he told me he was going to Oklahoma. So . . . ?"

"So, he's not returning phone calls."

"Why not?" I asked.

"The police have decided that he's officially off the radar."

"Really?"

"Yup. Completely gonzo."

"You're kidding!" I exclaimed.

"Nope. It's true."

My head was spinning as I considered possible repercussions. "Why? Just because he's not returning phone calls?" I shrugged. "Maybe he lost his phone."

Wes shook his head. "It's not that, or not only that." He nearly vibrated, he was so animated.

"What else?" I asked eagerly, his enthusiasm contagious.

"The company he told the police he was going to work for—you know, that big hospitality company?"

"What about them?"

"They say they've never heard of him," he stated dramatically.

It took several seconds before Wes's words registered. "How can that be?"

"Bingo. That's the question. Sounds like he's on the lam," he said, excited.

"Wow," I said, "I just can't believe it."

"Kind of amazing, huh?"

"Now what?" I asked, nodding.

"Now the police get serious about locating him. They've applied for search warrants—they're going to try to track him down by his cell phone info, his bank accounts, his change-of-address forms, and so on. If he's filed any change forms at all," he said doubtfully.

"But I figure it'll be a washout even if Eddie's on the up-and-up, 'cause if he's relocating, he probably doesn't even have a new address yet."

I nodded. "Good point, Wes. That sounds right." I thought of my conversation with Max. *The police are limited in what they can do, but I'm not.*

Wes started to speak and I held up a hand to stop him. "Wait," I said, thinking, passing my idea through a sieve of potential obstacles.

"What is it?"

I shook my head and turned away. I could see no objection and no difficulty. "It's possible," I said aloud.

"What?" Wes asked eagerly.

I smiled like a cat who swallowed a canary. "I've got an idea."

CHAPTER FORTY-THREE

F ifteen minutes later, I implemented my plan—calling Eddie from my office phone so his phone would display a number he'd recognize.

I escorted Wes in through the rarely used side door, peeked into the warehouse and saw no one, and, with my heart pounding, led Wes across the concrete span and up the spiral staircase to my office. We made it unseen.

As I got settled at my desk, Wes stood in the middle of the room, examining my office with interest.

"You like chickens, huh?" he asked, pointing to a bamboo and glass cabinet filled with a collection of metal, wood, and porcelain roosters.

"They're roosters," I responded, "not chickens."

"Oh, yeah?" he said indifferently, then turned toward me. "You ready?"

"Piece of cake," I assured him, and picked up the phone.

I dialed Eddie's cell phone number and, as expected, got his voice mail. "Hi, Eddie, it's Josie. How ya doing? Listen, you know how we always pay you right away upon receipt of the invoice, right? Well, looks like we were too quick off the mark this time. My accountant tells me we shorted you for five people at the Gala, and since I got the full amount from the Guild, we need to be sure you get your share. Call and tell me where to send the money, okay? Talk to you soon!" I said, and gave my phone number.

I hung up, turned to Wes, and said, "And now we wait."

"How long do you think it'll be before he calls back?"

Even before I could respond, Sasha called on the intercom to tell me that Eddie was on the line. I blew on my nails and rubbed them on my lapel, bragging.

"I bow before you," Wes said, and did so. "As a con woman, you've got potential."

"You know, I've often thought the same thing about myself. I don't know if that's a good thing or not."

"You all set?" Wes asked, smiling a little at my comment.

I was jump-out-of-my-skin excited, focused, and ready. "You bet," I said with confidence. I punched the line-one button and activated the speakerphone function. "Eddie?"

"Sorry I missed the call, Josie, I was just walking out of the john. So how's it going?"

"Pretty good, Eddie. Pretty good. Well, truth be told, you know how it is—things are actually kind of crazy around here, what with the murder and all."

"Sure, sure. Any news?" Eddie asked, his tone solemn.

"Nope. Nothing yet."

He sighed but didn't respond. I heard the muffled blare of a truck's air horn in the distance.

"How about you?" I asked. "Are you with the cowboys yet?"

He chuckled. "You're kidding me, right? According to the sign on the highway, I'm only in Springfield, Missouri. This is one big country we've got here, you know?"

"Well, all things considered, you sound pretty good, Eddie."

"Thanks, Josie."

"So, Eddie, for when we figure this thing out and I need to send you something, do you have a forwarding address?"

"Not yet. I've got the post office holding my mail until I get a place."

"Tell me again where you're going."

"Briar Ridge."

"That's in Tulsa, right?"

"You got it."

"So do you want to call me when you're settled in?"

"Sure, I could do that. Or you could send the check directly to my bank in New Hampshire," Eddie said.

"No, we can't make deposits. Why don't I just send it to you care of your job? That'll work, right?"

"Yeah, I guess. That would be fine."

"Briar Ridge," I repeated. "You got the street address?"

"Sure, just a second." I heard rustling papers; then Eddie said, "You ready?"

"Yup."

"Briar Ridge Inn, 5862 Dalworth Street."

"Tulsa, right?"

"You got it."

"What's the zip code?" I asked.

"It's 85353."

"Perfect! Let me talk to my accountant tomorrow and I'll call you. Okay?"

"Sure," Eddie said. He lowered his voice to a radio-persona pitch and added, "This is your friend Eddie, heading west and signing off. Good night and good luck."

Without speaking, I brought up a browser and entered the zip code into the search window. When Tolleson, Arizona, came up, my mouth opened but no words came. I looked up at Wes, his eyes fiery-alive.

"Well?" he asked.

"He's going to Tolleson, Arizona. I guess it was my mistake to hear it as Tulsa and fill in Oklahoma."

Wes spread his hands and shook his head. "What do you think it means, Josie?"

"I don't know."

He paused. "Now what?" he asked.

"We look at him—but we look at other people, too," I said as I stood up and started for the stairs.

Wes paused at the outside door and said, "Like Britt, right? As a suspect, I mean."

I thought about his question. A droplet of water dripped on me from the gutter above the doorway. I stepped back inside, shaking my head, shivering in the afternoon chill. The rain had stopped, but the sky remained thick with dense clouds.

252

"I thought Britt was out of it. You told me that there was no indication that he transferred the money to Maisy, right?"

Wes nodded, deep in thought. "Right."

He marched toward the parking lot. He looked less rotund from the rear, and less young. After a few steps, he turned to face me. "We're back to knowing nothing, you know?" he said.

I nodded but didn't speak. I couldn't think of what to say.

"Let's talk soon," he said, and stomped away.

I called Max as soon as I got back to the office and filled him in about Eddie.

"Curiouser and curiouser," Max said.

"Yeah," I agreed.

When he arrived later, about a minute ahead of Rowcliff, I asked him if he had any new thoughts.

"No," he said, "but we're close to answers. I can smell it."

I smiled at his unwarranted optimism.

"I'll tell the detective about Eddie's call," he said.

"Okay."

When Rowcliff arrived and we were settled upstairs, Max turned to the detective and said, "Josie spoke to Eddie a little while ago."

Rowcliff tapped his foot for a moment and glanced at me. "Oh?" he asked, turning the word into an accusation.

"He called about a money issue," Max explained.

"What did he say?" Rowcliff asked me.

Max nodded, indicating I could respond.

I took a deep breath. "Not much. Except that he's still on the road. He said he was just passing Springfield, Missouri. And I was wrong—he *is* going to Arizona, not Oklahoma. I heard Tulsa, when what he was saying was 'Tolleson.'"

Rowcliff nodded and paused. "He just called for no reason?" he asked.

"I'd left him a voice mail and he called me back."

"Why did you call him?"

"I might owe him some money," I fibbed, "so I needed his new address."

Rowcliff's eyes narrowed and I sensed heightened interest as he leaned forward. "Did you get it?"

I shook my head. "He doesn't have one yet. But I got his business address." I handed over the paper on which I'd written the Briar Ridge Inn's address. "He said I could send a check to him there."

Rowcliff transferred the information into his notebook and handed the paper back to me.

"When was this?"

"About an hour ago."

He excused himself to make a call. I heard him give Eddie's address to whoever answered on the other end. "Call them now and find out when he's supposed to start work," he instructed.

While he spoke, I turned and looked outside. The sky was brighter and it looked as if the mist was lifting.

Rowcliff slapped his phone closed and slid it into his jacket pocket. "What else?" he barked.

"Nothing," I responded, hiding my irritation at Rowcliff's confrontational attitude. "I'm glad to have helped."

His face reddened, and I got the impression that thanking me wasn't high on his "to do" list.

"Detective?" Max piped up, apparently trying to head off sparks.

"Yeah? What?"

"You asked to meet with us. Why?"

Rowcliff shifted position and his leg began to jiggle. "There are two things I want to discuss with you," he said to me. "I'd appreciate your assistance," he added, as if he'd rather jump off a cliff than ask.

"If I can, I will," I said.

"First thing I need is a list of who was at the Gala."

"I don't understand. You got the list right after the murder."

"No, what I got was a seating chart. What I need is to know who was actually there—you know, maybe someone brought a friend because his wife got sick, or maybe someone forgot to RSVP and just showed up. That sort of thing. I need to know exactly who was there and who wasn't."

I nodded. "I don't know everyone. Actually, I don't know most of the people, so I can't help. To tell you the truth, I don't think that anyone tracked it that closely."

Rowcliff nodded. "Who might have noticed?" he asked.

"Britt Epps."

"Who else?"

I thought for a minute. "I'm not sure. Probably, there were lots of people there who could help you—people who were more involved with the Guild, or who've lived in Portsmouth longer than I have. But I don't know them."

He sighed deeply, signaling disappointment. "Turn my question around. Was there anyone you expected to see at the Gala who *wasn't* there?"

I didn't know what he was driving at. "No," I said. "Why?"

"Just looking for anything out of whack. Okay, then. Next subject: We found what we think is the source of the fake tureen."

"That's great!" I exclaimed.

Max shot me a *be quiet* look.

"It's only great news if we can ID the buyer," Rowcliff said sharply. "There was one sold locally—at Weston's here in town— on Friday, for cash. None was sold at any of the other stores and shops located within the hundred-mile range we set within the last week."

"Who bought it?" Max asked.

"A man, and since it was bought for cash, there's no record of his name. But the store's register tracks the time of every purchase, so we know that the sale occurred between noon and one."

"Lunchtime," Max said.

"Right."

"Do you have a description?" Max asked.

"Yeah. He's tall, young, kind of gangly, with sandy-blond or even lighter-colored hair. And he's soft-spoken." Rowcliff turned to me. "Does that ring a bell?"

Eric? I thought, shocked. *No,* I protested to myself. Pushing aside my instinctive objection, I reminded myself to consider the possibility objectively. Was it conceivable that Eric could and would do such a thing? Self-deprecating Eric? It was hard to imagine that

255

he'd have the wherewithal to pull it off. But still, the description fit.

"How young is 'young'?" I asked, hoping Rowcliff would state an age older than twenty.

"Somewhere between twenty-five and thirty-five. But that's not a sure thing. Could be younger. Could be older."

"How come the description is so vague?" Max asked.

Rowcliff stopped tapping and shook his head, looking disgusted. "The clerk is nearsighted and her glasses are out of date. We're lucky to have what we got. All I can tell you for sure is that he was a tall, thin, young Caucasian male with light-colored hair."

I was having trouble breathing. The description exactly matched Eric. But *why* would he do such a thing? What possible motive could he have?

"From the description," Max said, "it doesn't sound like either Britt or Eddie."

"Right. We showed the clerk their pictures. Not even close."

I felt sick and turned to look out the window. Fog was thickening, obscuring the view. The storm wasn't over.

"Josie?" Max asked gently. "Does the description ring a bell?"

I stayed still, trying to think what to say.

"What?" Rowcliff urged when I didn't immediately respond.

"Eric," I whispered. "But it's absurd," I said, meeting Rowcliff's eyes. "I know him. He'd *never* do such a thing."

Right, Rowcliff's face conveyed, *and the check is in the mail and I'll love you in the morning.*

My eyes smarted at unexpected tears.

"Where was he last Friday, at lunchtime?" Rowcliff asked.

I breathed deeply until I felt able to answer. With Max and Rowcliff staring at me, I called up our on-line schedule. "Friday, he was here all day—setting up the tag sale."

"When did he take lunch?"

"I don't know. I don't track it that closely."

"Got a photograph of him?" Rowcliff demanded.

Without commenting, I reached into my bottom desk drawer and sorted through miscellaneous photos. I found one from about four months ago, taken by a waiter. I'd treated my staff to a night out, and you could tell by our unposed smiles that we were having a good time. I handed it over. "That's him. On the left."

Rowcliff took it, and after a quick glance, he slipped it in his pocket. He stood up. "I'll be in touch."

CHAPTER FORTY-FOUR

J ust after Max left, Gretchen buzzed up to tell me that Ty
was on line two.

"Hi," I said, punching the button.

"How's it going?" Ty asked.

"Okay," I responded, and filled him in.

"Sounds like Rowcliff is being thorough. How about you? You okay?" he asked.

"Yes. More or less."

"Anything I can do to help?"

"Not now," I said softly, "but thanks."

"You let me know, okay?"

"You're going to be sorry you offered. By the time you get home, I'll have a long, long list."

He laughed and said, "Good. I work well with lists."

I smiled and asked, "How about you? Are you okay?"

"Same as you. Yes—more or less."

"How's Aunt Trina?"

"The doctors keep reminding me that she's almost ninety."

"That's awful."

"Is it? Or is it realistic?"

He sounded sad, and I understood why.

"Both. It's both," I said, and then I added, "I understand." After I hung up, I realized that I'd spoken without thought, and suddenly I felt sick.

It had been perilously easy to utter the conventional words of acceptance—*I understand*. And as it happened, I *did* understand why Ty had posed the question—"Or is it realistic?" He was bracing for Aunt Trina's death—without fruitlessly lashing out at the doctors or indulging in childish wishful thinking. No, he was a decent man doing the right thing, practical and competent, but it made him sad.

But that wasn't why I'd said it. My motivation was less altruistic and more self-serving—I hoped to please him, and that could only mean that I was more invested in him than I'd thus far admitted to myself. Apparently, I was willing to say whatever I thought he wanted to hear. In this case, the words were true, but what about the next time? *If necessary to keep his love, would I hide my feelings? Would I pretend that everything was okay even if it wasn't? Just how far would I go? How many lies would I tell?*

I'd seen what happened when friends lied to their boyfriends or husbands under the guise of protectionism, hoping to preserve their egos or hide their own needs or ambition: They were lulled by the continued appearance of intimacy into thinking that all was well. But I knew that deceit wore through the fabric of a relationship as surely as a moth destroys wool, and inevitably, the women found themselves in the chasm of isolation they'd lied to avoid.

I pivoted to face the window and examined the newly bare branches on my maple tree through the misty fog. I looked to the left, to the west toward Los Angeles, over the barely visible tops of the birch trees that ringed my property, past the spire of the Presbyterian church. *I'll never lie to you, Ty,* I promised. *Not once.*

The route I followed to reach Mrs. McCarthy in Dover took me directly past the old Victorian house where Eric lived with his ill-tempered mother. About halfway there, I spotted Chi's blue car, far back.

As I went by Eric's house, I saw that while it was in as bad shape as I remembered, apparently repairs were under way. There was a sign in the front yard declaring that Wallace Contractors were on the job, but I saw no workers. *The rain,* I thought. *They'll be back at work tomorrow.*

Knowing how seriously Eric took his responsibility to care for his mother, I could only imagine what a great sense of accomplishment it must be to him to be able to make repairs. I hoped his mother would appreciate his efforts, but having witnessed her morose discontent, I doubted it.

All at once, I felt my heart begin to race. *Four hundred thousand would fund a lot of repairs,* I thought, appalled. *Eric? No way.* I chased the depressing thought out of my head.

I parked in front of Mrs. McCarthy's elegant center-entrance Colonial, and as I walked up the pathway, I glanced around. I saw nothing unusual. No sign of Chi or his blue sports car, nor of anyone else. I rang the bell.

"Come upstairs, dear," Mrs. McCarthy said, and led the way to a small room at the back of the house. "You can't imagine how surprised I was to discover this thing! I'd forgotten all about it. I haven't seen it in years!"

She pointed to an enormous, elaborate black—tarnished silver, probably—epergne. An ornate temple stood in the center, completely surrounded by a detailed jungle scene. There were tigers, elephants, and lions; palm trees, bamboo, and willowy flowering plants; and sepoys and palanquins were positioned here and there in and about the jungle. Eight leaf-capped branches twisted throughout the panorama, each branch ending with a circular brace, all but one of which supported a bowl with a gadrooned border—the same style of bowl Fred had shown me—and each bowl cupped a cut-glass dish. The seven bowls were all black. I extracted one of the bowls and turned it over, silently praying, *Please, God, let the hallmarks match.* And there they were—the same anchor, lion passant, and lower case *a* that marked the bowl back at the office.

Turning to Mrs. McCarthy, who was eagerly awaiting my judgment, I said, "When it's polished, it will be spectacular."

"Do you think so?" she asked skeptically.

"I'm quite confident," I replied. "Do you know where it came from?"

Mrs. McCarthy looked embarrassed. "I'm afraid not. It's so big, I've never displayed it. I don't even know what it is."

"It's called an epergne. Believe it or not, it was used as a centerpiece. Can you imagine how big the table must have been to support it!"

"With all those wild animals," she said, pointing to a lion squatting on his haunches, poised to pounce, "it doesn't seem suitable for family dinners, does it?"

I laughed. "Depends on the family, I guess. But actually, it probably was used for ceremonial dinners."

"Really? How do you know?"

"Well, that's just an educated guess. I may be wrong. We'll know more when we look into it."

"Do you think it's very old?" she asked. Knowing sellers, my guess was that her question was euphemistic and what she really wanted to know was how much it was worth.

"Most likely, it dates from the early nineteenth century. I suspect it's quite valuable," I said.

"I'll keep my fingers crossed," she said, "that it sells for a lot."

"You know I'll do my best to get a good price for it," I promised.

She watched as I packed it carefully, using supplies I'd brought along, and signed the updated consignment agreement. I thanked her, feeling enormously gratified that she trusted me and my company with her treasures.

Ty called to say a quick good night, and after hanging up, I found myself filled with restless energy. I swept the kitchen floor and did a load of laundry, and then, desperate to relax, I took a long lavender-scented bath, and it worked. Not even my constant fretting about Eric's possible role in the tureen theft kept me from sleeping well.

Following instructions to vary my route into work, I took Route 1. As I exited the Old Post Road, I thought I saw Chi's blue car glint by, but I couldn't be sure.

I greeted Gretchen after her day off, then went to the tag-sale room and helped Eric organize a large display of Christmas-themed decorative and household items—from pottery Santa Clauses to vintage Dickens village houses and from fake trees to sets of dishes festooned with boughs of holly and berries. Around ten o'clock I returned to the main office and sat with Sasha and Fred to brain-storm how to research Mrs. McCarthy's epergne.

"The jungle suggests that it was created for someone who lived in one of the British colonies—India, probably," I said.

"Or someone who'd been there and felt nostalgic—it was made in Birmingham, after all," Fred commented.

"Yeah," I agreed, "that's possible. Maybe someone who made his fortune in India and then returned home to England. How will you start to trace it?"

"With the maker," Sasha said. "Some of them kept records of their important pieces."

I nodded. "Sounds good. Keep me posted."

I left just after noon to drive to Dora's Literacy Matters luncheon at her boyfriend's beachfront house in Rye Beach. The weather was far sunnier than the day before. It was perfect for a fall event—bright and crisp. For reasons that seemed to have more to do with a good night's sleep, pleasing conversations with Ty, and the weather than confidence that Rowcliff was close to solving the crimes, my mood was sunnier, too. Regardless, I was relieved to be feeling better

Hank's house was small but spectacular, traditional in design and built on stilts to maximize the ocean view. I recognized Hank by his blond ponytail as he stood with his back to me just inside the ground-level garage, which had been converted into what ap-peared to be a workshop of some sort. Barnlike doors stood open and I saw a dozen or so trombones, trumpets, and other brass in-struments suspended on Peg-Boards affixed to the back wall.

As I walked across the street and up the driveway, I glanced around and saw Dora's gold Jaguar, but none of the other cars ranged along the street or in the driveway looked familiar.

"Hi," I called.

Hank turned around. "Hi, there," he said.

"I'm Josie. We met at the Gala."

"Sure," he said, "I remember."

"I don't know if I ever got a chance to tell you how much I en-joyed the music." He'd been the trombone player in the small group.

"Thanks."

"You don't play all those, do you?" I asked, gesturing toward the instruments hanging in the back.

"Hardly. I do instrument repair."

"Really? Like what?" I asked.

"I work on brass instruments—you know, a little of this and a little of that," he said, and shrugged. "I knock dings out of bells, replate mouthpieces, adjust valves, that sort of thing. Mostly repairs on school instruments."

"Interesting," I said, smiling. "Is Dora upstairs?"

"Yeah. Take the stairs by the front."

"Nice seeing you again."

I looked toward the ocean as I climbed the steps and paused on the half landing. Hank had an unobstructed view of the dunes and the ocean beyond. Dune grass and late-blooming sea roses swayed in the easy breeze, the sapphire-colored water sparkled in the bright sun, and white-tipped waves rolled in with the tide.

Dora opened the door before I reached the top. "Josie! I'm so completely thrilled that you're here!" She held the door open so I could enter. "Let me look at you! Aren't you a quick healer. If I'd been through what you've been through—well, I wouldn't look as good as you do, I can tell you that!"

I was flustered by her comment and didn't know what to say, so I simply smiled and murmured, "Thank you." She whisked me in and introduced me to the other attendees, none of whom I'd ever met. The six other participants were women, all older than I, and all were pleasant. The conversation throughout the luncheon was varied, but if the truth be told, superficial and, I acknowledged to myself, boring.

It was only after lunch was finished and donations had been solicited and received that I had a chance to fully appreciate Hank's house. Standing on the jalousie porch that jutted out toward the ocean, I could hear the peaceful sound of thunderous waves even through the closed windows.

"What a great place," I commented to Dora.

"Isn't it? It's been in his family for generations, and it's hard to imagine a more beautiful spot," Dora replied.

"He seems very nice. I spoke to him briefly on my way in."

"We're good together," Dora said, staring pensively at the beach. "He's quiet, kind of introspective. He has lots of substance below the surface." She laughed suddenly and turned to me, her charm bracelet jingling. "They say opposites attract, right? Well, we know I'm neither quiet nor introspective. But that's where the opposite commentary stops!"

I smiled. "Absolutely," I responded as if on cue. "Everyone knows there's great substance to you."

"Forced you into that one, didn't I?" she said with a chuckle.

I shook my head, smiled, but didn't respond. I was never comfortable with teasing chat.

"Have you heard anything from the police? Are they making any progress?" Dora asked after a moment.

"Not that I know of," I replied, "but I'm not sure they'd tell me. I think they have several lines of investigation they're pursuing."

"Like what?"

I shrugged. "I think they're making progress on the purchase of the fake tureen. And they know the make of the car that tried to run me down."

"That *is* progress, isn't it?"

She didn't look at me, but kept her focus on the ocean, as if answers would wash in along with the roiling waves. I followed her gaze, and we stood without speaking, two friends sharing a private moment.

I laughed and she turned to me, smiling, eager to share the joke.

"I'm laughing," I explained, "because you just finished telling me that you aren't introspective—yet here we are, both of us lost in our own thoughts."

"Oh dear!" she said with a soft laugh. "I'm found out!"

"Your cover's blown. There's substance, and you're introspective, too."

"Thank you, Josie." She was going to add something, but the moment was shattered when my cell phone beeped, alerting me to a message. I felt myself tense as I listened to Max ask if I was free at four o'clock for a meeting with Rowcliff. *What now?* I wondered.

CHAPTER FORTY-FIVE

A s I entered the front office around 2:30 P.M., the phone was ringing. Gretchen mouthed hello to me and handed me two messages, then answered it with her usual cheery greeting, "Prescott's! May I help you?"

Zoe had asked that I call her back when I had a chance and a woman named Amy Lorne had wanted information about appraisals.

Before heading upstairs to return the calls, I took a quick spin around the tag-sale venue. The place looked great—well stocked with interesting items attractively displayed. Our Prescott's Instant Appraisal booth, complete with computer hookup, stood ready to go. Every Saturday, Sasha, Fred, and I took turns manning the booth, providing on-the-spot, quick-and-dirty informal appraisals of whatever anyone brought in. It was a popular feature, generated good publicity as well as valuable leads to buy antiques and collectibles, and it was a lot of fun.

I watched as Eric, atop a six-foot ladder, strung vintage Japanese lanterns from one side of the room to the other, the cords passing over displays of silver teaspoons, model airplane kits, wicker baskets, dictionaries, writing implements, souvenir shot glasses, and porcelain teacup and saucer sets.

Eric, I thought, *could you be working hard and betraying me at the same time?* I didn't believe it, but knew it was possible. *Anything is possible,* I told myself, *most anything, at least.* I took a deep breath and prepared to carry on as if everything was fine.

"Hey, Eric! Those look great!" I called, pointing to the rice-paper lanterns.

"Thanks."

"Looks like you're almost done," I added, scanning the room.

He nodded. "Yeah. I think we're in good shape."

"I'll be in my office if you need me."

"Okay," he said, and returned to his task.

Upstairs, I dialed Zoe, and she answered, sounding breathless and harassed.

"Yes, I'm both out of breath and harassed," she agreed, laughing, when asked. "No surprise, since I've been chasing two tireless beings for what seems like hours."

"Well, at least you sound cheerful!"

"Yeah, and the truth is that I love it! Guess that makes me crazy, huh? Anyway, I was wondering about dinner tomorrow night—can you come?"

"Absolutely. Sounds great."

"Let's barbecue," Zoe said, "and drink martinis."

"Perfect."

I told her that I'd see her at seven tomorrow, and crossed my fingers as I dialed Ms. Lorne. My luck held. She was interested in learning more about the process of appraisals, which I explained; then she invited me to come and see her nineteenth-century snuffboxes, clowns, African masks, and pewter vases

"That's quite an eclectic array of collections," I remarked.

"I've indulged my varied interests for a lot of years," she said proudly, "and it's way past time to make sure that I've got enough insurance."

"I'll look forward to seeing everything."

When I called Max, his assistant told me he was in a meeting, so I left a message that I'd expect him and Detective Rowcliff at four o'clock.

I entered the amount I'd written to Literacy Matters into my check register and realized that I was too filled with nervous energy to start any project that required concentration or precise thinking. Instead, I dusted my rooster collection, the bookshelves, and all the flat surfaces in the room, and still it was only 3:50 P.M.

I picked up Detective Rowcliff's Mitsubishi listing and idly flipped through the pages. With a sigh, I turned to the first page and began to read, once again, each name and address, just in case I'd missed something.

And there it was—right in front of me.

I stared at the entry, shocked, my mouth gaping open. I couldn't breathe. Once I recognized it, it was so obvious. *Henry Avery on Old Locke Road. Hank. Dora's boyfriend, Hank.* Synapses sparked in my brain as previously unrelated facts linked into one cohesive chain of events. I didn't know why, but now I knew who—Hank.

He owned a black 2003 Mitsubishi Lancer ES. And he fit the sales clerk's description of the man who purchased the reproduction soup tureen—he was tall and quiet, with light-colored hair.

I couldn't believe it. I couldn't even conceive of such a thing. *Hank? What did I ever do to him?*

With Max and Rowcliff due any minute, I picked up the phone, my hand trembling.

"Max," I said when I had him on his cell phone. I choked, suddenly so dry that I couldn't speak. I gulped some water.

"Hey, Josie. I'm just pulling into your lot. You okay?"

I coughed. "Hurry upstairs. I need to talk to you before Detective Rowcliff gets here. I'll tell Gretchen." I hung up, then got Gretchen on the line and told her to send Max right up but to buzz me when Rowcliff arrived.

"Sure," she said. "Also, Bridgewater Elegant Junque would like to know if you want to bid on their barn. They're closing the shop and moving to Florida, and they're looking to sell everything as one lot."

I heard the words, but they made no sense, and I didn't know how to respond. I couldn't think. I forced myself to focus. An entire barn's worth of stuff for sale. I knew the place. It was a dump, and nothing in the place was worth much. But I knew I should take a look regardless. "Yes. Make me an appointment for Monday," I said.

"Sure," she responded, sounding concerned. "Are you okay?"

"You bet!" I lied, not wanting to be burdened with explanations.

Max hurried into my office and sank into the yellow guest chair nearest the door, not taking his eyes from my face. "Tell me," he said.

I pushed the listing across the desk and pointed. "The second one down. That's Dora's boyfriend, Hank, the trombone player at the Gala. I was at his house at a luncheon Dora hosted today. I saw him. He's tall, thin, blond, and quiet. He *has* to be the one."

Max stared at the printout, then at me. "It doesn't seem logical, does it?"

"I just can't imagine. I can't think. I mean, I—" I raised a hand, shut my eyes, and forced myself to breathe. *Don't talk until you can control yourself,* my father once warned me. *Otherwise, people will only hear your emotion, not your message.*

"Sorry about that," I said, looking at him, and trying to smile. "One possibility is that Hank learned something about Maisy from Dora and tried to blackmail her. Maisy threatened to go to the police—or to Dora—and he killed her to eliminate the threat."

"But how? How could he have killed her? He was in the back, wasn't he? With the band?"

"Not really. He was only sitting with the musicians when he was playing. Otherwise, he was with Dora, and I've talked before about how Dora is an absolute master of working a room. I mean, I can't say for sure, but I'll bet you that she stopped at every table—including, I assume, Maisy's. If I'm right, that means Hank was near Maisy's wine and could have poisoned it."

"But you remembered Maisy drinking her wine and being okay." Max shook his head, perplexed.

"That's right." I shrugged. "I don't know. I remember the waiter clearing glasses, but the truth is that I've sort of lost track."

"It's incredible, isn't it?"

"Yes," I agreed, thinking hard. "I wonder where his car is now."

Max nodded and made a note on his legal pad. "Astonishing to think of," he said, sliding the papers back toward me. "Is that how Hank could afford a house on Rye Beach? By blackmailing Maisy?"

I shrugged. "I don't know. I don't think so. According to Dora, his family has owned the house on Rye Beach forever. Maybe he comes from money." *Wes can find out,* I thought.

"But why would Hank try to kill you?"

"Or steal the soup tureen?" I added, shaking my head. "None of it makes sense."

I was struck by a sudden thought: *If Hank's in, Eric's out,* and I felt weak with relief.

Gretchen buzzed up. I glanced at Max and he gestured to proceed. "Send him up," I told her.

"Do you know what Detective Rowcliff wants?" I asked, almost as an afterthought.

"Only that he has some photos he wants you to look at."

"Photos of what?"

Max shrugged and shook his head. Before I could respond, I heard Detective Rowcliff's feet pounding up the stairs. *He sounds angry even when he walks,* I thought.

He sat first, then said hello. "Did Max tell you I have some pictures to show you?"

"Yes," I managed to say, shaking a little as I reached for my bottle of water. "No problem."

"Before you start," Max interjected, "Josie recognized a name on the Mitsubishi list."

"Tell me," Rowcliff instructed.

Max explained, and Rowcliff looked at me, assessing something—I didn't know what—for more than a minute. I drank more water.

"Why didn't you pick up on him before?"

"I only met him at the Gala—and he was introduced as Hank, not Henry. I've never even heard his last name. If I hadn't looked at the listing immediately after driving down his street, I don't know that I would ever have noticed it."

"We cross-referenced the Mitsubishi owners with the invitation list—and he wasn't on it. Why not?" Rowcliff growled.

"He was working. No one who was there to work was on the list."

He stared at me, as if he was considering whether to believe me. I stared back.

"What do you know about him?" he demanded after a long pause.

I glanced at Max and he nodded, indicating that I could answer. I took a deep breath. "I spoke to him today for the first time."

"And?" Rowcliff waggled his fingers, wanting more information.

"We chatted about his business. In addition to playing in a quartet, he repairs brass instruments. Trumpets and tubas. For schools, mostly." I shrugged. "Nothing special."

Rowcliff shifted in his seat and began tapping his foot, staring into space, thinking. Max and I watched him for what seemed like a long time.

"I've got some snapshots," Rowcliff said, "taken by a Gala guest." Rowcliff pulled a manila envelope out of an inside pocket, unfolded it, and extracted a Ziploc bag stretched taut, filled with four-by-six glossy prints. "In a minute, I'm going to ask you to comment on each one, but first, point out Hank Avery." He flipped through the photographs, found one showing the brass quartet posing in a formal stance, their instruments in their hands, and passed it to me.

Hank's tux fit him as if it were custom-made; his smile was crooked, kind of awkward and very appealing; and his gaze conveyed understanding. He looked like a really nice guy. "That's him," I said, pointing, "on the right."

Rowcliff accepted the photograph and pulled out his flip phone. He pushed a preprogrammed button, and when someone answered, he said, "Two things. Send someone out to visit Henry Avery—the second entry on the Mitsubishi list. . . . Do you see it? Right. . . . Old Locke Road. Confirm the whereabouts of the car, but don't spook him. You know the drill. Routine, right? Also, I want someone to go to Weston's pronto with a photo array. Use the guy on the far right from photo number"—he paused to turn over the photo—"nineteen."

Smacking his phone shut, he turned to me. "In the meantime, take a look at the photos one by one. Tell me what you notice."

He slid the pile toward me.

The first dozen or so were shots of the gathering crowd, and nothing in particular struck me. Pointing to one shot, I commented, "See what they're doing?" I pointed to a jovial group gathered near a small rosewood table, one of the antiques that had been offered for sale. "That's mostly what people did until dinner—they looked at the antiques, greeted their friends, and drank."

The next photo showed Maisy standing off to the side, next to Pam, viewing the room, a goofy expression on her face. A few photos later, Maisy, still grinning happily, stood next to her husband, Walter, who stared disapprovingly into the far distance.

There were several photos of Dora chatting with people, all with Hank by her side. One shot showed her brushing up against him as she laughed at something out of view. Hank's face was far less expressive than Dora's—the reserved demeanor of a quiet man. Pam appeared in two pictures. In one she was seated near Maisy, raising her glass in a toast, and in the other she was chatting to a man I didn't recognize.

I paused to sip some water and noticed that my trembling had stopped. The shock had passed and my ability to concentrate had returned. I continued my narration.

"Look at this!" I exclaimed. "It's just like I described! Britt is leaning over my glass, handing something, or indicating something, to Dora. And there she is looking at the bid sheets."

Gretchen called up, interrupting my commentary. "Eric's left and asked that I tell you he'll be in by seven o'clock tomorrow."

"Is everything locked up?"

"I did it myself—and I set the alarms in the tag-sale area and the auction room. Sasha and I are getting ready to go, too. Should I set the phone or ask Fred to cover it?"

"How long does he plan on staying?" I asked, aware of Rowcliff's irritation.

I heard her relay the question.

"For at least an hour," she said.

The clock in the corner of the computer monitor read 4:30 P.M.

"Go ahead and set the phone, and would you ask Fred to call up when he leaves?"

"You got it! Can I bring you anything before I head out? You want some tea?"

I thanked her, and said no. I didn't know what I wanted, but whatever it was, I doubted that she'd be able to provide it. I was able to act the part of a helpful citizen, but beneath the surface, I was seriously shaken.

I did the only thing I could think of—I turned my attention back to the photos.

In two go-arounds, considering the photographs one by one, I noticed nothing unusual or unexpected. Rowcliff asked me no questions, but he seemed attentive throughout the process, making an occasional note. I tried hard to describe everything I saw, but after a while, it began to seem like a senseless exercise.

Just as I was finishing my commentary, Fred called up to say that he was leaving, and I told him I'd see him in the morning.

Rowcliff's phone rang. "Bring him in," he said to the caller. He stood up, tapped the pile of photos against my desk to line them up, and slid them back into the plastic bag. "I'll be in touch," he said as he headed for the door.

"Wait! What did you learn?" Max asked.

"Nothing official," he replied evasively.

"Understood," Max said, standing up and walking toward him. "We won't hold you to anything."

They stared at one another; then Rowcliff replied, "Henry Avery refused to talk about the car. The clerk's ID was positive."

Max and I followed Rowcliff as he clomped down the stairs and strode through the warehouse to the front office and out into the parking lot. A man on a mission. After locking the door behind him, I turned to Max.

"What do you think it means that Rowcliff is bringing Hank in?" I asked.

Max looked at me for a long moment. "Best guess?" He shrugged. "It means that Detective Rowcliff thinks Hank Avery knows something. Something significant."

CHAPTER FORTY-SIX

I called Ty and got him.

"Can you talk?" I asked.

"Yeah. I'm at a coffee shop down the block from the hospital. I decided to stretch my legs."

I heard fatigue in his voice, and something else. *What? Anxiety. More than that. Deep worry. Maybe even more than that, too.* I wished I could see his face to better gauge his mood. "How's Aunt Trina doing?" I asked.

"Seems she's taken a turn for the worse."

"I'm so sorry."

"Yeah. Well, according to the doctors, some people don't get better." His words were brusque, but his intonation expressed frustration, not anger.

"That's not very comforting, is it?" I said.

"No."

"What else do the doctors say?" I asked.

He paused before responding. "They say I should stay close."

Ominous words, calmly spoken. "Makes sense," I replied, ashamed for feeling disappointment at the delay in his return. I chastised myself. *How selfish is that, to even think of such a thing while Aunt Trina lies gravely ill.*

He cleared his throat. "How about you? You okay?"

"Yeah. Much to my amazement, I seem to be holding up all right. Actually, there's new info."

"What?"

I explained about Hank and asked, "I figure it's good news, right? Rowcliff bringing him in for questioning, don't you think?"

"It could mean anything—or nothing," he said, hedging his bet.

"It sounds like a solid lead, though, and I bet Rowcliff was hungry for one of those."

We talked about small nothings for a while, then said a quick good-bye and I hung up, wishing I could do more to help him. *He's such a good man,* I thought. *Good and strong. Like my dad.*

Back in my office, I swiveled and looked out of the window. Through the mostly leafless trees that gave onto the main street, I saw Chi talking to a man in a brown sedan hidden in the deep shadows, and felt simultaneously frightened and relieved.

Why would Hank want to kill me? I shook my head, troubled and annoyed. I needed more information. *Wes.*

I dialed his number from memory, and he answered in his usual rush, sounding as if I'd caught him on the run.

"Wes," I said, "it's me. Josie."

"Whatcha got?"

"News. And questions. We need to meet. It won't take long, but I'm not comfortable asking on the phone. Can you be at the Blue Dolphin in about fifteen minutes?"

"No problemo. At the bar?"

"Yeah."

"Done. See ya in fifteen."

I called Chi and told him I would be making a stop before going home, and he thanked me for the heads up.

Walking to my car, I shivered in the growing evening chill and noticed that Chi was gone, but the brown sedan was in place and its occupant met my eyes and nodded in my direction. The sunny day had given way to a cold, moist evening, shrouding the distant trees in a mist.

As I drove up Market Street, I felt my heart begin to pound, and I had trouble catching my breath. I was terrified. The last time I'd been to the Blue Dolphin, I'd nearly been killed on the street outside.

I found a spot a hundred feet away from the restaurant and sat for a moment trying to calm myself. As I watched, a woman in a trench coat passed through the deep shadows cast by the sharp white conical glare of a streetlight. It was unnatural-looking. I glanced around. Two couples were laughing as they entered a restaurant across the street. Three young woman, dressed in goth black, strutted into a dark, small bar on the corner of Bow Street. An older woman wrestled open the heavy door of the Blue Dolphin and went inside. A tall man walked a wire-haired terrier while smoking a cigarette and talking on his cell phone. No one paid any attention to me.

I took a deep breath and stepped out, ready to proceed despite my anxiety. Inside, I paused in the entryway and took several more deep breaths, then entered the lounge. There were half a dozen people scattered around in pairs, talking quietly. Wes was waiting at the bar. He didn't look well. His features were puffy, and he seemed pale.

Jimmy, the red-haired bartender, came over and asked if I wanted my usual. I didn't. I was upset, and I wanted my mother's chicken soup, not a drink.

"Just water right now, okay, Jimmy?" I replied.

"You got it," he told me, and placed a tall glass of water, no ice, in front of me.

"How ya doing?" Wes asked. He scooped a handful of mixed nuts from the small bowl at his elbow and stuffed them in his mouth.

I wanted to whip the nuts away and order him a salad. Instead, I said, "I'm okay." I cleared my throat and sipped water. "Listen, Wes, did you hear that the police have brought in Hank Avery for questioning?"

He stopped chewing and aimed his laser-focused eyes on me. "Why do I know that name?" he asked.

"Dora Reynolds, the chair of the Gala—Hank's her boyfriend," I explained.

"Huh. Really. What did he do?"

"He bought a reproduction tureen—presumably the one that was put in the display case to hide the theft of the antique—and he owns the same model and color Mitsubishi as the one that tried to run me down."

His eyes rife with speculation, he pulled a folded wedge of pa-

275

per out of his pocket, found an unmarked corner, and wrote something. "This is good news," he said. "It may be the big break in the case—nice and dramatic for my article. I could title this section 'The Final Chapter.' What do you think?"

I restrained myself from answering his question honestly, and only said, "I'm glad you think the information will be useful in your writing—but right now, we still have work to do."

"I'll check this Hank guy out. Anything in particular I should look for?" He dug another handful of nuts out of the bowl and tossed them into his mouth.

I glanced over my shoulder to be certain no one was eavesdropping, and still I hesitated, wondering if it was all right to state openly what I wanted to know, then decided that I had nothing to lose by telling Wes the truth. "Is there any way you can find out if Hank and Maisy were, you know, an item?" I whispered.

He nodded, his interest engaged. "Maybe. What else?" he asked.

"Whether he transferred the money—so we can figure out whether he was the one Maisy was blackmailing."

"Hank Avery," Wes said aloud as he wrote the name down.

"Henry. His full name is Henry Avery." I gave him the Rye Beach address.

"What does he do?"

"He's a musician," I told him.

"Would a musician have enough money to pay Maisy off?"

"I don't know." I thought about it for several seconds while I drank some water. "He owns an oceanfront house in Rye Beach. Dora told me it had been in his family for generations, so maybe he comes from money."

Wes nodded. "I can find out."

"Also, he owns a small business, repairing brass instruments."

As soon as I spoke the words, I knew the answer to the puzzle. Instrument repair—brass instruments. "Oh my God! I remember!" I exclaimed, grasping the bar rail for support. "One of the things instrument repair people do is plating."

"What?" Wes asked, his eyes bright with intensity.

"I'd only been thinking of jewelers! It never occurred to me!"

"What are you talking about?"

"Hank repairs brass instruments," I whispered. "Get it, Wes? He *plates* things. He told me so himself."

Wes was pulsating with excitement. "Now we're cooking. Okay, so he owns the same kind of car as the one that hit yours, he bought the same tureen as ended up in your place, *and* he has access to cyanide—the poison that killed Maisy. Looks like we got a killer in our crosshairs." He was almost salivating.

"Wes," I told him, "you sound positively ghoulish."

"I'm not ghoulish," he protested, offended. "I'm diligent and passionate."

"Well, don't be quite so passionate while you're being diligent. It's unseemly."

"*Unseemly*? What kind of a word is that—*unseemly*?"

"It's a perfectly good word to describe your morbid fascination with murder."

"I thought you wanted to find out who killed Maisy!" he objected, hurt.

I sighed. "I did. I do. Forget it. Sorry. The one thing we don't know is motive. Why in God's name would he have killed Maisy and tried to kill me?"

"What's the mystery?" Wes responded, sounding only marginally less bloodthirsty than before. "Same motive, different person. Maisy had something on him. She blackmailed him, and he decided to kill her. Bada-bing, bada-boom."

I shook my head, dismayed at the thought that Hank was a killer, but relieved at the implication that Eric was in the clear. Wes ate some nuts. *What about Eddie?* I wondered.

"Eddie's in the clear, too, right?" I asked.

"It looks that way," he replied, with a little shake of his head. His feverish excitement had stilled, replaced by a quiet intensity. "I don't know. What do you think? Remember, his company's never heard of him."

I shrugged. "Bureaucracy. He hasn't started yet, so the local place hasn't filed the paperwork with headquarters."

"That makes sense," he acknowledged. "Which leaves us where?"

"It leaves us with Hank."

"Right—so, how about Hank's opportunity?" Wes asked. "Did he have access to Maisy's wine?"

I nodded. "Yeah, he was beside Dora the whole night, except when his group was playing, and Dora visited every table, including Maisy's. As I recall, Maisy drank some wine and was okay after Hank was at her table—but I'm not sure. It's all confused in my head. Still, I guess it's at least conceivable that he poisoned the wine."

"So, where are we?" Wes asked.

I recapped. "We need to know whether he transferred four hundred thousand dollars, and whether he and Maisy were an item. Right?"

"Right," Wes said. "And why she might have been able to blackmail him. Or if there's any other connection between them that might provide a motive."

He slid off his bar stool and wiped the palms of his hands on his pant legs. *Gross,* I thought.

"I'll get right on it and call you ASAP," he said, shrugging into his navy-blue pea coat. "I may even have news tonight," he added. "You gonna be home?"

"Yes," I said, and with a buoyant wave, he left.

I sat for a minute longer, still shaken. *Hank did plating.* I couldn't believe the implication. I was too frightened to move, yet I felt too agitated to sit still. I stood up and leaned against the railing, trying to imagine Hank as a killer.

"Jimmy," I said after several minutes. "I've changed my mind. I'll take that drink after all."

"You got it, babe," he called back cheerfully.

I sat and sipped my Bombay Sapphire, my thoughts a million miles away from the Blue Dolphin. Hank seemed to dote on Dora. I recalled seeing him with his arm around her shoulders several times during the Gala. And talking to him earlier today, I'd certainly witnessed no consciousness of guilt. I shook my glass, swirling the last of the ice and lemon, and finished the drink. I needed to talk to Max.

CHAPTER FORTY-SEVEN

I arrived unannounced at Max's door, and immediately second-guessed my decision. *I should have called,* I thought. I heard canned laughter from a television comedy in the background. *I'm here now. It's important.* Taking a deep breath, I rang the bell. The laughter stopped abruptly. Someone must have muted the TV. The door opened. It was Max.

"I'm sorry to just show up on your doorstep so late," I said, "but it's urgent. Do you have a minute?"

"Sure. You okay?"

"Yeah, I'm okay. But, I mean, I want to . . . well, I need to—" I stuttered to a stop, incapable, it seemed, of expressing my thoughts clearly.

"Come on in. Let me introduce you to Babs, my wife."

"Another time, Max. Thanks, though. I can't stay. It's just . . ." I paused, searching for the words to express my inchoate theory.

"Step in at least. Let me close the door."

We stood on a braided rug in the front hall. The house was warm and smelled of spiced tea, or maybe cinnamon-rich apple cake.

"What is it, Josie?" Max asked, concern darkening his eyes.

"I realized something—Hank does plating." I looked at him, waiting for his reaction. He looked blank. "He uses cyanide in his work."

Understanding registered. "How do you know?" he asked.

"I saw his workshop earlier today—he repairs musical instruments, and instrument-repair people do replating. I just didn't get the significance of it right away."

"This is major," Max said. "I'll call Detective Rowcliff. He probably already knows about Hank's repair business, but it can't do any harm to remind him how cooperative we're being."

"Thanks, Max," I replied, and my tension dissipated like mounds of snow in a January thaw.

"Come on," he told me, and led the way into a small room off the hall.

I wondered if Max called it a den or a study.

Gesturing that I should sit on a love seat, he moved behind a small desk. I sank down into the plaid upholstered cushions and looked around the room. There were bookcases packed with law books and best-selling romance novels, a television with a built-in VCR resting on a wheeled cherrywood cabinet, and a globe atop a tall stand in a corner.

Max dialed a number from memory, and when someone answered, he introduced himself and asked for Detective Rowcliff. After a short time on hold, Rowcliff took the call. I could hear his booming voice from across the room.

Their conversation was brief. After reporting my observation about plating, Max mostly listened and agreed to things. I heard the smacking sound of Rowcliff slamming down his phone, Max turned to face me.

"Hank's been arrested," he announced.

Hank? "I knew it!"

Max shook his head in mute agreement.

"What's the charge?" I asked softly.

"Material witness. But that's probably just until they gather more evidence."

I stared at him, speechless.

"There's something else," Max said.

"What?"

"Detective Rowcliff asked that we come to the station."

"Now?" I questioned.

"Now. I said okay. I know it's late, but I think we ought to go."

"Why? Do you know what he wants?" I asked, my anxiety level spiking.

"Not exactly. He said he thinks you can help sort things out."

"Me?"

"That's what he said." Max smiled. "You've done a lot so far. Let's see what he has in mind."

Suddenly, it felt hard to swallow.

Wes called as I was driving to the Portsmouth police station. Max and I decided to take separate cars, and he was just ahead of me.

"You said you were going to be in all night," Wes complained. "I tried you at home."

"Something came up."

"What?"

"Why are you calling, Wes?" I asked, ignoring his question.

"You asked me to," he whined.

"Does that mean you learned something?" I asked, eager for information.

"One yes, one no."

"Tell me," I said, wishing he'd be less circumspect.

"Which do you want first, the yes or the no?"

Bad news first. "The no."

"No to the couple," he said discreetly.

I'd wondered whether Maisy and Hank had an affair. "Are you sure?" I asked.

"Absolutely. According to my source—he is a one-woman man and she wasn't that woman."

"And the other one, the one we know about, is, in fact, *that* woman?" I asked.

"Yup. The early reports say so."

Apparently, Hank and Dora were as much in love as they appeared to be.

"What's the yes?" I asked.

"Money, honey."

"Really?" I asked, astonished. Quiet, unassuming Hank had paid off Maisy? It didn't seem possible.

"Yup. Two transfers from one of his accounts. One for three hundred K last August, one for a hundred K last week."

I couldn't imagine it, yet I didn't doubt Wes's facts. Hard as it was to believe, I'd just learned that Hank had a killer motive for murder.

I called Dora, feeling awkward but determined not to desert her as so many so-called friends had deserted me during the price-fixing trial. I didn't envy her the coming days and weeks, during which she'd learn bit by scathing bit the extent of Hank's treachery.

"Dora," I said, "I heard about Hank. How are you holding up?"

"Not so well, actually," she responded flatly. "The police won't let me talk to him."

"That's tough," I said.

"I'm getting ready to go to the police station. I'm going to wait there until they let me see him. I can't just stay at home."

"I understand. If there's anything I can do," I said, knowing there was nothing anyone could do.

"Thank you, Josie," she said sadly.

Dora's dismay communicated itself to me and I found myself becoming increasingly fretful as I drove through the drizzling cold, braced for I knew not what.

Moving as quickly as my injured ankle allowed, I made my way into the station house, trailing behind Max. Before I could say anything, Detective Rowcliff's head appeared through a door on the left; he waved his hand to indicate that we should go that way, and I followed Max inside. Rowcliff led us to the same conference room where we'd met before. Officer Johnston was already in place, ready to take notes. A video camera was set up to record our interview.

Rowcliff stated the date and our names, then said, "I want to talk to you about Henry Avery, known as Hank."

"Okay," I agreed.

"Has he ever been to your house?"

"No—at least I don't think so," I replied, confused.

"Why are you asking that?" Max interjected, gesturing that I should be quiet.

Detective Rowcliff tapped his pencil. "We're checking all angles," he said, as if we should be satisfied with his nonanswer. "It would be very helpful to the investigation if we could search your house."

"Why?" Max demanded while I sat in perplexed silence.

"Information received," Rowcliff said importantly.

"What information?"

"I'm not at liberty to say," Rowcliff said. "Can we search?"

"No," Max responded.

I leaned over and said in an angry whisper. "Max! I'm innocent. Shouldn't we let them look?"

"Not now. Maybe never."

I didn't argue, just sat back, fuming, my hands clenched into fists.

"I don't think you're the murderer," Rowcliff said, as if I ought to be grateful. "But what if, for example, Hank Avery managed to plant some cyanide in your place?"

"Why would you think that?" Max asked as fear prickled the back of my neck.

After a thoughtful rat-a-tat-tat, Rowcliff shrugged. "I'm not saying I do. But either someone thinks you're involved," he said, fixing me with his eyes, "or someone is trying to involve you. And it looks as if that someone is Hank." He shrugged. "You're sure Hank wasn't ever at your place?"

"Not that she knows of," Max interjected.

"Right," Rowcliff said, sounding as if he was making a huge concession, *"that she knows of."*

"It sounds like you're convinced Hank's the one," Max remarked.

"Convinced is too strong a word," Rowcliff said, and shrugged. He looked annoyed and stared hard at Max, hoping, I suspected, to win a change of heart and get Max to agree to the search. "Look, I'm making a reasonable request."

"Sorry," Max responded, dismissing the idea. After a pause, he asked, "So, what can we do for you, Detective?"

"Other than let us search for cyanide?"

"Right," Max said calmly, "other than that."

Rowcliff tried to stare me down as he tapped his pencil, and I felt my pulse begin to race. *Many people lose their tempers merely from seeing you keep yours.* I recalled my father passing on that nugget from *The Colby Essays.* I half-smiled, assuming a relaxed position in the chair, hoping my seeming insouciance would further irritate him. He looked away, shifting his attention to Max.

"Means, motive, opportunity. We've searched Hank's house, and we've found what we think will test positive as potassium cyanide. As you said, he does instrument repairs and uses cyanide in the plating process." He glared at me.

I wondered if he was upset that I hadn't realized the significance of Hank's plating business for so many days after Maisy's murder—or that I'd realized it at all, stealing his thunder.

"So what you're saying is, that's means," Max said. "According to Josie, Hank stayed close as Dora made her way from table to table, so he was near Maisy's wineglass—although maybe not in time to poison her wine. And that is, at least, a possible opportunity."

Rowcliff tapped his pencil, looking from Max to me, then back again.

"And what about motive?" Max asked.

"Maybe money."

"Really? In what way?" I asked.

"Do you know?" Rowcliff countered, his voice dagger-sharp.

"Me?" I leaned forward, shocked. "No."

Rowcliff shrugged and tapped his pencil. "We're working on it."

Max asked who was representing Hank, but I didn't listen. Instead, I stared into space, my brain in a whirr. *The photograph. The angle was wrong.* I couldn't speak. I opened my mouth, but no words came out. I tried again. I gasped.

Think. Breathe. Never be positive, never be wrong, my father had warned. I shut my eyes, forcing myself to think, to remember. *I'm not wrong,* I thought.

"What is it?" Rowcliff demanded, his eyes fixed on my face.

In a flash of clarity, I knew that Hank wasn't guilty because I'd seen the killer administer the poison. I was positive. And I *wasn't* wrong. Better yet, I knew how to prove it.

CHAPTER FORTY-EIGHT

H ank didn't do it," I announced.
Rowcliff and Max stared at me.
"He couldn't have," I declared.
"Why do you say that?" Rowcliff pressed.

"I told you, remember? Maisy and I drank wine *after* she left her table—Hank was already at the back with his quartet, getting ready to play the fanfare. I kept going back over it again and again, thinking that maybe I was confusing one glass of wine with another. But I wasn't."

Max rubbed his nose, thinking.

Rowcliff said, "That's what you came up with?" He snorted. "Alibis are rarely conclusive. Until I see a minute-by-minute schedule definitively excluding Hank—well, even then, I want it notarized before I dismiss him as a suspect."

"There's more. Do you have those photos?" I asked. "The ones you showed me before? I think I know what happened, but I can show you quicker than I can tell you."

Rowcliff picked up the telephone to make the request. In less than a minute, a uniformed police officer knocked once, then stepped into the room to hand Detective Rowcliff the plastic bag containing the photos. Opening it, Rowcliff shook the photos loose and spread them across the table. "Be my guest," he said.

Sorting through them, I quickly found the photo I sought—the one where Dora stood with her head tilted to the left, looking at the bid sheets.

"This is it," I said, and laid it on the table so they could see it. They both leaned forward to gain a better view. "Do you remember how I told you what happened? It was during one of our first interviews. . . . I told you how I was admiring Dora while Britt reached across the wineglasses. Well, this shows what I was looking at—Dora. Except she wasn't focused on the bid sheets. Look." I waited for them to follow my finger as I indicated what I was referring to. "I can barely fathom it—and I can't believe I'm saying it aloud—but the truth is that if you look at this picture, I think you're seeing Dora in the act of adding poison to the wine—right here." I touched the spot, then looked up at the detective. "The last time I'd looked at this photo, all I noticed was Dora's dress—just as I did at the Gala."

"And now?" Rowcliff asked.

"Do you remember how I said that I thought Dora's shawl was too close to the wine? So I moved it aside?"

"Right," Max concurred. "I remember that."

"Except that if you look at this picture, Dora's shawl *wasn't* too close to the wine—the angle is wrong. That's what I *perceived,* but this photo shows it isn't true." I pointed to Dora's arm, indicating where the shawl was draped *over* the wine. "Do you see?" I asked. "There's a tiny bulge here—near her wrist. At first, when I looked at the photo, I thought it was her purse. But if you look here—wedged under her left elbow—*that's* the purse. *So what's the bulge?*" I raised my eyes to Rowcliff's. "Dora had the poison in her fist at that moment. Right there."

"Maybe," Rowcliff acknowledged.

"And," I said, reaching for another photo, one that showed her black envelope-shaped clutch purse, "I bet she kept the poison here until she was ready to use it."

"Why?" Rowcliff asked.

"Where else could it be? Look at her dress and shawl. There're no pockets, no hidden flaps or anything. It would be too risky to tuck it down the front of her dress and have to pull it out in front of everyone, but no one thinks anything about it when a woman opens her purse and pulls out a tissue or a hankie."

He picked up the two photos and stared at them one after another, tapping them against the wooden table.

"She's here, right?" I asked as he considered what I'd said.

"Dora? Here?" Rowcliff asked. "Why would you think she's here?"

"I spoke to her and she told me she was going to come here and wait until you let her see Hank."

After a short pause, and without a word, Rowcliff slipped the photographs into his shirt pocket and left the room. Max and I exchanged glances but didn't speak. I felt uncomfortably aware of Officer Johnston's observant presence.

When he returned, Rowcliff seemed more confident and less adversarial than before. "I'll have information about Dora soon," he said.

Maybe, I thought, *he uses antagonism as an investigative tool, and now that things are coming together for him, he doesn't need to act mean.* I was white-hot curious about what he'd done when he left the room, but instead of asking questions that I knew he wouldn't answer, I focused on his words.

"In the meantime," he said, "let's continue." He shifted position and tapped a short sequence with his pencil. "Let's start at the beginning. There are three issues—the murder of Maisy, the attempt to kill Josie, and the theft of the Chinese pot."

"Tureen," I said.

"Right. Tureen. From what you've said, it seems that Dora Reynolds *could* have poisoned the wine. She was there, and the photograph could be interpreted as you suggest. She was in and out of Hank's house all the time, so she had access to the cyanide. We're back to motive. Do you have any idea why she would want to kill Maisy?"

"No." I felt suddenly sad and lonely. I *liked* Dora. Was it possible that she was a murderer? Was it possible she was a thief? Had she tried to kill me, too? I took a deep breath, trying to shake off my gloom.

"What will you do now?" Max asked.

Rowcliff shrugged and tapped his pencil. "Talk to her."

I crossed my arms protectively at his words. I didn't envy Dora that conversation. "There's still the question of how she could be certain Maisy would get the poison. And not me," I said.

"You moved the glasses aside, right?" Rowcliff asked.

I nodded, remembering.

He shrugged again. "Dora kept her eye on them and made sure Maisy got the one she wanted her to get."

"Maybe she was trying to kill Josie all along and it's *Maisy* who died by accident," Max observed.

"Josie?" Rowcliff asked. "What do you think?"

"I don't know. Maybe Dora targeted Maisy because Maisy was blackmailing her, not Hank."

Rowcliff's open manner slammed shut. "What do you know about blackmail?"

I froze. *What am I supposed to know? Keep it vague,* I warned myself. "Nothing. I don't know where I heard that Maisy was blackmailing someone. Maybe I read about it in the paper."

Rowcliff stared, trying to wither me. I stared back, trying not to show how intimidating I found him.

"Okay, then," Rowcliff said. "*If* Maisy was blackmailing someone, what do you think she might have been blackmailing Dora about?" he asked me.

"I can't imagine," I said. *But I bet Wes could figure it out,* I thought. "Did the money come from Hank's accounts?"

"From their joint account."

Dora had a ready-to-go defense—blaming Hank. I wondered how Hank would handle her betrayal. Neither Max nor I spoke.

Rowcliff tapped a steady beat for a long minute. "Let's talk about the second issue—the attempt on Josie's life. Have either of you had any additional thoughts?"

"It doesn't make sense, does it? If Dora was targeting Maisy, why did she try and run *Josie* down? *If* it was Dora behind the wheel. Was it? Do you know?" Max asked.

"We think it was Hank's car," Rowcliff hedged.

"Assuming it was Dora who drove the car, there's a chance that she didn't know that I *hadn't* seen something," I volunteered. "Maybe she was convinced that I was a threat—that I would reveal something she thought I *might* have seen at the Gala, or maybe she was worried that I would blackmail her myself."

"All possible," Rowcliff acknowledged. "Here's another possibility. Maybe she *wanted* us to think it was Josie who was targeted."

"Interesting," Max responded, thinking aloud. "You're saying she tried to kill Josie because she wanted us confused."

"I'm saying it's possible. Maybe Dora was afraid that if we looked hard enough at people's motives for killing Maisy, we'd find hers. She wanted us to think that Josie was the intended victim to turn the light off of Maisy."

And if it would have worked, I speculated, *if she would have killed me, you might have stopping trying to trace the money.* The implications began to dawn on me. "Wait! You're saying that *I* was a *decoy?*" I asked, appalled.

"Yeah," Rowcliff agreed, "maybe."

"Could she have just taken Hank's car? Wouldn't that have made him suspicious once he heard what happened?"

"Hank's not talking much, but he did say that Dora took his car Monday evening, telling him that hers was in the shop. No big deal. They borrowed each other's cars all the time. Later that night, she said she'd hit a deer, that she was okay but the car needed work and that she was having the repairs done. She came home in a rental."

"Are you suggesting that after all that, Dora switched plans and decided to try to make you think I was the murderer?"

"No way to know until we talk to her," Rowcliff said, shrugging. He gave a little tap-tap with his pencil and seemed about to continue speaking, when there was a discreet knock on the door.

The same uniformed police officer who had brought the photographs stepped into the room and handed Detective Rowcliff a single sheet of paper. Max and I watched as he scanned it. A cynical smile appeared on his face and he nodded slowly. "Well, well. It seems that Dora Reynolds has been picked up just over the Massachusetts border. She was on her way to Logan," he said, naming the Boston airport.

"She was fleeing?" I asked, this new shock rocking my brain.

"With a ticket to Houston in her purse. A *one-way* ticket," Rowcliff said, highlighting the phrase.

I realized that Dora must have hung up the phone after talking to me and immediately headed south.

"So, is Dora en route back?" Max asked.

"It'll take a while to get through the legalities. But," he said, glancing at the sheet of paper that had just been delivered, "we should have her prints within the hour." He turned to me and added, "Then we'll know more about her—and, maybe, *you.*"

CHAPTER FORTY-NINE

I sat in near-frozen silence, terror at Rowcliff's insinuation settling over me like a shroud.

"Why do you say that?" Max asked.

Detective Rowcliff tapped his pencil. "We can speculate all we want, but until we know *if* Dora is the killer, we can't know how Josie fits in. There are too many question marks."

Max nodded. "Fair enough."

"Let's talk about the soup bowl," Rowcliff said, changing the subject.

"The soup tureen," I corrected.

"Right. The tureen." Rowcliff tap-tapped. "We've confirmed that Hank bought the fake one. What I want to know is how it got into your auction room. Could Dora have made the switch?" he asked.

I thought about that day with Britt and Dora. We placed the little Post-its on the display cases. *Of course,* I thought. "You know how I said Britt Epps could have replaced the tureen when he went to the rest room with his oversized pilot's case in hand?"

"Yeah."

"Well, Dora was on her own in the auction venue—with a huge tote bag." I shook my head. "And I didn't think anything of it. She would have had plenty of time to make the switch."

"Okay, then." Rowcliff almost smiled.

"Why would Hank have bought it?" I asked.

Rowcliff shrugged. "He said she'd asked for it for her birthday."

"But why?" I asked. "*Why* would she have stolen it?"

Rowcliff shrugged. "Maybe to get herself a chunk of cash to start a new life in Houston."

Dora? I still couldn't believe it. I didn't *want* to believe it. My perception of Dora told me that it *couldn't* be true—*and if you can't trust your perceptions, what's left to trust?*

The legalities must not have taken as long as Rowcliff expected, since Dora was being led in as Max and I were heading out. Max had promised to produce me for another round of questioning if and when Detective Rowcliff requested it.

"Dora," I called without thinking.

She turned to me. "Josie," she said. "It's all right."

"No, it's not," I responded.

She smiled angelically but didn't answer.

I called Wes on my way home.

"I can't tell you anything," I told him.

"Then why are you calling?" he asked, sounding hurt.

"If you wanted to check out someone else—well, I can't tell you the name."

Wes paused, processing my comment. "I already looked at Hank and Britt."

"I know."

"And Maisy."

I stayed silent.

"Dora," he said.

"Good night, Wes."

"I'll call you in the morning," he said, barely able to contain his excitement.

Ty called and left a message saying that Aunt Trina was continuing to weaken. His voice delivered the sad news in measured and quiet tones. Poor Ty. Poor Aunt Trina. I wished she would recover quickly so Ty could come home. It would be a relief to have his strength nearby to supplement my own. I dialed his cell phone. It went to voice mail.

"I'm so sorry that Aunt Trina's worse. It must be so hard for you to see her decline. Ty, I'm here and going to bed soon, but if you want to talk, call. Otherwise, we'll speak tomorrow, okay?"

Too tired and too confused to eat, I skipped food. Instead, I took a hot shower, crawled into bed, and within seconds was asleep.

At seven o'clock on Saturday morning, Wes called.

"I know it's early," he said, anticipating my complaint.

"Not on a Saturday," I told him. "Saturdays are tag-sale days. They always start early."

"I got some information. We gotta meet."

We settled on connecting at the tag-sale entrance in an hour. With Chi following in the distance, I grabbed a cup of coffee and a bagel from a deli en route. When I arrived, I found Wes waiting by the door.

"I only have a sec," I told him. "What's going on?"

"I found out about Dora."

"And?"

"It's kind of funky."

"What do you mean?" I asked, hating his habit of building suspense.

"Dora Reynolds's records only go back a few years."

"What does that mean?" I asked, perplexed.

"I don't know," he said. "It looks like she got a new identity three years ago."

"Do you figure she was getting a fresh start?" I asked, thinking of Gretchen, secretive about her past since the day I met her.

"Maybe," he ventured, eager for drama, "she's on the run."

I looked away, staring deep into the forest, seeing nothing. Maybe that one fact—that Dora had assumed a new identity— would lead to an understanding of her motive. People with innocent reasons for changing their identities don't kill—unless they're threatened by the very thing that made them start over in the first place. *What would Dora's past reveal?*

"I guess it's possible," I acknowledged without conviction. "But her reasons could be completely innocent. Sometimes people start over to escape an abusive husband, for example, or maybe she's in the Witness Protection Program."

"Makes sense," Wes replied as I thought again of Gretchen.

Is that why Gretchen ran—to escape violence? I wondered. *If so, I hope she's safe—and I hope she knows she can tell me if she's not, and that I'll help her in any way I can.*

"We need to know more. Were you able to find out anything about her previous identity?" I asked.

"No," Wes said, frustrated. "I'm still digging." Putting his notebook away, he added, "I have a separate question for you."

"Okay," I said, and waited.

He seemed unsure how to begin, or how to ask what he wanted to know.

"What's up, Wes?" I asked after a long pause.

"Well, there's this girl. She was really helpful, you know, in getting me some information. So, like, I want to take her to dinner."

"That's a good idea," I told him.

"Where?"

"Where what?" I asked, confused.

"Where should I take her? Someplace nice, you know?"

He kept his eyes down and I realized he was embarrassed to consult me. *Wow,* I thought. *Wes has a date. Imagine that!*

"What kind of girl is she?" I asked. "You know, kind of wild and crazy or more sedate? Formal? Informal?"

He looked at me helplessly. I could have been speaking Swahili. "She's nice," he said.

I nodded. "Take her to Connolly's Pub. Do you know it—on Route One? It has a good menu, decent prices, and the atmosphere is okay—you know what I mean? It's not too rowdy or loud, so you can actually have a conversation. But it's still pretty informal."

"Thanks," Wes said. "That sounds exactly right."

At eleven o'clock, I was in the Prescott's Instant Appraisal booth, tactfully explaining to a disbelieving man that his nineteenth-century decoy was, in fact, worth very little—maybe twenty-five dollars.

"I heard some decoys sell for hundreds of thousands of dollars," he argued.

"That's true," I acknowledged, "but this isn't one of those, I'm afraid. It wasn't carved by a famous maker and it's in pretty rough shape."

"Well, if it isn't worth anything, it isn't," he said, quickly resigning himself to disappointment. "What can you tell me about it?"

"It's a blue-winged teal drake decoy, dating from the late nineteenth century. I would classify it as folk art."

"Twenty-five bucks?" he asked.

"At the most, I'm afraid," I said ruefully.

He thanked me and got up to leave.

A woman clutching an old pine turned bowl entered on his heels and I invited her to have a seat.

The wood had no chips or cracks and I was able to tell her that probably it would retail for over two thousand dollars. She was thrilled and left chattering to her husband, holding the bowl as if it were made of gold.

When Fred arrived to take his turn in the booth, I decided to take the plunge and ask Eric about the call from Gretchen and renovating his house. Not knowing was like an itch I couldn't scratch. He was at the cash register, so I waited for him to finish ringing up a sale.

"Can I ask you something?" I said, smiling to diffuse any potential anxiety.

"Sure. What?"

"The other day, Gretchen called in to talk to you on her day off. What did she want?"

He looked embarrassed. "It's nothing—just a work thing."

"What?" I asked, still smiling. It was unusual for me to demand to know about a phone call, but not extraordinary—after all, I owned the place. I became increasingly anxious as I waited for his response.

He took a deep breath. "It was about that job description. She's like a maniac about it, you know, listing every little thing I do. She thought of something and wanted to tell me right away."

"That's great!" I said, relieved that the subject of the call was innocuous and delighted at hearing an example of Gretchen's loyalty to the company. "Gretchen is doing the right thing, Eric. It might be hard for you to understand, but Prescott's growth is tied to your producing a detailed and accurate job description."

"I guess."

I tapped his shoulder affectionately. "Consider it to be a necessary evil, okay? Listen, I drove by your house the other day," I said, changing the subject and keeping my tone light and airy. "I saw the contractor's sign. Congratulations on doing some work on the place."

He frowned a little. "We had no choice, really. The roof was leaking, and, well, we had to. Did you get a call from the bank?"

"What do you mean?"

"We got a home-equity line of credit to pay for the repairs," Eric explained, "and I was thinking that they might call to verify my job, you know?"

"Oh, I see. Guess they didn't need to. Anyway, congratulations to you and your mom."

I nodded politely at another customer, who was ready to pay for her glass animals, and left Eric to his task. Glancing around as I walked, I saw that the tag sale was busy, and I smiled. *Excellent!* I said to myself. *Buy, buy, buy!*

Stepping into the main office, I saw that Sasha's eyes shone with excitement.

"I have good news about the epergne," she said.

"Tell me!"

"It was commissioned by the East India Company and presented to the fifth earl of St. Erth in 1794."

"That's terrific. So it's as important a piece as we thought it was."

"Absolutely. I think it's going to be of interest to museums. It's unique."

"What figure did you put on it?" I asked, crossing my fingers for luck.

She smiled. "A hundred and twelve thousand dollars."

Yowzi! I thought. "And the provenance?" I asked, keeping my cool.

"Easy as pie," Sasha said. "It was in the family until 1957, when it was sold to an antique store in Harrogate and subsequently bought by Mrs. McCarthy's aunt Augusta. Mrs. McCarthy kept all of her aunt's receipts."

I gave her a thumbs-up.

Between the rare epergne and Mrs. McCarthy's other pieces, we had a solid foundation for an important auction, one that would be a milestone in Prescott's history. In addition, we were currently building collections of rare books, Victorian tear catchers, grape scissors, and Regency snuffboxes. I controlled myself, but what I really wanted to do was shout "Whoopee!" and click my heels in the air.

Ty called midafternoon to tell me that Aunt Trina had died. He sounded completely worn down.

"Oh Ty!" I exclaimed. "I'm so sorry."

"Yeah."

"What do you do now?"

"Clean out her place. Plan her funeral."

"I can fly out there and help."

"Thanks. But I'm okay."

"Are you sure? I'd be glad to."

"Thanks, Josie. If I needed you, I'd ask. The truth is that Aunt Trina sold off most of her things before she moved into the assisted-living place, so it's going to be pretty easy to clean out her things. The funeral . . . well, she wanted to be cremated. But you know what?"

"What?"

"I thought maybe when I got home, I'd contact the VA and organize a memorial, an interment, you know? I mean, Aunt Trina was a veteran. She was a nurse in World War Two, so I figured I'd have 'Taps' played and the flag thing done and all. And that way, she'd be near me, so I could go visit."

Tears welled up and I swallowed twice. "That sounds wonderful, Ty. It would be an honor to attend with you."

"Thanks, Josie."

He said he'd schedule his flight home for later in the week. After we hung up, I sat for a while, feeling dejected, then sighed and reached for the phone to call Zoe and confirm dinner.

"Great! Listen, would you please tell Jake that you're not going to wear jammies to dinner."

I laughed and said, "Sure."

"You need to wear your jammies," Jake announced imperiously.

"I'm going to wear jeans," I told him, "not jammies."

"No. You need to wear jammies!" he insisted.

"I'm sorry, Jake. But I'm not going to."

He dropped the phone and it made a hollow clattering sound that hurt my ear.

"Sorry about the dropped phone, but thanks for standing your ground," Zoe said.

"No problem," I replied, giggling.

CHAPTER FIFTY

Max called me at home on Monday morning to tell me that Dora had been arrested for Maisy's murder and that therefore it would be appropriate for me to allow the police to search my house. I agreed.

"Your volunteering will look good," he said, "and it may help them build their case."

"In what way?" I asked.

"Detective Rowcliff told me that the reason he asked to search your house in the first place was that he received an anonymous tip. The person who called said you're the murderer and that they'd find proof in the form of cyanide if they looked."

"Oh my God!" I whispered, remembering that I'd left Dora alone in the kitchen while I retrieved my purse from the stairs, when she'd stopped by to show off the donation she'd received at her breakfast meeting. *Was that a fake, too,* I wondered, *like so much of Dora's story?* I felt myself becoming throw-things-against-the-wall angry. I just couldn't believe it. "Dora planted cyanide in my house to frame me?" I asked, incredulous.

"Yeah," Max said.

He told me whoever placed the anonymous call disguised his or her voice and that the police considered it a dead end. It could have been a woman trying to sound like a man—or vice versa.

"Well," I said, swallowing ire. "If there's cyanide here, I sure hope they find it."

I got myself settled on the window seat in my kitchen, opening the shades to enjoy the morning sun. With Dora under arrest, I could once again sit by a window with the curtains open.

"Detective Rowcliff made another request."

"What now?" I asked, immediately wary.

"Dora has asked to see you, and Rowcliff would like you to meet with her."

"What?" I said, shocked. "Why would she want to see me?"

"I have no idea. But the conversation will be taped, so whatever admissions she might make may be very useful to the police. How's this afternoon?"

"Okay," I agreed, still uneasy, and added, "Have they searched Dora's place yet?"

"I assume so. Why?"

"I want my tureen. The real one."

"I'll ask," Max said.

"Can I call Chi and cancel security? What do you think?"

"Good point. Now that an arrest has been made, I guess that's it."

"Kind of anticlimactic, you know?" I commented.

"But a relief."

"Yeah."

As I hung up the phone, I noticed that my hands were shaking.

Gretchen was already deep in the tag-sale financial reconciliation when I arrived at work just after nine.

"You're here bright and early," I said.

"That's me—an eager beaver!" she responded with a small laugh.

I smiled. "Thank you for helping Eric with the job description, by the way. He told me that you called in on your day off with something for the list. That's way above and beyond the call of duty."

With streaks of sunlight glinting on her copper-colored hair, she looked magnificent, like the subject of a classic portrait. *Rembrandt,* I thought, *or Vermeer might have used her as a model in a painting depicting contentment.*

She laughed. "He hates thinking about himself, so I have to help him," she explained. "I don't know why, but I was eating breakfast and I suddenly remembered that he oversees the guys who clean the gutters twice a year." She rolled her eyes. "And I couldn't risk forgetting *that* important task, could I?"

I laughed a little. "Would you call Eddie for me and tell him that the payment he got is correct after all?"

"Oh, was there a problem?" Gretchen asked, confused.

"No, everything's fine. Just give him the message, okay? Tell him that I was wrong and his invoice was correct."

"Okay." She made a note.

"And call Chi for me, will you, and thank him for me. I already called and left him a message, but please do it again—and tell him where to send his invoice."

"Got it. Anything else?"

Before I could reply, Britt Epps set the chimes jingling as he came into the office.

"Hello, my dears," he said. "I was driving by and thought I'd stop in to check on the pledges. I was so shocked to hear the news of Dora's arrest."

"Oh, me too!" Gretchen said.

I listened while they exchanged astonished views, until they ran out of revelations to share. I noted that Britt never actually mentioned the pledges again. *That gave him an excuse to stop by,* I thought, *but what he really came for was the scandal chat.*

"Have you heard about Larry Willis?" Britt asked.

"No," I said. "I don't recognize the name."

Gretchen shook her head.

"He's the managing director at Arthur's," Britt said, lowering his voice reverentially as he named one of the most prestigious engineering consulting firms in town. "He's been promoted, and he's moving to London. I was thinking that he might be planning on selling some things." He winked at me. "Couldn't do you any harm to call him and ask."

"Thank you, Britt," I said. *He's just a tittle-tattle,* I thought. *Nothing less. Nothing more. Just as my ex-boss, Trevor Woodleigh, is just an opportunist bent on rehabilitating his image, not a murderer out for vengeance. Just as Eric is a devoted son, not a thief, and Eddie left New Hampshire for a fresh start, not an escape. Sometimes,* I told myself, comforted at the thought, *my perceptions are on the mark.*

After a while, I excused myself and left Gretchen to deal with him. The last thing I heard was her asking, her voice hushed, "Do you know any details about the sale of the Winton Farm to developers? I heard that old Mrs. Winton is having a hissy fit about it."

"We need help," a striking assistant district attorney named Celeste McGowan said to me and Max that day just after noon. She wore a kelly green suit and spike heels, and looked like she hadn't taken a wooden nickel in a year or two. "The case is weak."

"How can it be weak?" I asked, astounded.

She looked straight at me for a moment. "There are many ways to interpret facts. For instance, Dora Reynolds doesn't deny that she had access to cyanide—in fact, she's acknowledged being in the workshop with the purse she carried at the Gala. She's very believable when she explains that the cyanide must have fallen in accidentally."

"That's absurd," Max objected.

"I agree. But you haven't heard her. She's a very persuasive talker. Plus, she's lovely. She'll make a fragile-looking and credible witness. I'm telling you: We need help."

Max nodded and stroked his nose. "It seems Dora did, in fact, have access to Josie's kitchen."

"Oh?" ADA McGowan replied. "Do tell."

Glancing at Max for an okay to explain, and getting it, I recounted my memory.

"We gotta look," Rowcliff insisted.

"Josie has agreed to let you search her house."

"Thanks," ADA McGowan said, "maybe we'll find something useful."

"How about other people at the Gala?" Max asked. "Did anyone see her slip the poison into Maisy's glass?"

"No one we can find so far. It was an audacious act and she got lucky."

"It's hard to believe. What do people say?" Max asked.

"Detective?" McGowan said, turning to Rowcliff.

He gave a tap-tap of his pencil before speaking. "Greg Davis, who was at Josie's table, was talking to the couple next to him about Barbados. They liked it; he didn't. The woman on the far side of Josie—Lori, her name is—she and three others were talking about having trouble finding reliable baby-sitters." He shook his head, looking disgusted. "And it was more of the same at Maisy's table. Her husband, Walter, was talking about baseball with the guy next to him. The couple sitting to Maisy's right were speculating about the auction bids with a woman named Pam. You get the picture. No one saw anything we can use."

Max nodded. "Do you know why Dora wants to talk to Josie?"

"No," Rowcliff said, and both Max and I turned to ADA McGowan. She made a *beats me* gesture.

"One thing before we proceed," Max said.

"What's that?" McGowan asked.

"Did you find the stolen tureen?"

She nodded and looked at Detective Rowcliff.

Rowcliff said, "We found it in the rental car—the one she hired after she allegedly hit a deer in Hank's Mitsubishi. The car she was driving when we picked her up."

"Okay, then," Max said. "I presume we'll get it back in due course."

"Certainly. We have it properly vouchered," McGowan said.

"Where is the Mitsubishi, by the way?" Max asked.

"Some junkyard in East Boston, probably," Rowcliff said.

As we were walking to the visitor's room, where I was scheduled to meet with Dora, I whispered, "Won't that help their case? That Dora was fleeing with the tureen in her possession?"

"Probably not. She could deny knowing it was there and blame it on Hank. He had access to the car—and he's the one who bought the reproduction tureen that was left in its place."

"There's one other thing you need to know," McGowan said.

"What's that?" I asked warily.

"Up until three years ago, Dora Reynolds was known as Alice Reddy."

The change in identity Wes discovered. I schooled my features to look confused and interested. "What?" I asked.

"Are you saying that Dora Reynolds is really Alice Reddy?" Max asked.

"Probably Alice Reddy is an alias, too," Rowcliff said.

Max shook his head. My mind was reeling.

"We're just beginning to piece it together now," Rowcliff continued. "She's under indictment in Oregon."

"For what?" I asked.

"Some kind of pyramid scheme—selling stock options to little old ladies."

"Dora?" I said. It seemed inconceivable.

"Yeah. She paid off past obligations with new sales revenue. The postal authorities initiated the investigation."

"Is that why she changed her name?" I asked.

"Probably," McGowan said. "And we found evidence indicating that Maisy was doing a little investigating on her own. Her Internet history showed her on Web sites featuring Alice Reddy on lists of most-wanted criminals."

"Which explains the blackmail," I commented.

"But no proof," McGowan pointed out.

"Didn't you find a record of money changing hands?" I asked, knowing the answer.

"Yes, but not directly. It was a joint account—she'll argue that Hank is the one who moved the money to Belize."

"And from there?" Max asked. "Where did it go after Belize?"

McGowan shrugged. "Who knows?"

"What does Hank say?" I asked.

"He's in shock, poor guy. Pretty much, he doesn't know which end is up."

He trusted her, I thought, *and now he'll never trust that way again.*

I shook my head, told them I was ready to proceed, and opened the door.

Dora entered from the far corner with a glittering smile, as if she were greeting a favorite guest at an important dinner party, not seeing an acquaintance for unknown reasons while under indictment for murder.

"Josie," she said, sitting on the other side of the divided area. "Thank you for coming."

"How are you, Dora?" I asked. I wondered where the microphones were hidden. I spotted nothing, and could only trust that they could hear us clearly.

"I've been better," she said, laughing a bit.

"You asked that I come to see you," I ventured.

She nodded. "The hardest part of being here is the limited access to information."

"What do you want to know?"

"Have you heard anything that might explain this terrible mistake?" she asked earnestly.

"Mistake?"

"Yes, of course. You don't think I killed Maisy, do you?" She looked stunned. "Or that I tried to kill you? And stole the tureen? You couldn't!"

I didn't know what to say. "The evidence," I said finally.

She waved it away. "It's all a misunderstanding. And that means the real murderer is still out there—I assure you."

I understood what ADA McGowan meant. For whatever reason, I very much wanted to believe Dora, and even though I knew she was flat-out lying, I was ready and willing to hear her out.

"I have no information," I said. "I'm sorry."

"You don't believe me," she said, looking me square in the eye. "But you'll see—sooner or later, they'll find the *real* killer."

She's setting me up at the same time as she's preparing her defense. That's why she snuck cyanide into my house. I bet they'll find it. She did it just in case she was arrested. She's giving her lawyer an alternative theory of the crime—me.

"What about the stolen tureen?" I asked. "It was in your car."

Tears glistened on her beautiful eyelashes. "Hank," she said sadly. "I had no idea he needed money so badly. If only he'd confided in me."

McGowan is right: They're in trouble. If I were on the jury, I'd definitely have reasonable doubt.

304

"And Alice Reddy?" I asked.

"Identity theft," she said, sounding pensive. "That's all I can think of. I'd never even heard that name until yesterday. You've got to believe me."

I almost did. "Is there anything I can do for you?" I asked.

"Help me learn the truth. *Please.*"

I found myself falling under her spell, and I stood up quickly, suddenly desperate to get away. "I can't help you. I've got to go. You take care, Dora."

Once we were outside, I turned to Max and said, "Max, can I ask you something?"

"Sure."

"Is Dora insane?"

"Nope. As near as I can tell, she's major-league clever. And you never know—she may just pull it off. I don't envy McGowan one bit." We walked a little farther. "I have a question for you," he said. "Do you have any idea how Maisy discovered that Dora used to be called Alice?"

"No. I wondered about that, too."

Max shrugged. "Since Maisy's dead and Dora's not talking, I guess we'll never know."

Recalling how I'd nearly stumbled when Rowcliff had asked me what I knew about blackmailing, I said, "It's nearly impossible to maintain a lie indefinitely, so if Dora tripped up and Maisy noticed, that might have been the beginning of the end. Maisy grabbed the end of a thread and Dora's story started unraveling."

"Yeah," he agreed. "It probably happened just that way."

"Makes you think, doesn't it, Max?"

Later that afternoon, I sat at my computer, brought up a browser, and searched for the name "Alice Reddy" and "most wanted."

There were eighteen hits. I shook my head. "It's true," I whispered.

The top listing took me to a site run by the post office's investigative arm, and when I clicked on Alice Reddy's name, Dora's photo appeared as clear as day.

I stared at it for a long time.

Another site showed the criminal trial's docket number, and when I clicked on the entry, up came a summary of the court proceedings. I backed out of the official record, clicking instead on an Oregon newspaper article.

Embedded in the article was another photograph of Dora. In this one, she was standing next to her lawyer outside the courthouse, earnestly staring into the camera.

The caption read: "'I can't imagine how this terrible misunderstanding occurred. It must be identity theft,' Alice Reddy said upon leaving the courthouse. She was released on $500,000 bail."

Another article was about how she'd jumped bail.

I closed the browser, sickened at her pretense, disgusted with myself that I'd fallen victim to her charm.

"People see only what they are prepared to see," Emerson wrote. I wondered what had motivated him to record that observation in his journal. Had he cared for someone who had deceived him and then, later, tried to analyze his role in the duplicity? Had *I* missed cues that could have—that *should have*—warned me that Dora was a fake? There was no way to know. It hadn't ever occurred to me that she was a phony. I wanted a friend, and she was kind, so I perceived a friend.

Was there a lesson to be learned from this experience? Yes. If people see only what they are prepared to see, the lesson is to prepare to see the truth.

I picked up the phone to call Ty.

CHAPTER FIFTY-ONE

T y dropped a copy of a U.S. newspaper on my chest. "Check it out," he said.

I looked at him, shielding my eyes from the blazing Bahamian sun, and said, "I don't want to work that hard. You read it to me."

He picked it up, flipped it open, and said, "It's just two sentences. It says, 'Alice Reddy, also known as Dora Reynolds, found guilty last month of first-degree murder, today retained well-known celebrity attorney George Norwalk. Norwalk announced his intention to file an appeal immediately and expressed confidence that "This dreadful miscarriage of justice will soon be overturned."' In other words, the show goes on."

"Wow. I thought it was over."

"You kidding? With people like Dora, it's never over."

"Do you think she'll win her appeal?"

"No chance. There's too much forensic evidence."

"Like the cyanide in the Tupperware container she left under my sink?"

"Right. No one will think it's credible that her fingerprints are on the container because she thought she heard water dripping and moved it aside so she could check your pipes. Give me a break." Ty laughed.

"One look at Dora and you know you're not dealing with a plumber," I agreed.

My pulse began to race as I recalled Detective Rowcliff telling me that they'd found the cyanide in my kitchen. Within an hour of getting permission from the police, I'd discarded every food product in my kitchen—everything. Within another hour, I'd scoured every flat surface with bleach. By the end of the day, every dish, pot and pan, utensil, and glass had been washed.

"Her lawyer's just grandstanding. I doubt there are any issues to appeal. The case was tight—and Dora's guilty as hell."

I relaxed a little at his words. She'd been convicted, and there was no reason to think it would be any different next time around.

"I wonder how Hank is doing."

"You saw that photo of him in the *Seacoast Star*," Ty said.

"Yeah. He looked brutalized."

"He'll get over it. We all get over it." Ty stared out over the ocean, maybe thinking of Aunt Trina or some distant hurt that he'd had to overcome.

I focused on the timbre of the waves as they crashed and receded, the sound of time.

"Ty?"

"What?"

"How many little umbrellas do we have so far?"

"Not counting the Planter's Punch by your side? Twenty-one."

"Excellent," I said, and rolled over, reaching for his hand and holding on tight.